High praise for Josepha Sherman's award-winning fantasy

The Shining Falcon

"Magic sparks and glitters through *THE SHINING FALCON* like sunlight on the floor of a great Eastern forest . . . A spellbinding story"
Tom Deitz, author of *Windmaster's Bane*

"Enchanting . . . With wild magic, *THE SHINING FALCON* takes on a life of its own."
Locus

"A gloriously rich tapestry of pageant, adventure, and magic, with wonderfully intriguing and believable characters"
Esther Friesner, author of
The Chronicles of the Twelve Kingdoms

"A richly detailed novel with all the charm and readability of a fairy tale. Highly recommended"
Library Journal

"Darkly brilliant and shimmering with magic"
Morgan Llywelyn,
author of *The Lion of Ireland*

"Wonderful . . . Exotically rich and different . . . A delight from beginning to end"
Salem News

Other Avon Books by
Josepha Sherman

THE SHINING FALCON

THE HORSE OF FLAME

JOSEPHA SHERMAN

AVON BOOKS ◆ NEW YORK

AVON BOOKS
A division of
The Hearst Corporation
105 Madison Avenue
New York, New York 10016

Copyright © 1990 by Josepha Sherman
Cover art by Kinuko Craft
Published by arrangement with the author
Library of Congress Catalog Card Number: 90-93184
ISBN: 0-380-75815-6

First Avon Books Printing: December 1990

AVON TRADEMARK REG. U.S. PAT. OFF. AND IN OTHER COUNTRIES, MARCA REGISTRADA, HECHO EN U.S.A.

Printed in the U.S.A.

RA 10 9 8 7 6 5 4 3 2 1

With sincere thanks to Chris Miller,
my editor at Avon Books,
for prodding me with,
"Yes, but *why* does the magic work?"

1

❖

ASTYAN

THE GIRL MARYA HUDDLED in shadow, pressed in terror against the cold stone of the wall, her heart pounding so wildly she thought she'd be sick. Dear Lord, why had she come down here? Why had she ever tried to follow her father down to this lowest, most secret, level of the royal palace? No matter how curious she'd been, she was old enough to know magic wasn't a game! And she certainly should have known the elaborate rituals he'd been undergoing these several nights could only have meant he was going to attempt some great and terrible sorcery.

Now it was too late to run. Her father had already begun shouting out sharp, twisting Words of Power, Words that flickered and flashed blindingly before Marya's eyes, Words that pulsed with a painfully building tension . . . To run now would be to be blasted by that Power. The girl's slender body shook with involuntary shudderings, because something was forming . . . Something raging and evil was being drawn to this place—

And she saw it. Staring at that terrifying Other her father had ensnared, the being that was all the more frightening for standing tall and proud as any warrior, for bearing a shape that was almost human—save for the eyes, those cruel, wise, hating eyes—Marya knew

1

her only hope of safety lay in immobility. If the evil
one became aware of her, and she without a single protective charm or circle about her . . . The girl fought
down her shivers, trying to will herself to not even
breathe until that savage, evil Thing was bound.

Could it be bound? It burned, it blazed with force,
fiercely battling her father, alive with its hate, alive with
psychic fire, sorcerous fire, alive with an alien strength
beyond anything merely mortal—

Oh, Father, Marya pleaded silently, *why did you begin this?*

He'd brusquely mentioned something about safe-
guarding his people from supernatural peril.

But there wasn't *any peril! The Thing didn't even
know we existed until you dragged it into our world.*

Her father showed no sign of fear. For all that his
eyes were wild with strain, his face deathly pale, he
stood proudly, arms outflung, commanding, prince and
magician in one, fighting back that raging Other, holding back the darkness, shouting blazing Words of Binding. And for a time Marya dared believe he was going
to win.

But the man had gone too far. His magic was innate,
finite, fueled only by his own inner strength and will.
The Power he fought to control was much stronger than
anything merely human. Clenching her jaws till they
ached, Marya bit back her frightened sobs, *feeling* her
father's exhaustion, *feeling* his sudden, sickened realization that he'd doomed himself. Akh, how she ached
to run to him!

But that would do no good at all. She had inherited
no magic of her own. Marya bit her lip in shame, remembering the long, frustrating, futile hours of her
father's testing of her, remembering his barely contained rage and disappointment that this, his only living
child, should bear within her nothing but the smallest,
most useless scraps of Power. How she'd struggled for
his love! She'd learned everything she could, states-

craft, weaponry, trying to make up for that one sorry lack.

What use is it all now?

She would rush the Other, and distract it, and—and at least die with her father—

No. Deep within her, a bluntly honest voice was crying, *You must survive. Magic or no, you are your father's only heir.*

The girl closed her eyes in painful acceptance. For the sake of Astyan, for the sake of her land and its people, she must survive.

But—oh, Father! Father!

Her eyes shot open again. Helpless, anguished, she saw wildfire engulf him, psychic fire, saw him twist in agony in the blinding flames of Power blazing loose, out of control, heard him cry out, despairingly:

"My people! Oh, my people, what have I done?"

But then, even as he stood dying on his feet, the arcane fire burning at his being, the prince found one last, desperate reserve of strength, tearing free what his daughter knew must be the very stuff of his life-force, hurling it at the Other with a final, ringing Word of Binding—

And the Binding held.

The heavy, terrible sense of Otherness vanished. Silence fell, total, terrible silence. For a moment more the prince stood, swaying. And then he fell headlong, and lay motionless. With a wordless cry of pain, his daughter rushed to his side, seeing the last embers of life flickering out within him even as he looked vaguely up at her.

"Marya . . . ? Marya, girl . . . ?"

"Y-yes, I'm here."

"Forgive me . . . I was too proud . . . Tried to save our people from *all* harm, even . . . even only possible harm. Too proud . . . Not enough strength or skill . . ."

A trembling hand reached painfully up to touch her cheek, then fell away again. "Marya . . . Never meant

. . . for you to have to rule so soon . . . And you so young . . . Daughter, I—''

He broke off, convulsing in sudden agony, and Marya cried out faintly, "Father!"

"Not much time . . ." Gasping, he forced out the words. "Have to tell you—You must keep watch! The bindings . . . Hadn't the strength to make the bindings . . . eternal. They can be broken—Oh, Marya, forgive me!"

"Hush, Father. I—it's all right, I—"

"No! You must keep watch . . . Never let Koshchei escape! Promise me . . ."

Koshchei. At the sound of the Other's earthly name, Marya felt a wild shudder race through her, and wanted very much to scream that no, she couldn't, she lacked the Power. But the princess forced herself to say, almost calmly, "Yes. I—I promise. Oh, Father . . ."

But he couldn't hear her any longer. Eyes staring blindly, the prince repeated over and over, voice slowly failing, "Never let Koshchei escape! Never!"

"I won't! Oh, Father, I won't!"

With that frantic cry, Marya, princess, ruler of Astyan, awoke, shivering helplessly with horror. What—

A dream. Only a dream.

Ah, dear God, she thought she'd gotten over them! It was a full seven years since that terrible night, and she was no longer a girl, but a young woman.

A badly shaken young woman, aching with the grief she thought she'd laid to rest. Trying to steady her trembling hands, Marya worked to disentangle from about her neck and arms the silky, clinging strands of long black hair that had freed themselves from their braid in the night. She hesitated a moment, then, grimacing at her weakness, forced herself to pull aside the heavily embroidered bed curtains and stare boldly out.

No demons lurked. The royal bed-chamber was chilly, the colors of everything from enameled night table to the usually bright reds and blues and golds of the vines and flowers painted on walls and ceiling looking strangely washed out and wan in the pale grey light of very early morning. There wasn't a sound. Or, realized Marya after a moment, there *almost* wasn't a sound.

At least now I know I didn't scream aloud! the princess thought with a touch of wry humor, glancing down to where her lady-servant, plump, pretty Olga, still slumbered peacefully away on her pallet at the foot of the royal bed. Olga was the daughter of petty nobility, accepted into Marya's service more as a kindness to the young woman's father—who'd once done a favor for her own father—than anything else; Marya suspected Olga's parents hadn't been thinking so much of the honor to their daughter as of the chance of having the sensual, shallow-brained thing under royal supervision till a husband could be found for her. Marya looked down at the pink-cheeked, childish face and shook her head.

I wish I could be that trouble-free!

The horror of the dream was still clinging to her, fight it though she would. Marya sighed, rubbing a hand over her eyes, feeling ages older than Olga, for all that they were almost the same age. God, she'd thought she had conquered her inner demons long ago, those twin specters of useless guilt at herself for having lived when her father had died, rage at her father—akh, yes. There were times when she could hate her father for what he'd done, for falling prey to his pride, for getting himself slain, for destroying his daughter's childhood and leaving her with a double weight of crown and that other, arcane burden of which, for the sake of the land's safety, no one else in all Astyan must ever know . . . In those seven years of her rule, she had, indeed, managed to keep guard over her father's demonic captive. In those seven years, despite his ragings and inhuman guile, the Other had never been able to break free.

But just how long would those bindings remain true? What if her dream hadn't been merely a memory? Her scraps of inherited Power had grown a bit stronger as the years went on; if she stared full into someone's eyes and concentrated till her head ached, she could *feel* truth from falsehood; and sometimes there were unexpected psychic warnings—

As her dream might have been a warning?

Dear God, no!

Marya knew the proper spells to keep the bindings fast. Her father had managed to pass them from his mind to hers before he died. But she hadn't inherited his Art, his talent for magic.

What if I make a mistake? What if they don't even work for me?

Fine. Here she was, trembling like some little fool of a scared child. And what was she planning to do? Up and run away? Abandon her people to Heaven only knew what vengeful evil?

"All right," the princess said softly. "The job, as the peasants say, isn't going to grow shorter for the waiting."

Heart pounding, Marya slid into a silky caftan, brushed back her hair with impatient, not-quite-steady hands, and slipped silently out of her chambers and down the long, weary way to the palace's lowest level.

TO AN OUTSIDER'S EYE, the dark, dank, stone-walled chamber would have seemed totally featureless, a vast, empty room far below the ground. But Marya, standing grimly at the bottom of the stairway, could plainly see the faint outline of a doorway on one wall. Her father's magic had planned it that way. Only she, or one linked to her by ties of love or blood, could ever see either that doorway or the hidden room that lay beyond—with its dark captive.

The Other knew she was there. She could feel its thoughts, chill as the touch of some foul, lingering death, brushing her mind, calling to her, gently, seductively, calling to her . . .

"Oh, no," murmured the princess dryly. "You don't get me, demon. Not yet."

But—the Other was laughing at her, immortal scorning mortal. *"Wait,"* the chill voice told her. *"Wait, little thing. These foolish bindings bar my essence from your world for but a short, short time."*

Marya, checking the binding spells as her father had taught her, shuddered in disgust at the touch of those thoughts, and tried her best to block them out. But still they continued, like the caress of a gently cruel ravisher's hand:

"Soon I shall be free, little thing."

Damned if she'd let the thing know how he was frightening her! "Boast away, devil," she said lightly. "You're not getting out just yet."

To her unutterable relief, the bindings were still intact, and Marya determinedly shut her mind to the thought that someday they might not be. Instead, she turned sharply and began to climb the stairway as swiftly as she could while still clinging to her dignity, feeling a shadow of the Other's laughter echoing in her mind until she'd finally managed to get beyond his reach. Even so, Marya didn't slow her climb until she stood at last, winded and gasping, back in the palace proper.

"And to think," she murmured dryly when her breathing finally began to steady, "that once upon a time I actually *envied* Father for his magic!"

Drained, the princess leaned back against a wall, feeling, as she did every time she came in contact with the Other, unspeakably soiled, painfully alone . . .

Lord in Heaven, if only this could be *over!* If only there were some way to slay that demon, truly slay him! But Koshchei, the princess wearily admitted, wasn't called the Deathless for nothing.

Enough of this. Fiercely blinking back a surge of hot tears, Marya shouted at herself not to be a fool. Things were as they were, and weeping wasn't going to change them.

Yes, and she must remember caution: *What if someone saw me climbing up here?*

This stairway was tucked away in a deliberately obscure corner of a deliberately obscure hall, and as far as she knew, no one knew about her visits to her demonic captive, but even so . . . even after seven years, not all the people of Astyan were comfortable with the idea of a young woman alone on the throne. Marya gave a sharp little sigh. The last thing she could afford if she meant to keep her crown secure was to have her name linked not with innocent magic but with out-and-out sorcery.

Still, if someone did chance to go down that stairway, all he or she would find would be that chilly, apparently quite empty room; they'd never even see the doorway.

Unless, of course, that someone is of my blood, or is my lover. Assuming, of course, she added with a touch of dry humor, *that I had one.*

A tactful cough made Marya whirl, hand groping frantically for the weapon she wasn't wearing. "Olga."

"My Princess." The lady-servant made a quick, graceful curtsey. "I didn't mean to alarm you. But—had you forgotten that you'd granted an early morning audience to the *boyar* Vasilev?"

"Damn." She *had* forgotten. And thanks to her grandfather's long-ago passion for a noble's wife, Vasilev bore a token share of royal blood, which meant he couldn't just be ignored, tiresome and foolish though he was. He'd arrived late yesterday, too late for any meetings, and she had indeed promised him this audience.

Dear Vasilev could just cool his heels till she had bathed and been properly garbed. "Convey a message to the *boyar*, Olga. Tell him he shall be summoned to the Krasny Chamber in three turns of the glass."

Olga curtseyed again. "It shall be done, my Princess."

Marya raised a brow. "So formal, Olga? Is something wrong?"

The fair, plump face reddened. "Nothing, nothing at all."

"Really?" Marya studied the young woman thoughtfully, a stirring of her unpredictable Power letting her sense something about Olga . . . "One might almost wonder if you were feeling guilty about something."

"Oh, no, my Princess!"

The *feeling* of guilt radiating from her was growing stronger. Marya sighed in sudden anger. She could have forced details from Olga, now, while the surge of Power lasted. But why bother? The truth was all too plain as it was. The last thing she wanted to have to do right now was deal with the silly girl's romance, but deal with it she must. "You were sleeping amazingly deeply this morning. Almost as though you were exhausted from having spent the night elsewhere."

"I—I—wouldn't—"

"Olga, please. Don't try to lie to me." Marya bit the words off sharply, struggling against her growing rage. Damn the girl! If Marya shouted at her, Olga would almost certainly burst into hysterical tears and not hear a word she said. Besides . . . wasn't it partly her own fault that the flighty thing had managed to slip out in the night so easily?

Yes, but what about the guards who had supposedly been guarding the royal quarters? How dare they neglect their duties! How dare they think that just because she was a woman, and young, they could—

No. That wasn't true. She knew they respected her well enough. What it came down to was simply that she'd been lax in supervising them.

I hadn't thought they needed it. Without warning, a surge of stark, painful loneliness overwhelmed her.

Dear God, isn't there anyone I don't have to oversee?

Of course not—that was part of being royal. Marya let out her breath in a sigh of frustration and turned back to the nervous Olga. "Look you," the princess began, voice rigidly controlled, "I'm responsible to your parents for your well-being. And I'm trying to arrange a respectable marriage for you. You know that. I can't have you trysting in shadows."

Olga's start of alarm told her she'd read the young woman correctly. "Uh, no, my Princess."

"I'll put it simply. God knows I don't begrudge anyone happiness. But as long as you are lady-servant to the crown, you aren't free to do what you will. Olga, you just can't be so indiscreet! There can be no more midnight visits." Sensing the young woman's sullen hostility, Marya continued, more severely, "Disobey me, and I shall be forced to return you to your parents." She saw Olga wince at the thought of such a disgrace, and smiled thinly. "Is that understood?"

"Yes, my Princess." It was a subdued whisper.

"So. Now, go and convey my message to the *boyar*."

OLGA KEPT HER RESPECTFUL POSE till the princess was well out of sight, then straightened indignantly. "Indiscreet," was it? Well, if Her so-honorable Highness knew with whom her "indiscreet" maidservant had spent the night . . . The young woman shivered with delicious memories, recalling the magic of those searching, skillful hands, that demanding, teasing, honey-smooth body against her own . . . She had dreamed of this reunion for so long, ever since that day years ago when she'd been barely out of childhood, when she had chanced to meet him in the forest, when he'd been hunting, and she—she had been playing at being a fine lady. How splendid he'd been, tall and fair as some god of old! She had never dared imagine that so noble a man would deign to look at her; his rank was so high, while she was barely more than a commoner.

But what had happened between them that day and night had had nothing to do with rank. It had been better, finer, than any of the stableboy's fumblings, finer than all the songs of love she'd ever heard, all the old, pagan tales of passion. She'd told her parents some hasty lie about getting lost in the forest and spending the night in some woodcutter's hovel. And they had never suspected!

After that brief, fiery time, he'd gone his way, and she had been sent to court. To serve with Her most honorable Highness. But now he'd come here, and—oh, wondrous—he remembered her. Better than that: this night he had admitted that he loved her!

Olga hugged herself in rapture. Why, the man had even told her of his hopes for the future, of how mighty he would become—with her aid. Of course he could never marry her, she hadn't ever expected that. But there was no shame in becoming the royal mistress. And that, she would be. She would share his glory. The glory of the *boyar* Vasilev, cousin to the Princess Marya, and soon to be her husband. Even if Marya didn't know it yet.

But now Olga knew she must prove her worth. Biting her lip, the young woman glanced nervously about, wondering if anyone was watching . . .

No. She was alone. Carefully she started down the mysterious stairway up which she'd seen the princess climb. This was how she was to help Vasilev, by spying out anything suspicious, anything sorcerous, anything that he might use against Marya, anything to make her yield to him.

Olga's breath caught in her throat. What if some people thought she was committing treason . . . ? No, that was ridiculous! She wasn't actually doing anything to hurt Marya, just easing the way for Vasilev.

Who would soon enough be ruler of Astyan.

BOYAR VASLEIV VASILOVICH STARED at himself in the small mirror of polished metal his servant held, pleased with what he saw. Tall, elegant of face and form, eyes of the clearest blue, golden hair touched here and there by such distinguished streaks of grey . . . The splendor of his brocaded caftan was so nicely calculated, not one gold thread too ornate, not one gem too ostentatious for his rank. All in all, he decided, a vision to turn a delicate young maiden's head. Even if said maiden was his less-than-delicate cousin.

Akh, Marya!

To bed her would be like bedding a steppes barbarian, all angles and fierceness. But bed her he would. He would do a great many less pleasant things for the throne of Astyan!

When he'd been younger, less sensible, he had wasted time in hating his father. After all, bastard or no, the man *had* been Prince Grandfather's eldest child. With a touch of properly placed ambition . . . But the man had apparently been born without the slightest desire for a crown, content with a quiet life and whatever shreds of reflected glory came his way. *Father, you were a fool!*

Vasilev had finally accepted that, thanks to that paternal shyness, the title of Prince of Astyan hadn't a chance of descending to him. For a brief time, he had actually considered rebellion.

Ah, but then he'd taken a long, hard look at the magician-prince, Marya's father, who had legitimately inherited the throne, and decided it would be safest to find himself a throne elsewhere.

He'd nearly done it, too, by sheer, blond charm—and by lying a touch about his status. But then his royal fiancée had caught him in . . . embarrassing circumstances, and Vasilev had fled in panic back to Astyan.

And there he'd found the prince safely dead, and Marya on the throne—his safely magicless daughter.

His unmarried daughter.

Vasilev grinned wolfishly, secure in his ability to charm even the most regally cold of women. Last night . . . Remembering last night's bed-sport, he felt his grin widen. It had been quite a stunning surprise to find Olga here at court, but flattering to have her mooning after him after all these years. What luck that he'd managed to remember her name! Yes, and the circumstances under which they'd first met, too.

But then, it would have been difficult to forget that sensual little thing cavorting in the forest like some buxom wood-sprite. He'd been shocked to learn, after

the fact, just how young she'd been—barely old enough
to . . . properly know a man—and more shocked to
realize that he hadn't been her first.

Some women were just made for one skill, after
all . . . Last night—Akh, it had been like sinking into
a feathery bolster, all that soft, pink flesh, but not unpleasant at all. And she was such a compliant little fool,
believing everything he said, going off earnestly to spy
for him. Ha! Even should she tell anyone here the truth,
who would believe her?

And as for Marya . . . Vasilev remembered a
scrawny, dark, intense little foal of a girl, but Marya
had grown up to be lovely—in that thin, fierce sort of
way—and a brazen little warrior, handy with sword or
bow.

Vasilev's grin thinned to a cold line. Warriors could
always be disarmed. And if the disarming should prove
less than successful, if she should be stubborn about
sharing her throne or becoming properly subservient
after their marriage—well now, everyone knew that
warriors did meet with all manner of accidents.

Some of them quite fatal.

II

THE ESTATE

EMELIAN BROUGHT his sword frantically up to parry, panting in the chill early morning air, the shock of blade against blade jolting through him painfully. Aie, now the hilts had locked! The young man wrenched his sword free just before it could be pulled out of his grip, but before he could recover his balance, his opponent was after him again.

He had to turn things around, had to attack, but there wasn't time. He was being driven helplessly back, the other man grimly raining blow after blow on him. As his foe's sword came whistling down at his head, Emelian, desperate, tried to spring lithely aside. But his foot slipped on the wet grass and went out from under him, sending him sprawling, struggling to raise his sword, to get his feet under him because, merciless, Serge was continuing the attack and he'd never be able to defend himself in time—

But all at once, the stern-faced man was drawing back, lowering his sword, shaking his head ruefully.

"If I'd been an enemy, young master, you'd be dead."

Gasping for breath, Emelian got to his feet, impatiently brushing back sandy hair from his sweaty face. "You're not, and I'm not," he muttered. "And what would an enemy be doing out here in the middle of nowhere?" Serge raised a disapproving brow at this, and Emelian sighed, contrite. "Akh, no, man, I'm not belittling your training, really I'm not. I know it's taking precious time away from your family."

The other man stiffened proudly. "Time well spent! You are a *boyar*'s son, young master. This would have been my duty back when I was still captain of your father's guards in . . . better days. It's still my obligation to see that his only son learns the skills proper to one of his rank."

Skills over twenty years out of date! Emelian was too fond of the grizzled old soldier to say that aloud. *We don't even know for sure if this is still the proper style of swordplay!* He forced a grin. "Ah well, I suppose I'll learn in time."

Serge shook his head. "You already show the signs of making a fine swordsman. You just must learn not to be so—so—"

"So impulsive?" the young man finished for him. "Yes. I know. I've heard that from you before. And from my father." Emelian stirred impatiently. "Serge, thank you. But now I'm afraid I'm going to have to put aside the skills of a nobleman and go help said father repair the chicken coop."

Serge winced. "That a *boyar* should come to this!" he said softly.

"And what do you expect?" snapped Emelian, then added gently, "Nobility's all well and good, but it doesn't hire servants. And a penniless *boyar*, fine blood or no, has no choice but to—Ahh, never mind, Serge. You know the old saying: 'What is, is.' The past can't be changed, now, can it?" Emelian slapped the man lightly on the shoulder. "Go on, get back to your own affairs. And a good day to you."

"And to you, young master."

Hands on hips, Emelian watched the old warrior leave, and gave a bemused little smile at the thought that Serge, for all his snobbery and concern about the proper order of things, had ended up married happily to a peasant woman in a peasant village.

The whole wooden palisade surrounding the estate shook ominously as Serge shut the gate behind him, and Emelian's smile vanished.

"Dammit, not that, too!"

He fought down the urge to give the wobbly fence a savage kick. Something else to be fixed. When he had the time.

The time, ha! He could have had the whole palisade strengthened already, had his father not insisted he waste so much of that time learning to be a proper *boyar*.

Emelian snorted, looking about him with honest eyes, seeing the ramshackle old mansion falling slowly to pieces, the sagging outbuildings. Estate? Farm—and a failing one at that! He'd often suspected it hadn't been mercy that had made Prince Svyatoslav grant Emelian's father exile here—rather than slaying or imprisoning him—but a rather nasty sense of humor. The young man had heard often enough what his parents had found on their arrival: a hastily vacated estate, with all its portable valuables vanished with the caretakers. That hadn't mattered too much at first; his parents had managed to hurriedly pack sufficient gold with them to buy servants from the village. But over the years, the gold had run out, and with it, the servants.

Not that Emelian truly blamed those peasants; they had their own lands to tend, their own families to feed. Only the rich could afford charity. In the past five years, it had come down to him and his father trying to run the place all by themselves, shutting up all the rooms in the drafty mansion save for those three small enough to be easy to heat, farming only enough of the increasingly stubborn land as would keep them alive.

Emelian looked down at his rough, work-callused hands. "A *boyar*!" he repeated softly.

Why would his father never face facts? The old man would never be able to return to Stargorod and the way things had been. And as for his son . . . Emelian sighed. He knew his father meant only the best for him, but these lessons in swordsmanship, these ridiculous lessons in the manners and mores of the nobility . . .

He'd never even seen Stargorod! He'd been born here, soon after his parents' arrival. At first, after the tragedy of his mother's death, Emelian had followed his father's wishes—no matter how dubiously—simply because he'd been too young to do otherwise. There'd been just the two of them, alone save for each other. And for Serge, of course: kindhearted, but a living reminder to the exiled *boyar* of what he'd lost.

Emelian stirred restlessly. He wasn't a wide-eyed boy anymore. By now the only things keeping him obedient were love and a painful pity for a man clinging with such terror to his past.

But how far could pity stretch? *Father, I love you, but I've my own life to lead!*

Assuming that he could figure out what his own life should be. The young man glanced down at himself and grinned ruefully. He wasn't ever going to be more than of medium height and, lessons in nobility notwithstanding, his inelegant life had left him sturdy and sunbrowned as any peasant.

Maybe that's it, thought Emelian, only half in jest. Maybe he should have been raised as a peasant. After all, he had friends in the village—for all that his father disapproved—and they seemed content with their lot, knowing exactly what they wanted out of life and how to get it.

Akh, ridiculous! What they wanted—no, *all* they wanted—were good harvests and fertile beasts and wives, with never a wondering about what might lie beyond the edges of their fields.

But that's not what I want! Wild, wondrous images flashed through Emelian's mind: shining palaces, bustling cities, visions lent him from wandering peddlers' tales. *I want—oh, God, I want to get out of here!*

Yes, and to get his father out, too. If only Emelian could get him away from these crumbling old ruins—

maybe they couldn't go to Stargorod, but there was a whole world out there.

But so far the old man stubbornly refused to leave this last reminder of his former life. Emelian sighed. He could hardly sling his father over his shoulder and walk off with him. But he couldn't simply abandon the man either, no matter how great the temptation, not when he was so worn and aging and alone . . .

Enough self-pity, Emelian told himself sternly, and set out in search of his father.

"AKH, WAIT!" Emelian rushed forward in alarm. "Don't try to lift that whole side of planking by yourself!"

His father tried to shoulder him aside. "No, it's all right, I can manage—"

"You shouldn't try to—"

With the two of them struggling against each other, they quickly lost their hold on the planking, and it fell, breaking apart into individual boards once more.

"Oh—damn it!"

"Father, I told you I'd help you!" Emelian's anger died in birth as he studied the man, seeing his own features reflected there, the same brown eyes, the same broad cheekbones, but so painfully sharpened by age and deprivation. *How frail he's become, how old . . .* "You shouldn't have tried to do it all yourself," Emelian finished lamely. "I could have helped."

"It's all right, boy." The man's voice was as soothing as though he were talking to a child, and Emelian flinched.

"Father—"

"Your session with Serge was more important. Tell me, how did it go?"

"Well enough. But . . ." Emelian hesitated, trying in vain to control himself, then gave up, exploding, "What's the point of any of it?"

"What do you mean?"

"You've taught me how a *boyar* talks and acts and

handles a sword—*please*, just once, see things as they really are! We don't have any fine estate, we don't have *versts* of land. All we have is this one little ruin of a farm!'' Emelian stopped to catch his breath, and managed to continue more calmly. "Instead of studying those high-and-mighty ways, I'm going to do what I should have done years ago: go to the villagers and learn proper farming from them. They've already told me how poor the soil is here—that's one reason we've been having so much trouble—but maybe with their help I can still find a way to turn this place into—''

"No!'' His father's eyes blazed with insulted rage. "You are a nobleman, not some filthy peasant! Some day the summons will come, returning us from exile, and then you must be ready to take your place as my son.''

Emelian winced. "It's not going to happen,'' he said as gently as he could. "Prince Svyatoslav is quite secure on his throne. Those travelling merchants told us that just the other day. Remember?''

"They lied! That—tyrant! His cousin should be Prince of Stargorod, not he!''

"Father, please . . .''

But, lost in his memories, the old *boyar* had already begun retelling the all-too-familiar tale: how he'd sided with Svyatoslav's cousin, Prince Rostislav, during that ill-fated revolution more than twenty years past; how Rostislav had been defeated, and fled.

Leaving his loyal followers to face death or exile, Emelian thought dourly.

Aching with pity, he glanced at his father, anguished at seeing only this frail and lonely shadow of the strong, loving man of his childhood.

"And so your mother and I came here,'' the *boyar* was concluding. "Here you were born, and here, soon after . . .'' He paused, blinking fiercely. "My poor Xenia . . . You do remember her, boy, you must.''

Emelian did, vaguely, a small boy's memories of a slight, gentle, loving Someone, and the three of them laughing together . . . Now, with older eyes, Emelian could see how fragile his mother had always been; it hadn't been the shock of exile that had killed her so much as the fact that she'd never quite recovered from his birth.

But his father, blinded by grief, wouldn't accept that. "Her strength was never the same after that terrible day of exile." The old man straightened fiercely. "Another crime to be laid at Svyatoslav's feet. He slew her as surely as any executioner!"

"I loved her, too," Emelian began carefully. "But . . . Father, she died over fifteen years ago. We can only live in the present."

The man simply stared at him. Overwhelmed by a rush of love and despair, Emelian cried out, "This place is nothing! Let's leave it, you and I!"

"Indeed." His father's face went still and cold as stone. "And where would you have us go?"

"I don't know . . . We still have kinsfolk, don't we? Kinsfolk unallied to either Svyatoslav or Rostislav . . . Ha, I have it! There's Maria, Maria . . . Danilovna, that's the name! She's my—what?—my third or fourth cousin, something like that, and she's supposed to be the wife of Prince Finist of Kirtesk—Kirtesk isn't an ally of Stargorod, not really. Surely we'd have shelter there—"

"As penniless beggars."

"Oh, come now! We wouldn't be—"

"I will not accept charity! This is my land, *mine,* poor though it may be. And I will *not* leave it to become a beggar!"

"But you—I—"

"No! Enough of this. Emelian, enough! We have work to do."

EMELIAN SAT on a rock in the middle of a peaceful grove, surrounded by warm springtime, by soft stirrings of leaves and dappled sunlight, sat with anything but peace in his heart.

He'd fled into the forest on the pretext of gathering firewood, after their quarrel had gone fruitlessly on and on, because there had come a point where his rage and despair and frustration had gone beyond bearing. Had Emelian stayed, he would surely have said or done something both his father and he would have regretted.

With a weary sigh, the young man sagged, head in hands. It always ended like this. Every time he tried to reason with his father, they wound up shouting at each other.

I can't stand this anymore. I've got to get out of here!

But how? How leave his father alone, helpless? Emelian groaned, despairing. There wasn't even anyone to whom he could turn for advice. Serge would tell him sternly to obey his father, no matter what. The peasant folk would either quote proverbs at him or simply refuse to consider the problems of *boyars*.

God, where was the way out of this tangle?

A loud squeal of anguish cut sharply into his misery. Emelian straightened, identifying: *rabbit*. Some predator must have made a kill.

But the anguished squealing went on and on, and the young man got reluctantly to his feet. What a wonderful day *this* was turning out to be! The unfortunate beast must have gotten itself mangled by some hunter's trap, and now Emelian, out of humanity, was going to have to put the poor thing out of its pain.

It's a worse day for the rabbit, he thought, and set out. Judging from the sound, it couldn't be too far away. Somewhere down this path, he guessed . . .

Odd. Now the sound seemed to be coming from the right, instead of straight ahead. Could the rabbit have torn itself free? No, if that were so, the injured beast would be hiding in silence, not continuing those nerve-shattering shrieks; Emelian knew that much woodcraft. If he parted these bushes, he should be able to see . . .

With an alarming suddenness, the screams stopped. Emelian gave a relieved sigh. The rabbit must have died of its injuries, and he didn't have to be its butcher. Now, all he had to do was retrace his steps . . .

Could he retrace them? Emelian stopped, puzzled. Surely the path he'd been following had run in a reasonably straight line, west to east. There couldn't have been this many twists to it—and he *knew* there hadn't been a branching to it!

Feeling the first cold tricklings of fear, Emelian whirled, trying to find some familiar landmark, struggling to get his bearings. Akh, which way was which? He had suddenly lost all sense of direction. The sun— but he couldn't judge direction by the sun, because the leafy branches overhead cut off almost all the light, leaving him alone in green dimness.

No need to be alarmed. All he had to do was climb a tree till he could reach sunlight and see just where he was.

But the first branch Emelian tried to grasp somehow seemed to raise itself just a bit higher than he could reach.

The wind, Emelian told himself, trying to ignore the fact that the air down here seemed perfectly calm.

But the second tree apparently had raised its branches out of his grasp too, and when he tried to shinny up the trunk of a third tree, it let him fall back to the forest floor in a shower of dead bark and bits of twig. Panting, Emelian picked himself up, fighting panic.

All about him, the forest seemed to be holding its breath, making him abruptly aware of being surrounded by a presence very alien to his humanity, a presence that fairly quivered with . . .

With *humor?*

Emelian froze in sheer disbelief. Humor! Paths that changed as though deliberately trying to get him lost. Trees that seemed determined to shake him off. But— not out of malice, he realized slowly. None of this, frightening though it might be, was being done out of malice. Rather, it was almost as though some nonhuman creature was trying to play a joke on him!

And just then, as though to settle his doubts, the path before him softly shifted direction. Emelian gave a laugh of out-and-out wonder, his panic forgotten.

"All right," he called out, "you win! I believe. Only a *leshy* could have the power to do something like this!"

He'd first heard about the *leshiye*, those shape-shifting, quicksilver-humored beings who were lords of the forest, from the peasantry. At the time he'd merely laughed, sure that he was being teased. But now, surrounded by forest and that inhuman sense of amusement, he had to wonder . . .

There hadn't been a rabbit at all; the screaming had only been a lure to draw him into this snare. There was a way out of this, though, unless the peasants had lied . . .

Feeling like a fool, Emelian sat down and began undressing, turning trousers and tunic inside out, dressing again with everything on back to front. A burst of wild laughter made him jump up, nearly stumbling in the shoes he'd placed on the wrong feet.

"Clever!" crowed a voice like the whisper of wind in leaves. "Oh, a lovely, silly jest!"

And with that, Emelian abruptly felt his confusion vanish, leaving him knowing exactly where in the forest he was. The tales were true, he realized with relief: give a *leshy* a good laugh over human foolishness, and he'd let you go. "Uh . . . thank you, my lord *leshy*," Emelian called out uncertainly. "I'll be going now, with your permission."

For a moment, he could have sworn that wild, bright eyes were staring down at him from the leaves overhead. "Ha," said the wind-whisper voice. A faint rustle, hardly audible; then, "Wait." Now the being was somewhere directly before him, hidden in shadow. "What are you?"

Emelian blinked. "Why, a man! Your pardon, but I don't—"

"No, no. City man, country man, you smell of both and none. What *are* you?"

"I wish I knew," Emelian muttered. *"Leshy,* my father came from a city. I was born here. I'm sorry, but that's about as much as I can tell you."

"No!" For a heartbeat's time, the being allowed himself to be seen, a strange, skinny, green-furred creature, horned like a goat and— No, that was wrong, the *leshy* was a smoothly blue-skinned little man who— No, that wasn't it, either. But before Emelian could be certain of what he had seen, the being was gone into shadow again. "Not enough. You do not belong here. Why?"

For a moment, the young man could only stare, trying in vain to make out even a vague outline of his questioner amid the bushes. None of the tales had ever mentioned anyone actually having a conversation with a *leshy!* And for all the being's bizarre and seemingly harmless form—or forms—there was a casual air of Power to him that made Emelian wonder uneasily what would happen if his answers weren't satisfactory.

"It's true," the young man said warily. "I suppose I don't really belong here. My father is—was—is a nobleman, from a city, yes, and he—well, he trained me to be a nobleman of a city, too. But he's in exile here— ah, do you know what 'exile' is?"

"A human punishment. Nothing to do with me." The wind-whisper voice was now coming from a thicket to Emelian's left, though he hadn't sensed even a hint of motion. "Go on, city-country human. He must stay here, yes? His punishment. But you?" The questions were coming swiftly as a squirrel's chatter. "Why must you stay? Are you in this exile, too?"

"No, but I must stay. Father's no longer young, and there's no one to care for him save me." A wave of despair swept over him. All at once Emelian was furious at the *leshy* for these light, uncaring questions that raised such pain, and he cried out, "Oh, *leshy,* I don't know how much of this you're understanding, I don't even know if you're really interested in what I'm saying, but: Do you understand 'love,' *leshy?* I *can't* leave him!''

There was a long pause during which Emelian became certain the being had grown bored and left him. But then he was showered with a rain of twigs and leaves, and looked sharply up, just in time to catch a glimpse of those wild, mad eyes.

''That is yours, that strange, ugly farm? The one with the old man? He is yours?''

''Yes,'' said Emelian warily. ''Why?''

There was another long pause. The vaguely seen, green-furred head tilted sharply to one side, listening to something beyond mere mortal hearing. ''So . . .'' It was the faintest whisper of sound. ''I think you no longer have a problem of staying-going, human.'' There was a strange undertone to the alien voice—almost, thought Emelian in sudden alarm, of pity.

''What are you saying?''

''Sorrow. Joy. Go and see.''

''My father—has something happened to my father? Tell me!''

But the *leshy* was gone.

Heart racing, Emelian started back towards the farm, the familiar trail suddenly seeming to be more overgrown than ever, at least now that he was in a hurry, each delay adding to his growing panic till he was tearing his way with frantic impatience through the tangled underbrush, feeling like a man in a nightmare struggling through a never-ending maze. But then he was in the open, and running full out. Ahead was the farm's sagging palisade, and Emelian nearly tore the gate off its hinges in his haste.

''Father? Where are you? Father!''

The farmyard held only a few disinterested chickens. Emelian raced into the house, glancing wildly about, running frantically from room to room—empty. But the axe was missing from its place on the wall. Had the old *boyar* gone into the forest? They'd known they'd eventually need more logs for repairs. Had he, trying to work off anger at his son, thought to cut trees down all by himself? Emelian ran back out through the rickety palisade gate, praying to hear the sound of the axe, listening instead to terrifying silence.

"Where are you? *Father!*" A flash of color caught his eye, the blue of the old man's caftan, and Emelian hurried forward in wild relief.

"Didn't you hear me calling you? Why didn't you . . . Father . . . ?"

His steps faltered.

His father had indeed gone to cut wood. There were the marks of his axe on a tall larch. But a dead branch had apparently been jarred loose by the blows. It must have fallen from a great height. And it had struck the old man on the head.

For a moment, paralyzed by shock, Emelian couldn't do anything but stare at the crumpled body, thinking helplessly:

He—he can't be dead.

Then suddenly the paralysis shattered, and he was running forward, hurling himself down at his father's side, taking the frail body in his arms, seeing without really accepting the terrible head wound. The man must have died instantly, without pain, at least there was that. But Emelian couldn't think about it yet. He couldn't do anything but huddle where he was, too anguished even for tears.

Gradually it came to him that he was being watched, and Emelian glanced up, glaring at the glimpse he caught of bright, wild, *leshy* eyes. And, driven by grief far beyond the point of caution, he cried:

"He was an old man! What harm could he possibly have done to you?"

"Why, no harm!"

"Oh, don't sound so innocent! You knew what I'd find! This is all your doing, isn't it?"

"No."

There seemed to be such genuine surprise in the being's voice that Emelian's anguished rage cleared enough for him to add, almost pleading, "But this is your realm . . . Couldn't you have . . . ?"

"Stopped him?" The *leshy* stirred in sudden sharp impatience, and the branches about him stirred, unnervingly, with him. "Stopped the tree from being a tree, or the natural laws from being laws?" There was an angry edge to the being's voice, like the sharpening of wind that marks the coming of a storm. The forest seemed to waken all about him, tense with waiting, and Emelian shivered in spite of himself.

"I did not kill the man," the *leshy* continued coldly, "nor did the tree kill him. A branch fell. He was beneath it. That is all." The being paused. "Human, I will forgive you your words. For now. But—be wary. Press me too far, and things may happen in the forest that are *not* mere chance!"

Emelian was no fool. "Forgive me, my lord *leshy,*" he murmured. "I meant no insult. It's just that . . . my father . . ."

Gradually the sense of inhuman tension lessened. There was the faintest breath of a sigh. "Why do you human-folk mourn so wildly?" the *leshy* asked plaintively. "You grieved to me of his imprisonment here. Now the man is free of that foolish thing of exile. Why do you mourn his freedom?"

"Akh, can't you understand about death?"

"Death? Death? After forest-death comes forest-rebirth! What more is there to it? Ha, and think, human! Now you too are free—free to find your own destiny."

"Destiny," echoed Emelian dully. "What would you know of that?"

"I know! Do you dare think the forest is bound to your petty ideas of time? Phaugh, why do I bother with you?"

There was so long a silence that Emelian was sure the being had vanished. Putting the *leshy*'s bizarre words aside, he looked down at his father's body again, nearly sobbing aloud to see it so frail, so diminished . . . But it wasn't quite time for mourning yet. First he must see to what must be done, the burial, and the—

Without warning, the wind-whisper voice spoke up again, just as though there hadn't been a pause. "And it will be a strange destiny, human."

"Why tell me this?"

"Oh, why, indeed? Perhaps because you tried to show mercy to a rabbit-that-wasn't. Perhaps because I sensed the hint of a strangeness-to-be about you." The *leshy* stirred in renewed impatience. "Enough! Listen, human: this destiny of yours may well be deadly. But then again, it may prove splendid."

With that, the *leshy* was gone, and this time did not return. Emelian, alone, was horrified to feel the stirrings of something besides grief, something that was almost . . . relief.

God, what sort of creature am I, to be glad my father's dead!

And yet, despite himself, a faint, hopeful, inner voice kept repeating the being's words:

Now you are free to find your own destiny. And it may prove splendid.

"No," said Emelian bitterly.

But still, that thread of hope remained.

III

DISCOVERIES

"BUT DO YOU REALLY THINK this is wise?" *boyar* Nikolai asked yet again.

Marya sighed. Nikolai, head of her Inner Council, was that rarity: a clever, honest man absolutely content with his position in life. And he had been a great comfort to her in that dreadful time right after her father's death. But, being twice her age, he did have an annoying tendency to patronize her. She glanced at the slender, middle-aged man with his scrupulously clean caftan and scrupulously neat hair and beard. *Neat!* the princess thought in amusement. *Were our Nikolai to fall into mud, he'd convince it not to stain him!*

"*Boyar*, what's bothering you? That I'm agreeing to meet him without having the full council present? Or that I'm meeting with Vasilev at all?"

"He's a risky sort . . ." Nikolai began carefully.

"He's a fool! Come now, what harm can he possibly do me?"

"My Princess, you haven't seen the man for over seven years. That is a long time, and—"

"And Vasilev might have learned some sense during it? Oh, Nikolai! I have my spies watching his estate, just as you recommended. Vasilev was and remains a fool! The only thing I really regret is that this meeting is taking time away from any of my people who might

29

really need my help. So let me get it done as quickly as possible!''

As VASILEV SWEPT down in an urbane bow, Marya, seated in impressive if somewhat uncomfortable splendor on the huge, square-sided ivory-and-gold throne chair of the Krasny Chamber, studied him covertly, wryly amused to realize she really had come quite a bit from that girl of seven years ago who, even though she'd been bright enough to recognize his shallowness, had still been just a bit awed at the sight of that handsome face and graceful form. And Vasilev was still a fine sight, what with that elegant face and those limpid blue eyes.

Witless blue eyes.

He might happen to be her relation, thanks to Grandfather's romp many years ago, but that didn't mean she had to like the man.

Still, she must be polite. "So, Vasilev," Marya said sweetly. "Good morning. And why are you here?"

He gave her a mildly reproachful look. "Why, my dear Princess, you yourself invited me!"

"Of course I did." This time the politeness was a touch forced. "At your request. Come, why are you here?"

The man glanced about the audience chamber, with its rich blaze of carpeting, its brightly painted walls— and its ever-alert guards. "Cousin Marya, I must speak with you. In private."

"I think we have little to discuss."

"Please. It's about us—and Astyan."

"Is it, now?"

Vasilev smiled a gentle, sympathetic smile. "I know you tend to rise early—virgin beds are such . . . lonely things—and I thought that if you were gracious enough to grant me an audience now, before the crowds are about, surely we'd have time to speak alone."

Marya fought to keep her face carefully blank. *"Virgin bed," is it? Cousin, you never were noted for your tact.*

But stupid men could still be dangerous. Particularly

stupid men with both ambition and a share of the royal blood . . . Marya knew she should be careful. But after the sheer evil of the Other, Vasilev seemed so trivial that before she could stop herself, she'd snapped, "Don't waste that wounded look on me, Vasilev! I'm not one of your silly little conquests!"

"Marya!"

"Vasilev, please. Stop pretending. You don't like me, and I don't like you. I know you hate your father for having been born of illegal blood and not letting you be the heir to the crown. I know you despise my being both a woman and your junior. There, now. What else is there to say? That you want me to marry?"

Ha, that stunned him! Hadn't he realized how transparent he'd been?

No. Vasilev being Vasilev, he hadn't realized it at all. And now he was trying to regain his poise, stammering, "I—uh—yes! It's not wise for a young woman to rule Astyan all by herself. Women aren't meant for such burdens! Look what it's doing to you, turning you into a bitter creature, you who should be full of joy and life—"

"And light-headedness?" completed Marya wryly. "Go on, Vasilev. I'm fully aware that I must wed. But whom are you suggesting?" she added delicately. "Yourself, perhaps?"

He drew himself up, insulted. "And why should that be so ridiculous an idea? I am free to wed, and of the blood royal. We're not such close kin—why shouldn't I be the one to wed you?" Vasilev glanced at the blank-faced guards, and his voice sank conspiratorially. "And I know the paths of pleasure, Marya. I could show you joys of which you've never dreamed."

"And in exchange for these joys, you'd want what? A consort's chair? Would you be content with that, now?"

He fell right into her trap. "Why, no, we'd rule together! Co-rulers, of course we would!"

"We would *not!*" Marya's voice was sharp enough to make him flinch. "I am ruler of Astyan, Vasilev;

that is my sacred trust.'' Blazing with rage, she continued, ''And I will not abandon it, I will not share it, I
will not see it lessened or shamed or belittled, not for
you, not for anyone! Now, unless you have some other
business to discuss with me, cousin, you have my permission to leave!''

RAGING, Vasilev stormed out of the Krasny Chamber.

That—that—that little *bitch*! Sitting there so kiss-my-
feet proud, scolding him as though he were some little
boy—

And he'd had to just stand there, and bow, and pretend nothing was wrong. For a moment, Vasilev tried
to picture Marya humbled, in his bed— No, no, as his
servant, his slave, huddling at his feet in terror.

Dammit, some of the guards were following him, just
as though he were some criminal! Vasilev whirled to
face them. ''Get out of here!''

''Ah . . . we—''

''Do you think I'm going to steal something? Get out
of here! Leave me alone!''

At least they were obeying him. Fuming, he watched
them go, then turned to stalk away with as much dignity
as he could summon. But a small hand was catching at
his sleeve, a woman's voice was whispering urgently:

''Vasilev! Vatza, please!''

Akh, Olga. He wasn't in the mood for her plump
silliness right now. But before he could say anything to
be rid of her, the young thing was pulling him back into
the shadowy niche with her, babbling:

''I've found something, at least I think I have!''

''What *are* you talking about?'' Vasilev glanced
around warily. ''And did anyone see you—''

''No one. I've been careful, I swear it, Vatza.''

He winced at the pet name. ''What did you find?''

''Well, I was watching, just as you told me to, and I
saw Princess Marya come up a staircase, that one over
there, and she was pale and trembling, though naturally
she pretended nothing was wrong when she saw me.''

"And?" Vasilev prodded impatiently.

Olga gave him an indignant glance. "Well, once I was alone, I went down there to see what was frightening her, you know."

"And?"

"And there was nothing down there, nothing at all!"

"Idiot!" But Vasilev hastily bit back the word. Foolish to alienate the girl when he still might need her. "Forgive me, Olga. I didn't mean you."

But he was wondering, *What could possibly have frightened that tough little witch?*

Witch, indeed . . . Maybe she didn't have any of her father's magic. But what if she had been toying with something forbidden, something sorcerous. Something he could hold over her head as a threat. Vasilev chuckled at the thought. Why, the throne might still be his! He caught the startled Olga in his arms and kissed her till he felt her melt helplessly against him, then released her, chuckling anew. Oh, maybe Olga *thought* she hadn't seen anything down there, but he couldn't expect the silly creature to know truth from fancy.

"Thank you, sweetheart," Vasilev said lightly. "I'll go down there myself and see what I can find."

That was, he realized in sudden unease, before dear cousin Marya sent guards looking for him to throw him out.

In a place far beyond the physical, a plane of endless, formless darkness, a presence stirred in restless anger. Long and long he had struggled against the bindings, fighting to free himself, to reenter the human world . . . But though his spirit roved free throughout the empty plane, his mortal shell remained imprisoned, held fast by charms and iron.

If only I had struck first—aie-yé, how I'd have tormented that fool!

But the magician had fled from any chance of vengeance, escaped into mortal death.

Death. The presence considered that for a time. He

could vaguely recall what it had once meant to be human, to live every short day knowing he must eventually face that ending. Now, humanity abandoned after long and terrible sorceries, he need never know true death.

But, whispered a shadow in his mind, *you will never know true life again either, or joy, or peace . . .*

What of it? The Power was all! Long ago he had accepted that no Power was gained without a price. And the price he must pay was simple enough: if he wished to walk in mortal realms, he must wear a mortal shell. Without it, his essence would be no more than so much vapor, to scatter the first time he tried to enter a world, all his Power useless as mist upon the winds.

The presence hissed in anger. Were he to abandon the human shell that lay trapped behind spells and chains, he would be free. But creating such a human-seeming form was no easy thing. Each shell he'd worn over his long existence had taken slow, painful ages to build, formed bit by patient bit from the fine mists of matter sometimes found where Nothingness chanced to brush against a mortal realm.

Oh, he'd made a fool's mistake with the last-but-one of those shells, warding it against the touch of any man's weapon, only to have it destroyed and himself banished by a knife-wielding woman. This time he'd taken care to place such spells and restrictions on his shell that no mortal creature, man *or* woman, could ever slay it.

Even so, there is always mischance.

The presence shuddered, darkness rippling soundlessly about him. Should his shell be destroyed, he would face once more the long and anguished fall into the Outer Dark that would trap him in despair till, eons later, he had tediously managed to build a new shape.

No, the presence thought bitterly. The magician—curse that human fool!—had sensed and snared him even as he reentered the physical world. There had barely been enough time to fit mind and newly completed shell together! *No,* the presence repeated. Imprisoned this

form might be, but after all those painfully slow ages
of its building, he wasn't ready to yield it:

Not while there was still a chance of freedom—and
revenge.

VASILEV DESCENDED the small stairway warily, uneasy
in the dim light, carrying no torch because the light
would have certainly brought the guards down after him.
Still, he had never liked such close, dank places. What
if some sorcerous thing should chose to pounce on him
right now, when his only weapon was an ornate and all
but useless dress-dagger?

Nonsense—if a silly fool like Olga could come down
here unhindered, so could he.

Of course, Olga probably didn't have the sense to
know when to be afraid.

Akh, enough. Here was the bottom of the stairway
at last, and not the slightest sign of life. Hand still on
the railing, Vasilev paused. Now, why would Marya
ever want to come down here? This place was dank and
cold and clearly empty of anything that—

But it wasn't empty, not quite. If he strained his eyes
to peer intently, he saw nothing, but if he let his vision
wander . . . yes. There at the corner of sight was the
hint of a sealed doorway. Though why he couldn't seem
to see it clearly . . . Puzzled and uneasy, Vasilev took
a wary step forward.

THE PRESENCE STARTED as sharply as though hot metal had
touched him. Someone had drawn near his mortal shell!

Swiftly the presence dove through empty darkness,
pouring smoothly back into that shell. There was a moment's confusion, a dizzying sense of being so suddenly
bounded by the finite after all that infinite nothingness.
Grimly the presence struggled for control.

All at once he felt his center of focus shift: now the
dark emptiness seemed alien, mortal limitations quite
normal and natural. The transition was complete, and
he was Koshchei once more.

Now he must concentrate only on the human. Koshchei tensed, listening intently with human and inhuman senses.

Aie, the feel of this aura—could it be? Shivering with savage hope, he tightened his scan . . . Ahh, yes! This wasn't that stubborn, strong-willed little magician's daughter; this was a weaker, far more foolish mind. But it did belong to one of the right blood.

Quickly Koshchei sent out a tendril of mental force, delicately probing, and felt the human mind flinch. A more intelligent personality, even one untrained in magic, would have been complete enough in itself to shut him out. But this weakling was no more a total entity than a child. *Oh, yes, soon I will be free* . . . Aching with anticipation of that freedom, Koshchei increased the strength of his probe, calling cajolingly:

"Come to me."

On the other side of the door, Koshchei sensed, the human froze, then whirled. Koshchei could almost read the frightened thoughts: there was no one in the room with him, yet someone had just spoken to him—and spoken without words!

"What's that?" Vasilev cried. "Who are you?"

Koshchei answered, as gently as scant patience permitted, *"No one to frighten you."*

"You—you're talking in my head!"

"In a manner of speaking, yes."

And then he had to wait for the torrent of terrified thoughts to stop tumbling through the human's mind. "This is impossible!" It was a wail. "I—I've gone mad, or— Where are you?"

Ah! Delicately, now: *"Here. Trapped behind this door. Can't you sense me here?"* The human fool did, or they wouldn't be able to speak together. *"Come, touch the door and you will see it clearly."*

But instead, Vasilev cringed away. "The demon! You're the demon the prince confined, the one that slew him! God, no, leave me alone!"

In another instant, he'd be running in panic. Fiercely

Koshchei increased the force of his probe, lashing out at the man's weak essence. *"Fool! Free me, and I will grant you wonder! What are your dreams, little man? Let me see . . ."* The man's fragile psychic walls crumbled easily before the Deathless's skillful mental touch. *"So-o!"* Koshchei said in triumph. *"You would rule, would you? Splendid—you shall have your throne. Only free me, and it shall be yours!"*

But he'd pushed the foolish mind too far. Terrified of him, of the very thought of demonic pacts, it was curling madly in on itself, shutting him out.

Raging, Koshchei tore blindly past his victim's weak, untrained defenses, overwhelming the human mind.

"So you want the throne, do you, fool? Then you shall fight for it! You shall take your funds and buy yourself men, and fight your cousin!"

But human minds broke so easily! Panting, Koshchei brought himself back under control. Had he slain the man?

No. Vasilev was still alive and mostly sane, though the Deathless's fury had burned away segments of his reason. What remained of that weak personality . . . Koshchei smiled thinly. His rage had hit on the fool's own inner dream: Vasilev as conquerer, Marya at his feet. Now, his mind damaged, the man wanted only to achieve that dream. He gave no resistance at all to Koshchei's sorcerous commands.

Beyond the door, the Deathless felt Vasilev turn and leave, white-faced and mute, fierce with sudden new determination, never once seeing the foolishness of it.

And the fool would gladly fight, making war on Marya. One would win and one would die—which, it hardly mattered. Either way, the winner, weak and drained from battle, would have no resistance to fight Koshchei's proddings.

"I will be free!" the Deathless shouted. "At last, *I will be free!*"

IV

FOREST MURMURINGS

"BUT WHAT ARE YOU GOING TO *do?*" Serge asked plaintively.

Emelian paused in his packing to glance up at the man. Struck by the genuine concern he saw in Serge's eyes, this time he answered honestly. "I don't know. But there's no place for me here."

"Your father . . ."

The young man sighed. "My father has been dead for nearly three months now. I—I've had my time to grieve. Akh, man, don't look so grim! What h-happened, happened." That hadn't come out quite as smoothly as Emelian would have liked. He hurried on: "The estate is yours now, to do with as you will. I brought in those witnesses from the village to swear to it, so there shouldn't be any trouble for you."

"I'm not worried about myself! But you, setting out into the world like— Your father wouldn't have wanted—"

"Serge, please. We both know Father never meant for me to be a farmer. He trained me to be a *boyar.*" Emelian looked down at his plain, serviceable clothing with a wry smile. All he had to prove his noble birth were his manners, his sword, one rather worn silken caftan carefully packed away, and a few odd bits of jewelry. "Well," he added with a sort of desperate cheerfulness, "I'm going to see if I can find myself a court position somewhere out there and try my hand at actually *being* a *boyar.*"

"Not in Stargorod!"

"Oh, hardly!" Emelian had no intention of getting involved in feuds begun before he was even conceived. "I think I'll try Kirtesk first. At the very least I can pay a courtesy call on my cousin Maria." *Always assuming*, Emelian added dryly to himself, *that she'll acknowledge such a poor relation.*

God, the whole thing sounded so naive. Emelian straightened, adjusting his pack to a more comfortable position. Biting his lip, the young man looked about the estate with a fondness he'd never felt before, reluctant at this last moment to leave the only home he'd known.

Enough. If he hesitated any longer, he would never have the courage to leave. Now was the time to go, while summer still lingered. And how ridiculous it was to wax nostalgic about a place that had always made him miserable!

Emelian took a deep breath and turned resolutely away. "So. Let me be off before the day gets any older."

Serge's face was rigidly impassive. "Be well, young master," he said formally.

"And you, Serge." In a keen rush of affection, Emelian caught the startled old soldier in a quick, fierce embrace. "Akh, don't worry about me! I'll be all right."

"God willing."

"Indeed. Well, now. Serge, farewell!"

And Emelian boldly turned his back on his old life and set out into the world to find his destiny.

EMELIAN STOPPED to wipe back unruly strands of hair from his face, glancing about yet again at the forest all around him, listening to birdsong and the rustling of leaves, wondering if he was ever going to see another human face again.

Once he had gotten over his initial unease, things had gone well enough—at first. The thrilling, frightening sense of being truly on his own, for the first time in his life responsible to and for no one but himself, had turned the first day of walking into an adventure. For all its discomforts, the first night's camping by the side of the road had been something of an adventure, too.

But the second day had brought muscles stiff and cramping from the unaccustomed hiking, bruises from sleeping on what had felt like every rock in the forest, and a reluctant admittance that he'd been listening to too many songs about the joys of the wandering life. Particularly when it drizzled all afternoon, and he couldn't find enough dry wood for a fire.

By the third day of his journeying, any exuberance Emelian might have felt about travelling afoot was long gone. The weather had turned clear again, but there was a nagging chill to the air that heralded the end of summer.

Things would have been a good deal easier on horseback. If he had a horse.

Might as well wish for an escort while I'm at it, and a wagon of food.

Food: Emelian suspected he was going to run into trouble there. He'd heard there were villages from which he could buy supplies all along the way from here to Kirtesk. But he was becoming uncomfortably aware that those stories hadn't been told by anyone who'd ever actually *been* to Kirtesk. All he had seen so far was the narrow road before him and the walls of trees on either side. Somebody had to be maintaining that road, but so far there hadn't been a sign of human life.

Ah well, he might have been gullible when it came to believing tales, but at least he knew how to forage for food.

Emelian wasn't worried about getting lost; he knew the forester's trick of keeping on a straight line through wilderness by sighting from tree to tree. But gathering berries was one thing, gathering food long-lasting enough to be carried with him was another.

Nothing to worry about . . . yet.

He wasn't on any strict schedule, after all. And even with that warning chill to the air, the weather was still being cooperatively warm and—at least for today—clear. Emelian shrugged. If he could find signs of rabbit warrens, he would simply set up camp long enough to snare himself some dinner.

ODD. This type of forest, with all the tangled underbrush so well-loved of rabbits, should be fairly teeming with life. Yet so far Emelian had seen no traces of any sort of animals at all. And the deeper he went into the forest, the more difficult it seemed to be to keep the straight sightings clear in his mind . . . Akh, he had better turn back now, before he got himself lost.

But which way *was* back? Surely he'd passed that larch with the bent trunk, and that clump of saplings, surely the road was—

Gone. Instead of standing on open ground, the increasingly bewildered Emelian found himself in the middle of a small, mossy glade that he certainly hadn't seen before. But something seemed to be penetrating his fuzzy memory . . .

Akh, yes! He had been through this before! *"Leshy!"* the young man called out. "My lord *leshy*, please! I haven't come here for games!" He paused, listening only to silence, feeling the confusion of magic still binding him. "Have I offended you?" Emelian asked the silence. "I'm sorry, I didn't mean to—ah—to trespass, so if you'll just be good enough to show me the road again, I'll be on my way—"

A creaking little rustle of a laugh cut into his words. A strange, shadowy figure that might have been clad in greenish fur seemed to beckon. The *leshy*! Emelian hesitated, well aware of the being's reputation as a trickster. But surely the joke of reversed clothing wouldn't amuse the quicksilver-humored *leshy* a second time. He didn't know what else to do to break the spell on him, so Emelian sighed and followed his elusive guide.

This isn't the way back to the road, I'm almost sure of it!

But the *leshy*'s spell lay heavily upon him. Unable to think clearly, unable to resist, Emelian could only hurry after the being, the branches somehow never catching his clothes or lashing his face, the tree roots never tripping him, on and on through unending forest . . .

And then, without warning, the compulsion was gone. Returned to himself with shocking suddenness, Emelian swayed with a weariness of which he was only now aware. Blinking, confused, the young man looked warily around, shivering in air growing increasingly chilly. As far as he could tell, he was still surrounded by trees, but it was difficult to see even the nearest trunks clearly in the rapidly fading light. The *leshy* had kept him moving nearly all day.

Why did he do this to me?

Emelian knew, in an unquestioning way that could only be the residue of *leshy* magic, that it hadn't been mere trickery on the being's part. The *leshy* had had a definite point in leading him here. But what was it?

He sagged wearily in the darkness, wondering if the *leshy*, having the forest's own undying strength, was even aware that mere humans didn't share that strength. Akh, if the *leshy* had deliberately brought him this far, he was going to trust that the being wouldn't let anything get him during the night.

With that, Emelian wrapped himself in his cloak, sank to the ground, and slept.

HE WOKE with a start the next morning, to find himself quite alone—

And surrounded by a featureless world of grey.

V

OF BATTLEFIELD AND
FOREST

THE LITTLE MEADOW WAS a confused tangle of noise
and smell and color, of the clashing of sword on sword
or shield, of horse-sweat and man-sweat, of the brightness of livery and blood in the late afternoon sunlight.
Surrounded by a ring of loyal guards, weighed down by
her helm and mail shirt, Marya sat her uneasy horse,
hand clenched on the hilt of her as-yet-unbloodied
sword, and determinedly vowed not to be sick. General
Simyan might swear that this wasn't a true battle, only
a skirmish—the attack had apparently caught Vasilev
completely by surprise, and the royal forces outnum-
bered the would-be usurper's disorganized men by more
than three to one—but it was bloody enough for her. It
was one thing to study warfare on parchment and practice swordplay against friendly opponents. It was quite
another to see men actually dying . . .

Marya straightened in the saddle. She would not—
dared not—show any weakness, not when she already
had two counts against her, being both young and female, not when all her men were looking to her as a
sign of royal strength, not when this was the first genuine trial of her reign.

Wild shouts to her left made Marya start, instinctively raising her sword. The firm circle of her guards shattered as a wild-eyed demon of a warrior slashed his way through—

Riding straight for her.

Her training saved her. All at once no longer afraid, Marya parried his first wild blow, though the force of it knocked her back against the high cantle. Ignoring the confusion about her, she struggled back into the saddle, countering with a fierce cut that threw his sword out of line, her mind calmly saying, *There, at his throat. Where helm and shirt don't quite meet.* Two-handed, Marya lashed out, feeling her blade bite into flesh, seeing the man's blood spout, hearing his bubbling gasp of horror—

Then her escort had regrouped, and the would-be assassin was falling, being trampled beneath their horses' hoofs. Someone was asking her frantically:

"Are you hurt? Oh, my Princess, are you hurt?"

It was a long moment before she could force down her shudders enough to do more than merely shake her head.

"Eh, look at that!" said a surprised voice.

Marya straightened sharply.

Vasilev's men were sheathing their weapons and fleeing into the surrounding forest.

"General Simyan! Is this a trick?"

The old warrior turned to her with the swiftest of reverences. "No, my Princess. The traitor hadn't time to gather other *boyars* to him. These are mostly mercenaries, and mercenaries don't risk their lives in lost causes, certainly not for free. And"—Simyan gave her a quick, fierce grin—"it would seem that word has reached them that the traitor's funds have just run out."

"But where *is* Vasilev?"

"Oh, we'll take him, don't worry."

"You don't understand!" Marya fought down the hysterical edge to her voice, shivering in the chill, dank breeze. "It can't be long till nightfall. If we don't take him by then, we'll lose him in the darkness, and have all this to do over again some other time!''

And who knew but that in the interim Vasilev might not be able to form alliances? Maybe the next time wouldn't be a mere skirmish, but a full-out battle—

Murmurings from her men brought Marya abruptly back to the present. *Oh, dammit, no!*

The breeze had been a warning. A wall of fog was rolling in, thick, blinding fog, the timing so terrible it was almost as though her cousin had found the magic to summon it.

''We can't give up now! We've got to find him before it's too late!''

But it was already too late. Surrounded by greyness, all she and her men could do was set up camp in the sudden silence, post guards, and hope Vasilev was as helpless to escape as they were to overtake him.

Surely the fog would be gone by morning.

VASILEV LICKED dry lips, looking wildly about the small tent, fighting down a renewed surge of panic that told him he had been hiding here too long, this day and night and day again, panic that screamed at him to run, run blindly, run anyplace but here.

How could everything have gone so wrong? He'd been so positive when he'd left the palace, so sure of himself. (*Too sure*, insisted a small, sane voice at the back of his mind.) Granted, none of the *boyars* he'd contacted seemed to have any interest in joining his rebellion; granted, most of them had thought him mad. (*Of course they did*, the inner voice continued. *You should have been more cautious; you should have spent more time feeling out the situation*.)

But there hadn't been any time for caution. Vasilev shuddered, dimly recalling a dark, empty chamber . . . a demon . . . The memories slid smoothly away before he could grasp them, and Vasilev shook his head impatiently, now remembering only how he'd left the palace blazing with determination. After that . . .

Damn, he couldn't seem to get facts straight in his mind!

After leaving the palace, there was only that wild, terrifying rush of excitement sweeping him along. All he'd known for sure was the certainty that he must act quickly, empty his coffers to buy mercenaries, storm the palace with whatever men he could get to join him—

But somehow Marya had found out what he planned. Spies, he realized slowly. She must have had spies watching his every move. That was how the little bitch had been able to bring her own troops storming down on him yesterday, before he'd gotten more than a few *versts* from his estate.

It hadn't even been a decent battle! Yesterday his funds had run out, and so had most of the mercenaries, right there and then, leaving him and those few servants remaining loyal to him to run for their own lives.

But he couldn't run any further, not with the pathless forest so near and this cursed fog all around him. Vasilev risked yet another peek out of his tent, and groaned. It was still as dense and blinding as it had been last night—

Surely this was sorcery. He had thought Marya Powerless, but plainly he'd been wrong.

Vasilev sank to his camp stool with a moan. What was he to do now? Oh, God, what *could* he do?

But before he could get lost in self-pity, the man felt a wave of cold emotion sweep over him, a rush of cruel, alien mockery that was never his own. For an instant, wild with terror, Vasilev clearly remembered the terrible, sorcerous mind tearing at him, for that instant he *knew* it wasn't his will moving him, these weren't his ideas flooding his brain—

The instant passed. As though a door had been swiftly shut in his mind, the encounter was forgotten.

Vasilev straightened with something of the cornered beast's desperate courage. He wouldn't run anymore. He was a *boyar*, not some cringing little peasant! But if he didn't run, he must think of something convincing to say when Marya and her cohorts overtook him. If only there was some charge he could level against her, with all her people listening . . .

Akh, yes. Since Marya seemed to really be working sorcery, what better charge for him to make than:

"This is *your* doing. You sent your demon to possess me, to force me to rebel so you could be rid of me!"

Ha, *that* should make her flinch, and that sanctimonious Nikolai too. Vasilev grinned sharply. Who knew? Marya might actually believe him! And even if she didn't:

Why, she won't dare have me harmed, not and risk having people say she murdered me to keep me from telling the truth!

But . . . little Marya was no fool. What if she didn't believe him? Worse, what if her people didn't believe him either? What if she and they laughed at him? Vasilev's grin faded as he pictured himself forced to kneel, surrounded by mocking foes, the fatal sword raised sharp and shining over his neck, ready to drop . . . God, no! He wouldn't die like that!

If she doesn't believe me—dammit, I will go out fighting!

And, let a demon strike him down if he lied, he would take the little bitch with him.

SURROUNDED BY FOG that glowed eerily in the morning light, Marya struggled with her horse as the animal danced nervously beneath her, snatched at the wild wisps of hair that had worked their tickling way down from under her helmet, and tried in vain to wriggle the heavy mail shirt into a less chafing position. Overwhelmed, she spat out a few words that would have shocked prim *boyar* Nikolai.

It was either rage or admit to herself that she was frightened. And right now, lost as she was, it would have been very easy to be frightened.

Vasilev. Think only of Vasilev.

Akh, yes, Vasilev, who had cobbled together the

whole little revolt in such mindless haste. It didn't make sense! Hadn't he realized that not even the most rebellious *boyar* was going to support him? Was he *that* much of a fool?

Fool or no, so far he had managed to elude her. Marya frowned. It should have been easy to overtake him. It *would* have been easy. But this disgusting fog persisted. And in the grey confusion, unable to tell friend from foe, Marya had become separated from her men. Vasilev and what remained of his forces were, as far as she knew, still free, only God knew where. If the man should stumble over her now, he just might be able to turn that ridiculous shambles of a revolt into a victory.

Her horse wasn't any help. Prancing, eyes rolling wildly, it seemed determined to find monsters lurking amid the greyness no matter how Marya tried to steady it with hands and voice.

"Easy, now. Nothing to be—"

A twig snapped behind them, sounding like a thunderclap in the stillness, and the horse was off, grabbing the bit in its teeth, running in blind excitement. Marya clung to its back, crouching as low as she could, hoping the beast could at least sense where it was going. Akh, now they were in the forest, trees looming up about them like so many grim specters. Marya tried to flatten herself even more, picturing a low branch sweeping her from the saddle, or cracking her skull. What was one supposed to do with a runaway? Pull its head around so the horse would run in one big circle?

In the middle of a forest? And have it run full into a tree?

At least her mount seemed to be tiring. Pretty soon she'd have won control again, and maybe—

With a wild cry, a dimly seen, strangely *greenish* someone sprang up under the horse's nose. The startled animal reared, and Marya went flying. She landed with a thump in a pile of dead leaves, barely missing a sturdy larch. For a stunned moment, she lay still.

Aie, but what about her mount? Marya struggled to her feet again, just in time to see the horse gallop eagerly away.

The sound of hoofbeats faded into silence.

Marya was alone and lost, on foot, in the middle of who knew how many *versts* of fog-shrouded wilderness.

AFTER THAT FIRST, panicky start, Emelian sank back to the ground with a weak chuckle. Fog. Day had come, and the glowing greyness was only morning fog.

Chilly, though!

He scrambled to his feet, dancing in place, trying to get his blood flowing freely again. Warmed, Emelian stopped to glance about once more. The fog did seem to be shredding a bit, allowing him tantalizing glimpses of the forest. Common sense told him he should stay where he was and wait for the fog to lift, but Emelian liked the idea of having to stay put against his will almost as little as he'd enjoyed being moved through wilderness against his will.

All at once, two glowing green eyes were piercing the fog, steadily watching him. Emelian snatched wildly for his sword, then froze.

"So. My lord *leshy*," the young man said flatly. Sheathing his weapon, he swept a dour arm about the foggy wilderness. "And is *this* what you wanted for me? Dragging me halfway across the forest— Why? What have I done to you?"

It wasn't the safest of tones to take with a *leshy*, but the being never stirred. "Your destiny approaches." Was there a touch of alien humor in the wind-whisper voice? "Since I do not tell lies, I needed to . . . push it a bit to make my words come true. Now I am done with you, human."

With that, the glowing eyes vanished as swiftly as an extinguished candleflame.

"Wait!" Emelian began, futilely. "Where am I and—"

Something large and in a hurry tore through the bushes to his left, and he whirled, sword in hand before he'd even realized he had drawn it.

A horse! Some wealthy somebody's horse, complete with expensive saddle and bridle, plainly headed at full speed back to its home stable, the fog not hindering it at all . . .

In the next moment, the horse was gone, so swiftly Emelian could almost wonder if he'd dreamed it. But dreams didn't leave broken branches or hoofprints behind.

And what about its rider? The man must have been thrown, might even be lying somewhere, badly injured. The fog was rapidly lifting now, at least enough for Emelian to follow the horse's trail back the way it had come, so he snatched up his pack and set out.

There, now. Ahead of him was a little glade where crushed grass indicated someone had fallen. And wasn't that flash of red a torn scrap of clothing?

"Hello?" Emelian asked tentatively. "Can you hear me?"

No answer. The rider really must be hurt, maybe knocked unconscious. Emelian had a sudden anguished flash of memory: the fallen branch, his father limp beneath it. With a stifled gasp of horror, he hurried forward—

Only to trip and fall flat over someone's outstretched leg.

"Hey!" Emelian squirmed about indignantly to see who'd tripped him. But then he froze, staring up from where he lay.

The point of a sword was at his throat.

VI

SMITTEN

BOUND AND HELPLESS, Koshchei raged. What was happening? Where was his tool, that idiot human? Vasilev had fought, the battle had occurred, that much of a disturbance had affected the man enough to let a psychic echo come trailing back to the Deathless. As far as Koshchei could tell, Vasilev was still alive. But it seemed to him that the magician's daughter still lived, too, which meant that nothing had been gained.

But I can't be sure!

Frustrated, the Deathless stared blindly ahead, suddenly overwhelmed by a longing for something to *see*. There hadn't been anything for these seven years: If he stayed within his physical self, there was only the lonely expanse of blank stone walls. If he abandoned the physical, there was worse: that vast, black, emptiness that was the only realm of the spirit open to him. Koshchei had long ago realized he could forget that human fear of madness; his mind would not break from simple external deprivation.

Akh, but it would look back on the past, remembering.

For a moment his simple longing swelled into a bittersweet ache of loss. For a moment he remembered poignantly the sharp scent of autumn, the golden taste of mead, the silken touch of womanflesh . . . Tricked by memory, he knew again—or almost knew—what it had been like to be human, truly alive, surrounded by sight and sound and color . . .

To be Powerless! Abruptly back to himself, Koshchei hissed. Had he sunk to this, envying humanity? Puny, useless, *mortal* humanity—damn the lot of them!

Savagely he forced down that weak, ridiculous ache for what-had-been till there was only the Deathless, only the Power, only the burning need for revenge.

All softness banished, Koshchei drove his will outward, seeking Vasilev, the tool of his freedom.

BOYAR NIKOLAI ABSENTLY BRUSHED stray hair back from his face, looking desperately about the foggy field yet again. And yet again he moaned:

"I knew she shouldn't have come. A young princess never should have been allowed on a battlefield."

General Simyan shot the *boyar* a contemptuous glance. Pretending to adjust his peaked iron helm, he muttered, "Seems to me you're the one with no business here! Should have stayed back in Astyan, where you'd be nice and safe."

"What's that, man?"

Nikolai's voice had a warning edge to it, and Simyan belatedly remembered that the man was, after all, head of the royal council. He said neutrally, "Princess Marya isn't a little girl anymore, *boyar*. She's our rightful ruler, and her place was here. She *had* to be here, show folks right away she isn't some ninny afraid to do what's got to be done."

"Yes, I know. Don't quote politics at me." Nikolai stirred nervously in his saddle. "But—dammit man, where is she?"

General Simyan winced. "At least she isn't Vasilev's prisoner. We'd have gotten word from him, fog or no fog, if he had her." He gave the *boyar* another quick glance, seeing the concern on the elegant face, and said with rough good cheer, "Our princess is no fool. She can take care of herself. We'll find her alive and well, no fear.''

Very softly the old general added to himself, "And may Heaven protect her till then.''

EMELIAN, flat on his back, stared up the length of the sword that held him pinned to the ground. Beyond it was a warrior, small and slender, clad in stained but expensive high boots, mail shirt, pointed helm. And framed by that helm . . .

She was fierce and sharp and beautiful as a falcon, this young warrior-woman. And her face, her wonderful, fine-featured face with its dark eyes and that long black wisp of hair come loose across one cheek—how he ached to brush back that wisp, touch it, touch her . . .

My destiny, Emelian thought, bewildered and joyous at what had just happened to him.

"Who are you? Why are you here?"

She must have asked that three times, voice sharpening with each repetition, glance wary, dangerous, before the words penetrated Emelian's daze.

"Who . . . oh. I am Emelian, lady. Emelian Grigorovich,'' he added, seeing no reason to lie. Surely this falcon-lady had nothing to do with old Stargorodian politics. "Ah . . . could you move that sword, just a bit?"

"Names are easy. Who do you serve?"

He blinked. "Why, myself!" Remembering a line out of the ballads, he added, quoting with deliberate bravado, " 'Brave men serve only their own wills!' "

That startled the smallest of chuckles out of her. The blade drew back a bit, and Emelian raised a wary hand to his throat.

"Lady, I don't know who your enemy might be, but I assure you, I have nothing to do with him. I don't even know for sure where I am!" He hesitated, looking up at the fierce eyes. Blue, by Heaven, not black as he'd first thought, but the deepest, most wonderful blue . . .

"Look you, either run me through or let me sit up. I'm lying right on a very unfriendly rock."

This time she really did laugh, a short, choked-off sound as though she was wary of making too much noise, and backed off enough to let him get slowly to his feet. The sword swung up to follow his movement, and Emelian sighed.

"All right. I admit, you don't know me from—from a *leshy*. I don't know who you are, either."

The young woman hesitated a moment, studying him carefully, though her sword never wavered. "You really don't, do you? Marya. Call me that."

Marya, Emelian echoed silently. *How lovely.* Even if it was only part of her real name.

"So," he said. "Marya. Suppose I swear an oath of some sort. Would that satisfy you?" On what could he swear? Emelian didn't want to risk rummaging through his pack for the holy medal Serge had slipped in there, not with the woman so edgy. "Here, now, look: do you know anything about the peasantry? Yes? Well, this is what they do when they want to swear a vow. It's supposed to be something from the old days, quite sacred in a . . . well, an old sort of way."

Oh, fine. And what if she were a fanatic about religion, the type to cut down anyone even mentioning pagan ways?

Ah, no, his lady could never be so short-minded.

His lady . . . ?

You romantic idiot! Emelian told himself.

She was watching him calmly enough, one brow raised skeptically. Emelian shrugged. Slowly he bent to touch bare ground and, remembering the words he'd learned as a boy from the peasant children, recited:

"By Warm Mother Earth, I swear this oath: I don't know this warrior-lady, Marya, or her enemies. I have never seen her before, or heard her name. While we're on the subject, Warm Mother Earth, I also swear I really don't know where I am. And may the Earth not receive me when I die if I'm lying.'' He glanced up at the young woman. "Good enough?''

The corner of her mouth crooked up in a sardonic little smile. "For the moment. Unless you're a far finer actor than any I've seen at court.'' She slid her sword back into its sheath, though she let a hand rest purposefully on the hilt. "Now, suppose you tell me about Emelian Grigorovich, this man who professes so much ignorance, swears oaths like a peasant, yet speaks like a fine *boyar*.''

"A *boyar*, eh? My father would be grateful to hear that. And you, *boyarevna* Marya, or whatever your true name might be, are no peasant, either. Don't give me that hostile stare! Not too many peasants carry swords or wear anything as expensive as mail.''

"Granted.'' Her voice was flat.

"Oh, look,'' Emelian exploded in an impatient burst of honesty, "what I am is the son of a nobleman who managed to get himself exiled from Stargorod. You know Stargorod?''

"I know of it.''

"Ah. Well, I never saw it, myself. Don't really want to, either.'' Oh, damn, listen to this—one glance from those fierce, lovely eyes, and he was off and chattering like a fool! Emelian began again, more slowly. "My father . . . died recently. I'm on my own, trying to see something of the world and make something of myself.'' Akh, there he went, chattering again. Well, he might as well tell her everything. "Since I have remote blood-ties to Maria, wife to Prince Finist of Kirtesk—''

Both black brows shot up in surprise. "Kirtesk!''

"Did I say something peculiar?''

"Let's just say that I have certain ties to Kirtesk myself.''

Emelian hesitated, wondering. She had already let slip something about being "at court.'' *Royal* ties, could it be . . . ?

Before he could speak, the sudden sharp rustle and

crash of a falling branch made them both start. Two blades flashed out, Emelian overwhelmed by a sudden urge to protect the lady, the lady plainly quite able to protect herself. For a moment they stood in tense silence, then Emelian let out a long sigh.

"No one there. Look you, *boyarevna* Marya, whoever you are, you're clearly in need of help." Gazing into those deep blue eyes, he thought, with a surge of passion that nearly stunned him with its suddenness, *Oh, my dear, let me help you!* and echoed aloud, carefully neutral, "Let me help you."

She gave him an uncertain glance. "Eh, I'd might as well try this."

With that, she stared at him, fixing his gaze with hers, looking into his eyes with an almost mystical intensity.

Mystical? Emelian wondered. Or . . . magical? She was, after all, a woman with ties to Kirtesk, which was as good as saying with ties to that ruling line of magician-princes . . . He wasn't afraid of magic, not if it was wielded by this, his heart's sudden delight . . . Royalty, though, was another matter . . . But he couldn't concentrate on that, not now, not with her eyes so wide and lovely, her face so close to his . . .

Abruptly she broke contact, those deep blue eyes confused. "But that's ridiculous," he heard her murmur to herself.

"Lady? Is something wrong?"

"No." But she turned sharply away.

A totally bewildered Emelian tried to recapture his train of thought. Kirtesk . . . magician-princes . . . He and his father hadn't been completely isolated from news of the outside world, not with peddlers turning up from time to time. There was something he had heard about a young woman who ruled . . . Emelian hastily searched his mind for that one elusive scrap of news—

"Ha, I've got it! You're Marya, all right: *Princess* Marya of Astyan! That is it, isn't it?"

She whirled to him, even as Emelian was thinking in

dismay, *A princess. Boyar*'s son though he was, how could he ever dare love a princess?

Refusing to even consider it, he forged boldly ahead. "But what in the name of all the saints are you doing here all by yourself?"

"I should have known I couldn't hide for long." Her tone was wry. "Yes, I am Princess Marya." She paused, eyeing him thoughtfully. "And even if I'm not a magician like Cousin Finist," she added, "I still have enough Power to tell when someone's lying."

"I wasn't—"Emelian began indignantly, but she cut him off, smiling:

"I know you weren't. I don't quite understand you, Emelian, but at least I've seen you are an honest man."

She paused again, and for an instant her cool control slipped, just enough to give him a glimpse of a very human young woman close to the edge of her endurance; the magic must have wearied her more than she would admit. Aching with sympathy, Emelian longed to take her in his arms.

Marya continued levelly, "But just how honest are you? Honest enough to help me against a traitor?"

Fight a traitor? Why, he would fight demons for her!

Then Emelian felt himself redden. God, if she had been able to read his truthfulness, maybe she'd also seen this sudden love of his, too. "Of course," he said as evenly as he could. "But where is he?"

"That," Marya murmured, "is something I mean to discover." She glanced about. "The fog is lifting. We should be able to find our way."

"With enough mist left to screen us," Emelian added.

She gave him a quick, speculative glance. "You should be aware of what you're doing. I'm going to try to rejoin my men. But if I fall upon my enemy instead— The traitor is my cousin, Vasilev. He wants my throne. If he should capture us . . ."

Emelian got her point only too clearly. Were her cousin any sort of a man of honor, Marya might be sent to live out her days in a nunnery-prison. At the worst, she would die quickly. But he, without the protection of wealth or a powerful family . . . Unwelcome memories raced through Emelian's mind, stories told to him by his father of torment at royal commands, of cruel, slow death.

But to desert Marya . . .

No, he couldn't bear to lose her, no matter what the risks!

"He won't catch us," Emelian said belatedly, and hoped he spoke the truth.

EMELIAN AND MARYA HUDDLED together behind a natural wall of bushes, looking out over a muddy field. There, swathed in fading ribbons of mist, was a ragged tent, surrounded by sagging men-at-arms.

"Is that . . . ?" breathed Emelian.

The princess nodded grimly. "Vasilev's tent."

"Your cousin doesn't seem to have very many men."

"Not after yesterday's battle." Marya's eyes were fierce. "If only I could get to him, I could end this here and now."

Emelian studied the fog, which was being swirled in confusing veils by the wind. After a moment, he smiled. "Princess Marya, I do think you can."

VII

DEMONS

IVAN PACED nervously back and forth, uncomfortably creaking in leather armor grown stiff and dank in the damp air. Spear clenched in his hand, the guard forced himself to continue his rounds, keeping one wary eye on his master's tent.

Already most of *boyar* Vasilev's men had deserted, slinking off into the night and the fog. And if it weren't for the fact that if he fled he'd have nowhere to go, Ivan would have been off and running a long time ago. Maybe Vasilev did provide him with a roof over his head. But how much loyalty could a man hold for a master who was growing more irrational with every passing moment? Ivan touched the little amulet hanging about his neck; he was of peasant stock, and the peasant folk knew all about such things as possession.

Possession, yes—how else to explain Vasilev going from terror to battle-rage to apathy all in the same turning of the hourglass? It was almost as though some demon were controling the man.

Ivan shuddered, glancing about him at a world still grey and vague and bewildering despite the morning sunlight trying to pierce the haze. The princess's troops hadn't found them yet, but it was only a matter of time. But there was worse than plain, honest warfare; there was the forest so close about the camp. The princess's father had been a magician, everyone knew that. Maybe the princess herself had sworn strange pacts with the Old Ones! Who knew what demons might be lurking out there, safely screened by fog against the demon-slaying sun? Maybe the men hadn't deserted after all, but had been . . . taken.

I shoulda stayed in my village. Dull life or no, I shoulda stayed and raised chickens and . . .

Something moved. Ivan hastily raised his spear with both hands, but it was only Vanka, the other guard. Ivan lowered the weapon again with a shaky laugh. He started to call out a friendly greeting to the man—

And froze, as a dark, dimly seen Something swarmed over Vanka, dragging him to the ground. Ivan managed a strangled gasp, and a face turned to him, a fierce, fine-boned, fiery-eyed face— It could only be a demon come for Vasilev!

Ivan threw down his spear. "That's it," he said flatly. "*Boyar*, you're on your own. I'm goin' home to raise chickens!"

VASILEV HUDDLED in his tent, hands over his face. Dimly he knew he hadn't a chance of eluding Marya's troops, not unless he abandoned everything and ran. But he couldn't run, he couldn't move, he couldn't even think clearly. Something was pulling savagely at his mind, trying to get him to ignore safety and blindly attack—God, that would be the death of him! He struggled to hold fast to his hot determination of fighting Marya with clever words. But how could he be clever now, when he couldn't even choose the thoughts racing through his head?

Who are you? he cried silently. *Why are you doing this to me?*

"Destroy Marya!"

The sudden answer was faint but fiercely clear within the confines of his mind. Remorseless, it continued:

"Destroy the magician's daughter and be free of me!"

Hopeless, drained by fear, Vasilev huddled blindly in

his tent, and wished only that it would all be over and he be at rest.

A discreet cough brought him to his feet, snatching for his sword. Swallowing dryly, Vasilev managed to croak out: "Come."

Two figures entered, one a tall young man in plain leather armor such as the guards wore, dragging in the other, a slim, slight thing in expensive mail who stood with head bent, fairly radiating fury.

"Ah . . . *boyar,*" began the guard, giving Vasilev a flash of white teeth in a brown-eyed, good-natured face. "I . . . uh . . . stumbled on this woman. Thought you'd best see her."

Her? Vasilev stared, heart pounding. Oh God, could it be . . . ? "Raise your head!" he commanded the slim figure sternly.

Sullenly, she obeyed. He caught a glimpse of a fine-boned face, dark, fierce eyes—it *was* Marya, defenseless and alone, hands bound behind her.

"Wonderful!" laughed the savage voice in Vasilev's mind. *"Now you need only slay her!"*

In due time, demon! answered Vasilev. I *am master here, not you!*

"Of course, little warrior," the voice mocked. *"Believe that if it comforts you."*

Vasilev determinedly shut the voice out. This was *his* moment of triumph, dammit! Struggling not to be overwhelmed by the sudden, astonishing turn of events, he swaggered forward. "So, cousin. Things aren't turning out exactly as either of us planned, now, are they?"

Why was she smiling? "No, cousin," Marya purred. "Indeed they are not."

What was this? Her arms were free—she hadn't been bound, not at all! It had all been a trick! And now the sword in her hand was pressed right up against his heart!

"Emelian." Marya's voice was calm. "Take his sword from him, if you would."

Grinning, the young man obeyed. Vasilev stared. "You aren't one of my guards!"

"Oh, indeed I'm not." He glanced down at the ill-fitting leather he wore. "Poor armor you give your men. What's left of them, that is. We saw a whole party vanish off into the woods just a few moments ago."

Vasilev looked from him back to Marya, blinking in confusion. "But—but how did you get here? The guards—there *were* guards."

"They didn't even notice us," Marya said gently. "Too much fog, you see." Her voice hardened. "Vasilev, you fool, I don't know how you ever hoped to succeed. But you've lost. It's over."

Vasilev hardly heard her. Within his mind, the savage voice was raging, *"No! You must strike her down, now!"*

Dimly, he was aware of Marya's cry of shocked recognition, dimly he realized the demonic voice had been shouting aloud through his lips, but there wasn't time to waste. Neither his cousin nor that fool of a counterfeit guard had thought to search him. And though the small pen-dagger he wore in his sleeve was little more than a toy, it was sharp.

With a wild laugh of triumph, Vasilev snatched it out, and lunged at Marya.

BOYAR NIKOLAI CLUNG grimly to his saddle, aching to the very bones from the never-ending jolting. Surely the priests had it all wrong about places of eternal punishment; surely there could be nothing worse than spending an eternity bouncing about this apparently endless series of fields. After a troop had been sent back to Astyan with the wounded, the remaining men had fanned out on various scouting missions, but so far they'd found no clues to the whereabouts of either Marya or Vasilev. Nikolai grimaced, seeing ground so torn up by hoofs that it was impossible to trace anyone's movements. The men had managed to round up various former members of that so-called rebel army, most of them Vasilev's own peasants forced into service, more fright-

ened or resigned than defiant, and with no idea as to
the location of their ex-master or their princess.

Nikolai grabbed a handful of coarse mane as his
mount suddenly decided to jump over a bush. He
winced as the impact of landing bruised his already
bruised seat, and heard a stifled chuckle from General
Simyan. God, if only they could stop, if only he could
get down from this accursed beast and *walk*— Walk,
ha! He doubted he'd ever be able to stand upright again.
Simyan had been right, curse him—a counselor had no
business being out on a battlefield. He should have
stayed in Astyan where he belonged.

And abandon Marya?

No. Never that.

The *boyar* managed a thin smile, seeing in his mind's
eye not the strong young woman of the present but, as
he usually did, the princess of seven years back, the
grieving, frightened child desperate for comfort. Poor
little lass! He was glad he'd been there to help provide
that comfort. And no matter what jealous *boyars* might
have hinted, it hadn't been done out of any sort of
power-hunger, either. Granted, he thoroughly enjoyed
his position as head of the Inner Council; who wouldn't
enjoy the chance to make full use of his abilities? But
how could he have helped but feel genuine pity for that
skinny little thing, all staring eyes and gawky limbs and
frantic bravery? Indeed, thought Nikolai with a touch
of smugness, he had always been truly loyal to the father, and fatherly to the daughter.

The daughter who had become so foolishly independent of late, so—so imprudent, so—

"General Simyan!"

The suddenness of the shout brought Nikolai back to
the present with a shock.

It was one of the soldiers, prodding before him a man
in worn leather armor. "General Simyan, this is one of
the traitor's own guards."

Nikolai glanced from the stern-eyed Simyan to the
captive, and frowned. This hardly looked like a dan-

gerous warrior. The man stood submissively before
them, no more than a weary, plain-faced youngster.

"Please, my lords, I don't want ta cause any trouble.
Just want ta go home."

"Your name?" snapped Simyan.

"Uh . . . Ivan, my lord. Ivan, son of Ivan. Please,
my lord, I don't know anythin', I didn't even *want* ta
fight!"

"You were one of Vasilev's guards. Where is his
camp?"

The man's eyes flared white-rimmed as those of a
frightened horse. "I'm not goin' back there. Demons!"

"Demons," echoed Nikolai contemptuously.

"It's true! Saw one myself, snatchin' poor Vanka
down to Hell! A dark-haired woman-demon, it was, in
armor just like a man, with eyes like—like blue hell-
fire!"

Nikolai and Simyan exchanged startled glances.
"Marya," breathed the *boyar*.

"YOU MUST STRIKE HER DOWN, strike her now!"
As those hate-filled words spewed forth from Vasilev's mouth, Marya cried out in shock. That was never
her cousin's voice! Koshchei was speaking through him.

*Dear God, and here I was wondering why Vasilev's
plans all seemed so insane. It wasn't insanity at all, but
possession!*

That day when Vasilev had tried to propose marriage
to her . . . she had been so angry at him that she hadn't
marked where he'd gone. Why, oh why had she taken
him for granted? Why hadn't she remembered that,
stupid or not, he was of the right blood to sense her father's spells? Somehow Vasilev had found that magic-
hidden chamber.

Marya's unpredictable Power awoke with a start, a
bare instant before Vasilev leaped at her, dagger flashing in his hand. Alerted that split-second before danger,
Marya meant to sidestep neatly and strike her cousin in
passing. But Emelian, wildly heroic, pushed her aside—

"Emelian! No!"

Her warning came too late. Vasilev's dagger caught him full in the side.

As the young man staggered back, eyes wide with shock, Marya bit back her horror and, since she didn't have room to use the blade of her sword, quickly reversed it to hit her cousin a stunning blow with the hilt, right between the eyes. He went down as though axed, and Marya hastily turned her attention to Emelian, who was clutching his wound, disbelief on his face.

"Well struck!" he gasped.

"Never mind that. Let me see the wound."

"Oh, it's not so bad. A cut, no more." He made a sweeping gesture of negation. And promptly fainted.

"Emelian!"

Frantically she tore a length of cloth from the edge of her tunic, wadding it up against the wound, struggling to staunch the alarming spouts of blood. The dagger's blade had been small, but if it had nicked an artery . . . But after a horrifying time that seemed to stretch beyond bearing, the flow slowed, then stopped, and Marya sank back on her heels, shaking. Oh, God, Emelian had gone so still! There wasn't any justice, that such a gallant, *alive*, young man should die like this.

Akh, she couldn't let misery overwhelm her, not while she was still in the middle of her foes. And all at once, Marya tensed, listening fiercely. Hoofbeats thrummed on the earth, growing ever louder . . . Then the princess let out her pent-up breath in a relieved sigh. There weren't enough horsemen left to Vasilev's forces to account for the sounds. These could only be her men approaching, finally.

But as she looked down at Emelian's still, bloody form, Marya felt a sob escape her.

Help had come, but it had come too late.

VIII

SPELLS AND COUNTERSPELLS

"I FEAR I don't know what to tell you, my Princess."
The physician's voice was grim. "I'm afraid the young
man just isn't responding to treatment." He added defensively, "He *was* fairly weak when you brought him
here to the royal palace."

"I don't understand!" Marya protested. "The wound
itself isn't all that serious, and he hasn't lost all *that*
much blood."

"Ah. Well. The man is young and healthy, which is in
his favor, of course. But we don't know if the knife was
all that clean; there is always the chance of wound-fever."

"But he isn't feverish!"

"Mm. It's true that some scholars do feel there's no
such thing as wound-fever, that the problem stems from
the body's own natural reaction to the imbalance of hu-
mors that—"

He broke off abruptly at Marya's impatient sigh. "In
short," the princess said flatly, "you can't tell me
whether Emelian is going to live or die."

"Ah . . . no, my Princess."

"So. Leave me."

"But my Princess—"

"Leave me!"

He hastily bowed and obeyed.

Marya stood for a long time looking down at Emelian's unconscious form lying so pathetically still, the cheerful face pale and frighteningly composed beneath its tan.

And, despite Marya's worry, a foolish part of her mind began gossiping, *Well, he certainly isn't what you'd call handsome. But he's definitely a pleasing eyeful, as the servants would put it. Nicely made, too. Not so tall as some, but strong, broad-shouldered . . . A woman could enjoy being in the embrace of—*

Then she angrily silenced herself. This was a fine train of thought, with Emelian so ill!

But *why* was he ill? The knife hadn't been poisoned, she'd had that checked right away. *Vasilev* had been poisoned, diseased in mind if not in body thanks to Koshchei's touch . . .

Suddenly she knew: When Vasilev had attacked Emelian, he had spread a manner of arcane contagion—

Akh, no, such a thing could only have happened if Emelian had been of the same bloodline, or perhaps psychically linked to Marya. Which, of course, he wasn't . . . was he?

He loved her. Even with her weak Power, she had known that without a doubt. Amazingly, he had loved her from the first moment he'd seen her.

Of course she didn't return his feelings.

Didn't she? Just for an instant, there in the forest when she'd made contact with the mind behind those honest brown eyes, she had seen an inner image of the two of them together, joyous in each other's embrace, and it had been so warm an image, so wonderfully comforting . . .

Oh, you idiot!

She was a princess, not some little girl with her first romance. And even if she didn't have her people to consider—she *couldn't* be feeling anything for him, not so swiftly!

All right. Forget these silly maunderings. Pretend there *was* a linking, and a psychic infection. What could she do about it?

There was something . . . Marya winced, forcing herself to remember . . .

When her father had been trying with ever-increasing impatience to rouse whatever magic lay within his daughter's mind, he had taught her a good many spells. She still recalled them to this day, though most of them remained merely so many words to her; her father's testings had proven only too well that she hadn't the gift to transform words to Power.

Still, if memory served, among those spells learned so painfully by rote was one to save Emelian.

And yet she couldn't help but hesitate, painfully recalling all those struggles as a child, all those magicless failures. Her father had never actually blamed her, but he hadn't quite been able to hide his disappointment in her . . . Marya bit her lip hard, trying to banish the old ache of guilt, the inner voice that cried, *It's your fault he's dead.* If she'd had magic of her own, maybe she could have come to his aid on that fatal day. Maybe he would still be alive . . .

Akh, who was she trying to fool? Work a spell? She didn't have the Power.

But if she didn't try, then Emelian was doomed. Did she want his death on her conscience? Marya looked down at the still face, sure she was watching his life ebbing with every fading breath—

No—not *try*. If the spell was to have any hope of working, she must *know* it would succeed.

The princess took a deep, steadying lungful of air. During those dark, lonely nights after her father's death, she had worked out a technique to let herself sleep, banishing grief and loss by emptying her mind of painful thoughts, bit by bit. Now, forcing herself to calmness with every scrap of regal self-control, she used that same technique to banish doubt by simply refusing it room within her mind.

Carefully holding her mind blank of all but the intricate words of the spell, Marya knelt by Emelian's bedside. At least this magic required no special charms, no chalked circles or mystic tapers. She needed only the strength of her will, and belief. Softly she began the chant to narrow her mind's focus, to shut out the outside world and its distractions . . .

It seemed to Emelian that he had been wandering lost in this empty, endless world for eons. Weary to the very soul, he ached to rest, to sleep . . .

Except the moment he tried to rest, that dark, seductive Other would call to him again. He had no idea of its identity. He only knew it was evil—alien, conscienceless evil. Gasping, Emelian fought to win control, but the storm tore at him, raging, till, confused and burning with the force of it, he realized with horror that he could no longer resist the demon's call.

"But you can."

Could that be Marya? What would she be doing here?

"Emelian. Listen to me."

It was *Marya! Emelian froze, listening with all his might.*

"Shed fear and hatred," she murmured. "Let them fall as easily as you'd drop a soiled cloth."

"But . . . I don't . . . How can I . . . ?"

"You can. They are not your own emotions. They are being forced upon you. Shed them, Emelian."

The essence of her mind brushed his, gentle, soothing. Emelian felt the darkness enshrouding him begin to drift apart like so much mortal fog, and gave a sudden, joyous laugh of relief. With Marya's help, he could see that they belonged not to him but to the Other.

"And I will not be your slave!" he told it fiercely. "I will never be your slave!"

He felt the Other's rage, but now he knew it was harmless fury, powerless to hurt him—now that he could feel Marya's presence near him, and hear her murmur:

"Yes, the bonds are slipping from you. Follow my voice, Emelian. Come back with me. Come back to the mortal world, Emelian. Come back to Life."

* * *

EMELIAN STIRRED LAZILY. It seemed to him that he'd been peacefully asleep for countless ages. Akh, his eyelids felt heavy as two rocks. It would be far simpler just to fall back into slumber . . .

No, somehow he knew he *must* wake up.

And all at once, he *was* awake, and looking about him in bewilderment.

Where was he? A richly decorated room, walls gaily painted in intricate designs, the canopy of his bed heavily embroidered in silken threads . . . The last thing Emelian could remember was that tent, and the dagger, and then . . . nothing.

Except that fever-dream of being stalked by some demonic Thing. And there had been Marya's voice, and her gentle pulling of him back to his body and life . . . A dream, surely it was only that, and yet—

"Marya!"

Emelian sat up so sharply his head swam, seeing her lying crumpled at his bedside. He sprang out of bed, falling abruptly to his knees in dizziness, hardly feeling the bruising jar of impact, impatient with his weakness, reaching blindly out to her.

"Akh, Marya . . ."

At least she was alive and breathing regularly, with not a mark of a wound on her. Emelian knew he should do something, call for help, but for now all he could do was hold her, feeling her warm and soft in his arms.

Her thick black eyelashes fluttered. And then she was awake, her deep blue eyes unfocused and misty, her face looking so young and defenseless that Emelian could almost forget the fierce warrior-woman he'd first met. Aching with love and desire, he longed to hold her like this forever, to protect her, to kiss those slightly parted, tender lips . . .

Then Marya was pulling away from him, smoothing her rumpled caftan with unsteady hands. "Emelian! You're well!"

He gave the smallest of sighs for opportunities wasted. "Quite well. Hey, now, even the knife-cut is healed!'' Emelian stared at her in wonder. ''This was your doing, wasn't it? You worked a healing spell on me.''

''I . . . yes.'' She seemed even more amazed about it than he.

But whatever magic she'd worked had plainly exhausted her. Emelian leaned forward, blurting out, ''But you're all right? You haven't injured yourself?''

For an instant, they were so close that their lips nearly touched, and Emelian could have sworn he saw temptation flicker in Marya's eyes. But then she scrambled hastily to her feet. ''No. I'm quite well.''

He struggled up after her, but she was already at the door, face composed and regal. ''Emelian, I'm happy to see you recovered. And I do thank you for your aid against my . . . against the traitor. You are welcome to stay here at my court for as long as you wish. As my honored guest.''

''Marya—ah, Your Highness, I—''

''But now I must leave,'' Marya continued evenly. ''This is, as you might have guessed, the royal palace in Astyan.'' For a moment, their glances chanced to meet. Emelian froze, wonderstruck, at the flash of warmth he surprised. Then it was gone, and the clear blue gaze was hastily flicking away from his own. ''I— I have work to do,'' Marya stammered, and fled.

GUARDS AND COURTIERS ALIKE WERE STARING at her, curious as a herd of horses, and Marya forced herself to slow her flight to a more dignified pace. Akh, and what had she thought she was doing, running away like that? Maybe it wasn't proper for a maiden princess to be alone in a room with a young man not her relative—and she would be hearing lectures from good *boyar* Nikolai on *that* subject—but she certainly wasn't afraid of men.

Particularly not of Emelian, who was most definitely a man of honor.

At that thought, Marya felt a wicked little smile curl up the corners of her lips. Why, he hadn't even tried to kiss her in those first, bewildered moments of her awakening, when her guard had been so lowered that she just might have welcomed that kiss . . .

Oh, nonsense! The man really was what he claimed: a *boyar*'s son. If she'd needed any material proof, there had been that fine caftan in his pack—worn, but too elegant of cut and fabric to belong to anyone but a noble—and the signet ring that had fit his ring-finger perfectly. But they had only known each other a very short time. For all his noble blood, he was, as Nikolai would hasten to tell her, a nobody, with no valuable political connections at all. Worse, Emelian was the son of an exile, possibly even of a traitor, certainly no one for someone of her rank to consider even for a moment as a lover.

A lover! Marya stopped in dismay. Now, when had this happened? During the spell, while their minds were touching? Had she known he was to be hers and she his from that moment their eyes had first met— Nonsense. She was still shaken and weary from the magic, that's all it was.

The magic, yes: A shiver of wonder ran through her. To know a spell to be more than mere, dry words, to feel the exhilarating joy of it coming alive through her will . . .

But how had she done it? How had she ever managed to raise and control that surge of Power? There wasn't any stirring of magic within her now, any more than there had ever been. Marya bit her lip, not wanting to admit how diminished she felt by its loss.

Never mind that, the princess told herself sternly. How *had* she worked that spell?

She knew how. She was merely afraid to admit the truth—

Which was simply this: she never would have been able to work that spell, any more than she'd ever been able to work magics in the past, without the driving force of fear. Fear not for herself, but that she might lose Emelian so soon.

Emelian . . .

Love, she thought experimentally; then, *My Love.*

And then, too overwhelmed for anything else, *Good God.*

FOR A TIME after Vasilev's execution, Koshchei ached as though he'd lost a physical part of himself. The Other could do nothing but flee out of his body into Nothingness, dazed with shock.

But at last, surrounded by soothing blankness, he felt the worst of the trauma slip from him. Koshchei slid back into his physical self, adjusting to the finite once more with an angry clinking of chains.

The death of Vasilev was no great loss, though the Deathless admitted to himself that he'd been a fool to keep the psychic link intact after the human had passed the point of usefulness. But the man had accomplished nothing! Marya was still very much alive. Worse, the battle had turned out to be such a ridiculous shambles that it had left her no weaker of mind or body. Indeed, from what little he could sense from his prison, her strength actually seemed renewed!

The Deathless shook his head, confused. How could that be? How could his plan have gone so wrong? Could he have so misjudged human behavior?

Frowning, Koshchei tried to be logical about it, to take all the many facets of the human mind into consideration. First, there was . . .

There was what?

All right. Never mind. They acted as they did because . . .

Because why?

Aie, this was ridiculous! He'd *been* human! Surely he could recall what it was like to be—

Could he? A shudder shook the powerful frame. Could it be he'd come so far from humanity he could no longer think as humans thought, predict how they would act? Surely not. And yet . . .

Uneasy, the Deathless thought back to the last time he'd walked on mortal soil. It had pleased him to play the mortal lord, to build a fortress and control his human slaves, though now he found it difficult to fathom his own motives in such foolishness. His invasion had been a simple enough thing. But once the fortress was complete, he'd been stunned to realize he didn't remember how to act the part he'd chosen. What scraps he did recall of mortal life seemed so foreign now, so . . . trivial, standing in the way of his real reason for returning to mortal soil: the drawing of ever-new Power to him.

The humans had realized his confusion quickly enough. Yes, they were terrified of their unpredictable master, no mistaking that. But they were such sly and tricky creatures! Their unsubtle, unpredictable thoughts interfered with those attempts to gather Power, skittering about as they did, cutting into his concentration, slipping away from his psychic grasp like so many wisps of mist. It should have been easy enough to stop them: he had expected to control the fragile things with one surge of command. Yet he hadn't been able to find the proper spell to bind them. Unlike ridiculous Vasilev, their minds were complete, safe. And when he tried to find the way to tear through their innate human defenses, he'd failed: the memory of the proper patterns of a mortal brain kept eluding him. The slaves had been of no use to him as slaves, since he allowed no one within his chambers and needed neither food nor drink; or as sacrifices, either—he had long ago outgrown the need for such petty rituals.

At last, disgusted, he'd decided to destroy the nuisances. He had slain the lot—or thought he had—only to be slain in turn by that one vengeful woman his Power had overlooked.

I was a fool to waste my time, my strength, with so inferior a creature—

"I shall be free!" It was a howl of defiant rage.

He would *not* be defeated. He would find a way to force Marya to release him. And then, the Deathless swore, he would take his revenge on her and all her line—

No matter how long it took.

IX

OF POLITICS
AND ROMANCE

EMELIAN STOOD staring out of the small window of his bed-chamber at the city far below. Astyan was a pretty sight in the bright sunlight, there within its stout wooden palisade, a maze of log houses, one or sometimes two stories tall, roofs sharply gabled, doorframes and eaves intricately carved, painted in a riot of cheerful colors.

Emelian stood staring indeed, but what he truly saw was a mental image of a fierce, lovely face . . . deep blue eyes . . .

He sighed. He'd seen little of Marya in the past few days. That was to be expected, he supposed; she was a princess, after all, with the affairs of state to consider.

You couldn't just fall in love with a commoner! he mocked himself.

Well, as the poets said, love did strike where and when it would. Emelian sighed again, tormented by these never-ending dreams of Marya, embarrassingly real in his sleep, almost as distracting when he was awake, the images of her warm and loving in his arms, in his bed . . .

How could he forget that moment when she really had lain in his arms, eyes so wide and soft? There had been a bond between them at that moment, he was sure of it. And the way she'd so suddenly grown shy of him just after, and hurried away . . . Now and again he'd caught her looking at him since then, and thought he'd seen warmth flash in her eyes in the moment before she became all proper and regal. Maybe . . . maybe she did feel something of the same fire that tormented him?

Akh, enough of this. He'd been given permission to wander the palace, so wander he would.

It didn't help. Every room, every corridor, seemed to bear tantalizing hints that Marya too had passed this way. At last, to cool his head, Emelian climbed up to one of the narrow walkways rimming the many-domed roof.

And there, quite by accident, he found Marya, curled up in a secluded little niche like some lost and lonely child. She heard him approach and glanced up wildly.

"Uh . . . it's only me. Emelian. I didn't mean to intrude."

"Don't leave. I—I don't want to be alone."

After a moment's hesitation, he knelt at her side. "Marya, what is it? What's wrong?"

She was silent for a long time. Then: "Vasilev died today."

"I . . . know." He could hardly have missed the palace gossip on the subject, though he had certainly had no wish to watch an execution. Then all at once Emelian realized that Marya, as ruler, must have had to watch. "Oh, my dear, I'm sorry, I—"

She continued, unheeding, "The executioner took his head three turns of the hourglass ago. At my command."

Emelian searched his mind frantically for something comforting to say that wouldn't be a platitude. "There wasn't any other choice. You know that. He . . . ah . . . he *was* a traitor to the crown." When she didn't respond, Emelian stumbled on awkwardly. "I . . . know he was your cousin . . ."

Marya's glance was quick and fierce. "He hated me. I hated him."

"Oh. Well. I guessed at something like that, yes."

Emelian sighed. "Look you, you did only what needed to be done."

No answer.

"He would have killed you, you know, and . . ."

The faintest of stifled sounds made him look at her in surprise. Head turned sharply away, she was quietly, hopelessly, weeping.

"Oh, my dear!" said Emelian helplessly.

Forgetting who and what she was, he simply reached out and took her in his arms. She made one futile little attempt to push him away, then crumpled against his chest while Emelian held her and stroked her hair, murmuring soothing phrases.

But soon—all too soon, it seemed to him—she was straightening, wiping her face as best she could on a scrap of linen, throwing her disheveled black braids over her shoulders.

"Forgive me." There was only the faintest of quivers in her voice. "I . . . don't do that very often."

"No shame in it. You've been through a battle and its . . . its aftermath. My dear young woman, *anyone* is entitled to a few tears after all that!"

She managed a watery smile. "Akh, Emelian. How kind you are." It was said so tenderly that his heart sang. "You almost make me wish I was only a peasant lass, and you . . ." She reddened. "Never mind."

He grinned. "Go on, finish it."

"No."

"I dare you."

"No!" But she was smiling as she said it. Emelian laughed.

"Then I will," he told her, striking a dramatic pose. "You were going to wish us both peasants free to live happily ever after. No, no, don't deny it! Just pretend. See us, now, there in the middle of all the woodland, you with your pretty embroidered blouse and skirt and little bare feet, me with my leather pants and loose linen shirt—you sewed it for me, you know."

"Oh, I did, did I?"

"Mm-hm. Did a nice job, too. So, now. Here we are." He lapsed into the country dialect so familiar to him. "Marya, sweetun, I gotta nice milk cow. You got two fat pigs. Pa'll give me a good plot a ground for the growin', I need it. What about it? You want you 'n me to put my cow and your pigs in one barn?"

By this point, to Emelian's delight, Marya was giggling helplessly. "How romantic!" she gasped. But as she struggled to catch her breath, the light of humor slowly faded from her eyes. "What a pity that we aren't peasants."

Emelian sighed. "Poor lady. You never do get much of a chance to . . . well, to be young, do you?"

"I have my duty. I don't regret it. Usually. It's just . . ." Marya paused, swallowing convulsively. "It was simply that . . . this was the first time I ever needed to . . . sign a . . . death warrant and—oh, dammit all, I am *not* going to start bawling again!"

"No, you're not," Emelian agreed. Before he could stop to think about it, he leaned forward and kissed her.

"WELL, BOYARS?" Nikolai looked grimly about the council. "What are we going to do about this?"

There was an awkward pause. Then Yaroslav, youngest of the *boyars* at council, said tentatively, "She says she loves him. And he does seem to genuinely love her."

"Love!" exploded Nikolai. "What has love to do with it? This is Princess Marya of Astyan of whom we speak. Yaroslav, as a newly married man, you are hardly in a position to be sensible, but *think*, man: This—this Emelian Grigorovich—if that truly is his name—is certainly *not* the person to associate with a princess!"

"And are you going to be the one to tell her that?" pragmatic Dimitri asked lazily.

Nikolai eyed the *boyar*'s well-fed self and well-worn robes disapprovingly. One would think the man would, just once, consider dignity before comfort! *"Somebody must."*

"Oh, come now. It's not as though the two were actually bedding each other."

"Dimitri!"

Unperturbed, the *boyar* continued smoothly. "The young man does seem to be quite honorable. And our ruler is no fool. Let us not forget that she's young, though, and been through ordeals lately that would try a grown man. What harm in simply letting her have a little fun?"

"Fun! Have you gone mad, Dimitri?"

"Why, Nikolai, such venom!" Dimitri raised an eyebrow. "Could it be you're not merely interested in the proprieties? Could it be that you're jealous?"

"Ridiculous!"

"Mm? You are a widower of noble birth, close to the royal line. Perhaps you're planning to marry our princess yourself?"

"What—I—good God, no!" Nikolai exploded. "I think of her as a daughter!"

"Aha. And a rebellious one too, eh, Papa?" Dimitri grinned. "Do you recall what her late father—God rest his soul—was like when he got an idea set in his mind? She is truly *his* offspring, remember?" The *boyar*'s grin widened. "Go to it, man. Forbid our Marya to see her young dear again. And I promise you that the rest of us will come around afterwards to pack up your remains."

EMELIAN WAS leaning idly on the palace rampart's stone balustrade, admiring the view of Astyan and wondering if it would ever really be *his* city, when a voice startled him. Straightening, he turned to see a yellow-haired young man, not too far from his own age, the expensive brocade of his caftan proclaiming him nobleman.

"Boyar Yaroslav. Good day to you."

"And to you."

"All goes well?" Emelian asked.

"It does. All goes well with you? Yes?" The young *boyar* grinned. "There, now. We've gotten all the ritual greetings out of the way. Honor is satisfied."

His grin was infectious. Emelian found himself smiling back, even though he had to wonder aloud, "Might I ask what brought you up here?"

"I wanted to talk to you. Oh, don't look so hostile! I'm not old Nikolai, with his 'It just isn't proper!' " Yaroslav's eyes twinkled. "We did all warn him that the princess wouldn't take kindly to his lecture."

Emelian hesitated, feeling very much an outsider catching tantalizing glimpses of a private society. "These are the first informal words any *boyar* has said to me since I arrived."

"I . . . ah . . . know. That's why I came. Akh, look you, man, I don't know how much you know of our court. We're a wary lot, used to our city and its ways, bound up in its customs and traditions. When you burst upon us, a stranger from the outside world, worse, a stranger who actually dared love our princess . . . Well, the waves of shock are still breaking over us." Yaroslav waved a hand in a helpless gesture. "It's not your fault you weren't born and raised at court like the rest of us. And it is certainly not your fault you and Princess Marya fell in love!" His quick smile flashed. "I know all about how that goes. You see, I haven't been married all that long, but . . ." The fair skin reddened. "But I can't picture life without my Elenishka."

He was chattering like a man who in the normal course of things doesn't get much of a chance to express himself: the price of being the youngest *boyar* on the Inner Council, Emelian supposed. A little overwhelmed, he politely wished the man, "The best to you both."

Yaroslav dipped his head in thanks. "So, now. I really don't think we've been treating you fairly. God knows I've had to accept a good deal of coldness and condescension, coming into my estate and my place on the Inner Council as early as I did." He shook his head wryly. "Here I am, talking all around the point. What I'm trying to say is that I'm willing to give you a hand, as it were, tutor you in how things work among us. Well? What do you say?" He held out his hand. "Agreed?"

Emelian hesitated only a moment. "Agreed," he said, and took the proffered hand.

* * *

OF COURSE, Emelian and Marya couldn't be together as often as they would have liked. Marya must always give most of her time to her people, her city. Emelian could accept that; if nothing else, those years of poverty had taught him patience. Besides, he told himself, what time they could spend together became infinitely more precious to them both. Rejoicing in the wonder that had happened between them, they could speak and laugh together, and find that their so-different backgrounds didn't mean a thing in the face of love.

And yet, for all the joy, there were shadows. In the middle of a peaceful stroll along the palace ramparts, arm in arm with Emelian past smiling or bemused guards, Marya all at once remembered Koshchei, and felt the sharp autumn sunlight turn cold about her.

I must be in love, if I could forget that Darkness. Dear God, but do I dare expose Emelian to such peril?

"Marya? What is it, love?"

She swallowed dryly. "Nothing."

"Akh, you're shivering. It *is* cold up here. Come, let's go down."

Sheltered in his arm, Marya realized it was already too late for caution. She was in love, beyond all hope and reason.

Love, folk said, did conquer all.

Including the Darkness?

EMELIAN AND MARYA SAT TOGETHER on the garden bench, rich autumn foliage all about them, the air chill enough for Emelian to solicitously wrap his cloak about Marya as well as himself, for all the world as though they were an ordinary courting couple.

How lovely if they were nothing more than two plain little people, just as he'd pretended. He would ask for her hand, and she would accept, and they would spend their lives together happily on a farm somewhere . . .

Oh, ridiculous! Marya and he must face the truth: their joy just couldn't last. No matter how much he loved her, no matter how much she loved him, they couldn't hide who and what she was—and what he was not.

"Marya, love," he said reluctantly. "This isn't going to work."

"No?" she teased. "The cloak seems wide enough to me."

"You know that's not what I meant. I was talking about us."

"What's this? Tired of me already? I think that counts as treason—"

"Marya, please. From that first ridiculous moment I saw you, me lying there flat on my back with your sword at my throat, my heart was yours. I love you. I'll always love you. Don't ever, ever doubt it."

She stared at him levelly. "I don't. I won't. Emelian, what's the matter?"

"I was remembering that in some eyes, I'm the son of a traitor."

"Nonsense."

"I told you about my father's exile—"

"That was *his* exile, not yours. No one can possibly blame you for something that happened before your birth. Love, if it bothers you that much, I'll write to old Svyatoslav of Stargorod myself and have your name proven blameless."

"That's only part of it. All the goodwill in the world isn't going to hide the fact that I'm nothing more than petty nobility."

"Good God, man, have you never heard of patents of nobility? I can grant you any rank you want."

No, he hadn't heard of such things. Taken aback, Emelian asked, "But what about your people?"

She laughed softly. "They *like* romance. They will love the idea."

"Oh, I'm sure the commons will. But what about your *boyars?* Marya, love, I don't want to be a risk to you or your reign. And the fact remains that even the head of your Inner Council doesn't approve of me."

"Ha! I doubt he'd think you good enough for me if you were the King of the Eastern Isles himself. Good *boyar* Nikolai still thinks of me as a little girl." The faintest hint of iron entered her voice. "But I am his ruler, and he will obey me." There was a moment of tense silence. Then Marya grinned, and reached forward to kiss Emelian lightly on the tip of his nose. "Even if it means going along with my choice of such a shockingly disreputable soul for a husband."

"A—husband?"

Marya's eyes went wide with shock. "Akh, Emelian, I had no idea I was going to say that. Do—do you mind?"

"That depends. Did you mean it?"

Blushing fiercely, she nodded. "I wasn't sure about it till this very moment, but—I do. I want you beside me for the rest of my life." Marya paused. "Is that all right?"

She looked so terrified that Emelian, a little terrified himself, felt a dizzy surge of laughter well up and burst from him. "My dear, lovely, wonderful Marya, all this time I've been aching and agonizing over the fact that I couldn't ask *you* to marry *me!*"

"If you'd rather be the one to ask . . ."

"Don't be silly! I never would have gotten up the courage. Yes, I love the idea, and yes, I want to spend every second of my life with you, and yes, yes, yes, it's wonderful!"

And he accented every yes with a kiss.

NEITHER HE NOR MARYA WAS AWARE of *boyar* Nikolai standing in the garden's entrance, sheer, disbelieving horror on his face.

"AH, *BOYAR* EMELIAN. I must speak with you."

Emelian raised a brow, a touch annoyed at the grudging tone of that *"boyar,"* but managed a polite bow. *"Boyar* Nikolai. About what?"

"Wait. First . . ." The man looked about in a manner that was presumably supposed to be surreptitious, but looked wonderfully suspicious to Emelian.

"*Boyar* Nikolai, if it's privacy you're seeking, we can talk peacefully enough here in the garden. No sensible folk would stay out here in the chill, so we should have the place to ourselves. You were saying . . . ?"

"Ah. Yes. *Boyar* Emelian, why are you here?"

"I . . . beg your pardon?"

"I know, you were brought to the palace. But why do you stay?"

"Because of Marya! I love her!"

"Yes, yes, of course you do. But need I remind you who and what she is?"

Emelian frowned, wary. "No, you don't. But—"

"Surely you understand how difficult the life of a ruler can be. Particularly when said ruler is young and female. The last thing she needs is an . . . unnecessary complication."

"Meaning myself?"

"I do think we understand each other."

"Oh, no, we don't! Look you, I *do* love Marya, she loves me—"

"*Boyar,* please. We all know what love is worth."

"What—"

"I'm sure you're well aware that a marriage to you would only be an embarrassment for Princess Marya. Love is a pretty thing, but with nothing in common between the two of you, the prettiness wouldn't last very long. And you can't seriously be thinking just of marriage, can you?"

"I don't—"

"You would never get to rule, surely you can see that. Neither the *boyars* nor the military would ever support you. You could never be more than the royal consort. Hardly a position for an ambitious young man, now is it?"

"Ambitious! I'm not— The only thing I want to do is marry Marya and—"

"Of course. Now, as for wealth . . . Come, we can

take care of your wants without any silliness about marriage.''

"What are you saying?"

"Please, *boyar* Emelian, don't be coy. How much do
you want? How much will it take to see you quietly
away from Astyan?" When Emelian didn't answer right
away, Nikolai added impatiently, "Come, speak up."

"I'll speak up, all right!" Too furious for any tactful
rebuttal, Emelian exploded, "Look you, I was raised
to be polite to my elders, but if you ever dare try to—
to buy me off again, I swear I'll teach you a lesson
you'll never forget!" Struggling to get himself back under control, the young man continued levelly, "I'm going to say this only once, so listen well: I love Marya
for herself, *not* for her crown, *not* for her throne, *not*
for any royal wealth, *for herself!* Do you understand
me?"

"I—"

"Fine! Now, good day to you, *boyar* Nikolai!"

With that, Emelian turned and stalked off, leaving the
helplessly fuming *boyar* behind him.

"MY PRINCESS, we must talk about this."

"I have nothing more to say to you, Nikolai."

"Please. I realize the man is young and attractive—"

"Nikolai. I love him, he loves me. What more is
there?"

"But he's *nobody!*" It was a wail. "Yes, I know, you
gave him your . . . ah . . . late cousin's lands and estate, but—my Princess, *as* a princess, you should be
thinking of profitable alliances, politics, not . . . love."

He said the word as though it were something dis-
tasteful, and Marya gave a sharp, humorless laugh.

"I *have* thought of them." Her voice was clipped.
"Would you have me wed a prince, Nikolai?"

"Is that so terrible a thought?"

"Indeed? Would you have Astyan lose its indepen-
dence?"

"I don't see what—"

"*Think*, man. If I marry a ruling prince, I lose my own ruling status. By law, I become his consort. And that, Nikolai, makes Astyan his vassal state."

"But surely there are other princes who—"

"If I marry a weaker prince," Marya continued relentlessly, "say, a second son with little chance for a throne of his own . . . do you really believe such a man would be content as *my* consort? Of course not! And when he did try to overthrow me, it could only mean one of two things for Astyan: civil war, or war with my consort's father. Which do you prefer, Nikolai?"

"Oh, you exaggerate!"

"You're refusing to face facts, *boyar*! I am Astyan's ruler. I will not be less." Then the cold-eyed princess softened into the tender young woman. "Emelian has no regal ambitions."

"So he told me." The words were out before Nikolai could bit them back.

"You spoke with him about this?"

There was abruptly such regal warning in her voice that Nikolai flinched, seeing the strong-willed father suddenly reflected in the daughter. He hastily bowed in submission, fighting to get himself back under control; the *boyar* had no intention of telling Marya the rest of what had been said. At least Emelian had sufficient honor not to bear tales against him. "We . . . have spoken," the *boyar* said neutrally, and hoped that would suffice.

It did—barely. Marya eyed him suspiciously, then looked away with a sigh. "No," she murmured, "he has no regal ambitions at all. I know it; I saw it in his heart. Emelian loves me, not the princess, not the symbol of a throne. He loves *me*." She turned to the *boyar* with pleading eyes. "Nikolai, Nikolai, the crown is a heavy burden! Let me at least have some joy."

"Have I a choice?" murmured the *boyar*, defeated.

X

FAMILY REUNIONS

HIGH OVER THE CITY of Kirtesk, two falcons played in the crisp autumn air, easily looping and circling each other, their cries strangely like human laughter, their feathers silver-bright, dazzling against the intense enamel-blue of the sky. Then one falcon glanced down to the streets far below, to where a small group of horsemen rode towards the gleaming white royal palace. The falcon gave a wordless little murmur of surprise, and flipped up a wingtip in signal to its mate. Together, the shining falcons soared towards the palace, swooping through a wide window set high in one domed tower into an elegant bed-chamber bright with color. Its walls were painted in intricate designs of red, blue and green, while the two chairs and clothes chests were finely carved and gilded, but the room was dominated by the truly regal bed, a vast thing of shining, beautifully worked wood and silken hangings stiff with gold embroidery.

One bird came to a graceful landing on the smooth marble floor. The other landed with a squawk and a frantic flurry of wings on that princely bed. There, it quickly shimmered and grew into the shape of a ruefully laughing young woman, brown of hair and eye, tangled in a cloak set with silvery feathers.

"Finist, love, I don't think I'll ever get this right!"

The other falcon stirred smoothly back into human form. Finist, Prince of Kirtesk, tall, supple, and unself-consciously naked, stood brushing back wild silvery hair from his face, amber eyes bright with amusement as he watched his wife trying to wriggle her way free of the cloak.

"Why, I think you did beautifully, Maria! That landing right in the very center of the bed—I couldn't have done better myself. Of course, I'd be more impressed if you'd actually been *aiming* for the bed, but . . . Oof!"

She'd thrown a pillow at him. Finist threw it right back again, with an indignant, "Now, is that the gratitude I get for saving all those feathers for your cloak?" He frowned in pretended insult. "And at what are you giggling, pray tell?"

"Just picturing you moulting, that's all!"

"Impudent woman." Struggling not to grin, Finist said with regal dignity, "I do not moult. I . . . shed. And just remember this, my dear: without your feather cloak, you'd never be able to fly with me. Some people don't have innate bird-forms, after all."

"Some people don't have bird *brains*, you mean!" teased Maria. "Aie, Finist, no, the bed won't—"

He was already pouncing. The bed groaned under the impact, but held, and husband and wife tussled happily together until a tactful rap at the door cut into their play.

"Damn," said Finist. "We forgot about those messengers." He slid to his feet, slithering quickly into a heavily embroidered caftan, instantly self-controlled as only a magician could be. "Those riders were wearing the royal livery of Astyan. I wonder what Cousin Marya wants."

"I didn't know you *had* a Cousin Marya." Maria, flushed and tousled, was struggling to match her husband's calm. "No, now that I think of it, she was one of those who sent an envoy to our wedding, wasn't she?"

"Mm-hm. She must have been all of fifteen at the time. Marya's only a distant cousin, really, distant

enough to have apparently missed all but a touch of the
royal magic. Which is probably just as well, for Marya's sake.'' Finist's face had gone very still. "You see,
magic slew her father.''

Maria froze in the midst of dressing. "What do you
mean?''

"Don't give me that worried stare, love! It wasn't
some arcane plague, only a case of . . . Well, to put it
simply, the man overreached himself. He tried to Bind
too powerful a being. The magic he was trying to wield
tore free of his control.'' Finist hesitated. "You understand what that means?''

Maria shuddered. "Enough to know he died nas-
tily.''

He nodded. "As for the being: no one knows whether
he succeeded in Binding that one or not.''

"The . . . being?''

"Koshchei, the Deathless, who was once a human
sorcerer and is now . . . God only knows what. Maria,
love, don't worry. I have no intention of prying into
Astyani affairs. The last thing I want is to risk turning
the Deathless's attention towards Kirtesk. Unlike Marya's father, I do know my limitations.'' He paused, tilt-
ing his head to one side in a birdlike little motion. "But
now, I wonder: what does Marya want?''

Maria, who'd just finished braiding her hair up into
neat coils, stopped to study her husband. "There's only
one way to find out. Akh, wait.'' She reached out to
straighten the hem of one of the wide sleeves of Finist's
caftan. "There. Elegant.''

Finist ran his eyes lovingly over his wife. "And you,
my dear, are simply lovely.'' Waiting messengers or no,
he had to pull her to him for a quick kiss; even after
nearly four years of marriage, they'd never yet reached
the point of taking each other for granted. "Mm . . .
lovely, indeed.''

She turned her head away. "Finist, dear, the messengers . . .''

He released her with a sigh. "Ah well. Come, let's find out what Princess Marya has to say for herself."

THE MESSAGE WAS a written one. Finist took it from the respectful couriers, absently waving them off to rest and refreshment while he broke the seal and unrolled the parchment. After a moment of scanning the ornately ornamented, elegantly penned surface, he glanced up at Maria with a smile. "It's good news, love. You and I are invited to a royal wedding."

"Princess Marya is getting married? To whom?"

He consulted the parchment again. "The name means nothing to me: *boyar* Emelian Grigorovich." Finist paused. "Odd. You'd think a princess would be marrying someone of note, someone with political clout."

"Oh, you would, would you? Did you ever think that your cousin just might be marrying for love, like another royal someone we know?"

"Ah." Finist reached out to take his wife's hand. "Lucky woman, if that's so. Well now, I haven't been to Astyan since I was a child. What do you think? Shall we attend?" When Maria hesitated, he added cheerfully, "I told you, I'm not going to pry into matters magical or potentially dangerous. This would be a visit strictly for pleasure, I promise."

"I know. And I'd like to meet your cousin." Maria grinned. "And the fortunate bridegroom, too. I was only thinking of the journey. Astyan's so far away."

"Not for us, love!" Laughing, Finist let feathers shimmer along his arms for an instant. "Not for such as us!"

FOR ALL THE VASTNESS of the great Audience Hall in the Astyan royal palace, it was filled with such a crush of people that the splendid murals covering the walls, telling the history of the city in bold, bright colors, were half-hidden behind even brighter-hued, elegant caftans and robes of state. The colors perpetually shifted, now dazzling, now muted and vague, as the torchflames flickered wildly.

Thanks, thought Emelian in weary humor, *to the wind caused by everybody trying to talk at once.*

Everybody seemed to be wearing fragrances, too, floral concoctions the cost of which he couldn't even begin to guess, and these, together with the inevitable human-smell of too many people in one place, and the odor of torchsmoke, gave the air a thickness he could almost see. Emelian sighed shallowly, and shifted his weight subtly from foot to foot there on the royal dais.

To think that this was only the day *before* his wedding! What was tomorrow going to be like?

Feet aching (no, *all* of him aching, unused to the weight of this caftan that was so stiff with gold thread it could probably stand alone), Emelian carefully shifted position yet again.

Look at all of them, staring up at him as though Marya had chosen some alien creature for her fiancé. Little did they know he would have given every one of their pretty gems for a cool drink. By now his smile felt like a thing of paint and paste, meaningless as the polite murmurs of the throng. He'd never met so many folk in so short a time in his life.

God, it was warm in here! And his elegant new boots were definitely too narrow in the toes. Emelian drew a wary foot back, trying in vain to find a more comfortable position. His slight motion caught Marya's eye. The practiced, politic smile never wavering on her lips, she murmured:

"Say farewell to privacy, love. That's a luxury only the commons enjoy. Regrets?"

He glanced at her, wondering how she could manage to look so cool and at ease. Her slender, fierce loveliness was emphasized by her richly embroidered, cloth-of-gold caftan, and so fierce a wave of love surged through him that he nearly staggered. Emelian grinned. "None."

But she abruptly turned her attention from him. Surprised, Emelian followed her line of sight and straightened, almost forgetting his discomfort in sudden curiosity. Now, who was this tall, exotic creature with the silver-bright hair and those bizarre amber eyes? And why was Marya descending from the dais to greet him? Emelian hurried after her, just in time to see the man bend to give Marya the ritual three kisses, left cheek, right, left, that could only mean he was at least her political equal. And for a foolish moment, Emelian measured himself against that tall, elegant handsomeness, and felt a pang of jealousy.

Then he heard Marya saying, "Cousin Finist? It's been so long!"

The man was answering something polite, those astonishing eyes warm, but Emelian wasn't really listening. Finist? This must be the magician-prince of Kirtesk himself. And that meant that charming young woman at his side must be Maria Danilovna—*My own cousin, and the woman I originally set out to meet!*

The irony of it nearly made him laugh. Smiling, Emelian started forward to greet her.

Seen this close, Maria was no classic beauty; her face in repose could almost have been called plain. And for an instant, Emelian had to wonder what could have drawn the exotic magician-prince to her. But then she looked full at him, and the wit and the joy of life dancing in those brown eyes made him quite forget the formal speech he'd been preparing and say instead:

"Cousin Maria."

She blinked. "I'm sorry, I don't . . ."

"Akh, forgive me. Of course you don't know me; we've never met. But we're related through your mother's family: my father was Grigori Mikhailovich." He could have bitten that back as soon as he'd said it, seeing sudden comprehension flash in her eyes. His father's exile must have been common knowledge throughout the family.

But all Maria said was a careful, "I see."

"I'm sorry. I didn't mean to embarrass you."

She studied him for a moment, so steadily that Emelian wondered if she had managed to pick up a touch of magic from her husband. Then, as though satisfied with what she'd seen, Maria nodded, laughter glinting in her eyes.

"You haven't embarrassed me, I assure you. And you wouldn't be the first person to have had . . . difficulties with Svyatoslav of Stargorod."

"I don't understand."

"Why, my own father—" But then she broke off, glancing about the crowded hall. "This is hardly the place for kin to talk." Maria grinned. "Let's see if we can't find a quiet spot to sit and compare family histories."

FINIST WATCHED his wife go off, arm in arm with Emelian, and smiled to himself. With her good-humored powers of persuasion, Maria would soon enough have any information about the young man that she might want to know. He turned to look at his cousin again, and his smile broadened.

"This sounds banal, Marya, but good Lord, how you've changed. I recall a scrawny little girl throwing apples at me because I had magicked her toy sword up a tree." He rubbed his arm reminiscently. "She had good aim, too!"

Marya giggled. "I remember. And then I tackled you, and wouldn't let you up until you'd promised to fly up there to get the sword down again. My father was scandalized."

"So was mine." Finist paused for an instant, delicately scanning his cousin for traces of Power . . . No, no more than there had ever been. Smoothly, he continued, "And now here you are, a woman grown, and in love. It *is* love, isn't it? Akh, foolish question! You and Emelian fairly radiate joy."

"It is," murmured Marya, eyes glistening. "Oh, Finist, it is."

THE GREAT AUDIENCE HALL HAD BEEN TRANSFORMED
into a banqueting hall, filled to the door with tables
elegantly covered with white linen, around which
crowded what surely must be every man and woman in
the land with any pretension at all of nobility. There
was scarcely room for the servants to pass with the
wedding feast: course after course of meat and poultry
and fish, of bread braided and baked into exotic designs, of sweets fairly dripping with honey. The table
surfaces were crowded too, with bowls and goblets of
sleek grey stoneware from the southern quarries or delicate, priceless porcelain brought to Astyan by caravans
from oriental lands, or intricate salt cellars like so many
gold or silver castles. They caught and reflected back
the light of myriad candles, light that danced and glittered and dripped from noble earrings and bracelets and
necklaces till Emelian was so dazzled he didn't know
which way to turn.

Was this all really happening? Had the wedding really taken place, there in the royal chapel this very day?
All that remained in his mind was a dizzying blur of
light and rejoicing and song, the steadiness of Marya's
hand in his as the rings were exchanged—the chill of
her fingertips giving the lie to her apparent calm—the
warmth of her lips against his . . .

Emelian swallowed dryly, thinking suddenly of the
night to come, and glanced shyly at Marya. But she
was speaking with great animation to one of the *boyars'*
wives, the thickness of her high, pearl-encrusted head-
dress effectively blocking her face from him. Eh, well,
he'd have plenty of time to see her face later tonight.
Her face, and all the rest of her—

Oh, God.

Dry-mouthed, Emelian snatched up his golden goblet
with shaking hands and took a healthy swallow of potent mead, then rather wished he hadn't. Having had
no appetite at all, he'd been sipping at that mead all
through the feast instead, and now, between the mead

and the noise and the warm, crowded air, his head was beginning to swim.

There was a faint chuckle beside him. "Never thought I'd get through my wedding day, either," Finist of Kirtesk murmured in his ear. "But things get better. Believe me, they do."

Under normal circumstances, Emelian imagined, he never could have felt so at ease with a man who was both prince and magician. The mead must have been helping. Helping him, anyhow. Finist's goblet contained merely water. Of course—wielding Power as he did, the man would, for safety's sake, have to remain sober.

Feeling clever for having figured that out, Emelian turned to tell Marya about it—only to realize the place on his left was empty.

Marya was gone.

"Where . . . ?"

"Don't worry." Finist's eyes were amused. "I daresay you'll be joining her soon enough."

Soon enough, it was. Surrounded by a laughing, torch-bearing, bawdy company, Emelian found himself being virtually dragged off to the royal chambers. Not-quite-steady fingers pulled at his wedding robes, stripping his finery away, heedless of his protests. For a moment he was left bare and shivering, then someone had slipped a long silk shirt over him, and he shivered again as it slithered down his body. His laughing escort seized him again. A door opened. He saw a flower-strewn bed within, and drew in his breath sharply, but before he could say anything, he was shoved unceremoniously into the room. Emelian heard one last jest behind him, ribald enough to make his face redden. Then the door was shut behind him, and he was alone with Marya.

She stood statue-still, framed by the narrow, open window, the night sky deep blue behind her. Her long black hair fell sleekly down her back. Candlelight caressed her, hinting at the supple, lovely body beneath the thin shift, making her skin glow . . .

"I hope you know what to do." There was the faintest quiver to her voice; Emelian realized with a touch of sympathy that she wasn't at all as warrior-calm as she seemed. "All I know is what the old women told me."

"Ah. Well." His total experience consisted of a couple of feast day encounters with cheerful but hardly romantic peasant girls interested in learning if *boyars* were built like ordinary men. Emelian took a hesitant step forward, then another. Marya watched, motionless, eyes wide. He could have sworn he saw the faintest shimmer about her, a magical silver haze . . . No, that didn't make sense. It must be a trick of his confused mind. All at once the mead he'd drunk seemed to be rushing to his head. The very air seemed to quiver with tension as he reached out to Marya. She was so beautiful . . .

"I . . . think we can puzzle things out for ourselves," Emelian said, and swept his wife into his arms.

XI

CHALLENGES

FINIST AND MARIA EXCHANGED wry glances. After the disappearance of the newlyweds from the great banqueting hall, most of the guests had settled down for some serious drinking. The night was late, and neither of them wanted to stay here and listen to the increasingly drunken conversations. When *boyar* Nikolai started in for the third time in less than a turn of the hourglass on the same maudlin monologue about loving the Princess Marya like a daughter, husband and wife hastily made their excuses and fled to the elegant chamber Marya had assigned them, expelling a swarm of not-quite-sober servants.

"Alone at last!" Finist exclaimed melodramatically, bolting the door to their bedchamber with a flourish. But then he spoiled the effect with an immense yawn.

And in a short time, they were settled peacefully in bed, cuddled together in drowsy comfort.

Maria gave a soft chuckle. "It was a lovely wedding, wasn't it?"

"Mm-hm."

"And didn't they make a beautiful couple? The two of them, so much in love . . ."

"Mm. Only hope love's enough."

"What?"

"Nothing. Just a thought. Good night, Maria."

They were silent for a time. Then:

"Finist?"

"Mm."

"What did you think of Emelian?"

Finist sighed and rolled over onto his back, staring up at the dimly seen canopy. "Unfinished."

"*I* would have said innocent. He's been through a good deal of physical hardship, yes, but he knows nothing of the world."

"He'll learn." The prince slipped his arm about Maria. "Good night, love."

" 'Night," she echoed sleepily.

IT SEEMED to Finist that he had been asleep for only a few moments when a wild surge of psychic fire blazed through him, rousing his own Power to fever heat. Heart racing, he stared out into darkness, struggling till he'd managed to will himself back under control.

Now, what was that *all about?*

There was only one other person in all the palace with any Power. That outburst could only have come from Marya, were she under some extreme of emotion—

Oh.

Grinning, silently wishing the newlyweds all the joy in the world, Finist began to close his eyes again.

The he froze, suddenly awake, as a touch—faint but cold as midwinter ice—brushed his mind. Quickly he blocked it and felt it drift harmlessly away. Finist lay grimly still, eyes open, waiting. Someone else had sensed that wild burst of Power, but who or what that Someone might be . . .

The coldness didn't return. But the sense of hostile Other remained, like the thinnest ghost of smoke. At last Finist gave a resigned sigh and slipped carefully out of bed, trying not to wake his wife. Maria gave a puppyish little whimper, but slept on. The prince stood wistfully over her for a moment, aching to return to her warm embrace.

I'm sorry, love. I'm afraid I'm going to have to break my promise to you.

Donning the first clothing that came to hand, one of his light, silky caftans, Finist silently left the room, silently moved down dark, deserted corridors, turning the occasional sleepy guard from him with a gentle touch of will. Falcon-wary, he followed the thin, hazy psychic trail down an obscure spiral of a stairway, feeling his way carefully, the sense of cold Power increasing with every step. At last he had reached the bottom, and looked cautiously about a dank, stone-walled chamber.

As his eyes adjusted to the gloom, the prince could make out the shape of a doorway in what had seemed solid wall a moment before: a doorway outlined in blue fire, crossed and recrossed with glowing lines, some straight, some curling in spirals and swirlings intricate enough to dazzle any but a magician's eyes.

The chill sense of Other was centered behind that door. And it was beginning to look as though the stories of how the late Prince of Astyan had met his death were true.

Frowning slightly, Finist took a few slow, careful steps forward—then stopped with a sharp gasp, seized by so powerful a sense of despair and loss that he was nearly physically ill. This could only be the spot where another magician had died, leaving behind the psychic echo of his anguish.

Marya's father.

Who, apparently, hadn't been a complete amateur. Fighting the residue of emotion, Finist straightened, studying the magicked doorway. After a moment, he nodded. The Power spent in creating that Binding had been fierce enough to kill the man, but at least the Binding had been completed. And if it lacked the elegance that came with true skill, it had been completed well. The captive behind that door was there to stay.

Was he? Finist hesitated, very well aware of the

Power and hate smoldering in the being. How long could such as That be held?

Slowly a heroic image began to form in the prince's mind. He saw himself boldly breaking that Binding, casting open the door . . . saw the Other, a horned, demonic shape, looming over him in a stormcloud of Darkness . . . He saw himself standing proudly erect, calling forth spell after blazing spell, rending the Darkness asunder, destroying evil—

Finist's scornful laugh cut into the silence. "Oh, no, old Deathless! I'm not so easily snared!"

Of course the Other had known Finist was there from the first, sensing the Power in him. For an instant, the prince felt that chill, alien intelligence test his mind, trying to probe him for information. He slammed shut mental doors, picturing his inner self shielded behind a smooth, seamless wall, feeling the Other's mind slide helplessly away.

"So, Deathless. I think we understand each other a little better now."

Smiling thinly, ignoring the sickening psychic reek about him, Finist set about reading each and every one of the intricate lines of Binding.

At last he drew back, relieved. They were quite secure. Marya's father really *had* done a good job. The only way Koshchei was going to get out was if someone let him out.

That someone wouldn't be Marya. If the Deathless had been able to control her, he would have been out years ago. Thanks to the restrictions her father had woven into the Binding, the only other person who might be able to free the Deathless was himself, and that, of course, was—

But what about Emelian? He wasn't of their blood, but if he was as truly Marya's love as he seemed . . .

Nonsense. Oh, his love was real enough. And the young man might be every bit as innocent as Maria believed. But he was no fool. Finist sighed, and began the long climb up again, glad to be out of that sad place.

There was no reason to worry. Bound as Koshchei was, the Deathless hadn't the strength to lure Emelian down to him. And as long as Marya never told him about it, the young man would almost certainly never even notice this dark little stairway, let alone find a reason to come down here.

Still, accidents did happen . . .

Uneasy, Finist paused at the head of the stairs. What if he set his own Ban, just enough to make Emelian uncomfortable if he came too close to the stairway? The prince raised a tentative hand, Power flickering about it . . .

No, dammit! Though the Binding had been complete, it had been an amateur's job. If he set any magics working here, they would conflict with it, possibly even start to unravel it. He would just have to trust to Fate and Emelian's common sense to keep the young man safe.

Finist wearily made his way back through the silent corridors to his room. Maria was awake and waiting for him, sitting up in bed, a cloak clutched about her shoulders.

"I was beginning to wonder if I should call out a search party . . . Finist? What's wrong?"

"I was down in the palace cellars. Marya's father really did work a Spell of Binding down there. And it killed him."

"And . . . the Deathless?"

"Oh, he's down there too, safely bound."

"Akh, love, you're shivering."

I should be. I lived another man's death, and spoke with Evil, and was very much afraid . . . "It was cold down there. In more ways than one."

"Come to bed."

He obeyed gladly, grateful for the warmth of her arms about him. But after a moment she drew back, studying him. "Finist? Is there something you aren't telling me?"

He hesitated just a moment too long, and Maria tensed. "There's danger, isn't there?"

"Yes—no. Maria, I honestly don't know. Let's just say that there's the potential for danger."

"To your cousin?"

"To your kinsman."

"Emelian! Oh, Finist, he wouldn't stand a chance against sorcery! Can't you . . ."

Finist sighed. "I'm sorry. There's not much I can do."

He had already attracted more of the Deathless's attention to himself than was wise. Should it ever come to warfare between That One and himself . . . In order to defeat an enemy's magic, a magician needed to know the name and shape and class of that magic. Finist thought of the cold, alien, *nameless* Power that had brushed him, and shuddered. Akh, and it wouldn't be merely his own life at stake . . .

"Maria, I *am* sorry. But I can't risk Kirtesk's safety, not even for Emelian." He paused. "Still . . . tell me, love. Would you mind very much if I made him a present of that lovely dagger you gave me?"

Maria glanced at him. "Not if it keeps him safe."

"I . . . can't promise that much," Finist said honestly. "But I can at least try to give him some protection."

EMELIAN AND MARYA BOTH LOOKED so sleek and contented that Finist couldn't keep from smiling every time he glanced at them.

"Eh, well, my wife and I must be leaving now," he told them. "Good fortune to you both. Marya, remember the mirror-spell I taught you, should you ever need to contact me in haste." Then the prince stopped, as though suddenly struck by an idea. "Emelian, now that we are kin, why don't we follow the old formula of friendship and exchange daggers?"

Emelian's hand fell to the ornate knife at his belt, a flicker of reluctance in his eyes; the knife had obviously been a gift from Marya. But Finist noted, not displeased, that the young man had already learned enough politics to favor alliances over sentiment. "Gladly, kinsman."

As Finist took the knife, he fought down a smile. He had been wondering how he was going to cast an unobtrusive spell, what with the iron of the blade fighting him; iron, unlike other metals, being linked to the wild Power of Earth alone, was all but impervious to mere mortal magic. But the hilt of the knife was Moon-linked silver, that metal most responsive to magic.

Thank you, Cousin Marya!

The prince pretended to fumble with the knife, just enough to nick Emelian's hand with the blade. "Aie! Forgive me!"

Amid Emelian's hasty reassurances and Marya's attention to her husband's little wound, neither of them noticed Finist's lips moving in a silent incantation. Neither of them noticed how the dagger glinted blue-white for an instant as the small bloodstain faded into the shining silver of the hilt.

With a quick, secret smile at Maria, the prince slipped the dagger into its sheath. He had just used the Power of blood—a potent force indeed—to link Emelian's essence to the knife; if ever the man fell into sorcerous peril, the bright blade would seem to blacken, alerting Finist.

It was as much help as he could give Emelian.

Finist glanced at his wife again. "Maria, love, it's getting late. Marya, Emelian, I'm afraid we're going to have to"—he grinned—"fly."

XII

WINTER DREAMS

Vasilev slowly climbed the steps of the platform, his face ashen. Guards moved hastily to surround him as he swayed at the sight of the executioner and the block. But after a moment, he drew himself proudly erect, pulling contemptuously free of their rough support. Carefully he knelt, servants spreading out the folds of his ornate robes behind him. He began to lower his head, then hesitated, eyes sweeping the murmuring crowd. His gaze met hers. His lips whispered her name. Then Vasilev obediently lowered his head to the block as the blindfold was fastened over his eyes. The executioner raised his sword, the sharp blade glinting bright and cruel in the sunlight. It came whistling down—

OLGA CAME AWAKE with a gasp, shaking violently.

Vatza. Oh, my love, my lost, murdered love.

It had been her name he'd whispered on that last, fateful day, she was sure of it. Vasilev's final thoughts had been only of her.

Olga sat up in her bed there among all the other beds of the unmarried women of the court. All about her, the night was silent save for the sound of soft, regular breathing, and bitingly chill even with all the shutters drawn fast. Olga huddled amid the tangle of her bed-clothes, clenching her teeth till they hurt, willing her-

self not to weep. She had wept enough in the months
since that dreadful day, tears all the more painful because she knew the princess pitied her. Pitied her!

Aching, Olga thought back to that first, dreadful night
after Vasilev's death, when she had been completely
shattered, unable to hide her weeping, and the princess
had found her like that . . .

"OLGA? What is it, girl? What's wrong?"

Olga scrambled to her feet, choking down sobs, frantically trying to scrub her eyes dry. "N-nothing, my
Princess. I . . . I . . ."

She couldn't come up with any convincing excuses.
Before she could even try to pull away, Marya was trap-
ping her head between gentle hands, studying her with
magic-bright eyes. Olga froze, terrified, held by that
unblinking blue gaze into which she was sinking . . .

Then the spell shattered. With a faint, sad smile, the
princess released her.

"So *that's* it. I was a fool not to have known."

"I d-don't know what you mean."

"Your mysterious lover was Vasilev."

Olga gasped. Oh, God, Vatza had died as a traitor!
What if she too was accused of treason, just for telling
him about that stairway . . . ? "No, I—"

"Yes. And you're mourning him." Marya reached
out a hand to her. "My poor dear, I'm so sorry."

Olga could have cried out in relief. Plainly the princess's gifts didn't let her read *all* the truth about a body!
Besides, the girl argued with herself, she hadn't done
anything wrong, not really.

Relief turned to anger. Sniffing, Olga pulled away,
muttering, "What have *you* to be sorry about?"

It was a foolish tone to take with a princess. Marya
straightened, eyes losing something of their warmth.
"As a ruler, nothing." There was a hint of iron behind
the flat words. "But I am a woman, too. Olga, I don't
blame you for having been attracted to Vasilev. He *was*

a handsome man. But . . . oh, my dear, didn't you realize he was only using you?''

''That's not true! He loved me!''

''Vasilev loved no one and nothing but himself.''

''He *loved* me!''

There was a long silence. Then Marya asked quietly,
''Would you like to be sent home?''

''No!'' It was a heartfelt cry; if she went home now,
disgraced as she was, her parents would keep her under
lock and key till they could marry her off to the first
taker. ''Please, no.''

The princess sighed. ''Don't beg, Olga. You may
stay. But I'm afraid you can no longer serve as my personal lady-maid. Room will be made for you in the
ladies' quarters. You have my leave. Go.''

Olga bowed wordlessly and obeyed. But the princess's call made her stop and turn back.

''Believe me,'' Marya said, ''I understand your grief.
But the pain will grow less with time, I promise you.''

How would you know? Olga thought bitterly. *You
cold-hearted witch—how would you possibly know?*

HUDDLED IN HER BED in the present, Olga gave a silent,
humorless laugh. A good deal had changed in those few
months. Now Marya knew what it was like to hold a
man in her arms. Now she knew what it was like to be
hopelessly, mindlessly in love.

Curse her! So superior, so full of that false pity—
well, she was going to learn to suffer, too. Olga would
see to that, somehow. She would find a way to use
Marya's love against her, no matter how long it took,
and then:

*She'll weep, just as I wept. She'll ache, just as I
ached. And my poor Vasilev will be avenged.*

THE DEATHLESS NEVER SLEPT, not as mortal creatures
reckoned sleep. But he did slip into an empty blackness
of trance from time to time. And it was from such a
trance that he awoke now, in his mortal shell, all his

faculties instantly alert, to ponder what had been happening in the palace above him.

Up to this point, Koshchei had *felt*, every now and again, the slight tingling of Power, not quite as tangible as the prickling of mortal skin before a storm, from the accursed magician's daughter, frustrating because there was never enough of it for him to use.

Yes, but lately there had been an interesting change. Koshchei's lips curled back in a thin, cold smile as he remembered that first startling burst of Power. If he was correctly interpreting what stray scraps of thought and emotion drifted near enough for him to snatch, the surge meant that Marya had found herself a lover.

The Deathless's smile tightened. Even as the rules woven into the Binding would have it: his liberator need not be of the royal house, merely someone linked to Marya.

A magicless lover: Someone to be nicely susceptible to Koshchei's wiles.

Aie-yé, how wondrously ironic if his enemy had woven into the Binding the very thread that would free him!

The Deathless gave a sharp, impatient hiss. This gloating was all well and good, but it accomplished nothing. The princess's lover still had to come down here of his own free will if Koshchei was to make use of him. And that, the man wasn't likely to do, not with Marya protecting him.

Surely she wouldn't protect him forever. Right now, it was true, they were living in such sickening bliss that echoes of that mindless happiness drifted all the way down here to torment him. But they were merely human, after all. The first hot flames of delight would fade, the first wedge come between them—

Aie, yes, but how long would that take? In the time since his capture, the only one to pay him a visit—discounting that fool Vasilev and Marya herself—had been the stranger, the man who wore Power like a cloak and was of the proper blood . . .

Koshchei settled back against the wall, chains clinking softly about him, and considered. He hadn't been able to learn much about Finist of Kirtesk, but it had been enough to intrigue him.

Indeed. The man's contempt had rankled; it rankled still. But it hadn't been the light bravado of a fool. There had been that unmistakable sense of true Power; but behind the Power had been the faintest metallic tang of fear, the understanding of danger . . . Power and fear. A perilous, fascinating combination, uniquely human, uniquely unpredictable.

Koshchei stretched the limbs of his mortal shell as best he could. How long had it been since there'd last been a human with sufficient strength to challenge him? This one should make an interesting foe indeed.

Let me get free, the Deathless mused. *Only that. Let me get free.*

The great Audience Hall was crowded with folk, boyars *in their rich court robes, ambassadors in colorful, exotic silks and furs. But all of them were raging, fighting each other to be first to speak with her. Overwhelmed by their angry shouts, Marya seized the arms of her throne and screamed:*

"Silence!"

There was a low rumble like the growling of some vast and hostile beast, then they were quiet. But all those angry eyes stared at her till Marya was hard-put not to shrink back into the shelter of the throne like a frightened child.

"Why have you come here? What do you want?"

A tall, red-bearded man, fierce and powerful as a bear, pushed his way through the throng. "I am the Ambassador from Nestera," he announced.

Nestera? Marya bit her lip in alarm. She'd never heard of any such land . . . "I—I'm sorry, I don't know which country—"

"Ha! Ignorant girl, do you give me insult? You yourself invited me to your court!"

"Oh. Of course." Marya struggled desperately to regain her composure. "Pray forgive me, my lord Ambassador. What would you?"

"Reparation! I told your husband that a great storm had sunk our trading fleet. I asked him for advice. And do you know what he did? He laughed, and told us to plant wheat instead!"

"And I—" Another man pushed his way forward, round as a berry, red as a berry in his ruby-studded robes. "I am the Prince of Syrenia!"

Syrenia! Oh, God, she didn't remember any Syrenia, either!

The prince glared at her. "Some peasants blocked my coach's path, but when I ordered them to step aside, your husband told them not to move! He said that they were just as good as I—no, better, because they at least raised food, while all I raised were taxes!"

He looked so silly in his rage, his plump face gone the color of his robes, that Marya, horrified, felt herself starting to laugh.

"You dare!" gasped the prince. "Let us see how you laugh when Syrenia declares war on you!"

"What of us?" yelled the boyars. "Your husband has insulted all of us, too! He mocks the proper rules of the court! He doesn't know a council meeting from a festival!"

"You made a mistake." It was Nikolai. "You never should have married him."

"Oh, but Nikolai, I—"

"You have failed me," said a grim voice. "Once again you have failed me."

Marya sprang from the throne, staring. "Father . . . ?"

"You married for yourself, not for the crown's sake."

"Emelian's a good, kind, clever man. He just needs time to get used to the proper procedures here at court, that's all. He'll learn, you'll see."

"You should have married well. You should have borne my magic. You should have saved me!"

"I couldn't! Father, I—"

"You wanted the throne. You let me die."

"No! That's not true! Father, please, you know that's not true!"

MARYA CAME STARKLY AWAKE, gasping. A dream . . . ? Akh, yes, thank Heaven, nothing more than that.

She turned to look at Emelian slumbering beside her. Odd, she wondered, dazed. In these four months of their marriage, had she never really noticed how he looked asleep? Without that good-humored, gentle smile brightening his face, he looked almost . . . common.

What nonsense! She was letting that ridiculous dream get the better of her. He never had been conventionally handsome. What of it?

Yes, and as for what had been going on at court . . . Well, it was true that Emelian had made some foolish blunders, confusing rank, proceedings, but those had been honest mistakes, nothing that couldn't be corrected in time. He loved her well enough to prove a quick student for her sake. And of course she loved him.

But for a long while, Marya lay awake, unable to shake the unhappiness of her dream, staring at the man who all at once seemed such a stranger.

For one confused moment, Emelian had no idea where he was. Forest . . . a ramshackle old house . . .

Home! He was back in his childhood home. And, oh, could it be? His father was coming to greet him, smiling.

"You're alive again!" Emelian cried in delight.

But then he saw those cold, empty, lightless eyes, and knew with a thrill of horror that he was very, very wrong.

"You abandoned me." His father's smile had vanished. Voice cold and flat, the old man accused, "You left my grave and forgot about me."

"That's not true! I mourned you, I mourn you still. But, Father, life must go on, you once told me that yourself. I'm married now, to a princess, and—"

"You wed in haste, without the proper chance to earn her. Now your only hope is to become a true boyar. Serge and I will teach you. Serge! Now!"

The old warrior stalked grimly forward, sword in hand, and Emelian gasped to see that it wasn't a dulled practice weapon, but a true warsword. His father was forcing a similar blade into his hand.

"Fight him, my son, kill him!"

"This is insane! Serge, I'm not going to fight you. Stop it."

But the old warrior continued to advance, a cruel, merciless light in his eyes . . . Emelian dropped his sword, shaking his head in denial.

"You can't be Serge! And I can't be here!"

—And he wasn't. This wide, flat square was part of Astyan's marketplace, and he was all alone.

No. A harsh laugh made Emelian whirl . . .

The hulking warrior loomed over him, so close he could smell the man's unwashed stench. As Emelian drew back in disgust, the barbarian grinned, showing stained, broken teeth.

"Afraid, little man? You should be. The Princess Marya doesn't love you. She can't love. She's a witch."

"Liar!"

The barbarian continued to grin. "But witches are still women. Do you know what I'm going to do to her when we conquer Astyan? I'm going to—"

"Stop it!"

Somehow a sword had formed itself in Emelian's hand. Wildly he swung out at the barbarian. At the touch of the blade, the hulking form dissolved into a little pile of dust. As Emelian stared down at it in horror, a voice exclaimed peevishly:

"No, no, no, that will never do."

"Nikolai."

"Do you know what you've just done. You've killed

*the Ambassador from the East. Now there's going to be
a war, and it's all your fault.''*

"But I . . ."

*"Silly little boy, you should have stayed at home and
raised turnips.''*

"No, I—''

*"Go home, I say. Go back to the farm where you
belong.''*

"No. I— No!''

And with that, Emelian came awake, panting, staring
up at nothing. Beside him, Marya slept on, and after a
moment, he turned to look at her, at the sweet curve of
one cheek half hidden beneath a liquid fall of long black
hair.

God, what a ridiculous dream that was!

But something of the grue of it remained . . .

Since he had been here at court, only one of the
boyars, young Yaroslav, had shown the slightest sign of
friendship towards him. Oh, Emelian didn't doubt that
he could easily have made friends with any of the common folk working in and around the palace or down in
Astyan's streets. But of course such . . . lowly friend-
ships were discouraged.

Those things didn't matter. With Marya's love to
comfort him, what more did he need?

The young man sighed. What more, indeed? For all
his father's desperate lessons in nobility, Emelian realized all too clearly the gap between customs twenty
years or more out of date and the intricate ways of a
modern royal court.

What *was* he doing here, after all? Even after these
wonderful months of marriage, he still hadn't figured
out all those courtly intricacies. He had already made
some ridiculous mistakes, calling people by the wrong
titles, confusing orders of precedence. Surely it was
just a matter of time before he did something really
stupid to endanger Marya or the busy, cheerful city he
was coming to love almost as much as she.

Marya stirred, then opened her eyes to stare at him in alarm. "What is it? What's wrong?"

Emelian sighed. "Nothing, love. Go back to sleep."

"You cried out."

"Sorry. I didn't mean to disturb you. It was only a dream."

"You had a nightmare, too?"

"Akh, yes."

Her gaze was wild. "Emelian, tell me, was it . . . about us?"

"How could you know—"

"Then it was!"

"In a way."

Marya moaned. "And in it, were we . . . wrong for each other?"

"Well, yes, but—Marya, it was only a dream!"

"You don't understand. I dreamed, too. About us. It wasn't a happy dream."

"So? Coincidence. Or maybe you, my magical dear, accidentally influenced my sleeping mind." He frowned. "You can't be taking it seriously! The dinner last night was too rich, that's all. Hey, now, even the peasants don't believe—"

"Oh, Emelian, don't start that again!"

"What—"

"It's always 'the peasants do this,' or 'the peasants do that.' I don't *care* what the peasants do!"

He frowned. "You sound like my father. The peasants are your people as much as the nobility."

"Don't lecture me."

"Akh, Marya! If you don't want me to talk about them, why didn't you say something to me before this?"

"Because I didn't think it would be necessary! I thought surely a *boyar*'s son would have the sense—"

"Forgive me!" Emelian snapped. "From now on, I'll be careful to watch what I say so I don't offend—"

"I didn't mean that! Emelian, you've got to remember you're not a peasant, but a royal consort."

"Are you saying you're ashamed of me?"

"No!"

"Then what is it? Marya, love, we were so happy these past months! Are you . . . having second thoughts about us now?"

Say no, he pleaded silently. *Oh, please say no.*

Marya wouldn't meet his gaze. "I—I don't know," she murmured at last. "I do love you, truly. I always shall. It's just . . . Oh, Emelian, we've known each other for such a short while. We're such different people!"

"Of course we are," he said with forced gaiety. "I'm a man, you're a woman."

"I'm not jesting! Could Nikolai have been right? Were we in too much haste to wed? Did we make a mistake?"

He winced at the misery in her voice. "Oh, love, no, never. Look you, can you picture us apart?"

"No . . ."

"Your Power showed us together, and happy." But, deep within him, his own doubts were stirring . . . "Marya, I—"

"No, please!" she cried out wildly. "No more talking. Hold me. Just hold me."

For a time, they clung together in an embrace that had more of loneliness than passion to it. At last, her head cushioned on Emelian's shoulder, Marya slipped back into sleep. But he remained awake, thinking of his dream, thinking of his marriage. Staring blindly up at the bed's canopy, he silently counted off the long, lonely hours, and slept no more that night.

XIII

SPRING AWAKENINGS

THE LITTLE GARDEN in the royal palace was bright with
sunlight and early flowers, brighter yet with the reds
and blues and yellows of the caftans and embroidered
sarafans of that group of *boyars'* wives and daughters:
boyarinas, boyarevnas. They and their lady-maids sat
with sweet-stringed *gusla* or harp or needlework, chattering away like so many sparrows, all of them glad to
be out in the open air this first warm day of spring,
happily spreading gossip and shredding reputations.

Olga, still grieving for her lost Vasilev, sat somewhat
apart from the other women, as always; they and she
both knew she'd lost precious status by being demoted
from lady-maid to the princess back to mere petty noble's daughter.

*Spiteful cats! Well, I don't care. Let them ignore me.
All I want is for my Vatza to be avenged.*

True, almost half a year had passed without her being
able to come up with a single plan for that vengeance
. . . Still, if the latest rumors were true, Princess Marya
and her consort were already on the way to making
themselves miserable. Olga looked warily about, wondering if she dared discuss those rumors . . . The
women had already talked over everyone any of them
knew (anyone who wasn't actually in that garden, of
course). The girl burst out:

"What about the princess?"

There was startled silence.

"What about her, dear?" asked *boyarina* Ludmilla, wife to Dimitri of the Inner Council.

Fat and sloppy she might be, but Ludmilla happened to be the only councilor's wife in the garden just then—which meant that she was of higher status than anyone else here. And aware of it. Forcing down her distaste, Olga said in wide-eyed, nicely feigned innocence, "Oh . . . I was just wondering . . . Are the stories true? About her and her consort, I mean? And their . . . troubles?"

That, of course, was all it took to spark a new session of gossip. Eyes dancing with delight in their daring, the ladies chirped and chattered gaily:

"I heard they have a quarrel every night."

"*I* heard they aren't even sharing the same quarters anymore."

"Or even," giggled someone, "the same bed."

"Oh, how could you know that?"

"Well, the servants say—"

"You mean, you listen to servants' gossip?"

"It's all because of him, you know," murmured the *boyarina* Anna suddenly, and the others granted her a moment of respectful silence. Elegant, elderly, the thin reed of a woman had been a widow so long none of the others could even recall her husband's name. She glanced around, enjoying her moment of power. "He's a nobody, really."

That set the women off anew.

"I heard he does foolish things," said plump little Manya. "Sometimes he gets people's titles mixed up."

Tall Ilenka looked down her long lashes in delicate malice. "Is that all? If I recall, dear, you did the same thing when *you* first arrived. Your husband was furious."

Manya blushed. "Well, yes. But Emelian does worse things than that!"

"Such as what?"

"Such as favoring the common folk too much. Why, he even worries about the peasants!"

"Not surprising," said Anna. "After all, the man practically *is* a peasant!"

Olga stifled a sigh of frustration. All this talk about Marya's love-trouble was satisfying enough to make her gloat—

But if the troubles aren't of my causing, how can I ever call it revenge for my poor Vatza? I must find my own way to make her suffer!

Ignoring her sudden thoughtfulness as they usually did, the others continued:

"I heard he's not even noble."

"*I* heard he really *is* a peasant!"

"I heard," cut in Ludmilla lazily, "that theirs is a very young marriage, full of the trials and flames of any young marriage. My husband and I fought every day the first year we were wed, no secret about that. Ah, but the reconciliations every night . . . "

There was such a sensual purr to those words that all the women shivered, giggling. The *boyarina* let it continue for a moment, then added, almost as an aside, "I also heard a group of silly women gossiping about their betters. Now, ladies, don't you think we can find something more suitable to do?"

There was the faintest edge of warning to the lazy voice. Suddenly everyone became very interested in music or needlework.

"I thought you could," said Ludmilla, and smiled.

"DIMI? Are you asleep?"

"Yes."

"Dimi!"

Boyar Dimitri of the Inner Council of Astyan groaned, rolling over in bed to lie on his back, eyes determinedly shut. "Don't tell me you aren't satisfied. Woman, one of these nights you're going to burn me out."

Ludmilla chuckled, delighted. "No chance of that!

But that's not what I want—well, not right now. I mean, Dimi, love, you know no other man could ever please me as you do.''

"Good. Good night."

"Dimi! I want to tell you what the women were discussing today."

"Akh, 'Milla. Can't it wait till morning?''

"No! Dimitri, they were chattering all about our princess and her consort, saying how they do little but fight all the time— Oh, of course it's true that things haven't been going so smoothly for them; they're both very young, and only human, after all. Still, to say they aren't even sharing a bed— Now, I happen to know that isn't true, my little Sasha being friends with one of the women of the princess's bed-chamber. But there must be *something* behind all that gossip, don't you think?''

"Mm."

"Dimi! Don't go to sleep yet. I haven't finished. Now, I didn't think the situation between them was so very bad, but of course I might have been mistaken. Unless the whole thing really *is* just gossip . . . The princess keeps such a private tongue in her head, you never can tell what she's thinking, but— Dimi, what do *you* think? Do you think the royal marriage truly is in trouble?''

"What I think, wife," said Dimitri sternly, "is that this is scandalous talk, unbefitting a *boyarina.*"

"Oh, but—Dimi!"

"Don't pout, woman. Listen to me. You are not to spread gossip. Is that understood?''

"I wasn't—"

"Is that understood?''

Ludmilla sighed. "Yes, Dimi," she said in reluctant obedience.

THE MEMBERS of the Inner Council of Astyan sat in secret, uneasy, meeting. "Dimitri?" asked Nikolai warily. "Why have you asked us to gather?''

Dimitri looked about at his fellow members of the Inner Council for a long moment, then began. "*Bo-*

yars, much as I hate sounding like some gossiping servant, I'm afraid there is a matter we must discuss: the state of the royal marriage.''

Nikolai groaned. "I *told* you she shouldn't marry him. But no, leave her alone, you said. Let the girl have her fun, you said."

"I never expected her to actually marry him!"

"But she did!" Nikolai groaned again. "I tried to warn her, but she wouldn't listen to me."

"*Boyar,* please. Self-pity isn't going to solve anything."

"Self-pity!" The man sat bolt upright in indignation. "Very well, *boyar* Dimitri, if you're so wise, what would you suggest we do?"

"Akh, I don't know. We must think of the princess's welfare, of course. But first and foremost, we must consider the well-being of Astyan."

"Emelian *is* her consort," young Yaroslav reminded them. "He can't merely be bought off like some simple adventurer. And . . . maybe we're all being too hasty," he added hesitantly. "After all, they do love each other."

The others gave him contemptuous glances. Dimitri said flatly, "We're thinking of the welfare of our land, *boyar,* not of whether or not a minstrel's tale has a happy ending."

"Of course. I only meant—"

"*Boyar* Yaroslav, I know you like the man. Not surprisingly; you're nearly of an age. And it's to your credit that you've been tutoring him in courtly ways."

Yaroslav stirred uncomfortably. "I admit I'm young, but pray don't patronize me."

Dimitri frowned. "All right, then, no gentle words. Teaching the man pretty phrases and proper forms of address isn't going to solve our problem!"

"*What* problem? We don't—"

"Oh, come, *boyar*. It was bad enough when Princess Marya insisted on marrying the man. Astyan will become a laughingstock among nations when word gets out that not only did she wed a nobody—she wed a quarrelsome, ignorant lout to boot. If Astyan's image suffers, trade suffers too, and—''

He was interrupted by Yaroslav's wordless exclamation of disgust. ''That is the most farfetched excuse I've ever heard! First of all, Emelian isn't the boor you're painting him, and you all know it. Second, there isn't going to be any trading disaster just because Astyan's princess was romantic enough to marry for love. If anything, the whole thing should be wonderful for Astyan's economy: people love romance!''

''Of course.'' Dimitri's voice was bland enough to be blatantly insulting. ''Well, *boyars*, what do you think?''

''But—''

''Please, *boyar* Yaroslav,'' Nikolai said gently. ''Give someone else a chance to speak.''

Yaroslav, still too young not to be polite to his elders, fell silent, fuming.

Just then, Yuri, quiet, middle-aged, so grey in personality that the others tended to forget he was there, cleared his throat sharply, making them start and stare in his direction. ''The man really can't be bought off?''

''God, no!'' said Nikolai fervently. ''Wouldn't *that* do wonders for Astyan's image? Besides,'' he added reluctantly, reddening, ''I already tried that once, before the wedding. Without success.''

''He . . . could meet with an accident,'' someone suggested softly, and Yaroslav cried, ''No!''

''No,'' agreed Nikolai. *''Boyars,* we've all done what we must over the years, for the sake of the land. But I, for one, draw the line at murder.''

Dimitri straightened suddenly. ''Annulment. That's the answer.''

''Annulment!'' echoed Yaroslav. ''On what grounds?''

''Akh, what does it matter? An acceptable excuse can always be found when royalty is concerned. Get Princess Marya to admit she's made a mistake, have her agree to an annulment, and—our problem is gone."

"But we don't *have* a problem!" Yaroslav insisted. "Emelian's not a fool, or abusive or foul in looks or manners. If he and Princess Marya quarrel from time to time, that's no one else's affair! *Boyars,* there's not the slightest bit of shame in his being the royal consort. And yet you insist on disliking the man just because he doesn't happen to have any convenient political ties!" Overcome by his own emotion, the young *boyar* continued fiercely, "I don't think you're concerned about Astyan's well-being at all, not when it concerns Emelian. No, I think you're only interested in soothing your injured pride because the Princess Marya didn't come to you for advice before following her heart, and—Wait!"

None of the others were listening to him. Before the furious Yaroslav could muster his thoughts, he found himself alone in the council chamber.

YAROSLAV PAUSED in mid-stride, staring down at the courtyard below him, and those within it. And after that first, startled moment, he began to grin.

Emelian and Marya were duelling down there, fencing with practice swords. Yaroslav knew the princess liked to keep her not-inconsiderable skill in weaponry fresh whenever possible, but he had never seen Emelian as her fencing partner.

It was a ridiculous bout. Evidently, they'd been jesting as they fought, and by now the two of them were laughing so much they couldn't keep their weapons in line. At last, totally oblivious of curious courtiers and servants, Emelian went down on one knee in ostentatious defeat, casting aside his sword. Marya, the gracious winner, knelt beside him to administer a kiss of peace—a kiss that turned into something a good deal warmer than peace. Yaroslav's grin widened.

So their marriage is in trouble, is it? Look at this,

you condescending boyars, *look and learn! Annulment,*
ha!

Still, it might not be a bad idea to warn the princess
of her councilors' plot . . . He would send his wife to
her; no one ever took offense at Elena, his sweet Elenishka. And he himself would warn Emelian . . .

Later, thought Yaroslav, *when he's alone.*

YESTERDAY THINGS HAD GONE so smoothly. Yesterday
things had gone so happily!

Emelian leaned moodily on the rampart's balustrade,
thinking that these sudden jumps from joy to gloom
were starting to be all too typical of his marriage.

No more brooding, he told himself sternly. Far below
him was what had drawn him to this spot in the first
place: perhaps the finest view of Astyan. The young
man looked out over the cheerful confusion of log
houses that, now that spring was here to stay, were
freshly painted in every bright color of the spectrum,
and smiled in spite of himself. What had once seemed
an impenetrable maze no longer held any mystery for
him.

He leaned out a little farther, looking over the line
of the palace wall. There was Masha the baker, just
opening up shop now (remarkably late for Masha; but
then, he and his wife had a new baby, and had probably
had little sleep last night), and down Market Street went
Yuri the horse trader with five of his charges in tow.
Two doors down from Masha, Leo the rug merchant
was sitting peacefully by his exotic, half-unrolled mer-
chandise, the smoke from his pipe a thin white feather
in the still air . . . no, now it was wavering as he sa-
luted Ivan the gem-seller, who was making his wary
way down the street, closely trailed by the bodyguard
he'd never yet needed . . .

Emelian straightened. By now, he realized, bemused,
he could call most of the citizens of Astyan by their
names and occupations.

Which, unfortunately, was more than he could say

about the *boyars*. Those supercilious, patronizing, tradition-bound idiots . . . The worst of it was that they'd influenced Marya. Oh, he had done his best to show her that Astyan wasn't all fine manners and snobbery, he'd taken her on secret tours of the city outside the royal palace, and she had seemed to enjoy herself. And yet . . .

Emelian's hand stole to the silver amulet hanging on its chain about his neck. Marya's gift . . . Within it was a lock of her black hair and three drops of her blood: an old charm, she'd said, only half in jest, to bind the two of them together. Even now, as he held the shining little thing, he fancied he could feel a soft warmth to it, as though instead of hard silver he was touching Marya herself . . . Ah, Marya!

These constant quarrels were as much his fault as hers. Emelian freely admitted he could be as infuriatingly stubborn and impatient as any peasant from around his father's estate.

But at the same time:

God, if only there was something for him to *do!* Everyone, even friend Yaroslav, seemed to think he was feeble-witted, capable of doing nothing but sitting quietly at the princess's side and smiling vacantly. Granted, Emelian had realized from the start that as royal consort he wasn't going to be taking an active part in Astyani government. Fine. He could accept that. But—dammit all, he wasn't a toy for Marya to dress in pretty clothes and show off like a little girl with a new doll!

Yes, but every time I try to prove myself, I seem to end up doing something stupid. Emelian groaned. *How, in God's name, can I ever hope to be worthy of her?*

Just then, a voice burst out with: "But you two looked so happy yesterday!"

Emelian spun about. "Yaroslav."

"Forgive me. I didn't mean to startle you. But . . . After yesterday, I did think everything was fine between you and Princess Marya."

Emelian raised a brow, struggling to control a sudden

stirring of anger. "You were watching us?" he said carefully.

Yaroslav shook his head impatiently. "I wasn't spying, if that's what you mean. I chanced to pass by while you and she were duelling, that's all. But . . . Well, what went wrong this time? I felt sure you'd be in the Audience Hall, listening to the litigants with Princess Marya."

"I should have been. That's exactly why we quarrelled."

Yaroslav blinked. "She . . . didn't want you there?"

"Oh, no. Marya invited me, all right. I just didn't want to go." Emelian held up his hands in supplication. "These aren't folk really in need of help, you and I know that. They're nobles arguing over hairs. I had a picture of myself sitting there for hours, doing nothing but listening to elaborate orations, a look of deep wisdom fixed on my face . . ."

"But—dammit, man, that's part of what being a royal consort is all about!"

"I know it."

Yaroslav wasn't finished. "To refuse to take your place at her side, just to save yourself a few turns of the hourglass of boredom . . . Do you realize what you've done?"

"Only too well."

"You've made her look weak! You've made her look as though she didn't even have the power to control her consort, let alone her land— Emelian, how could you ever have been such a fool?"

"Easily! I usually am!" Emelian turned sharply away, leaning on the balustrade. "I love her so much . . ." He reached up a hand to tenderly touch the little silver amulet again. "And yet I seem to be doing my best to tear us apart. *Damn!* Why am I always doing something stupid? Ha, 'too impulsive,' that's what Serge would say."

"Serge?"

"A man I used to know. Back when I was still nobody, living in the middle of the forest. Back when I could still afford to be naive!'' He slammed his hand down on the balustrade with such force that he saw Yaroslav wince.

"Emelian . . .''

"Never mind. I'm not going to sicken you with any more self-pity.''

"I didn't mean—''

"Wait. Let me finish. I admit I didn't realize when I married Marya that I was also wedding Astyan. But I do love Marya, and I've come to love this land as well.'' He gave Yaroslav a quick, faint smile. "You should get out into the streets and fields more often, all you *boyars* should. Staying locked up here with your traditions, you can't really know Astyan. You have a charming people down there, full of energy, bustling about working deals, making sales, enjoying their lives to the fullest.''

"I . . . suppose they do,'' said Yaroslav slowly. "I never really thought about it.'' He eyed Emelian with new respect. "And I never realized you felt so strongly about Astyan.''

"I do.'' Emelian's voice faltered slightly. "It's the first time in my life I've felt a place was truly my home . . . Akh, enough of that. I have to remember to think about court matters as well. I promise you this, Yaroslav: from now on, no more thoughtlessness. From now on, I will do nothing to disgrace myself or my wife. And,'' he added ruefully, "the next time Marya asks me to do something, I'm going to do it, whether I hate it or not. I'm not going to risk hurting her again.''

"I . . . only hope it's not already too late,'' Yaroslav murmured. "Emelian, the Inner Council met secretly yesterday. They're going to try to convince Princess Marya to . . . have your marriage annulled.''

"They *what?*'' Overwhelmed by shock and rage, Emelian floundered helplessly for a moment. Then, with a low, wordless cry, he started fiercely away.

"Wait!'' Yaroslav cried plaintively after him. "Where are you going?''

"To Marya. Her meeting should be finished by now. Yaroslav, thank you for the warning."

"But what are you going to do?"

"I don't know yet. But I'm not going to let the Council spoil my marriage. I intend to stop them. No matter what I have to do!"

THE MEETING in the Audience Hall was long over. At her command, she had been left alone amid the dim, smoky silence. But Marya still fumed, half at the litigants who had wasted so much of her time, half, though she tried to deny it, at Emelian for having so lightly escaped them.

The rage wouldn't be denied. Blazing with frustration, the princess clenched her fists till they ached to keep herself from hurling a priceless vase across the room.

Curse it, Emelian, how could you run off like that?

Just this week, now that the spring floodings were done and the roads were passable again, preparations would begin for her yearly tour of the land. Marya had planned to have her husband riding proudly at her side, but now— He would probably decide that, too, would be too boring, and want to go hunting instead!

Oh, Emelian, I love you, but— Damn you, there are times when I could wish I'd never seen you! When are you going to accept your responsibilities and—

"My Princess?" said a shy voice.

"Yes?" Marya snapped. "What is it?"

When she got no immediate answer, the princess hissed in anger, turning so sharply that the slim little woman who had spoken cringed away.

"P-please excuse me, my Princess. I didn't mean to interrupt your thoughts."

Akh, Yaroslav's wife. Pretty, shy, gentle little Elena, with her long blonde braids and (even after a year's marriage) incredibly innocent blue eyes. Marya sighed. God knew what Yaroslav saw in the woman. "Sweet" was the politest word that could be applied to her.

"Vapid," Marya thought dourly, would be more accurate. But one could hardly take out one's anger on such a gentle creature; it would be like kicking a puppy.

No, that wasn't quite fair. Dull, Elena might be, but there wasn't a bit of malice or callousness to her. Unlike all too many others at court. She also was no spreader of gossip. Again, unlike all too many others.

"Forgive me, *boyarina* Elena," Marya said, contrite. "I didn't mean to shout at you. What is it you want?"

"It—it's none of my affair, really, but . . . Oh, please, don't be too angry at the royal consort!"

"What's this?"

Blushing, Elena nevertheless continued doggedly. "He loves you, he really does."

"And how would you know that?"

The guileless blue gaze met hers without blinking. "I'm not as sophisticated as some of the other *boyarinas*, I know that. And maybe I'm not as bright or as clever, either. But I'm not a fool."

"My dear, I never thought you were," Marya lied tactfully.

"I know love when I see it. And I've seen Emelian's eyes when he looks at you—my Princess, he adores you."

"Ah. Well. I trust you didn't come here just to tell me that."

"No . . . I wanted to ask you . . ."

"Come, out with it. What did you really want to say?"

The blush returned, brighter than before. Her voice little more than a frightened whisper, Elena blurted out, "That—that you shouldn't be too hard on Emelian."

Marya frowned. "What's this? Are you accusing me of acting unjustly?"

Elena's eyes widened in horror. "Oh, no, never! I only meant . . . He truly is trying his best to fit in."

"Don't lecture." Marya turned away from the pretty, earnest face, arms about herself. "I know he is."

And to her amazement, she found herself over-whelmed by memory, all at once seeing not the dull reality of the quiet, empty Audience Hall, but the bustle of Astyan's main square as it had been that market day a month or so past . . . At Emelian's insisting, she and he had daringly escaped from the palace to go, dis-guised in hooded cloaks swiped from servants, down among the commons, jesting with them, listening to their complaints and joys. Emelian had bought her a fairing that day, a silly, pretty bunch of red ribbons for her hair, as though she'd been no more than a little peasant girl. And when she, laughing, amazed at the genuine delight she felt, had thanked him, Emelian had kissed her soundly, much to the approval of the crowd.

If they had realized it was their princess and her con-sort putting on such a show . . .

For a moment, the memory of that kiss, tasting faintly as it had of the golden mead they'd both been sampling, made her smile. Akh, she had learned more about her people in that one, short day . . . Marya shook her head. She mustn't let past pleasure distort her thinking. The fact remained that—

But she could feel Elena's eyes on her, and turned to find the young woman staring at her with such wild hope that the princess sighed.

"You and Yaroslav never fight, do you? No," she added wryly, seeing Elena's astonishment, "I thought not. But then, you two are hardly strangers to each other, betrothed as children as you were." Curiosity moved Marya to add, "You don't regret that, do you? Having no choice about who you wed?"

Elena smiled shyly. "No. Never."

"Mm. Maybe there's something to be said for ar-ranged marriages after all. Emelian and I barely know each other."

"Oh, but you know he's a kind man, and a gentle one, and a loving one, too, and . . . "

She went on from there, chattering simple, well-meaning words, all ignorant of the fact that her princess, lost in her own thoughts, had quite shut her out.

"You're right," Marya said abruptly, cutting into the earnest prattle, and Elena started and fell silent.

"My Princess . . . ?"

"I do tend to see only what he should be, and forget what he is. I married Emelian the man, not the polished courtier. I'm not ashamed of him. And I don't want to lose him!" Marya paused with a little sigh of regret. "It would have been pleasant to be able to show him off to the people when I make my tour. But Emelian doesn't seem to like such things. And . . . maybe he's right. Maybe this year, at least, it really would be better for Emelian if he stayed here. In my absence, he would have the freedom to learn about the royal way of things without having to worry about me hanging about his neck." She grinned at the other woman. "Oh, the clever man! That has to be exactly what he wanted; he just couldn't find a way to tell me. So! From now on, I'm not going to force Emelian into a role he can't play. And if some folk don't approve, the problem is theirs, not mine."

"I hope so," said Elena breathlessly. "You see, the *boyars* of the Inner Council . . ."

Marya frowned. "What about them?"

"They . . . Yaroslav said they . . . want you to annul your marriage."

"They would *dare!*"

The fury of outraged wife as well as princess was in that cry, and Elena shied away from the force of it. "Yes, I—I'm afraid they would."

Marya didn't hear her. All the rage and frustration she had tried to suppress over Emelian came blazing back to life, but the princess merely grinned: a sharp, humorless, almost predatory grin. "My councilors," she murmured, "my dear, prying, would-be controlling councilors, I think it time you are reminded once again: I am *not* to be controlled. I am not and never will be your puppet!" Savagely, Marya snapped, "Elena!"

The other woman started. "Ah . . . my Princess . . . ?"

"See that the *boyars* of the Inner Council are sent to me. Now!"

Elena curtseyed in nervous haste. As the little *boyarina* scurried off, Marya returned to her throne. Slowly she climbed the steps of the dais. Seating herself once more, the princess settled coldly down to wait.

EMELIAN STAGGERED as a small, hurrying form ran into him. "Oof! Gently, little one, don't—Elena? *Boyarina* Elena? What—"

"Oh, I, oh, forgive me, I'm sorry, I didn't mean to—"

"Hey, now, no harm done. Just tell me if you've seen the princess. The servants tell me she never left the Audience Hall."

"She's still there, but I don't—"

"Thank you, my dear. That's all I wanted to know."

Behind him, he could hear Elena's plaintive, "But . . . wait . . . " *No more waiting*, Emelian thought. Quickly he entered the Audience Hall through the private, royal entrance, that narrow doorway hidden behind the dais and the throne, brushing off uneasy guards who made halfhearted attempts to stop him.

"Marya, I—"

"Emelian! What are you doing here?"

It was hardly the reception he'd expected. "What in the name of—"

"You shouldn't be here, not now!"

"But I—"

"Please, just go."

"Marya!" Before she could interrupt him again, Emelian quickly continued. "I know you're probably still angry at me, and I don't blame you. But that doesn't give you the right to scold me as though I was a half-wit!"

"You don't understand—Akh, come up here on the dais so I don't have to shout down at you."

Emelian obligingly climbed the steps, stopping just below the level of the throne. "Better?"

"Emelian, listen to me. I haven't got time for a chat right now. But I'll be happy to talk to you later, so—"

"You're still doing it. I repeat, I am not a half-wit."

"Aie, Emelian!" It was a cry of sheer frustration. "Look you, I've summoned the Inner Council. They'll be here in less than a half-turn of the glass—"

"Then . . . you already know?"

Marya stiffened. "Know what? Are you trying to tell me you knew what they were plotting, and didn't bother to warn me?"

"Of *course* I didn't." Emelian couldn't keep the sarcasm from his voice. "I *wanted* to let them destroy our marriage. If we don't do the job for them. Dammit, Marya, I came in here to apologize to you! Are you going to let me, or not?"

The princess sighed. "No need for apologies. I was wrong. I never should have put you under so much strain that—"

"*I* haven't been under any strain! It's you—Marya, love, I want to help you. Let me."

"You do help, my love, just by being—"

"You're not going to say 'just by being you,' are you? Marya, dearest, please don't patronize me."

"I didn't mean—"

"Now, you listen to me. From now on, I will sit by you at every meeting, ride beside you on every journey, do everything a proper royal consort should. This, I promise."

"Don't be silly. I don't want you having to do anything you don't want to do."

"For the last time, Marya, stop treating me like an idiot!"

"Then stop acting like one!"

"*I'm* not the one who— All right. Let's not get into another argument. Agreed?"

After a tense moment, she nodded. Emelian sighed in relief.

"Now, quickly, before your *boyars* get here: I do intend to be a proper consort. When you leave on your tour of the land, I'll be at your side."

"No."

"Yes."

"No! Emelian, this is silly. We both know you don't really want to go."

"I never said—"

"Please. Let me finish. You see, I've come to agree with you. Emelian, there's no real need for you to tour with me, not this first year. No, I want you to stay right here."

"But—but that's ridiculous!"

"It's not! No, wait, give me a chance to explain. Without me, you'll have the time to adjust to your position, to see how Astyan is run, and—"

"To stay out of your way, you mean!"

"That's not what I meant at all."

Emelian stared at her. "Oh, really, Marya. Couldn't you come up with a more convincing excuse? What are you really trying to say? That you don't want your people to see us together?"

"Now that *is* ridiculous!"

But Emelian saw her glance drop away from his, just for an instant, and cried out in anguish, "My God, you're ashamed of me! That's it, isn't it?"

"No, never!"

"It is! You're ashamed of—"

"No! Emelian, I *love* you!"

"You have an odd way of showing it."

"Oh, my dear, believe me, I only want what's best for you!"

Emelian angrily slapped his hand down on the top of the dais. "Dammit, I told you not to patronize me!"

"All right, then! I tried to follow your wishes. I tried to explain why I agree that you should stay. Now I'm *ordering* you to stay! And I—"

A discreet cough interrupted them. The Inner Council was assembling, their faces a collective study in scrupulous innocence. Marya gave Emelian a quick glare, then straightened regally on the throne. "Ah, *boyars*. How kind of you to answer my summons so swiftly." She smiled charmingly at them. "Forgive us. My husband and I lost all track of time. Isn't that true, love."

"Oh, quite," Emelian forced out.

"We were just discussing the route of my tour," Marya continued blithely. "This one time, Emelian won't be riding with me. No, we have agreed that for the good of Astyan, he shall serve as Regent in my place while I'm away. With your aid, of course, good Nikolai. I'm sure my husband will find you as great a help as do I."

"Of . . . course, my Princess." Nikolai's face was a bland mask as he bowed.

Marya looked down at Emelian with so tender a smile he could almost believe its warmth. "And you, of course, will think only of what's best for Astyan. Isn't that right, dearest?"

With all the *boyars* watching him, looking for the smallest sign of weakness, what could Emelian do but agree? "Quite right, my love," he said through clenched teeth, and smiled.

XIV

PLOTS AND EXCURSIONS

THE SPLENDOR of the royal party was a sight for poets'
songs, all color and light. A brisk, clean wind caught
at the stiff, festive banners of royal red, making them
snap and flutter till the heroic figures embroidered on
their lengths seemed to dance, forcing the standard
bearers to struggle in their saddles, fighting to hold the
stanchions erect. The wind teased at the cloaks and
clothing of courtiers and soldiers alike, all of them
bravely clad in scarlet and gold and blues crisp enough
to rival the enamel-bright sky. Sunlight glinted dazzlingly back from sword hilts, spear points, iron helms
and bronze-washed mail shirts, from the brass and silver trappings of horses prancing nervously, eager to be
off.

And Marya—Emelian's heart ached with the sharp,
fierce beauty of her, slim as a swordblade in her shining
mail, regal red cloak whipping and flashing out behind
her like flame. Her eyes were brighter than the day, and
the line of her helm-framed face was so pure that his
hand fairly burned to stroke it.

Akh, my love! Their quarrels seemed so foolish now,
less than foolish, and Emelian had to force himself not
to shout out, *You can't leave me, I won't let you go!*
Instead, biting on the inside of his lip till it nearly bled,

he managed to keep still as Astyan's princess glanced about at those who were remaining behind.

"I cede you, my husband and consort, Emelian Grigorovich, regency of the throne of Astyan till such time as I return."

The words were mere formality; the actual ceremony of regency had taken place privately, with only the members of the Inner Council as witnesses. *Disapproving witnesses*, thought Emelian, and picked up his cue. "I, Emelian Grigorovich, husband and consort to you, Marya, Princess and ruler of Astyan, do pledge to hold the throne safe and unthreatened till your return. And may that return be swift and safe," he added earnestly, fixing his gaze on her face, trying to memorize every detail . . .

It was too much for Marya. She kneed her horse to his side and bent in the saddle. Emelian reached up and threw his arms about her as best he could, feeling the hardness of the clinking mail between them. Her lips pressed against his, warm and passionate.

Too soon she straightened, pulling away from his grasp, and turned her horse away. "Farewell."

Emelian nearly choked on the word. "Farewell."

He watched, helplessly frozen, as the royal party rode away. He watched till the last dust from their passing had settled.

"My lord?" Nikolai asked warily.

"Yes," Emelian murmured. "I'm coming."

The older *boyar*'s voice held an unexpected touch of sympathy. "She won't be away so very long, God willing. The entire tour shouldn't take longer than one cycle of the moon."

"I know."

Emelian didn't dare to say any more. Blinking his eyes fiercely till they were convincingly dry, he turned to follow the councilor slowly back into the palace.

WHAT WAS THIS? Puzzled, the Deathless straightened in his chains, suddenly alert, listening with senses that had nothing to do with the merely mortal. Where was the woman, the hated magician's daughter? All at once, the *feel* of her had vanished!

Odd, though, the faint psychic haze that seemed to linger after her . . . Almost as though she had some manner of arcane double . . .

Not a double, realized Koshchei with a shock, *a lover!*

Akh, what was this timeless place doing to him? Tricking his senses, tricking his memory— He had known about the man before this! How could he have so easily forgotten?

Koshchei shuddered in spite of himself. What if this mortal shell had somehow been damaged by captivity? What if . . . what if this arcane imprisonment had damaged his mind, his very essence?

No! This path was foolish, worse than useless! Grimly, the Deathless refused fear, shutting it out, replacing it, bit by careful bit, with rage.

They will pay for this, they will pay! And for a brief time, he allowed himself the luxury of hatred, glorying in the cruel, savage flames till his thoughts had cleared . . .

Enough. Now he must think only of the man, the pretty little lover: the key. There must be a way to lure the pet down here to him . . . The Deathless's lips peeled back from sharp white teeth in a thin smile.

OLGA, hidden in shadow, watched Princess Marya and her company ride away.

Leaving her husband here. All by himself.

The young woman nibbled nervously on her lower lip. Now was the time when she should win vengeance for Vasilev, dear Vatza. Let something happen to this— this upstart, this Emelian, let Marya know true grief . . .

But what could she do? What could one young woman alone, of no power at all, ever hope to accomplish? For a moment, Olga stopped gnawing on her lip, letting her tongue sweep languorously over it. She had been celibate since Vatza's death . . . What if she seduced Emelian? He was pleasant-looking enough. It wouldn't be unpleasant, not at all. Let Emelian learn what a *real* woman was like, not some skinny little girl who probably left bruises all over him every time they made love and—

Aie, no! Emelian was such a stupidly honest man. Suppose he told Marya the truth?

Besides . . . infidelity wasn't a terrible enough punishment. No, Princess Marya must learn the pain of losing a loved one for ever and ever . . .

Yes, b-but I don't want to actually kill *Emelian!*

Olga shuddered. She didn't dare go to anyone for aid. Even the plotting of violence against the royal consort was treason. It would be the axe for her, just as it had been for Vatza. Almost of its own accord, her hand stole up to touch her neck, and she shuddered again. Vatza . . .

Wait, now. There was something she was missing, something about Vatza . . . Olga forced her thoughts back to the time just before that terrible, fatal battle. Vatza had seemed so strange then, so fierce, so—so brutal. At the time, Olga had tried to convince herself that it was merely tension. But now that she really thought about it . . . It had been almost as though he were possessed!

Possessed?

When had the change really occurred? Olga frowned, struggling to remember. It hadn't been just before the battle, at that. No, he had been almost cruel to her right after . . . right after . . .

The staircase. Princess Marya's sorcerous little staircase. (And *I sent him down it,* Olga tormented herself. *But I didn't know it would hurt him! I only wanted to help!*) Vatza had gone down the stairs still the same warm, loving man. But when he'd climbed back up . . . Olga bit her lip, remembering now only too clearly. She had come running forward, anxious to find out what he'd learned. But Vatza had . . . ignored her, stalking away as though she hadn't even been there. And when she had caught at his arm, he—he had flung her aside as though she were some little servant girl, hard enough to leave her breathless on the floor. And even then, he hadn't spoken a word, only glanced at her with frightening empty eyes . . .

"Yes!" gasped Olga.

This was all Marya's fault. Olga had no idea of what dark magics the princess might have worked on that stair, but they had been enough to destroy Vatza. And now—what better revenge than this? No messy seduction, no risky violence: Olga would merely send Emelian down that same sorcerous staircase. When he climbed back up, no telling who or what he would be! Marya would lose her lover—and it *would* be all her own fault!

The time will come when Emelian is alone, with no one to see or hear.

And then, and then— Oh, Vatza would at last be avenged!

FINIST, magician-prince of Kirtesk, sighed in silent misery. If there was anything more maddening than lying wide awake and restless in the middle of the night, when everyone else—including his wife, here beside him—was sleeping sweetly, he couldn't name it.

Yes, but how could he sleep when this ridiculous sense of foreboding, vague and indefinable as a shadow, insisted on hanging over him?

Dammit, I'm a magician, not a seer! I never was any good at trying to read the future.

So far, the prince had done everything he could to analyze his unease during these long, silent hours, everything from arcane mental disciplines to mundane rationalizations. But the disciplines had failed to soothe him, and dinner had been innocuous enough to rule out simple indigestion. Do what he would, the misty weight of the premonition refused either to leave him or to clarify itself, remaining so maddeningly vague that Finist couldn't tell when or to whom it would apply.

Oh, not to Maria, please God! Finist glanced sharply down at his wife, her face relaxed and innocent in sleep. After an anxious moment, he smiled faintly. Whatever was going to happen almost certainly had nothing to do with her. Or with himself, either, he was fairly sure of that. Though, granted, the prince had never heard of anyone successfully predicting his own future . . . Finist shivered. Unfortunately, royal magic and royal fertility—or the lack thereof—did seem to be linked; his father had only had the one child, and that after six years of trying, while he and Maria hadn't yet been able to start a child between them. If something *should* happen to him, and leave Kirtesk without an heir . . .

Akh, this maundering was ridiculous! Impatient with himself, Finist slipped out of bed, shivering this time in genuine chill as cool night air struck bare skin, to stare out the open window. The moon was dazzlingly bright out there, the wind intoxicatingly heavy with rich green springtime scents, and all at once Finist gave a low cry of frustration and sprang from the wide sill, plunging out into the night, changing as he fell, catching the wind beneath him and soaring up and out on widespread falcon wings.

High over his city, the prince of Kirtesk circled and circled, moonlight spilling like liquid silver from his bright feathers. Far below, Kirtesk nestled sleeping and secure within the ring of its high stone wall, the neat, many-gabled stone houses all but indistinguishable in the deceptive moonlight, the only flecks of true color the occasional flicker of torch or candleflame. Scant chance of danger from those fires; there was little flammable material in Kirtesk. Finist, like his magical ancestors before him, upheld the pact made centuries before between the city and the surrounding forest; the only wood used in Kirtesk came from dead or diseased trees. In exchange, the forest and Those within it respected the city's boundaries. No small thing, that, considering the vast, alien Power within that ancient forest.

Finist wasn't at all concerned with history just then, or more than dimly aware of the city's peacefulness. Night flights, without sun-warmed air currents to ease his wings, were always more difficult. But, the prince told himself wryly, if he couldn't puzzle out what was disturbing him, maybe he could at least tire himself enough to let him sleep.

It wasn't working. His wings had never felt so strong. Finist had an image of himself circling and circling right through the sunrise, bleary of eye but still very much wide awake and nagged by unnamed fear, and sighed. All right. He would try narrowing down the scope of this stupid premonition once again . . .

Kirtesk, now . . . No. Apparently his city wasn't to be affected. He hoped.

The forest? Keen falcon-eyes studied the dark mass of it there beyond the newly plowed fields. Delicately, Finist expanded his psychic senses, feeling beyond the physical . . . He sensed the forest stir, responding to the touch of his magic, then quiet, recognizing him; Finist had friends in that forest, and most of them weren't human.

Not the forest, either.

What, then? Maybe . . . Maria! He had been so sure she wasn't the target, but— What if he'd been wrong, or too hasty, or—

In sudden sharp alarm, Finist went diving back through the open window of his bed-chamber, transforming in midair to stand in man-shape by his sleeping wife's side, studying her intently . . . After a time, he let out a silent sigh of relief. No darkness hung over her, he was willing to swear to it. She was safe.

Finist hesitated, frowning. Now that he had worn the edge off his impatience, he could almost sense something . . .

Uneasy, Finist moved to a small chest, removing from

it the dagger he had taken from Emelian. It looked quite unstained, there in the dimness . . .

Best to be sure. The prince closed his eyes, concentrating, quieting his thoughts, focusing his will, *feeling* the shape of his magic firm and sure in his mind. Opening his eyes once more, staring at the knife, Finist softly spoke a triggering Word. The silver of the hilt blazed into life, responding to this magic and the magic he had already worked upon it. It burned without heat or fuel, a cold blue-white light reflecting down the length of the knife, never quite touching the perilous iron of the blade, light clean and sharp as the knife itself.

For an instant he thought he saw chill shadow marring the blade—

No, there was nothing.

But Finist repeated his spell-Word again and yet again, fighting the iron in the blade that would dispel his magic in a moment if he let it break his concentration, feeling the release of Power pulling at his strength. Heart racing, the prince watched the light blaze up anew in response to each repetition.

The blade remained unstained.

Illusion, Finist decided at last, drained. He must have seen no more than a trick of the light, or the late hour, or his own imaginings. Emelian, too, was safe.

And yet . . .

"Finist . . . ?" complained a sleepy voice. "If you really must work magic now, please do it somewhere else."

"Akh, sorry." Finist spoke the counter-Word to put the dagger back to rest. The blue-white light winked out into darkness. The prince returned the knife to its chest, then wearily climbed back into bed. Beside him, Maria sighed softly and slid into sleep once more, but Finist, for all that now he was truly tired, lay awake for a time longer, musing:

Emelian . . .

XV

ESCAPE

EMELIAN, all alone on the royal dais, his gilded consort's chair just slightly lower and less bulky than the elegant throne, sat looking out over the vast Audience Hall and the ever-watching *boyars*, and felt more lonely than he'd been since the days following his father's death. There was no one with whom he could jest now that he was Regent of Astyan; even chattering, cheerful *boyar* Yaroslav, his prime defender, kept at a careful distance from him.

The young man sighed. Was this isolation, this sense of always being warily respected, a being set slightly apart from humanity, what it was like for Marya? If so, she truly had his sympathy now!

Marya. Emelian closed his fingers gently about the little silver amulet, her gift, feeling, warm as the touch of her hand, the sense of her presence, there across the distant *versts*.

A gift to bind us together, Marya told me. Bind us, indeed! I think this amulet could guide me right to her side.

Emelian glanced with wry humor about his watchful audience. Oh, the amulet's magic would guide him, all right. Assuming his watchdogs ever let him leave the palace.

Eh, well. Things could easily have been worse. At first,

Emelian had been terrified. Sitting up here on the royal dais, hearing ministers and petitioners, he had been sure he was going to make some disastrous mistake. But, bit by bit, the fear had left him. For one thing, Marya had evidently planned her tour to coincide with a time when little royal action had to be taken here at court. Outside the city walls, the planting of crops went on in the time-honored way, and the peasants neither required nor requested any regal intervention. Within the city, the routine of buying and selling continued as always. No foreign envoys were scheduled to arrive at the royal palace, and there were no treaties or controversial new laws needing the temporary Regent's signature.

And, much as he hated to admit it, Marya had been right. Miss her though he did—oh, he did!—and achingly lonely though he was, Emelian had to admit that now that his wife wasn't watching everything he did, now that he wasn't able to always turn to her for help, he was finally, perforce, getting the proper feel of things. In fact, he was finding that court affairs turned out to be, more times than not, no more sacred or complex than the problems of common folk—and just as solvable by sheer common sense.

Mm. If only our dear Nikolai would see it that way.

Emelian didn't doubt the councilor's good intentions or loyalty to the throne. But by now, realizing he was spending more and more time on trivial matters such as stolen crates of vegetables or deliveries of soured milk, the young man was beginning to suspect Nikolai of deliberately setting only the more inane cases before him.

Testing me? Or is he trying to show his contempt?

Either way, there wasn't much Emelian could do about it. He certainly wasn't going to make a fool of himself by accusing the *boyar* without proof!

No time for brooding. Right now, Nikolai was impatiently waving forward two more petitioners—farmers, judging from their plain, sturdy clothing and the faintest hint of barnyard hanging in the air about them.

Here we go again, thought Emelian.

Not that he, of all people, had anything against peasant folk. But bringing them before him here, in the royal court, came suspiciously close to being a studied insult.

Still, they might have a genuine grievance . . .

"Come, speak," Emelian told them, trying to keep his voice properly regal. He pointed to the man on the left at random. "You, first."

And, setting what he hoped was a determinedly stern frown on his face, he leaned forward to listen.

Unfortunately, it turned out to be pretty much what he had come to expect today, not a plea by commons for royal justice against noble injustice, but simply:

Farmer Bori had found five of Farmer Ivan's cows in his field and had confiscated them, claimed they'd eaten ten bushels of his growing spring wheat, tearing down his fence in the process. ("Since the wheat hadn't been harvested," Emelian commented mildly, "how could you know the exact figure?") Farmer Ivan agreed his cows had trespassed, but swore the fence was undamaged. The case was solved quickly enough when a witness testified the fence had a gate which—oh, shocking news!—Farmer Bori had neglected to latch.

"Bori, give Ivan back his cows. Ivan, try to graze them on the other side of your farm from now on. I fine you both five copper *kuni* for wasting the court's time." One *kuna* was a small enough sum; five should be just enough of a fee to make them think without imposing any real hardship. "Good day to you," said Emelian, pleased with himself. "And," he added, getting to his feet, watching the *boyars* reluctantly scramble to theirs, "good day to you all. Except for you." He pointed. "*Boyar* Nikolai, pray come with me."

He saw indignation flash in the man's eyes, but there was nothing for Nikolai to do but obey. Emelian led him to the first quiet, empty corner of the palace he could find, then turned on the older man, fuming.

"Just what game did you think you were playing in there?"

"My lord?"

"Oh, don't 'my lord' me! I know straying cows are no joke to farmers whose livelihood depends on the beasts, but—Dammit, man, you know as well as I that was a matter for common jurists, not for me!"

Nikolai's expression was a masterpiece of outraged innocence. "Why, Regent Emelian! I thought you were interested in the affairs of the commons."

"I am! But not at the expense of royal dignity!" Voice trembling with rage at the *boyar*'s delicate contempt, Emelian continued, "Just how great a fool do you think me?"

"My lord, I—"

"No! Let me finish. Look you, if that matter of the cows had been one isolated case, I would have said nothing. But every incident today has been like that: simple matters, silly things, cases you never would have dared bring before my wife. So, now, which is it? Are you trying to humiliate me? Or do you truly think I'm so feeble-witted I can't deal with any matter more complex than—than soured milk?"

"Please, my lord—"

"I admit I began badly when I first became royal consort. But if Marya trusted me enough to name me Regent—"

"She named you Regent," cut in Nikolai coldly, "because she knew you were safe. You have no real support, not from the military, not from the *boyars*—"

"I know that! I don't *want* the damned throne. But Marya did name me Regent. I represent her, and Astyan through her. And how dare you defy her?"

That got through. Nikolai flinched, his cool gaze flicking away from Emelian's rage. "I never intended—"

"Never intended? Never thought, you mean!" Emelian caught his breath with a gasp. "All right. I know what you're thinking: only peasants rant and rave. Nobles show their anger slyly, in petty malice. Well, I'm not malicious, and God knows I'm not sly. So I am simply going to say this: I look forward to Marya's return more than you can dream. When she does return, I will gladly surrender the regency to her. But till then, I am her voice, the voice of Astyan. And you will obey me!''

He surprised what might have been a grudging glint of approval in Nikolai's eyes as the *boyar* bowed compliantly, but just then was too angry to care. Knowing he would spoil whatever regal effect he had just created if he stayed a moment longer, Emelian turned in a whirling of elegant robes and stalked away.

NIKOLAI STRAIGHTENED SLOWLY, eyeing the young man's rapidly receding back. Had Emelian been aware that somewhere along the way he had picked up a properly regal tone and turn of phrase? Good God, he had sounded like Marya just now. Or rather, like Marya's father.

That strong-willed, stubborn, infuriating man. God rest him.

Unconscious mimicry on Emelian's part? Maybe. But the young man *had* been handling himself surprisingly well at court. Even under the circumstances.

Nikolai flushed, embarrassed to admit how eagerly he'd agreed with the rest of the Inner Council. After a brief, heated debate, they had decided, not without malice, to give Emelian only the simplest, most ridiculous of cases, matters that couldn't possibly be beyond his understanding.

The *boyar* shook his head slowly, wondering. Was it just barely possible that they had been wrong? Had they been underestimating Emelian all along? Nikolai smiled faintly, hating the thought that Marya might come to depend on someone other than himself, honest enough to finally admit it to himself.

Ah well, like it or not, they were stuck with Emelian.

Still, he admitted reluctantly, barring some unforeseen disaster, of course, it . . . just might not prove so terrible a thing at that.

WHEN SHE HAD HEARD the men approaching, Olga's first thought was to hurriedly get out of their way; it was hardly her place to meddle in the affairs of *boyars*. Particularly angry ones. But then the young woman stiffened. That was Nikolai's voice, surely. And that other, that furious voice, could only belong to one man: Emelian. Warily, hidden behind the bend of the hallway, she crept forward to listen . . .

Aie, Emelian was coming this way! Her thoughts racing about like leaves in a wind, Olga grabbed frantically at the first of them: Emelian was alone. He was finally alone, and now she could begin to take her revenge.

Vatza, for you, Olga told his ghost, and raced out into Emelian's path.

"Oh—my lord, f-forgive me," she stammered in not-quite-feigned fright, "I didn't see you in time, and I—"

The man's eyes were still blazing with rage, hot enough to add to her fear. But before she could stammer out anything foolish, he made a visible effort to control himself, giving her an almost convincing smile, even reaching out a helpful hand to steady her as she staggered. "No need to apologize, lady. I was the one not watching where . . . " His voice trailed into silence as he studied her. "I'm sorry. I can't seem to remember your name."

"It—it's Olga, my lord."

"Akh, of course. I should have . . . What's wrong, lady? You look terrified!"

I am! But Emelian was giving her just the chance she needed, and Olga plunged boldly ahead. "It's that . . . I saw something d-down in the palace cellars . . ."

"We have rats, do we?"

"N-nothing so normal. I—no, I can't talk about it!"

"Why not?" There was a touch of impatience to the man's voice. "Come, what did you see?"

She shook her head stubbornly and heard Emelian sigh. "So. Olga. Did you ask anyone else to take a look down there?"

"Oh, no, I—I couldn't." As if by accident, she added, "The princess would never—" With that, Olga broke off with a gasp of pretended horror at what she'd almost said.

"Go on," Emelian prodded sharply. "The princess would never *what?*"

"I can't tell you . . ."

"Olga!" His fingers tightened on her arms till she gasped again, this time in pain. Emelian hastily released her. "Sorry. But Olga, if this is something concerning the princess, something that might endanger her, you must tell me."

"I can't," she repeated. "I—I'm afraid."

"Akh, Olga!" He hesitated, and the young woman held her breath, hopeful and fearful in one. "All right," Emelian said. "If you won't tell me what's going on, let us round up some guards to go down there and investigate."

"No! You mustn't—I mean, you can't. No one else must know."

"Olga, please! This isn't some silly minstrel-tale!"

But she refused to meet his gaze, shaking her head stubbornly, and Emelian spat out something hot-tempered under his breath. "All right. No guards. We'll go take a look for ourselves. Will that satisfy you? Yes? Then, come."

She went, shyly as any timid maid, her heart pounding wildly. Soon, oh, soon . . .

They stood at the head of the winding stairway, its steps half in shadow. Emelian craned his neck to one side, plainly trying to get a better look down the dark, curving length. "Never noticed this stairway before. Obscure thing . . . This is it, eh?"

Olga nodded.

"Well? Are you going to show me what fearsome beastie is lurking down there?"

He doesn't believe me! He thinks I'm just a silly girl afraid of a mouse! "N-no, I . . . Please, no."

"No . . ." Emelian echoed thoughtfully. "The very thought of going down there again makes you shiver."

Had she been *too* convincing? What if he backed

down now? What if he went to get soldiers to help him? "The princess . . . " Olga murmured, and saw the man tense.

"There's only one thing that would terrify you like this," Emelian murmured, and Olga started, nearly blurting out, *I didn't want to do this, it's for Vatza*. But before she could say anything so foolish, the man continued. "It's something to do with magic, isn't it? The royal magic. That's what's frightening you."

"Yes . . ."

He glanced hastily away, but not before Olga caught a flash of horror in his eyes. And for a moment, Emelian's thoughts were clear on his face: maybe Marya had been trying to increase her Power. But why experiment down in that dank, dark, secret place? What had she to hide? Had she been toying not with clean magic—but with sorcery?

"Akh, well," Emelian said abruptly, "I . . . don't suppose that's a subject we want bandied about the palace." He gave Olga a quick, humorless grin. "Anything that wouldn't bother Marya won't bother me, either. Stay here, lady. I'll be right back."

No! Don't go down there!

But that warning scream was only in Olga's mind. Clenching her fists till they ached, hardly daring to take a breath, she stood at the head of the stairway and watched Emelian carefully descend. Silently, sadly, she told him:

Farewell. I'm sorry but—it's for Vatza's sake.

I sense him. The Deathless stiffened, fairly quivering with tension. *The man is approaching at last.*

Delicately, Koshchei sent out the faintest tendril of thought, daring no more, not sure what protection the magician's daughter might have placed about her lover . . .

Yes . . . There was something of her presence linking the two. But it wasn't nearly strong enough to pose a problem.

Koshchei drew back into himself, smiling. Still, this man had a more intelligent mind, more complete in itself, than had that fool, Vasilev. No simple temptation was going to work with this one; no brutal attack, either. He sent out a second sensitive feeler of thought, wondering . . .

Compassion . . . If he recalled human emotions correctly, that was what he'd sensed. The young man's weakness was compassion.

So be it.

Koshchei looked down at his imprisoned shell and concentrated. Though he couldn't free himself, though most of his Power was bound with him, there were still a few simple tricks left to him. For a moment, the human-warrior form blurred, altering, shrinking in on itself . . .

Satisfied, the Deathless leaned back against the wall in silent anticipation.

HALFWAY DOWN the dank, narrow stairway, the light fading with each step he descended, Emelian began to wonder why he had been so eager to come down here. And what had made him act in such a rush? It really would have been a nice idea to stop long enough to take a torch with him.

He hesitated on the edge of a step, toying with the idea of going back up to get said torch.

No, a voice whispered soothingly at the very edge of his consciousness. *No need for a torch. The space below isn't very large.*

"No need for a torch," Emelian muttered. "The space below isn't very large."

He stopped, bewildered. Now, how could he have known that? Still, it must be true. Otherwise Olga would never have had the nerve to examine it. He would be down and up again in no time regardless of what he found.

Which won't be much, the soothing voice hinted.

Which wouldn't be much. No matter what Olga thought she had seen, Emelian just couldn't believe there would actually be anything sorcerous down there. He knew Marya better than that.

He . . . did know her, didn't he?

Stop that! Emelian chided himself. To keep himself from thinking, he hurried on down the rest of the stairway, concentrating only on keeping his footing.

Ah. The room down here at the bottom of the stair was just as small as he had thought, and quite empty, nothing but bare stone walls and floor, the whole thing chill and dank in the dim light.

Maybe all Olga had seen was a rat. Rat eyes could glint demonically by torchlight. Or perhaps one of the kitchen cats had strayed down here and brushed her leg.

At any rate, the room was empty now, and—

Empty? As his eyes adjusted to the gloom, he thought he saw . . .

Impatient with himself, Emelian blinked, then raised a hand to rub his eyes.

The strange . . . whatever . . . remained, a thin rectangle of blue-white light there against one wall. *Magic,* Emelian thought, *aie, magic.* And though he had never been afraid of Marya's glimmerings of Power before this moment, now some vague dread made him turn to leave.

No. You must not leave.

No. He must not leave.

There's nothing here to frighten you.

This was foolish! There was nothing here to frighten him. All at once overwhelmed by a rush of curiosity, Emelian moved boldly forward. Now he could see that the far wall wasn't solid at all. He hadn't been able to notice this before amid all the darkness, but the thin ribbon of light was outlining a door: a heavily bolted door.

A . . . prison door? Here? The palace didn't have anything that could formally be called a dungeon; the last royal prisoner had been Vasilev, whose rank had entitled him to a tower cell, while common criminals, of course, were held in the city's own prison. But Emelian knew there was a row of cells off in the lower level of the main royal cellars. What would a solitary cell be doing in this isolated, unguarded room?

Puzzled, the young man reached out a tentative hand. Was the whole thing merely some bizarre illusion? But the cold, heavy wood his fingers encountered seemed real enough, and—

"Aie!"

Eerie light flashed up at his touch. Emelian shrank back, arm shielding his face, as cold fire blazed back and forth across the door in a blinding blue-white web, then just as abruptly winked out of existence, leaving a dark but unchanged door behind it.

Not quite unchanged. Though the door remained firmly shut, the bolts were gone. At least *they* had been illusion. Now all he had to do was pull the door open and—

Hey, no! He wasn't going to be *that* impulsive! "What's going on?" Emelian asked the air.

As though in response, a feeble voice whispered, "Please . . . help . . ."

The young man shied like a startled horse. "Who's there?"

"Please . . ."

The voice was plainly coming from the far side of the door.

"Who's there?" Emelian repeated warily. "Who are you?"

"Helpless . . ."

There was weary sorrow in the word like the grief of the world. All at once Emelian found himself aching with such pity *(Pity?* he thought, panicked. *How can I be feeling pity over a word?)* that his hands were pulling open the heavy door before he could stop them, and—

There wasn't a door! It faded from beneath his fingers, leaving only a doorway darker than the room around it. *Illusion, after all!* Foul, stale air rushed out, making him cough, and with it, such a chill that he hastily grabbed his robes about himself, every nerve shouting to him to run.

But that strange, intense pity still pulled at him, hold-

ing him in place. It was difficult to remember fear under
the weight of it. "I-. . . uh . . . I don't see you," Emelian called out. "Where are you?"

There came a faint clanking, as of heavy chains shifting. "Here." It was an ancient sound.

"Sorry. I still can't see—"

"Yes, you can." The cracked voice held a touch of
impatience. "Look again."

Something cold and harsh seemed to brush his mind.
All at once, Emelian realized that the darkness had been
replaced by light. Strange . . . He should be amazed at
the oddness of it, or frightened . . . He should be feeling *something*.

But in the next moment, Emelian's thoughts seemed to
slip sideways, and of course it was light in here. It had
never been dark at all, and he turned triumphantly—

And froze.

The chains were thick and heavy, ugly, intricately
wrought iron things surely strong enough to bind a dragon,
made all the more grotesque because the prisoner lying
helpless beneath their weight was an old man, frail as a
withered leaf, ragged and filthy, his dark eyes bright with
a light that could have been despair or madness.

"Who did this to you?" Emelian breathed.

"The usurper, the cruel usurper!"

"I—I don't understand. Who are you?"

"Are you foolish, boy? I am the prince of Astyan!"

Poor thing, he is *mad.* "I'm sorry," Emelian said as
gently as he could. "There's a princess of Astyan right
now."

"I know about that! She's the usurper's daughter."
The bright eyes glittered. "You don't know. Nobody
knows. I was the ruler of Astyan, once, once . . . He
came in the night, the usurper, the sorcerer, he tricked
and trapped me off my throne, took my rightful place,
and none was the wiser."

"Ah . . . how could that be?"

"I *said* the man was a sorcerer! He bespelled himself

into seeming the only proper prince, and worked his
foulness so well that no one could remember me!''

Of . . . course. Emelian hesitated, trying to find
something tactful to say, and the old man glared at him.

"You think I'm mad, don't you? But if I'm so mad,
why did the usurper keep me down here in silence, eh?
Eh? He was too cruel to kill me honestly, but why did
he keep me hidden all these years?''

"I . . . don't know." *God, he* can't *be telling the
truth!* But, the poor old man . . . Reminding him so
much of his father . . . His father, suffering all those
cruel years of exile, with no one to help him.

All right. Whether or not this pathetic old prisoner
was lying, Emelian wasn't going to leave that thin, worn
frame weighted down by those harsh chains. He glanced
about the cell.

"The keys . . . ?''

"There are no keys." The ancient voice was dull.
"The chains are welded fast.''

Emelian stared at him in horror. No crime he could
name was punished like this! "Well, they must at least
come to feed you and give you drink.''

A faint shrug. "At times.''

"God!" *Oh, Marya, you have some sharp questions
to answer!* "All right, you—you wait right here—''
Akh, stupid, where was the poor thing going to go?
"I'll be back.''

"Water . . . please. That's all I ask. It's been so long
. . . Clean, cool water . . . ''

Emelian couldn't stand the anguish in those burning
eyes. "Yes! I'll bring you water.''

"In a silver goblet . . . ?" the old man asked pite-
ously. "I used to drink from a silver goblet . . . ''

"Yes, all right, in a silver goblet. And I'll bring you
some food, too, and— I'll be right back, I promise.''

SOON, dazed, Emelian found himself returned to that
cell, a ewer of fresh water in one hand, a silver goblet
in the other, vaguely alarmed to realize he didn't really

remember where he had been to get them. There had been staring faces, startled glances . . . But they hadn't meant much to him. The image of the frail, pathetic captive was always before his inner eye, blocking everything else. All that had mattered was his returning here as swiftly as possible.

"Here—here you are," he panted. "Cool water, just as you wished."

"In a silver goblet?"

Emelian wondered at the sudden sharpness in that cracked voice. Madness, indeed, he decided. "Of course. Eh, drink slowly, now!"

Odd, how the old man seemed to be murmuring something into the goblet. A prayer, probably, Emelian decided, though for some reason the harder he tried to distinguish the words, the more they seemed to twist about, making his head swim. Odd, too, how the hair at the nape of his neck and all along his arms had begun to prickle. Almost as though the air was being charged with the tension that came just before a storm. Emelian frowned, feeling strangely numb, detached from the whole thing. He supposed he should be alarmed, but he just couldn't seem to muster enough emotion. Besides, there was really nothing alarming here; rubbing at his arms, the young man told himself he was merely reacting to the chill of the dank air.

The old man was holding out the goblet. "Finished?" Emelian asked gently.

"More, please, kind heart."

Heart aching at the pleading in the old man's eyes, Emelian quickly refilled the proffered goblet. Once again, the captive bent over it, muttering. Puzzled, Emelian found himself straining once more to make out the sense of the murmured words, feeling the meaning slip away before he could grasp it . . .

Akh, he couldn't listen anymore! All at once, the air had grown too thick and heavy to breathe. Dizzy, choking, Emelian fell back against a wall, the room spinning sickeningly about him. God, was he going to faint? He'd never fainted in his life! The old man was watching him, unblinking stare piercing through the haze, mocking, evil— Impossible. All this must surely be nothing more than the residue of illusion.

Yet now the old man was holding out the empty goblet once more, and though he could barely move through the heavy air, he must respond, he must . . .

Must? Why? *No* . . . realized Emelian vaguely. *This is not my will* . . . *Nor illusion, either* . . . His thoughts were coming painfully slowly. *Sorcery* . . . *I'm being bespelled* . . .

As though he'd heard that, the captive laughed, a soft, cruel, chilling sound, and waved the goblet slowly, tauntingly, before Emelian's eyes. To the young man's horror, he felt his body respond, for all his mind's frantic denials, watched his traitor hands move to refill the goblet.

"For the third time . . ." Emelian battled with his benumbed self to force out even those words. "Magic comes in threes . . ."

The old man laughed again, and this time there was no denying the cold mockery in his eyes. "That's right. It does." He sipped elegantly from the goblet, then smiled. "I was wondering how long I could hold you enthralled. Long enough, it would appear."

"Who . . . Who are . . . ?"

The other ignored his struggle. "But then, magic is such an odd thing, at times complex, at times deceptively simple, often dependent on bizarre wordings, strange demands, for its weaving or unravelling. The purity of water, for one. The touch of silver." He gave Emelian a coolly jesting salute. "And, of course, as you implied, the Power lurking in triple repetitions and the speaking of certain spells. Of such small things are Bindings broken." He sipped from the goblet a second time. "For this compulsive mercy of yours, and for this drink, I shall grant you a boon, young fool. But first . . ."

As Emelian fought desperately, futilely, to break the hold upon him, perspiration nearly blinding him, muscles trembling with strain, the other gave a short, harsh bark of a laugh, then bent over the goblet, murmuring words that pierced through and through Emelian with psychic anguish sharp as knives till only the spell upon him held him upright. Helpless, he watched the old man sip from the goblet one last time—

And then the man got smoothly to his feet in a swirl of dust and darkness as the heavy iron chains fell away from him, crumbling into Nothingness.

Illusion! Oh, God, what is he?

The frail and helpless victim was blurring, growing, changing, with a speed too swift for human eyes to bear. The force of sudden, unbound Power hurled Emelian from his feet, sending him crashing into a wall with stunning impact. Dazed, breathless, he crumpled to the floor, frantically blinking, trying to clear his tear-blurred vision, struggling to see—

What? Was this a warrior, a monstrous, dark-clad warrior taller, mightier, than any he had ever seen? Oh, this was more than mortal! Radiant with Power, he stood staring down at Emelian, and the young man gasped despite himself at those terrible, pitiless eyes—

"What are you?" he cried.

"Koshchei, little man. Koshchei the Deathless." Laughter echoed in the ringing voice. "Koshchei the free! More than that, you need not know." The being smiled thinly. "I swore to grant you a boon. It shall be this: I give you your life, little man. Cross my path again at your peril, but this once, I will not kill you. Of course, you may come to wish yourself dead. For now I go to avenge myself on your lover. Little man, farewell!"

The being vanished into a dark swirl of Power that tossed Emelian roughly aside. Gasping, he clung to his battered senses and managed to slowly pull himself erect. He must do something to stop this—this Koshchei.

But it was already too late. The Deathless was gone, and Emelian was alone in the darkness.

XVI

CAPTURE

Boyar Semyon, elderly head of the Inner Council of Kirtesk, sat with his fellow members in that elegant little meeting room, the Ruby Chamber, its red walls ornamented with delicate traceries of gold, its floor half hidden by priceless rugs, and pretended to be absorbed in the contents of a document pertaining to the taxation of wheat. All the while, though, he was covertly watching his prince, and smiling inwardly at what he saw.

There Finist sat in his royal chair, raised from the rest on only a few token steps, his head bent studiously over a scroll. The wild, silvery hair was working its way free from its confining coronet, as it usually did, gleaming locks falling forward to half hide Finist's solemn face. Save for that hair, he was the very image of princely responsibility. And Semyon would have believed that image had he not served the prince all these years. He knew what a mighty struggle Finist was waging to ignore the wind outside the room's wide window, the wind tempting him to drop regal responsibilities and spread his wings.

The old *boyar* hastily smothered his growing smile. Poor Finist! Eh, well, the meeting would be over soon enough, and the falcon-prince would be free once more. Perhaps charming Princess Falcon would go with him.

Husband and wife made such a pretty sight, flying together. Such a happy pair . . .

Semyon winced, grimly shutting his mind to thoughts
of Might-Have-Been, of his own dear wife, dead these
many years, of his childlessness. Akh, well, God's will
be done. At least there was Finist, dear to him as a son.
And there was always the hope that eventually Finist
and Maria would start a child between them. God grant
he live long enough to see it, perhaps even hold it, his
grandchild by love if not by blood . . .

A sharp cry shocked Semyon from his bittersweet
musings. The prince—

Finist had cried out in alarm, springing blindly up
from his chair, nearly falling from the low dais. The
old *boyar* moved with a young man's speed to catch
and steady him, seeing Finist's face frighteningly pale,
the amber eyes gone fierce and wild, plainly seeing
something far beyond normal human vision. Hastily,
Semyon waved the other *boyars* from the room, then
turned to his prince, uncertain.

"Is there anything I can—"

"He's free." Finist's voice was cold and remote. "I
felt the Binding break."

"I'm afraid I don't understand."

Life returned with a rush to the prince's rigid form.
He shuddered convulsively, pulling away from Semyon.
"I speak of Koshchei."

The *boyar* blinked, helpless. Politics he knew, affairs
of state, but these matters arcane . . . "The . . . demon?" he ventured.

"The Deathless!" Finist glared at him, eyes blazing
with sudden keen impatience. "Enough, Semyon."

"But—"

"I haven't the time for an explanation. The Deathless
is free—and I must see to our defenses!"

CHAOS SWARMED ABOUT HIM, a mad, senseless whirl of
not-color, not-shape, then abruptly, shockingly, sharpened and resolved itself into *weight* and *direction* and

color. The Deathless staggered, dazed by the extravagant waste of strength expended in escaping his prison, stunned by the residue of that wild, intoxicating rush into light and air and freedom. Freedom! He cried aloud in the ecstasy of Power awakening, pouring through his being, dizzying as wine—he was drunk as any mortal man on freedom, overwhelmed.

Ancient caution awoke beneath the wildness of freed Power. Though Koshchei realized with a shiver of joy that he could easily locate the oh-so-familiar aura of the magician's daughter, he forced himself into calmness. The sweet pleasures of revenge could wait. He had already risked rending himself apart, mind from shell, by that profligate leap through space and time without a focused-on point of arrival; he had no intention of risking himself again.

Eyes closed, Koshchei turned his Power inward, *feeling* the fit of deathless self within physical shell, finding it perfect, precise. He carefully studied the shell itself, going over every nerve, every muscle, first within, then, eyes open, without. *Functional*, he decided at last, satisfied, despite the long inactivity, *quite functional*. Not being shaped of human flesh-and-blood, the shell had suffered no loss of muscle tone or weight, and had shed its prison filth during that sorcerous leap to freedom.

The Deathless flexed arms and legs experimentally, and nodded. To all outward seeming, he was a tall, perfectly formed human male of middle years, perhaps a warrior, certainly of noble blood. His clothing (being, after all, formed from the same nonmortal stuff as his shell) was quite unstained, quite untattered; tunic, trousers, and boots all of a quietly elegant cut, half hidden by the folds of a great, dark cloak.

So. Now, let him learn where his mad rush had flung him, see how much the land had changed since last he had walked freely.

However long ago that might have been.

Hands on hips, Koshchei glanced about, pleased to realize he hadn't thrown himself all that far after all.

Behind him were the plowed and planted fields of As-tyan, while the city itself, some *versts* back, was a com-plex pile of domes and gabled rooftops behind its wooden palisade: unimportant. By the time anyone from Astyan came riding in search of the escaped prisoner, he would be far from here.

The Deathless smiled, the thin, cold smile of a pred-ator. Delicately, he opened his consciousness to *feel* the touch of the magician's daughter's aura once more, and focused on it, seeing it with his inner eye as a narrow silver thread, a path to lead him to her side.

A dark green mass of forest stood like a curving, living wall before him. The Deathless eyed it distaste-fully, sensing the wild, unstructured force of its primal Power, the very antithesis of his non-Natural sorceries. He *felt* that Power responding to his presence in a deadly surging of hostility. Koshchei curled a lip in contempt. Should he fear mere vegetable force? He, whose own sorcery held untold ages of strength within it?

Still, behind the forest's Power was the wild, bound-less force of the Earth. Or so it had been when last he stood on mortal soil. Caution stirred, warning him to take nothing for granted. He took a bold, experimental step forward—

There was a wild rustling in the forest, a hiss of sav-age rage, a rush of Power blazing up before his psychic sight in a thousand shades of green. Tree branches tossed in the still air and Koshchei drew back hastily, shaken by the unexpected force of that untidy, perilous Power. His psychic path was stopped by the blazing greenness, his physical way blocked by branches lash-ing together, bushes weaving into thorny barricades. The Deathless straightened, sensing a presence lurking behind them, a quicksilver intelligence.

"*Leshy*," said Koshchei, testing, "stand aside."

"You are not to pass."

It was a wind-whisper of a voice, prickling at his ears. *You would dare command* me? the Deathless thought. Staring in dawning anger, he caught a faint, tantalizing glimpse of a thin, fierce-eyed shape standing upright amid the maze of leaves, and repeated sharply:

"Stand aside!"

"Go aside!" mocked the *leshy*-voice. "Go away, you Thing, you not-man. Death-life, you have no place here."

Koshchei felt the prison-rage rise within him. But no chains bound his will or senses now. And the force of anger channelled, controlled and shaped, was Power in itself, a sweet darkness sharpening his perceptions. He sensed emotion behind the *leshy* mockery, and seized upon it, pushing:

"You fear me!"

Leaves quivered. "I do," the *leshy* admitted. "Ah, yes. The forest does. The forest is of life, even humans are of life. You, alone, are not, Death-life. You are a wrongness. And you shall not pass!"

Clinging to control was no easy thing after that will-softening time of imprisonment. Outraged at his weakness, Koshchei nevertheless lost his hold beneath the scourge of *leshy* contempt. His anger tore free in a blazing of: *Aie, how dare the thing defy him? He would rend the* leshy-*mind, rend it—*

Rend a being that *was* the forest? Behind the fury, cool logic whispered that for all his undeniable Power, there were still limits. Koshchei turned aside, struggling with himself. It would be so easy to burn the forest, burn all within it, so sweet! Yet he dare not strike. He wasn't vainglorious enough to attack the very Earth!

The Deathless caught at self-control. Rage turned with inhuman speed to cold calculation: he had learned all he needed to know about the forest. Staying longer would be foolish. He must fly . . .

Fly? Koshchei blinked, surprised, struggling with his recalcitrant memory. For an instant there had been a vague image of flight in his mind, of wind rushing all about him. Yet he had no gift of shape-shifting or levitation. Then how . . . ? There had been mountains, he was sure of it . . . the bitter cold of the upper air . . . There was . . .

Vyed'ma.

Vyed'ma, the Power-wielder, the Hag of the Rocks, unpredictable as the mountain winds: the one being who knew the secret of catching and binding those winds.

Koshchei's mouth tightened in distaste. He had once paid the price for her spell-weaving, spending long and long with Vyed'ma in her rocky, barren home as her lover. Oh, the Hag could put on a fair enough illusion of youth and beauty when the whim moved her; she hadn't always been unpleasant to the eye or touch. But, being what he was, deathless mind in constructed shell, mere animal sensation meant little to him. Koshchei had felt nothing during his enforced stay in the Hag's embrace, not the dimmest stirring of lust, not the slightest brush of pleasure, nothing but utter, endless, boredom.

Boredom spiced by fear. If that strange creature who was nearly his equal for Power had learned the truth about her lover, she would surely have slain his shell and banished him once more to the Outer Dark.

Perhaps it wouldn't have seemed such an ordeal had the Hag been inclined towards conversation, willing to discuss Power, or power, or—akh, even the mountain weather! But Vyed'ma had been as dull and silent as her rugged home.

Eh, but it had all been worth the tedious, perilous time of waiting. At the end of it, he had wooed Vyed'ma off her guard, and won what he had sought (though some might call it theft—Vyed'ma for one).

Now, if the Power of Vyed'ma's spell, cast those untold years past, still held true, he would have swift passage from here indeed.

But the *leshy* wasn't to be allowed to think it had defeated him. "Fear me," Koshchei said softly, and saw branches quiver. "I will be back. And I will take from you whatever I desire!"

He turned coldly away, staring with unblinking eyes

up into the wind-swept heavens, called out a Word, a
Name . . .

Nothing.

Frowning slightly, Koshchei tried again, his voice
ringing with Power. And this time, somewhere far beyond the range of mortal hearing, came a cry of despair.

"Come," the Deathless commanded.

No! It was a shout of hopeless defiance.

"Come. You must obey me even as in the past. I am
he who bound you."

Vyed'ma bound me, not you!

Koshchei stirred impatiently. "*I* hold your Name
now, as you well know. Therefore *I* bind you. Now,
come—or suffer!"

Ae-he, no, not again! Let me alone. Let me be free!

But anguish quivered behind each word. Koshchei
waited. And all at once, he felt resistance crumble beneath the force of his will.

As Koshchei watched in grim satisfaction, the grass
before him shook in a sudden whirl of wind, and fallen
leaves and bits of twig spun madly about.

"Shape yourself," the Deathless said shortly. "I wish
a steed."

There was the faintest of sad sighs. The wild whirling
of wind obediently thickened, visible now as a heat-
haze blur, now as an increasingly opaque fog, slowly
condensing into the form of a stallion, too lean, too
long of leg and arched of delicate neck to be mistaken
for mortal horse. Its pale mane and tail streamed out
behind it, whipping and tossing restlessly as flame over
the smooth, blue-white coat, and its tapering eyes were
colorless and wild.

Koshchei permitted himself a small, wry smile.
Vyed'ma's spell was an excellent one. He had never
been able to coax the exact details of the spell out of
the Hag, though part of its Power seemed to be the very
act of forcing a Name—and with it, a concrete reality—
onto the unNamed. But at least he'd managed to steal

this one Name from Vyed'ma, and this eternal servant with it. He leaped onto the shimmering back, feeling the powerful, newly formed muscles bunching beneath him. ''Hurry, slave,'' he told the creature, and with a mighty leap, it sprang up into the sky, racing with its master down the cold, clear paths of the winds.

MARYA SIGHED, stirring restlessly in the saddle. No matter how she tried, there was no longer any comfortable way to sit, not after all these days of journeying. And, no matter how nicely arrayed she might appear in her regal travelling robes (the rich brocade frantically cleaned and mended by her servants at every stop), the princess thought wryly that she would never be quite free of the smells of dust and horse.

And oh, how endless this entire tour had seemed, how thoroughly monotonous! Everywhere she had ridden, through village or town or nobleman's standing, it had been the same: the same courteous bows, the same curious stares, the same smiling faces—

Marya sighed again. Not a one of the minds behind those faces had guessed that though their princess had smiled in return and spoken wise and witty words, her thoughts were ever back in Astyan . . .

But good things came to those with patience. The tour was finally ended, and now the royal party could ride for home again.

Home to Emelian . . .

Lost in her thoughts, Marya barely noticed the sudden sharp rising of the wind. Even when it sent strands of her long hair whipping across her face, she merely brushed them back with an absentminded hand.

Emelian . . . Marya shivered with sudden desire, thinking of the long, lonely nights now to be ended. *Oh, my dear, how I've missed you.*

The alarmed shouts of her men brought Marya sharply back to herself. She glanced up, and nearly cried out. Impossible, this wild-eyed rider on a wild-

eyed, fiery something—was it a *horse?*—galloping down
the empty sky!

Marya's archers acted without waiting for their mistress's orders. But those arrows that struck shattered
against the skin of that demonic rider, or passed harmlessly through the body of its demonic mount. Hastily,
Marya whipped out her sword, wondering what good a
blade would be against an arrowproof foe.

As the rider reached down to seize her, the princess
struck at him with all her might—but with a screech of
tortured steel, the bright blade snapped in half. Marya
raised her hand to fling the useless hilt full in the savage, laughing face—

She knew that face. Koshchei! The Deathless was
free!

Marya hurled the swordhilt at him. He never even
flinched. An inhumanly powerful arm closed about her
waist and swept her, struggling helplessly, up from the
saddle. Oh God, they were climbing up and up into the
sky, and huge black wings reeking of Otherness were
closing about her (no, no, they were only the folds of
a great dark cloak), and she was so dizzy with the incredible speed, with the whirling of cloak and sky about
her, so crushed by the power of her captor's arm that
she couldn't breathe or think or . . .

KOSHCHEI GLANCED down at his captive. Dead? No; the
small thing still breathed, though her senses seemed to
have fled. Not from fear alone; the Deathless acknowl-
edged her fruitless courage. The swiftness of their passage down the wind-roads must have been too much for
the merely human to bear.

She will bear it, and worse.

Master? came the tentative not-voice of his spirit-
slave. *Where would you go now?*

Where indeed? Considering, Koshchei recalled his
last estate, a strong-walled, isolated place. It had been
long indeed since he'd last walked its walls, but the

stone had been sturdy. It should have survived the years since then.

BUT . . . THIS COULDN'T BE THE ESTATE, not this gaping, broken ruin, with its roof half caved in and its walls sagging, and the forest grown close up about it. For a moment, Koshchei could do nothing but stare at the desolation, overwhelmed by this undeniable proof of just how much time had passed since the days when he had been master here.

What of it? The walls of the estate were sound enough for his purposes, as was what remained of the roof. The forest posed no threat to him. This was no green and living woodland, but a strange, twisted place of thorns, writhing branches and scant, crumbling leaves, forest with nothing of the *leshiye* magic about it; unmoved by this dark ugliness as he was by beauty, the Deathless supposed that the natural growth had been warped by the residue of his Power.

He glanced down at the limp body of his captive, feeling only a certain cold satisfaction. A small human, this young woman, slender limbs scarcely looking strong enough to wield a sword. Or withstand torment.

Torment, yes . . . Koshchei considered the idea dispassionately. He might easily apply agonies sufficient enough to break the little creature's will and mind. And yet, the human body was such a frail thing; the amount of physical pain it could withstand, no matter how delicately or carefully that pain was applied, was finite. The woman would suffer most ingratiatingly, but only for a time. She would die long before the debt for his captivity was fully repaid.

But there was other than physical pain. Koshchei thoughtfully considered the possibilities available through Power. She did have some scant Power of her own—though not enough to fight him. In the days of his captivity, he'd learned that her Power was so scant it was barely worth the mentioning.

She had a kinsman with true Power, though: Finist

of Kirtesk. Now, there was one who might prove a worthy foe.

More than that. Marya's kinsman *and* a magician—Koshchei's lips tightened. There was a man he dared not let live!

The Deathless glanced down at his unconscious captive again. The estate, ruined though it was, would be sufficient to hold her, particularly after he strengthened it with Power. Revenge was not to be rushed. First he would attack the true peril: Finist. Then would be time enough to ponder the proper forms of vengeance on the woman.

And if the waiting itself proved to be torment for the little creature, why, so be it.

MARYA AWOKE from a nightmare into a nightmare. The room was dark and dank, heavy with the odors of mildew and neglect, and filled with what looked like the accumulated debris of centuries. The only light filtered through one narrow window, half-hidden by the crumbling pieces of what had once been shutters, and the roof sagged alarmingly. The broken, unsteady bed on which she lay was so badly decayed, festooned with webs and dust and shreds of rotted cloth, that she cried out in disgust and struggled to her feet—

To find herself face to face with her captor. Koshchei towered over her, his massive form wrapped in his great, dark cloak. For a brief moment, Marya could almost pretend he was nothing more than an unusually tall, unusually powerful warrior. But the Deathless radiated a Power that was so dark, so alien, she was sickened by the chill *feel* of it. And his eyes . . . Cold and remote and empty, they stared unblinkingly at her, as devoid of human emotion as twin holes into the Outer Dark.

Held by that unfeeling emptiness, Marya fought not to cringe. Instead she drew herself up as regally as she could and dragged her gaze away from those terrible eyes, glancing about the time-worn room with feigned contempt.

"Is *this* your estate?" The words came out almost steadily. "It seems sadly . . . lacking."

"It is sufficient. For now." The Deathless's voice was deep, almost rich. But the same emptiness hinting in the terrible eyes echoed within it.

"You are my captive, small one, as I was yours. The room, the estate, as your own slight Power should tell you, has been Warded against you; you may not escape. More, you need not know."

He turned indifferently away, leaving Marya alone in the decaying room. She waited, biting her lip nervously, till she was sure he wasn't going to return, then rushed to the window. The rotting wood crumbled to powder at her touch, leaving the window unblocked, and Marya eagerly leaned out . . . tried to lean out . . . tried to . . .

Suddenly so weary her legs refused to hold her, Marya stumbled back, struggling just to stand—

And as soon as she was away from the window, the weariness vanished.

A Spell of Binding, the princess thought grimly, *just as Koshchei boasted*, and set out to test its limits.

Some time later, she sat in a dejected heap on the cleanest corner of the bed.

The whole room was Warded, all right. If she tried to so much as approach the window, the door, or even the outer wall, that arcane weariness brought her crumpling to her knees. She hadn't the vaguest idea how one negated such a spell. Even if she had had the Power to attempt it.

She was truly, hopelessly, trapped.

XVII

DESPERATE NEWS,
DESPERATE PLANS

THE COURTIER, his hair and beard and clothing travel-stained and disheveled, threw himself to his knees before Emelian there in the palace courtyard, staring up at the young man with wild, anguished eyes. "Terrible news, my lord, oh, terrible!"

Emelian glanced from him to the others of the royal party, seeing that same anguish mirrored on all their faces. "What is this? Where's Marya? *Where is my wife?*"

"We—we don't know," the courtier said miserably.

"What!"

"It's true, my lord." The man swallowed. "Our Princess's tour was over. We were on our way home. The land around us looked peaceful and secure, with not a hint of trouble. But then . . . Out of nowhere, a—a demon on a fiery steed came plunging down out of the sky and snatched away the Princess Marya."

A demon. "Did this 'demon' look like a warrior?" Emelian asked grimly. "Tall, powerful, with terrible, cold eyes? Yes?"

Koshchei. It could only be Koshchei. Emelian could never forget that escape—the escape he'd allowed, curse him for a fool!—and the threat: *"Now I go to avenge myself on the magician's daughter, on her and all her kin!"*

"Oh God, Marya . . ." he moaned.

"My—my lord?"

"Did you not fight? Did you do nothing to stop him?"

"We tried, my lord. But our weapons broke against the demon's skin. And once he had seized our Princess, he was gone again into the sky, faster than thought."

Emelian clenched his hand about Marya's gift, the little amulet he always wore about his neck, feeling the smooth silver reassuringly warm against his palm. The warmth could be merely a reflection of his body heat—No, he would not believe that. "She's still alive," Emelian said. "I know it. Marya is still alive and unhurt. But we must rescue her, and swiftly, before . . . before she . . ."

He broke off, choking. *My fault. Dear God, all my fault.*

Nikolai was desperately trying to get his attention. "My lord, have you any idea where this—thing—might have taken her?"

Marya's amulet? She had said it would bind them together. Could he use it—akh, nonsense. He was no magician.

But someone else was. One of the wedding gifts from Prince Finist of Kirtesk and his wife had been the spell that, when spoken before a mirror, could be used as a means of speaking with the magician-prince from afar. He knew the spell. Marya had taught it to him, and apparently it was one that need not be recited by someone with Power to work . . .

Now, to find a mirror. Emelian whirled and ran into the palace, ignoring the astonished cries around him. Mirrors were rare, expensive things, none too common even among royalty, but he knew he had seen one, somewhere in the royal apartments.

Here it was, shrouded behind a protective velvet drapery. Carefully Emelian removed the cloth, staring for a nervous moment at his own wild-eyed face. If only he could remember the proper words . . . Feeling like a fool, Emelian recited the strange, twisting syllables.

Nothing happened.

Licking his dry lips, the young man tried again, speaking the spell as slowly and clearly as he could. Surely this time . . .

No. The mirror stubbornly remained only a mirror.

"Oh, please!" Emelian whispered. "Do *something!*"

He tried the spell once again.

Nothing. There wasn't even the faintest waver to his image.

"No, dammit, this has to work! Marya—"

Suddenly inspired, Emelian touched her little amulet against the glass, thinking that the small magics within it couldn't do anything but help. He held it there while he recited the spell yet again, eyes squeezed shut in concentration. Maybe if he tried to picture the Prince of Kirtesk as he'd seen him last: tall, elegant, sleekly silver of hair, coolly amber of eyes . . .

"Finist, please, Finist, where are you?"

"Enough, Emelian."

The sudden sharp voice made his open his eyes in shock. Finist was there in the mirror, seen almost as clearly as though through an open window.

But the sleek hair was wild as a falcon's ruffled feathers, those amber eyes were fierce with strain. "Hurry, Emelian. Tell me what's wrong."

"It's Marya. I—she—"

Emelian stopped short, seeing the impatience keen on Finist's face. Taking a deep breath, he managed to reorganize his panicky thoughts enough to tell the magician-prince exactly what had happened, from the moment he'd all unwittingly freed Koshchei to now, with Marya missing and almost certainly the Deathless's captive.

Finist let out his breath in a long, weary sigh. "Emelian, I already know all about That One being freed. I *felt* it the moment the Binding was shattered.'' For a moment, the fierce eyes closed, as though the prince were almost too drained to speak. ''And no, the blame does not lie with you, if that's what you've been thinking; That One merely used your humanity against you.''

''Thank you. But . . . Marya . . . ?''

''I'm sorry, Emelian. I . . . cannot help you.''

''No, that can't be! You—''

''Kinsman, believe me, if I could help, I would. But . . . I am That One's next target, as Marya's blood-kin and as magician; and Kirtesk my city with me. I can *feel* That One's approaching menace as clearly as you might feel a wave of heat, which is one reason I am not naming Names unnecessarily. Emelian, I cannot take my attention from the protection spells I'm weaving about Kirtesk. I dare not, or my people will be lost.''

Emelian couldn't meet that sharp, desperate stare. ''I . . . understand,'' he said hopelessly.

''No, wait. Listen to me: use that little amulet you wear to help you. Marya gave it to you, yes? And placed a lock of her hair and three drops of her blood within it? Oh, don't stare at me like that, I know the makings of such a charm! That amulet links you with Marya; the nearer you are to her, the warmer the silver will become. Use it to lead you to her.''

That was better than no hope at all. Emelian bowed. ''I shall. I . . . uh . . . hate to sound ungrateful, but I don't suppose you could give me some idea as to how far I'm going to have to travel?''

The amber eyes stared at him, all at once full of strangeness, more falcon than human. ''Far . . .'' Finist said abstractedly. ''Yet . . . not as far as it might seem . . .''

''Finist . . . ?''

The magician-prince shook his head as though to clear it of some arcane mist. ''No, I wasn't playing the seer. But I sensed . . . I don't think you'll need worry too much about provisions on your journey; I don't think it's going to take that long. Not if you are befriended by an unexpected ally on your journey."

That didn't make too much sense. But Finist's fine-boned face was so pale with weariness that Emelian didn't dare press him any further. "Thank you, kinsman. I didn't mean to take you away from—"

"Go alone," the prince interrupted. "Yes, I know the *boyars* won't like the idea, but it's your only hope. That One would easily detect an army, and destroy it with a wave of his hand. But he hasn't had the time to gather followers to him. And, for all his Power, whatever sorcerous defenses he's raised in this short span can be only rudimentary at best."

"Are you saying . . . ?"

"Exactly. One man alone—one bold man—just might be able to steal past those defenses."

"He might, indeed! Thank you!"

The image wavered and faded. But just before it snapped out of existence, Emelian heard Finist's parting words: "God be with you, kinsman. And with Marya."

"And with you, kinsman," Emelian echoed softly.

The mirror was now only a mirror. With a sigh, he replaced the protective drapery and turned away—only to stop short with a startled yelp. "Nikolai!"

"Forgive me, my lord."

"How long were you spying on me?"

The *boyar* winced. "Almost from the beginning. My lord, again, forgive me. But where the safety of our Princess is concerned— You can't truly be meaning to go alone, can you?"

"You heard Prince Finist. What other choice is there?" Now that he knew what he must do, Emelian was in a frenzy to get going. "Nikolai, you served as Regent once before, am I right? When Marya was a child? Well, man, you're going to have to take on that role once again."

"But—you can't—I mean— Akh, my lord, this is ridiculous! You can't—"

"I can. I will." Emelian had to snap out the words

to keep his voice from shaking. "D'you think I'm not afraid, man? Of course I am! But I can't abandon Marya."

"God, no."

"Come, Nikolai. Find me the swiftest horse in the royal stable. Prepare whatever statements need to be made for the—the transfer of power."

"But—"

"Do it! I leave today."

XVIII

JOURNEYS

THE HORSE WAS SWIFT, all right, so fast and fiery and full of himself that Emelian had a difficult time just staying in the saddle. The horse also had a mouth like the proverbial iron, and a prominent backbone that seemed designed to torment a rider. Breathless, struggling to keep both feet securely in the stirrups, Emelian wasn't really aware they'd reached the end of cultivated land and the edge of true forest till a branch dealt him a slap across the face that nearly sent him flying.

"All right, horse, enough!"

He threw his weight back in the saddle as Marya had taught him, pulling back on the reins till at last the horse deigned to slow, then stop.

"And look at you, panting and blowing. You can't gallop all the way, horse, you're only flesh and blood!"

At the back of his mind, he knew the animal was only reflecting his own frantic emotions. If they went the careful, sensible way of alternating walk, trot, canter, walk, trot, canter, it would take days just to get through this forest. Emelian raised a hand to Marya's amulet, feeling the warmth of it pulling at him. Through the forest they must go, as far as he could tell, and beyond—

"I don't care what Finist said!" the young man erupted. "We'll *never* get to Marya in time!" Then he gave a self-conscious snort. "Oh, fine. Look at me. Talking to a horse."

"*Only* to a horse?" asked a wind-whispery voice, and both man and horse started. As Emelian struggled to keep the animal from bolting, he glanced wildly about, thinking, *I know that voice!*

And suddenly Finist's puzzling words made sense: ". . . *befriended by an unexpected ally* . . ." Could this be . . . ?

"My lord *leshy?*" Emelian began warily. "Is that you?"

"*Leshy?*" the voice mocked, seeming to come from all around him. "Who is *leshy?* What is *leshy?* Is that you?"

"Please, my lord, I haven't time to play! My wife has been stolen away by . . ." The young man hesitated, wondering if he dared mention the name. "By the one who calls himself Koshchei the Deathless."

The forest abruptly grew very still. Not a leaf quivered, not a bird called. The air hung heavily around Emelian, so thick with silence he could hardly draw a breath.

"The not-man," said the *leshy* softly. "You are his foe?"

"I . . . . Yes. You could say that."

"You are of Life, human though you are, mortal though you are. You are not that wrongness." The *leshy* hissed, and suddenly the forest came to whispering, quivering life. "Yes. Come."

Come? Come where? The horse seemed to know, following their unseen guide at a walk, then a trot, then a full gallop.

"Hey, wait! You can't—"

But all at once, they were travelling at astonishing speed, the forest blurring about them. Emelian could have sworn the branches were actually lifting and stirring out of the way— Impossible! And yet . . . He gave up trying to puzzle things out, and simply crouched low in the saddle, blindly accepting whatever help the *leshy* chose to give him.

And at last the horse's mad pace slowed and stopped. The animal stood still, ears flicking nervously, blowing a bit but seemingly still fresh, none the worse for the wild trip. Then it lowered its head and began grazing frenetically on grass and leaves.

"There is no more living forest beyond this boundary," came the *leshy's* sudden whisper. "Only Death-life. Only—that."

Emelian looked, and shuddered. The living forest, as the *leshy* called it, ended abruptly. Beyond it lay a strip of bare earth, jarring in its barrenness after all the healthy green. And beyond that magical barrier began a forest out of nightmare. Trees were twisted into painful shapes, their branches reaching out like the arms of the starving. What leaves grew upon those tormented shapes were withered things, more brown than green. Only thorns seemed to thrive there; Emelian could see them standing out, sharp-edged as knives, from almost every branch.

"What is *that?*" he asked in horror.

"The Death-life spread Death-life to the Once-life."

It took Emelian a moment to make sense of that. "You mean Koshchei . . . Oh, he couldn't have done this deliberately!"

There was a rustling of leaves. "Who can say? Enough; I have brought you across my realm. Now you must go on, human-man."

And, "Go," the pull of Marya's amulet seemed to echo. Emelian sighed.

Impulsive to the end, eh, Serge? "My lord *leshy*, thank you for saving us ᴗ . . ah . . . however many days of travel it would have been."

"Repay us. Remove the Death-life."

As easily as that? But of course he knew better than to be sarcastic to anything as perilous as a *leshy*. "I . . . will do what I can," Emelian said carefully. His mount had finished its meal and seemed, amazingly, quite restored (more *leshy* magic, no doubt), so the young man sighed and gathered up the reins. "Come, horse, let's be off."

KOSHCHEI, mind turned inward, was only dimly aware of the world around him.

Finist . . . Finist . . .

He sent the first sly insinuation of his Power snaking out across mere physical boundaries, seeking a delicate, secret hold on that mortal mind. Once he had made even the most tenuous of contacts, he would erode the other's strength from within, subtly, carefully, till the man's Power was drained and he—

Aie! Koshchei straightened with a startled hiss. That first tendril of his Power had been met and blocked by a fiery wall of force.

The magician is wiser in Power than I thought. Not only does he know I am free, he has already prepared for my attack.

That meant this conquest was going to be more difficult than he had expected. Koshchei paused, considering. Odd. Surely he should be feeling rage at this unexpected obstacle. And yet . . . how long had it been since he last had faced a foe at all worthy of his time? Those had been wild, glorious days of combat, of triumph, long ages past. And even though those . . . human . . . extremes of emotion seemed alien to him now, was this not a stirring of pleasure he felt at the thought of Finist's defiance? Was it not a reminder that, distant from humanity though he was, he *could* still feel?

The Deathless smiled thinly. Even more pleasurable than the thought of Finist's defiance was that of his inevitable defeat, his despair as those around him shriveled into death. But such pleasures would have to be won carefully. There could be no simple mind-enslaving from afar, not with this one. To destroy him, Koshchei might have to travel to Kirtesk itself.

But what of my captive?

How much sweeter his vengeance after she had

learned the magician, her last faint hope, was dead, or perhaps mindless!

Yes, but she must not escape in his absence. Quickly the Deathless checked the strength of his Wardings. Good. They would last till he removed them (or, unlikely thought, till someone carried her away from them, breaking their strength). He had remembered mortal needs, as well. There was food and drink enough within those magical boundaries, and a place for waste; the woman would be alive and reasonably healthy when he returned.

Koshchei called out a Word of Power, a Name. With a wild stirring of the air, his slave-spirit was there before him.

Master?

"Shape yourself. I wish a steed once more. Come, hurry! We have far to ride!"

EMELIAN WINCED. What he wouldn't give for sound—normal, honest forest sound! There wasn't a bird or beast in all this twisted, ugly place, and the clop of his horse's hoofs seemed strangely muted, as though the very ground was rotten. Even the air smelled rotten, stale as the air in a room too long shut up.

At least the horse, though it kept its ears flat in resolute unhappiness and he had to keep prodding it with his heels, was still willing to keep going. That meant whatever peril had created this forest, the worst of it must have happened a long time ago. There wasn't any immediate danger.

Or so Emelian hoped.

But how long could a horse keep going on a foresty salad—no matter how augmented by *leshy*-magic—and no water at all? Emelian knew little about horses, but he suspected they were rather fragile when it came to such things as sufficient fodder. What if something happened to his mount, and he was left afoot in the middle of . . . this place? For that matter, how long could *he* keep going without rest?

Trying to combat the uncanny silence and his aching worry, the young man defiantly started whistling. But what should have been a cheerful tune sounded so flat and lifeless that he broke off with a shudder.

"Ah, horse, if only I hadn't gone down those palace stairs— Hey now, wait a moment. It wasn't *my* idea to go down them; that plump little girl persuaded me . . . Olga."

Olga, who had deliberately sent him into peril. Olga, who would have a good deal of explaining to do when he got back. If he got back.

"Why did she do it? What can she possibly have against me? Why would she want Kosh— ah, That One freed? Is she *his* servant? Or—"

Emelian broke off in alarm, flattening himself in the saddle, as a sudden savage burst of wind went roaring by overhead, sending the twisted branches lashing madly about.

Then they stopped, and there was silence once more.

"Now, what was *that?*"

But even as he asked this, Emelian remembered the courtier's description of "a demon on a fiery steed . . . plunging down out of the sky."

Koshchei!

The young man twisted about in the saddle, but whatever or whoever was already gone.

That *must* have been Koshchei. But . . . Marya? If the Deathless had taken her with him, surely the amulet would be turning cold. Instead, it was still warm, pulling Emelian forward. Could it be that the Deathless had left Marya behind?

"Hurry, horse, oh hurry!"

Without any warning, they burst out of one last thorny thicket into the open.

So much for the element of surprise, Emelian thought wryly.

Before him loomed what must once have been a fortress, though now the outer palisade was little more than rotting stumps and the walls and roof of the huge main building were crumbling and falling in on themselves. More of the scrawny, half-dead trees wormed their way between the broken stones. The whole scene was made even grimmer by the fact that the sun, which up to this time had been shining brightly, had gone behind an increasingly dark mass of clouds.

For all that he ached to rush blindly forward and snatch Marya out of that terrible place, Emelian forced himself to wait, sitting the nervous horse in tense silence. But, after a time, when nothing untoward happened, the young man let out a long, slow sigh of relief. That *had* been Koshchei winging his way overhead; if the Deathless had still been here, he certainly would have sensed the trespasser by now.

As Finist had guessed, there didn't seem to be any guards about, either. Emelian circled the grounds once, warily. When he saw no signs of life at all, he forced his unwilling horse through a gap in the briars.

Eerie. Normally, such a long-abandoned courtyard should have turned into a wilderness of weeds. But here, only a few scrawny bits of green broke the smoothness of bare grey earth.

Sorcery.

Suddenly Emelian couldn't stand the silence a moment longer. Abandoning all caution, he called out wildly, "Marya? Marya!"

To his heart-stopping delight, her face—pale but unmarked—appeared at a window. "Emelian!"

"Yes, love, it's me!" Laughing with relief, he blew her a kiss. "Don't worry, I'll have you out of there in—"

"No, no, that's impossible. Emelian, get out of her, *now!* If Koshchei catches you, he'll kill you!"

"The old devil's gone, love; I felt the wind of his passing." Emelian wriggled back onto the horse, out of the saddle. "Now, climb up into the windowframe, and you should be able to step right out and down onto this saddle."

"I can't."

Emelian looked up at her in surprise. "It's no difficult thing, love, truly. Don't be afraid, I'll catch you."

"I'm not afraid! Emelian, you don't understand. There's a Warding on this place. I literally can't leave it!"

"Ah. I knew things were going too smoothly." But then Emelian straightened. "Wait a minute . . . Spells have to be precisely worded to work, right? Good. The Warding is only on *you,* right? *You* can't leave?"

"Yes, but . . ."

"Ha! Maybe you can't leave—but there's no reason I can't simply take you away! Watch."

Hoping the horse was better trained about standing still than it was about stopping, Emelian gingerly stood up on the broad back. To his relief, the animal never budged, though a curious ear did flick back in his direction.

"Just stay put, there's a good boy."

The young man reached up carefully, just managing to catch Marya about the waist without overbalancing. He pulled. It was no easy thing; Marya was light enough, but, thanks to the spell, she was dead weight, unable to help him. Gritting his teeth, Emelian continued to pull—

And suddenly Marya was free, falling helplessly into his arms. The impact threw Emelian off his precariously held balance, sending them both tumbling to the ground.

"Oof! Are you—"

"All right? Are you—"

"Breathless. I— Oh, my love, my dearest!"

As the horse watched, ears pricked in strong equine curiosity, the two humans stopped babbling, instead embracing each other as though they would never again let go.

But at last Marya pulled free, glancing nervously about. "Akh, Emelian, we've got to get out of here."

"Yes." But he had to grin. "Thank heaven for carefully worded spells! I *told* you there was nothing that said I couldn't take you out of there."

"My clever love! Oh, but hurry; if *he* finds me gone . . ."

Emelian hardly had to ask who *he* might be. Quickly he climbed back into the saddle, Marya before him, and urged the horse into a canter.

"If we can make it back into the living forest, we'll be safe," Emelian told Marya. "The *leshy* there doesn't like old Death-life at all!"

"How would you know . . . ?" Marya twisted about to stare at her husband. "Don't tell me you actually spoke with—You did! Emelian, you never cease to surprise me."

He smiled, and wisely kept silent. But he was thinking, *Now, if only we can find our way back without the amulet to guide us.*

Looking around at all the twisted, thorny trees, all the apparently identical twisted, thorny trees, Emelian had a horrible suspicion that it wasn't going to be so easy.

XIX

THE FIRST ATTACK

THE SPIRIT-STEED SWEPT down the cloudy sky with the desperate speed of a slave forced to please its master, silently crying its despair as it rode the swift, chill winds and ached for freedom.

Koshchei ignored his slave's anguish. The damp, chill air whipped about him, tugging at the folds of his dark cloak, but he never shivered, unaware of anything as petty as cold. The pace as they sped over *verst* after *verst* of forest—dark green, hostile, far below them— would tear the air from the lungs of anything mortal. But mortality, he thought with a flash of dark humor, hardly applied to him.

Up ahead, the eternal greenness seemed to be thinning, the color lightening to a paler green, to browns and yellows, signifying cultivated fields. Koshchei brought himself back to the external world, grimly watching the colorful glimmer on the horizon that meant Kirtesk, and gathered his Power to him.

Soon, he told himself, *soon . . .*

FINIST, Prince of Kirtesk, stood atop the thick stone walls of his city, royal red cloak wrapped tightly about himself, silvery hair tossing in the wind, stood staring with unblinking eyes over the forest, *feeling* with every

magical sense the growing chill that had nothing to do
with mere physical weather.

Koshchei.

The forest and Those within it had already warned
him, sending nervous whispers of *peril,* of *not-life, enemy, evil,* well-meant warnings in their nonhuman way,
if not exactly helpful. Any danger so alien the Old
Magic of the forest feared it . . .

Eh, well, the prince refused to waste time or strength
in worrying over What Might Be. He knew he had prepared wisely and well. Old Deathless was going to have
a few surprises awaiting him; Finist wasn't the first
magician-prince to have placed protective spells around
his city—as many would-be invaders in the past had
discovered to their grief—and he had no intention of
being the last.

Soon, Finist told himself, and straightened resolutely.

WITHOUT WARNING, the spirit-steed staggered in the
air, slipping sidewards so that Koshchei had to make an
undignified grab at its neck to keep himself from falling, then righting itself so sharply he had to tighten his
grip.

"Idiot! Watch what you do!"

But, Master, the non-voice wailed, *I couldn't help
it! There was suddenly such an upsurge of Power—*

"*My* Power?"

Without waiting for a reply, Koshchei cast his will
back over the many *versts* towards the ruins of his estate. And what he sensed made him roar in such terrible
rage that the wind-spirit shivered under him and nearly
lost its shape.

Master . . . ?

"He dares! That foolish little mortal dares break my
Warding!" Grimly, the Deathless forced his seething
emotions back under control, freezing them beneath a
weight of cold, hating, logic.

Far on the path of Power though he'd come, it would
seem he was still capable of making mistakes. He had

underestimated the force of human determination; the moment the chains had fallen from him, back there in that dark cell, he should have forgotten about boasting and simply slain the man.

But what was, was. How, the Deathless wondered dispassionately, had the creature ever managed to reach the ruined estate? Determination, no matter how fierce, would hardly have been sufficient, not in so short a time. It would seem that the human had an ally. Finist, perhaps? Or that impudent *leshy?*

Koshchei's eyes glittered coldly as he considered the human, Emelian. Was the man fool enough to think he could steal a captive from the Deathless, and survive?

"I spared his life once," Koshchei murmured. "Now I shall correct that error!"

EMELIAN COULD NO LONGER DENY that he was afraid. Not so much for himself, but—Marya . . . Dear God, he had to get her out of this.

Every nerve in his body was screaming to him to run, to kick the horse into a mad gallop and go as far as they could, as fast as they could.

And have the poor beast die, and leave us as good as dead?

But how else were they going to get out of this dead forest? Granted, he had first lost almost all sense of direction when the *leshy* had sent him and his horse on that wild, mind-confusing ride. But it hadn't seemed to matter then; the amulet had drawn him straight for Marya. Who would have guessed it would be so difficult to retrace his steps? The ground felt so obnoxiously soft it should have held every hoofprint clear and sharp. But, bewilderingly, it held no tracks at all. And with the sun completely hidden behind the lowering clouds, making the air feel more like winter than spring, and all this ugly, dead forest looking so much alike . . .

Don't frighten Marya, he warned himself, and asked carefully, "I don't suppose you know where we are?"

She turned to give him a sharp glance. "No. I wasn't conscious when *he* brought me here."

Emelian bit back a groan. "I was afraid you'd say something like that." He reined in the horse. "Wait, I'll climb a tree."

It wasn't a simple thing to do, or painless. Scratched and bleeding from the knife-edged thorns that seemed to stud every branch, Emelian was glad to settle back down into the saddle again. "Couldn't see a thing," he told Marya, struggling to keep his voice tranquil. "Nothing but more of this dead place."

"Give the horse his head," Marya suggested. "Surely he'll find his way out of here."

Emelian obligingly loosened the reins. The animal took off at an eager trot, ignoring its double burden. "Ha, now, we're getting somewhere!"

Yes, but where? There still wasn't the slightest sign of greenness up ahead, not even a hint of that arcane strip of bare earth marking the forest's edge.

God, what if they were trapped? What if a spell lay over this land, and they'd triggered it by entering?

Akh, what nonsense. He was scaring himself like a stupid little boy. Of course there was a way out of this maze, and they would find it, somehow. Before Koshchei found them.

If only it wasn't so quiet in here! The silence pressed down about them with almost suffocating force, deadening their voices till Emelian and Marya gave up all attempts at conversation and fell silent, too.

The horse's willing trot was beginning to grow rough. Emelian clucked encouragingly and shook the reins, but despite all he could do, the trot slowed to a walk. The animal's head drooped, ears sagging.

Oh no, not now, horse; please don't give up now!

He didn't dare push the animal; he could already feel its sides heaving. *Leshy* magic might have strengthened the horse up to this point, keeping it from feeling true thirst or exhaustion. But, all too plainly, the last of the magic had just run out.

"We can't expect the poor beast to carry both of us," Emelian said, struggling against the deafening silence, and slipped to the ground. "We'll take turns," he called up to Marya, and started walking. Trying not to think what they would do if the night overtook them. Trying not to feel like one of the forever-lost, forever-hopeless damned.

There had to be a way out of this, there must. After all, things couldn't get much worse—

Oh, can't they? thought Emelian as a sudden fierce gust of wind brought Koshchei and his fiery steed plunging down at them.

"Marya, ride!" the young man shouted, and swatted their horse across the rump, hard.

But Marya, warrior that she was, leaped down beside him as the animal galloped madly away. "Emelian, the bare strip you mentioned—I got a glimpse of it as I jumped. It's just ahead of us. Come on, love, run!"

Hand in hand, they raced for the barren stretch of earth—and the living forest beyond.

Just a few paces more, Emelian told himself, panting. *We're going to make it . . .*

And then a blow that seemed to have all the strength of the wind behind it threw him to the ground. Ears ringing, head spinning, Emelian struggled back up to his knees, gasping for breath, hearing Marya's battle-scream echoing all around him. There was a dark, terrible shape—

Koshchei! The Deathless was there astride his uncanny steed, dark cloak flapping madly in the wind, there in the narrow strip between dead forest and live—there with Marya, struggling in fierce helplessness, trapped in his arms.

"*No!* Damn you, *no! You'll not take her!*"

Barely aware of what he was shouting, Emelian drew his sword in a screeching of metal and hurled himself at Koshchei.

The Deathless never moved. He let the sword strike him truly, and laughed as the blade snapped asunder.

As Emelian glanced about wildly for another weapon, a rock, a branch, anything to free his wife, Koshchei murmured, "I spared you once, little man. Not again."

He pointed, and spoke a Word that rang out in the chill air, heavy with Power. Emelian was hurled again to the ground, this time with such force that he felt his body break. The shock of it left no room for pain, for breath, for life . . .

The copper taste of blood sharp in his mouth, vision blurred, Emelian saw one last glimpse of his wife, her eyes wild with despair.

And then there was nothing.

XX

RESTORATION

PRINCE FINIST, standing rigidly alert atop the wall of Kirtesk, his roused Power a heat haze shimmer all around him, could feel the approach of Koshchei as a chill, colorless emptiness. The magician-prince expanded his senses to watch on the psychic level, and saw that cold-eyed, powerful warrior-form only too clearly. Koshchei, astride his eerie steed, was riding swiftly down the winds.

Heart racing, the prince braced himself for the combat to come. At any moment, the first of the protective spells ringing Kirtesk would spark into life. At any moment—

But without any warning, Koshchei reined in his wind-steed. As Finist stared in disbelief, the Deathless turned aside from Kirtesk and sped away.

For a time, the prince was too stunned to move, half expecting Koshchei to materialize out of the air around him. But nothing happened. The Deathless had apparently abandoned his attack before it was even begun, and at last Finist turned away with a sigh.

He snatched his cloak about himself as a stray breeze toyed with it. Now he would have to go before his *boyars* and tell them . . . what? That the peril was somehow gone? That it had been merely postponed? Dammit, what *had* the Deathless been about?

191

Something to do with Cousin Marya . . . ? Could she have managed to escape?

Akh, no. The poor thing was thoroughly snared, at least so Emelian had—

Emelian!

Fierce with sudden suspicion, Finist let his cloak fall where it would, hastily shifting shape to wing straight for his chambers in the royal palace. Maria, who had been standing tensely by the window, moved aside to let him enter.

"What is it?" she asked sharply, as he altered back to man-shape almost before his feet had touched the floor. "What about—"

"That One? He's backed off, at least for now. I don't know why for sure, not yet."

As he spoke, Finist opened the small chest that held Emelian's dagger—and gave a cry of horror.

"Finist?" Maria hurried to his side. "Oh, dear God, no . . ."

The dagger's bright blade had tarnished to a flat, dull black.

"I was right," the prince murmured. "He must have tried to free Marya. And That One sensed it." He caught his wife's hands in his own. "Maria, love, I can't wait. Emelian isn't dead, but if I don't help him right away—"

Finist broke off abruptly, eyes suddenly falcon-fierce. "He *mustn't* die!"

"Finist . . . ?"

"Ha, of course! The vague premonitions, the feeling of unease that had nothing to do with myself, or you, or Kirtesk— That's it, that's what's been bothering me all along: I've been *sensing* that if That One is ever to be defeated, Emelian *must* play a part."

"Oh, love, the danger . . ."

"To me? To Kirtesk?" The prince gave an impatient little shiver, sharp as a falcon ruffling its feathers. "It should be safe enough for me to leave, at least for the moment; I doubt That One will turn his attention back to us before he has checked and strengthened his spells around Marya.'' Finist gave his wife a kiss no less passionate for its desperate haste. "Farewell. I'll be back as quickly as I can.''

Before Maria could say a word, the prince was a falcon once more, and winging wildly out into the open sky.

IT HAD BEEN a long flight, and Finist was growing truly wing-weary by the time he located the ebbing *feeling* of Emelian's aura—and with it, the tense alertness of the living forest to one side of the bare, magic-guarded strip of earth, and the chilling, hollow aura of the deathly forest to the other.

Koshchei's doing, that unliving forest, the saturation of dark Power spilling out and around his fortress over Heaven only knew how many years, enough to slowly warp and kill an entire woodland . . .

The *leshiye* couldn't be too happy about it. But if even those incredible personifications of Old Magic couldn't move against Koshchei . . .

The falcon gave a low cry of dismay. There lay Emelian, arms and legs flung akimbo, for all the world like some doll thrown aside by a careless child. His face was deathly pale, and from this range, he didn't seem to be breathing at all.

Finist hastily swooped down to a landing, altering swiftly to man-form, kneeling beside Emelian, hardly aware of the chill air against his bare skin. But after the first wary examination, the prince sat back on his haunches, fighting despair. Emelian still breathed, though faintly. But the damage done to him . . . A mercy he was unconscious. How much longer could life continue to dwell in such a broken body?

But what can I do? Finist wondered helplessly. He could heal wounds, but not something as bad as this, not without help—

Help? The living forest held Power stronger than anything merely human, if only he could find a way to use it without burning out his mind in the process, or that of Emelian—

Emelian, who was going to die if he didn't do something quickly. Finist glanced sharply up at the shadowy mass of green, and realized he and Emelian weren't alone. The forest knew the prince was there. Leaves quivered without wind, branches stirred in response to his Power, and for all the weight of urgency, the prince said with wise caution, "I mean you no harm."

"Magic-man," whispered a voice soft as the rustling of leaves. "Magic-man, this is not your realm. What do you here?"

Finist scanned those dappled-green shadows. *Leshy,* no doubt about it. Not one he knew, though, not the forest-lord who ruled that particular portion of wilderness nearest Kirtesk.

"My lord *leshy,*" he said, forcing his voice to calmness, "I come in peace, surely you can sense that about me."

"I sense trouble, and worry, and human emotions. Pah, what a tangle!"

"Yes, but—" Finist bit back impatience. "My lord *leshy,* you know who harmed this man—"

"The Death-life." It was said sharply as a curse.

"That One is my foe, too, *leshy.*"

"So that sad human said. And look: he dies."

"No, no, he can live—*leshy,* he *must* live! He holds the key to That One's destruction within him!"

"He dies," the *leshy* said stubbornly.

"No! Listen to me: if you let me into the forest, draw its Power to me, through me, I can heal him!"

The *leshy* fell silent. Leaves quivered as though reflecting the being's uncertainty. "It . . . cannot be done," the wind-whisper voice said uneasily.

"It can! I'll show you."

Without waiting for the *leshy* to answer, Finist pulled Emelian's limp form, as gently as he could, into the forest shelter, wincing inwardly at the thought of the further damage he was probably doing to the young

THE HORSE OF FLAME 195

man. He could sense the forest's Power all around him, alien to anything human, and felt a spasm of genuine fear. How dare he presume he could bend the Old Magic to his use? And yet, that Power was somehow very comforting in its affirmation of life.

All right, no time to waste, Finist told himself.

He began gathering to him the Words of the strongest healing spell he knew, feeling the forest stirring wildly all around him, surrounding him yet separate from him, not giving him the Power he needed. Refusing to surrender, Finist gasped out, "You see, my lord *leshy,* it *can* be done! Give me your aid— He can be saved!"

"The forest is life and death and life, not this, not rebuilding— When a tree falls, is it restored? No! It decays, to feed new life!"

We're talking about a man, dammit, not a tree! But shouting at a *leshy* would accomplish only harm. "Please, my lord *leshy,* you want to stop that Death-life as much as I! Give me your aid!"

"No—"

"Yes!"

"No! It would bend the Old Magic, make it do what it should not, it would create imbalance—"

"I know, I will deal with it, see that the price is paid—just let me save Emelian!" Savagely, Finist prodded, "Come, my lord *leshy,* do you like that deathly forest on your borders? Do you want it to spread? It will, you know it, if you let That One reign unchecked. What say you, my lord *leshy?* Wouldn't that be worse than any small imbalance here and now?"

The answer came not in words, but in a rush of raw Power that blazed through Finist, making him cry out in painful ecstasy. Bit by bit, the prince won back control, by sheer will keeping his mind and sanity whole. The *leshy* was right, the Old Magic was never meant to be forced into the shapes he needed; it was pure Life, pure Growth, with nothing of healing-mercy about it, but Finist sent that fierce, raw Power coursing into the healing of Emelian's body. Shattered bones drew back

into their proper places beneath that savage flow, re-
forming themselves, new strength surging along their
lengths. Torn tissues and muscles wove themselves back
in place, organs were restored to strength. Finist, barely
in control, felt each new stage of healing stab through
his being as a wave of pain or pleasure, confusing his
senses, overwhelming his mind with Power till at last
mere mortal will gave way beneath the flood, and he
fell beside Emelian . . .

Emelian, who breathed cleanly.

No longer dying, Emelian stirred as though in sleep.
He yawned suddenly, and Finist sat bolt upright, startled. He stretched stiff muscles—

But they weren't stiff. He didn't ache, he wasn't weary
at all. By any rights, that wild rush of Power should
have burned out his mind. Instead, it had left him fairly
ablaze with energy. Why, he could surely fly straight to
Kirtesk and never even feel the strain! The winds were
calling to him—

Yes, but before he did any flying:

"Emelian?" the prince called softly.

Emelian's eyelids flickered, opened. He looked
blankly up at the prince for a moment, then frowned
vaguely, drawing a hand across his eyes. "How soundly
I've slept!"

"Almost too soundly," muttered Finist.

Emelian stared at him, eyes focusing.

"Kinsman! What are you— What am *I* doing here?"

"You don't remember?"

"I . . ." Emelian hesitated, shuddering. "It wasn't
a dream, was it? That demon snatching up Marya and
striking me—but that's impossible! I was dying. How
can I be alive and"—the young man glanced down at
his undamaged self—"and unharmed?"

"Magic," the prince said shortly, feeling the forest
Power racing through him, urging him to take to the
sky—

"*Imbalance* . . ." whispered the *leshy* in Finist's
ears. "*Restore* . . ."

"Let me be!" the prince muttered fiercely. "It shall be done." And in that moment, his own Power roused, he knew, without any doubt, exactly what must be done—and by whom.

Emelian was eyeing him warily, unaware of the *leshy's* presence, and Finist fought down a sudden surge of impatience, reminding himself that it wasn't the young man's fault he was magicless. "Emelian, listen to me. I can't stay with you very long." That came out far sharper than he'd intended, so the prince forced himself to add in explanation, "That One will soon be heading back to Kirtesk, and I must be there to defend it. Yes, you were dying. The only way I could save you was to . . . bend the laws of Nature a bit."

"What are you saying?"

Finist shuddered, fighting back the shimmering of feathers trying to form along his arms. "By keeping you from death, I created an imbalance. And I'm afraid the rules of Power insist that you're the one who must restore that balance."

"What does *that* mean?"

"Akh, Emelian, simply this: either That One dies within the year—or you do."

"But—but he *can't* die!" Emelian protested.

"Destroy his shell," the prince said shortly, getting to his feet. "It amounts to the same thing." He saw Emelian's eyes widen, registering his nakedness for the first time. "Kinsman, I'm sorry, I really must leave—"

"Please! Can't you at least tell me what I'm to do?"

The despair in that cry made Finist pause, head tilted thoughtfully to one side. If only he could think clearly! But the wind was calling to him, and Kirtesk needed him, and the Old Magic confused the paths of mere human logic. The prince forced himself to concentrate on Emelian as best he could. Emelian couldn't very well try to steal Marya away without a Powerful edge. And the shape of that edge . . . That wind-steed Koshchei rode . . .

"You can't defeat That One with a sword," Finist said quickly. "I hope you realize that. Your only hope lies to the north. There lives a . . ." He paused, frustrated at the limitations of nonmagical words. "Just call her a being. Vyed'ma. The Hag of the Rocks."

"The Hag . . . not human, I take it. No, of course not." Emelian shuddered. " 'To the north' is a rather vague direction, kinsman."

"Akh, yes." Words of explanation were so slow and imprecise! Instead, Finist reached out an impatient hand to touch Marya's amulet, still hanging from its chain about Emelian's neck. Eyes closed, *feeling* the warmth of his cousin's love lingering about it, he concentrated on Vyed'ma, the ancient, eerie Hag of the Rocks. Half entranced, Finist sensed soft Words rising to his lips, and murmured them, surrounding the amulet with new magic . . .

It was done.

The prince drew his hand back. "There, now, I've readjusted the Power within the amulet. It will guide you truly to Vyed'ma's mountain." He hesitated, hearing the winds singing to him, feeling the excess forest Power still burning within him, eager to be used, and fought to continue in bland human words. They came out in a tangled rush. "I don't know how That One stole a wind-sprite from her. She is perilous, she is of the Old Magic, and she is very, very Powerful. But— be brave, be clever. Maybe you can win a second wind-steed from her, win its willing aid. No mortal horse can run quickly enough to elude That One, not when he can use the speed of the wind. But with that second wind-steed, you and Marya—" Finist stopped short, struggling to control his runaway tongue. God, was this what it was like to be drunk? Feeling thoughts running about in confusion, and words pouring out in a flood— Was this weird plan logical, was what he was telling Emelian even possible? Yes, yes, the Old Magic was pushing him to continue, and Vyed'ma was of the Old Magic; this must be right; this was the only chance, the only hope—"With luck," the prince continued as rationally as he could, "the new wind-spirit will prove swift enough to see you and Marya safely to Kirtesk. Once you are behind the spell-walls I've raised, I will do my best to help you. More than that, I cannot promise."

Finist straightened, eyes wide, shivering beneath the renewed sense of a certain chill emptiness . . . "He stirs. Emelian, I'm sorry, I can do no more . . ."

That last word was dragged out into a falcon's shriek. Emelian stared, shaken, as a shining falcon soared up from where a man had stood. Finist looked down on him with vision now inhumanly keen, feeling a touch of pity at the dejected way the young man stood, so alone.

God go with you, kinsman.

The prince dipped a wing to him in salute, then sped out over the forest for Kirtesk.

XXI

DARK DAYS

THE MEETING in that small, private room in the Astyan royal palace was unofficial, and very secret, including as it did every *boyar* of the Inner Council—save one.

"Nikolai," muttered Dimitri. "Regent Nikolai. *Prince* Nikolai is more like it!"

"Oh, come now," Yaroslav protested. "Nikolai doesn't have any regal ambitions!"

"Doesn't he? Lording it over all of us as though we were peasants and he—the arrogant, oh-so-perfect son of a—" Dimitri choked on his anger, then managed to add, "Dammit, Yaroslav, the man doesn't simply *say* something, he *proclaims* it!"

"Well, yes . . . But that's only because he takes his regency very seriously."

Dimitri snorted. "Don't be so naive."

"I'm not!" Yaroslav blazed. "But this meeting is ridiculous! I mean, what are you all planning to do? Depose Nikolai?"

"If necessary," came a mutter.

Yaroslav shook his head. "Don't even think that! Nikolai was made Regent by the royal consort himself. To act against him would be treason!"

"Don't lecture us, Yaroslav," Dimitri snapped. "We've known the Laws longer than you've been alive."

"I didn't mean—"

"As long as Nikolai remains within the bounds of his appointed role," murmured Basil, "we will obey him. As we must."

"Yes," cut in Dimitri, "but let him, just once, attempt anything remotely resembling usurpation, and he'll learn all about the meaning of treason!"

"Oh, *boyars!*" Yaroslav protested. "Maybe he has been a little . . . overzealous—"

"A *little!*" someone scoffed.

"Never mind." The young man forged boldly ahead. "You're all making too much of the whole thing. Nikolai had a perfect chance to take the throne during the days of Princess Marya's minority. If he didn't want it then, why in the name of Heaven should he want it now?" He drew a deep breath, then continued before anyone could interrupt. "Look you, rather than gossiping like old fools, we should be spending our time doing the only thing we can: praying that Princess Marya is safe."

That hit the mark. Suddenly shame-faced, the other *boyars* refused to meet his earnest gaze. "Amen," someone murmured.

A little abashed at having silenced his elders for once, Yaroslav forced a grin. "And all this is only temporary, anyhow, only till Princess Marya and her consort return."

"When they return," murmured Basil.

"*If* they return," added Dimitri dourly.

BOYAR NIKOLAI, Regent-by-default of Astyan, sat moodily on the Regent's chair, alone in the great Audience Hall.

Chin on hand, he stared blankly out into the near darkness and wondered what could possibly go wrong next.

Dammit, I don't want *to be ruler!*

Why should he? It wasn't as though he had a son or daughter to place on the throne after him.

But Dimitri and the other *boyars* couldn't seem to see

that Nikolai acted sternly not out of any dreams of tyranny—God, no!—but only because he must defend the dignity of the royal house. No matter what he said, the *boyars* refused to believe he had been content with things as they were, with his position as Minister and counselor to the crown. Even if the crown hadn't seemed to need counsel quite as much since the arrival of Emelian . . .

Nikolai clenched his fists in frustration. *Emelian, you young idiot, how could you just run off like that, all alone and unprepared?*

Still, he had to admit, the man's arguments had sounded so logical at the time—as logical as anything amid all the hysteria. Particularly since they'd come directly from magician-prince Finist of Kirtesk.

Magic. Nikolai nearly spat. Magic was the cause of all this trouble. Magic had always been the cause of trouble in Astyan, right from the day Marya's father had gone and gotten himself killed while trying to prove he was the high and mighty sorcerer!

"God rest his soul," Nikolai muttered reflexively.

But his thoughts just then had nothing to do with salvation.

OLGA BIT BACK a cry of pain as she jabbed herself with the needle yet again, then glanced uneasily at the other noblewomen sitting in the sunny, fragrant palace garden. No one had noticed her clumsiness, it seemed—but who knew what the sharp, spiteful eyes of the ladies might or might not choose to see?

Oh, what difference did it make? How could she think about her needlework when her guilt preyed on her, day and night? When all she could see were the faces of Marya and Emelian, the people she had destroyed?

She was guilty of treason, guilty of releasing a demon, guilty of sending the princess and her consort to a terrible death . . .

Olga lowered her head, fiercely blinking back tears before anyone could notice. It was true she had longed for vengeance; but she had never meant any harm, not any *real* harm, certainly never anything as dreadful as this! Dear, merciful Heaven, if only there was some way to atone!

Vatza, it was for you, all for you!

But that silent, defiant cry no longer held any comfort.

Choking back a sob, the girl staggered to her feet and hurried away. If only she could confide in someone! But she didn't dare tell anyone the treasonous truth. Tormented though she was, she still didn't want to face the headman's axe.

Olga drew herself erect. No, there was no one in whom she could confide. She must live with her guilt, alone, always alone . . .

But how to keep anything secret when there were always curious, prying folk about? Unless . . .

There was only one place in which atonement could be found: she must enter a nunnery.

Eyes shining with sudden fervor, Olga pulled the folds of her ornate caftan about herself, picturing instead the simple grey or brown of a postulant's robe. She would leave the shallow life of this court and enter a nunnery. She would forget all about . . . sinful things, and spend her time praying for the souls of Marya and Emelian.

She must renounce the world.

And maybe then she would at last find peace.

EMELIAN, head craned back in panic, watched the shining falcon disappear over the tops of the trees.

"Wait!" he called uselessly after it. "I don't have any way to— My horse is—"

"No horse here!" a wind-whisper voice said, and Emelian started.

"No, my lord *leshy*," he replied, "I can see that. Judging from the way he was running, the animal is probably back in Astyan by now."

Yes, but he needed the horse now! Trying to fight Koshchei again would be suicidal, which meant that

Marya's only hope lay with this . . . Vyed'ma. But without that horse, the trip was going to take so long. For all he knew, Vyed'ma lived somewhere beyond the back of the North Wind!

And what happens to Marya in the meantime?

"Oh, God!" Emelian cried in despair. "What am I going to do? What *can* I do?"

"Walk?" asked the *leshy* helpfully.

"Yes, but—"

"That amulet the magician-man bespelled is an intriguing thing." For a moment, the being was so close that Emelian could almost see him clearly, a stick-thin, greenish figure among the underbrush. Then the figure was gone into the shadows again. "It will, I believe, show you the way." There was a quick rustling of leaves, then the whispery voice added, "You may find it far to travel, or maybe not so far. That is a strange realm, that of the Hag. Distance is different there."

It was scant comfort, but Emelian suspected it was kindly meant, so he bowed in the general direction of the forest.

"Thank you, my lord," the young man said, and set out upon his way.

THOUGH NO MORTAL COULD HAVE READ the slightest trace of emotion in his stance or expression, inwardly the Deathless was as close to confusion and despair as he had been in countless ages.

How much of himself had he lost during that time of captivity? Once, he never would have been so careless, so *humanly* sure of himself; once no mortal creature could have stolen onto his lands—let alone carried off a captive—without his knowing of the creature's every footstep. No matter that things had been corrected, that the woman was his prisoner anew, wrapped in ensorcelled sleep, and the foolish little man had been slain. The entire situation *should never have happened*.

Control, Koshchei told himself. *You are not diminished. You are whole, your Power is whole.*

Emotion cooled. Koshchei turned his full attention towards the Wards about the mansion. They must be strengthened before anything else could be done . . . He studied them for a time with physical and arcane senses together, seeing their weaknesses. Eyes closed, the Deathless pulled up Power from deep within his being, then opened his eyes once more and flung up his arms in command, calling out Words cold and grey as a winter sky.

And cold and grey as those Words were the Powerful lines that encircled the mansion, weaving a glinting web of force about it till not the slightest psychic gap remained.

At last it was done. Now, as surely as spirit and body belonged together, the woman was totally his captive. Now he could leave her here without the slightest qualm, and see to the destruction of the magician-prince of Kirtesk, the man who was the only genuine threat left alive and unbound.

XXII

AWAKENINGS

CAUGHT WITHIN THE WEB of Koshchei's sleep-spell, Marya stirred and struggled helplessly, dimly aware that somewhere beyond this soft grey nothingness was light, somewhere there was life . . . At first there seemed no way out: far easier to slide back into mindlessness. But gradually that awareness of Other grew stronger, and with it, the sense that the strands of that soft web were dissolving, sliding from her bit by bit. The waking world was real and firm and solid, and soon she would be free, soon she would awake and be a part of it . . .

And then, as the last of the Deathless's sleep-spell expired, Marya did awaken, all at once, alert and alarmed.

"Emelian!"

No one answered. And Marya shrank back with a groan. This was the decaying room in Koshchei's ruined mansion, the prison she had thought to escape. The bonds of sorcery were more strongly woven this time, so strong they pressed down on her like weights of lead. And Emelian—

Emelian was dead. She had seen him die, struck down without a chance to escape, crushed beneath the casually cruel Power that was Koshchei.

"Koshchei." The name was said as a curse. "Ah, Koshchei. You shall regret letting me live."

Easy words; but the spell held her fast for all her struggles, so tightly she could barely move, barely breathe, so tightly there was only the will, the burning, unconquerable will, and the Power—

The Power was real, and rising; hot and fierce as the grief and hatred and despair tearing through her, the Power was rending her being, rending the sorcerous bonds that held her, blazing till she screamed in terrified delight and—

With a shudder, Marya looked down at herself, standing before a bed on which lay—herself.

Somehow, through the force of fear or grief or sheer desperation, she had roused Power within herself. This eerie, immaterial state proved it: somehow she had pulled her spirit free from the prison of her body.

But that's impossible, her mind started to recite by rote, *I don't have any . . .*

But she did. Dizzy with the shock, Marya realized that all through those long, bitter years her father had been wrong. The magic had always been there within her, but dormant, buried so deeply he never had suspected it was there.

And, convinced of her Powerlessness, he had convinced his daughter, too . . . Marya shuddered, remembering the guilt, the sense of being somehow weak, unfinished, inferior, and all of it *wrong*.

But what good was it now? Lacking any genuine training, she had no idea how to free her physical self as well.

For that matter, how do I . . . ah . . . get back in again?

No, she wasn't going to worry about that, not yet. As long as she was . . . as she was, Marya intended to experiment a bit.

Warily, the princess tried to move, and nearly laughed aloud, astonished to realize that this astral self was weightless, unfettered by the pull of Mother Earth. But her feet remained firmly on the floor.

Or at least they *seemed* to be touching the floor;

though her senses remained keen, Marya couldn't feel a thing, not even the air moving through her lungs. (But of course she couldn't feel that! With a new twinge of shock, the princess realized that there *wasn't* any air in her lungs. Apparently this astral self had no need of breath.)

Maybe she couldn't really feel anything, but at least she could move, walking, or seeming to walk, by a mere flicker of will. Marya's eyes widened as the truth of it struck her. In this immaterial form, she could fly, actually fly, or soar, or slip right through a solid wall, all without the slightest bit of effort!

In this immaterial form nothing could keep her out.

Not even, if there was any justice at all, the Deathless.

All wonder fled. *So be it,* the princess thought. *If this is the only way I can stop Koshchei, then—Koshchei, beware!*

With only the barest glimpse back at the apparently sleeping body on the bed, Marya spread her arms, and took to the sky.

BOYAR NIKOLAI, Regent of Astyan, looked down at the plump young woman standing before him, her head modestly lowered, her hands clasped in childish supplication, and fought back a frown of distaste. This seductive little creature was Olga, once Marya's lady-servant, then banished to the company of the other noble ladies for some unspecified crime. Unchastity? Perhaps. The glance she'd given him before lowering her head had been knowing enough.

"Why did you seek this counsel?" Nikolai asked sternly.

"I—I wish permission to leave the court, my lord."

"Ah? Most ladies your age long to enter the royal service, not leave it."

"I know." Her plump face reddened. "But I—I mean, I—"

"What is it, girl?" the *boyar* cut in impatiently. "Have you a lover out there somewhere?"

Eyes red-rimmed from weeping shot him an anguished look. "No!"

So, now, thought Nikolai, *that struck close to home,* and continued coolly. "You have a lover here at court, then? Of course. And you've had a lover's quarrel."

"No! You don't understand." Olga stared down at her clasped hands as though they were something new and strange. In a voice almost too soft and rushed to be heard, she murmured, "I—I want to join a nunnery. I must."

Nikolai raised a surprised brow. "Why?" He hesitated, uncertain. "Are you with child?"

"N-no."

"What, then? Come now, *don't* tell me you received a sudden revelation from on high. My dear, willful child, I know too much about you to believe that."

He meant only that Marya had told him something about the girl. But Olga raised a striken gaze to him.

"You know . . ." she breathed in horror. "But—you can't . . ."

So! This terror was surely more than guilt over sleeping in the wrong bed. "Why not, Olga? What can't I know?"

"Nothing! I—"

"Come, Olga. What can't I know?"

"I . . . Oh, please . . ."

"Tell me, girl. What are you trying to hide?"

"I told you! Nothing!"

"Olga, child, I'm not a fool. Come, talk to me."

"I—I can't."

Nikolai sighed. Were this some recalcitrant manservant, he would have put the man to the question. But this was a noble's daughter . . . "Something is weighing on your conscience, and it's not just some silly girlish secret. Olga, if this concerns the crown in any way, I must know the truth."

She shook her head, biting her lip nervously. Nikolai

watched the plump face redden anew and the big eyes
grow bright with unshed tears, and forced back his impatience. *All right, my dear, if it's to be a waiting game,
so be it.*

He stared fixedly at her, the imperious stare that had
put many a rebellious *boyar* in his place. Olga squirmed
and tried in vain to look away.

In another moment, surely, she would break and run,
and then he would have to decide whether to let the
silly thing go or start the embarrassing turmoil of having the guards bring her back—

But all at once, something broke within Olga's spirit.
Slumping, she murmured hopelessly, "All right. I
should have known I couldn't hide the truth forever. I
couldn't bear it. Listen. And if this means my death,
well then, so—so be it . . ."

As THE GIRL FINISHED her sorry little tale of illicit love
and treason and revenge, Nikolai realized he was
clenching his hands on the arms of his chair so tightly
that they hurt, and slowly, deliberately, forced them to
relax. He didn't dare look at Olga.

The stupid, stupid girl! Letting herself be used by a
traitor like Vasilev, with never a thought in her head for
anything but love—ha, *love* had had little enough to do
with it; plain, old-fashioned *lust* was the word!—betraying her princess and the royal consort to God only
knew what arcane horrors, all because she had some
adolescent picture of herself as an avenging heroine—

Nikolai stopped short, studying the trembling girl.
Despite himself, a whisper of pity stole into his mind.
Adolescent, indeed. If only the little fool wasn't so
hopelessly young! Vasilev, for all his stupidity, had been
an adult, knowing perfectly well what he'd been about.
But this wasn't even a woman, only a girl, a child—a
child whose parents should have taken one look at those
sultry eyes and married her off the moment she had
reached the age of fertility!

The *boyar* took a long, shaken breath. Guilty she

was, no doubt about it. But if Marya—who, with her glimmerings of magic, must have known about Olga and Vasilev—hadn't executed the girl, Nikolai wasn't about to shed her blood now.

Relieved, he said quietly, "Olga."

She stared up at him with wide, terrified eyes.

"Don't look at me like that, girl. You're not going to die." As the girl sagged, stunned and red-faced with relief, Nikolai added coolly, "You wished to enter a nunnery. I agree. It shall be seen to at once. Now, go."

Silently, rigidly, he watched Olga leave, escorted by two guards. Only when he was once more alone did Nikolai at last allow himself to collapse, head in hands, mourning Marya, child of his heart, whom he surely would never, ever see again.

EMELIAN STUMBLED WEARILY to a halt, surrounded by the whisperings of leaves and heavy, spicy green scents of growth and rich soil. God, he had been walking north and ever north all day with hardly a stop for rest, and yet there was no sign that he had made any progress at all.

Marya, Marya, I'll never get back in time to help you!

Back to . . . where? A prickle of unease ran up Emelian's spine, making him shudder. Some time ago, as he'd been trudging along, there had been a very strange moment, a sudden shivery dizziness that had sent him stumbling to the ground, as though he had fallen through some arcane curtain, feeling as though the very world had subtly shifted about him . . .

Nonsense. Though he had looked warily about often enough after that, nothing seemed to have changed. There was still nothing to see save forest, and forest, and forest.

At least the pull of the magicked amulet had led him to a narrow path, overgrown with thorny bushes through which he had to tear his way, leaving scratches on him and bits of cloth on them. But following it was still far easier than fighting the denser wilderness on either side. The path meandered a bit, like a deer trail, but despite those occasional twists back upon itself, it seemed to be leading almost due north.

Emelian frowned, his peasant-trained eyes noting something a little disconcerting: while the bushes overhung the path in normal foresty fashion, the actual surface wasn't overgrown by so much as the smallest of weeds. Something odd about the soil, no doubt. Or maybe the bushes cut off too much light for anything to be able to grow beneath them.

Of course, the color of the path was a little odd, too: palest tan. Not the shade of normal earth at all. And there was a remarkable smoothness to that surface . . . Almost an unnatural smoothness.

Magic, whispered a superstitious little voice in his mind. Maybe the dizziness wasn't imagination. Maybe this isn't quite the human world anymore—

"And maybe I'll do something really stupid," Emelian muttered. "Like running away from good fortune and trying to hack my way through wilderness. Bah."

Enough fancy. The night was coming on: though the sky, glimpsed through gaps in the leafy ceiling, was still a bright, cheerful blue, Emelian knew from experience how quickly the forest could darken to black. A chill was starting to rise from the swiftly cooling earth, and he shivered. No help for it: he was going to have to make camp as best he could—a camp without supplies, without the means of catching dinner, without even a decent blanket to keep off the chill.

Physical discomforts, Emelian reminded himself, trivial things.

And what Marya must be facing was far, far worse . . .

As long as Emelian had been struggling his way along, there hadn't been time or energy to spare for thought. But now—how helpless he felt, trudging along like a peasant to market, while all the while she—she—

"Ah, God, Marya . . ." It was an anguished whisper. "Will I ever hold you again?"

To FLY, ah, to fly! Was this what Cousin Finist felt, soaring down the sky, this wild, wondrous freedom? Even though she felt nothing physical, even though she only vaguely sensed the cool, silken air sliding past her intangible self, Marya, racing fiercely on the winds, hunting Koshchei, knew how all too easy it would be to lose her hold on humanity, to simply soar—

But . . . what about her body, back there in captivity? Marya supposed it would be safe enough from any physical harm: no hungry wild thing or human peril was going to get past the Deathless's sorcerous defenses. As for anything else . . . The princess couldn't for the life of her remember how any of those tales of astral adventures ended. She could only pray that her body, in its current, comalike state, wouldn't want for food or drink.

Of course, Koshchei would almost certainly realize what she had done, and drag her back to herself.

Not if I get to him first!

But . . . what *about* her body? A prickle of fear shivered its way through the exultation. Now that she thought about it, from everything Marya's father had ever told her about astral selves and the like, there was supposed to be some manner of silvery thread linking spirit and body. Yet, when she looked warily back over her shoulder, she saw nothing of the sort.

I . . . can't be dead . . . ?

Nonsense. Of course she wasn't dead. She had left her body breathing freely, hadn't she? Besides, judging from every occult tale she had ever heard, no ghost could travel so easily, or so far, from the site of its death. No ghost could hold fast to mortal memory, either, or to such sharp, clear emotions as her storm of hate and grief and—

Akh, Koshchei! Where was he? And why had he left her, his longed-for captive—if not to take on someone the Deathless considered a greater foe? Someone, presumably, of her own kin, but with greater Power . . .

Finist.

Koshchei must surely be off to Kirtesk to battle the only one of her kin who could ever be a danger to him. Magical Cousin Finist.

Indeed. Now that the first mad thrill of flight was wearing off a bit, Marya found herself aware of a *feeling*, a pull. As she gave in to it, she found herself tugged forward like a child's kite in the wind.

Koshchei.

But . . . Kirtesk didn't lie in this direction. To judge by the sun, she was heading due north!

Odd. The land below her wasn't all that far from Astyan, yet it didn't look at all familiar. Forest, yes, but the proportions, the mix of trees, was all wrong, and— A strangeness rippled through Marya's immaterial body, almost as though she'd crossed an arcane boundary, slid through a gateway out of normal, prosaic time—

But the forest continued on in its unbroken progression of greenness, as it had all along, as did the narrow path.

The path that she hadn't noticed till this very moment, for all that it stood out against the green like a pale tan ribbon. The path that ran over slopes and under bushes, almost directly north, without a single hole or rut to mar its narrow smoothness . . .

Magic. Marya *felt* it with a renewed shiver. Not the darkness of Koshchei's Power, not like anything she'd ever sensed before, but undeniably magic just the same.

Where was it taking her? She was being pulled forward more strongly than before. And yet she wasn't afraid. Whatever this compulsion might be, there was nothing of Koshchei's evil to it, or of hatred, or of revenge. There was only this need to fly northward, following the pale, magical path towards:

"Emelian!" It was a shout of sheer astonishment.

But . . . it couldn't have been so loud at that, because

Emelian apparently hadn't heard it. He continued to sit where he was, there on a rock beside the path, his head down in dejection, and never even stirred. Marya came hastily spiralling down to his so-familiar, so-dear figure.

How could she have ever doubted her love for him? Heart singing with joy, she cried out:

"Emelian! My dearest, my own, you're alive!"

But still he didn't look up.

"Emelian? Can't you hear me? Emelian!"

Marya reached out a hand to shake him—

But her hand passed right through his arm. She shrank back with a gasp of horror. Dear God, of course! No wonder Emelian couldn't hear her. As long as she remained in this bodyless state, he couldn't hear her, or see her, or touch her.

She was less than a ghost to him.

XXIII

SHADOWPLAY

EMELIAN STRAIGHTENED. Odd . . . Though there wasn't another human soul anywhere in sight, just for a moment he could almost have sworn Marya was with him, whispering words of love in his ear.

Wonderful, he thought. *Now I'm hearing things.*

Wearily, he got to his feet. Time for sleep, if not for dinner. Emelian searched the forest on either side of the path, trusting the amulet's pull to keep him from getting lost, till he had found himself a level, sheltered spot under a larch. If he broke off enough of the springy branches and piled them up as carefully as the peasant folk near the old estate of his boyhood days had taught him, he could at least make himself a reasonably comfortable bed for the night.

Emelian reached up to close a hand around a likely branch. But after a moment, he lowered his hand again, empty. Somehow, he just didn't want to damage any of the trees.

Emelian shook his head, bemused. At any rate, he did have flint and steel with him; if he wasn't to have a bed, he could at least build himself a nice, cozy fire—

No, he couldn't. There wasn't any firm, logical reason for it, but again, somehow he knew that building a fire amid this forest, no matter how careful he was, was . . . wrong.

A little prickle of unease raced up Emelian's spine. These weren't *his* ideas . . .

Forest magic.

Feeling suddenly as though he was only here, unharmed, on sufferance, Emelian sighed and said aloud, not quite sure who or what might be listening, "All right. You win. I'll not harm anything, my word on it."

No answer.

But when he curled up under the larch, Emelian found a low, glossy green bush fairly covered with bright red berries. Warily, not sure of their type, he tasted one, then another, and another.

Delicious.

Belated caution made him pause. They *might* be poisonous— No; if the forest was offering him a kindness, he would accept it without worrying.

"Uh . . . thank you," he called to the forest and whatever was within it after he had eaten his fill (and prudently left a good many berries still on the bush). With the edge of his hunger assuaged, Emelian closed his eyes. He was too weary to feel the hardness of the earth under him, too weary to do anything but drift off to sleep . . .

MARYA, disembodied, hovered protectively over her sleeping husband like a mother with her child. The physical darkness was no barrier to her astral vision.

But she and Emelian weren't alone.

Staring at her coolly, plainly able to see her even in the darkness, even in her nonphysical form, were the twilight-hued eyes of what could only be *viliye*, nonhuman forest women of a race ancient as the *leshiye*-breed and just as dangerous—more dangerous to any man who chanced to catch their fancy or rouse their unpredictable anger.

They shall not touch Emelian, Marya thought defiantly, struggling not to let herself be cowed by their inhuman beauty.

The *viliye* were tall, slender, graceful, their pale elegance swathed in soft gowns the colors of the twilight shadows, their hair long, dark clouds about them. They fairly radiated Power, but it was a magic so old, the basic Power of forest and earth, that Marya, in her city-bred innocence, had thought it lost to the world long ago.

"Not lost."

The princess bit back a yelp. She hadn't realized she'd spoken the last aloud—or that the *viliye*, unlike human-kind, could hear her. The softest of laughs whispered from the shadows, and one *vila* repeated:

"Not lost." Her quiet, cool voice still held within it a hint of perilous alien humor. "Merely . . . re-treated."

From humanity, Marya guessed, unlike the sly, crafty *leshiye* who *were* the forest they inhabited and all the mischief within, who delighted in mocking tricks. No, the elegant *viliye* had retreated from humanity's smoke and noise and cruel, magic-slaying iron to this ancient realm outside the human world.

Fighting her growing panic, Marya glanced down at her sleeping husband, then defensively up at the watching *viliye*. *"He means no harm."*

"We know, magic-woman."

"I'm not a . . . well, yes," Marya added uneasily, *"I suppose I am."*

"We have no quarrel with him. For now." A touch of inhuman humor rested in the quiet words. "A *leshy* has aided him. And he shows the forest proper courtesy. But why do you and he travel here?"

Marya hesitated. *"I don't know,"* she said frankly. She bent over Emelian, stalling, then straightened with a puzzled frown. *"Someone has added a new enchant-ment to the amulet I gave him. Not Koshchei—"*

"Koshchei." The inhuman voice had gone so cold and hating that Marya couldn't help but shiver. "Forest-foe, life-foe that he is," one *vila* murmured. "He has passed this way once, to visit Vyed'ma, Hag of the Rocks. He shall never be granted passage again."

Vyed'ma? Marya knew the name only dimly, from half-remembered tales of magic. A witch, wasn't she? A creature of Old Magic? *"Ah . . . yes,"* she said vaguely. *"Exactly. We—my husband and I—are Koshchei's enemies, too. And I suspect,"* she added in sudden inspiration, eyeing the amulet again, *"that that new magic was added by someone else who hates the Deathless: my cousin, Prince Finist of Kirtesk."*

The *viliye* stirred impatiently. "That is nothing to us. We have no quarrel with your mate, as we say. Or with you, magic-woman." A delicate pause. "For now."

The glowing eyes vanished, two by two, as the forest women stole off into their realm. "But wise your mate was," came the fading words, quivering with menace, "to heed our warnings."

The *viliye* were gone. Marya and Emelian were alone.

No. Not quite, the princess realized with a start. Peering out from behind trees and through bushes were dozens of small wild things, attracted by the *viliye's* presence, magical little creatures in a bizarre profusion of shapes and sizes, some standing upright, looking almost like tiny human men and women, some on all fours, almost purely animal save for the gleaming of intelligence in their eyes, some with no apparent limbs at all. Marya caught glimpses of grey or brown or even green fur, of wings feathered or leathery, of forms to which she could put no name.

All the beings were alike in one thing, though: they all stared back at her with bright, shy, curious eyes.

Marya forgot her fears. She knew that the forests of her own experience harbored such sprites; she had even counted herself lucky enough to have glimpsed one or two on rare occasions. But she had never seen so many of them gathered together at one time.

"You aren't used to seeing humans, are you?" she asked, and bit back a laugh as they vanished with squeaks of fright. But curiosity was too strong for them; after a moment, they poked their odd little heads out of hiding once more.

At least, Marya knew, these creatures were totally harmless. And they were company of a sort. Particularly since she suspected she wouldn't need sleep in this disembodied form any more than she would need food or drink.

Settling weightlessly beside Emelian, Marya smiled at the curious little forest-things, and waited for the night to pass.

XXIV

DEBATES AND BATTLES

"No, BOYARS." Regent Nikolai's voice was firm. "The girl wishes to enter a nunnery, and so she shall."

"But—Nikolai!" Dimitri protested. "We're not talking about a serving girl who stole a loaf of bread. Olga was the mistress of Vasilev, an out-and-out traitor to the crown!"

"So he was. And he paid for his crime."

"But she was his *mistress!*" Dimitri glanced at the other members of the Inner Council, challenging them to argue. "I'm not spreading gossip; it's fact. My wife spoke with the girl, and Ludmilla can get the truth out of anyone."

A ripple of laughter swept around the Inner Council, dying at a cold stare from the Regent.

"No one is arguing the point, *boyar.*"

"He was a traitor, Nikolai," Dimitri repeated impatiently. "And that makes her—"

"A fool. A silly little scatterbrain who made mistakes more from lust and petty malice than genuine treason. I will not take her life."

"But the law—"

"I will not take her life!" Nikolai glared at the Council members, seeking resistance, and his stare locked with Dimitri's. For a long, tense moment no one moved or spoke. Then Dimitri, fuming, dipped his head to the

Regent in reluctant submission. Nikolai nodded, satisfied.

"The matter is settled," he said. "The girl leaves for the nunnery I have chosen within the week. Now, *boyars*, unless there is some further business anyone wishes to propose . . . ? No? Then I proclaim this session ended." He got to his feet, and the others followed suit more slowly, stealing wary looks at each other. Nikolai ignored them. "Good day, *boyars*."

"WELL, I say he's finally done it!" Dimitri hissed at his fellow *boyars*, who had stayed behind after the Regent had left. "I say Nikolai has finally overstepped all the bounds of his authority! Putting the girl in a nunnery—"

"Why not?" *boyar* Basil asked quietly. "To me, it seems a perfect solution. Declaring a pretty young girl a traitor, having her beheaded in public, with everyone forgetting the treason and seeing only the pathetic young victim—now, wouldn't *that* win loving support for the throne? No, this time I think Nikolai is right: far better to bury the girl secretly, as it were, behind the walls of a saintly prison."

"But, dammit all, Basil, the law insists—"

"The—the law insists," interrupted Yaroslav, tripping over his words in his haste, "that a condemned traitor be 'removed forever from the eyes of the world.' Granted, we all know that really means execution, but if you follow the exact wording of—"

"What's this?" Dimitri whirled on the young man in fury. "Has the boy suddenly turned into a greybeard, nattering about points of order?"

"Now, I hardly think—"

"Then don't speak!"

"*Boyar* Dimitri!" gasped Yaroslav. "You go too far!"

"Do I?" Dimitri glared at him with such savagery that the younger man flinched. "Do I, eh? What of you? You challenge every point I make!"

"Oh, I don't—"

"I mention the princess's marriage being a mistake:
you argue. I mention her consort: you defend him. I
bring up the very justifiable point that Nikolai is trying
to take over the throne—"

"He's not!" Yaroslav clamped his mouth shut, then
started anew, in a determinedly calm voice. "Look you,
this isn't the time for hasty decisions. I know you're on
edge; we all are, but right now the commons depend
on us. We mustn't start quarrelling—"

"Don't patronize me, boy."

"Dammit, I'm not a boy!"

"No?" Dimitri moved to stand nose to nose with the
younger man. "Then what are you, eh? A fool? Or—
are you challenging me, *boy?*"

Yaroslav's mouth dropped open. "To a *duel?* Good
God, man, no! We—"

"Then keep your mouth shut, youngling, and show
some respect to your elders!"

"I—I have as much voice on the Council as any other
boyar!" And I . . ."

But Dimitri was already sweeping angrily out the
door. Yaroslav looked at the remaining *boyars* in dismay, hands out in helpless supplication. But they refused to meet his gaze.

". . . AND THEN he as good as called me a coward."
Yaroslav paused in the midst of shedding his clothes,
too hot-tempered to bother with servants, gesticulating
with a shoe. "Dimitri practically challenged me to fight
him. And I—I could do nothing! As a *boyar* of the Inner
Council, I had to just—back down! Dammit, Elena, I'm
not a coward, or a fool."

"I know, love." His wife was already settled comfortably in their bed, blanket pulled up about her against
the chamber's chill. "Yari, that shoe has done you no
harm. Put it down, dear heart, and come to bed."

Yaroslav glanced down at the shoe in his hand, aware
of it for the first time. Face reddening, he let it drop,

then turned to look at his wife. Akh, lovely . . . her
eyes so warmly blue in the candlelight, her long yellow
hair so silken against the blanket's wool, no more silken,
though, than the perfect, pale skin of her bare shoulders, and the curve of her sweet breasts, hinted at there
where the blanket's edge had sagged . . . Stunned by
the impact of mingled love and lust, the young *boyar*
forgot his anger. Smiling, he moved into his wife's embrace.

BUT LATE THAT NIGHT, Yaroslav lay awake, Elena cra-
dled in his arms.

She stirred, blinking sleepily. "Yari? What's wrong,
love?"

"Elena, Elenishka, I can't forget what happened in
that council."

"You're not still angry?"

"No . . . Astyan is more important than my pride.
But . . . Elena, we nearly came to blows in there!
What's happening to us? Without Princess Marya, or
Emelian— None of them even mention him, none of
them care what happens to him."

"But you do."

"Of course I do! He's my friend. But I . . . have to
face facts. Suppose neither of them ever returns?"

"Nikolai . . . ?"

"Nikolai's a good, honest man. But I don't know
how long he could hold the throne in peace. Sooner or
later he and Dimitri would surely fight, or some of the
other *boyars* try to depose him . . . Astyan would be
leaderless while they battled. And then who would see
to our defense, our trade, our very survival?" Yaroslav
fought down a convulsive shiver. "I've studied history,
love, I've seen what happens to a land that loses its
leadership. Astyan might be torn by civil war, or—or
destroyed outright by invasion—"

"From whom, dear? We're such a little land. We have
no enemies."

"Akh, Elena! What we have is fertile fields, good

water, and access to no less than two trading routes. Realms have been desired for less. There are always ambitious princes, land-hungry second sons looking for principalities of their own—never mind. It doesn't have to be invasion. We could be destroyed by something as simple and disastrous as drought or famine, because with no one strong enough to guide us—'' Yaroslav broke off with a cry of pain.

Elena twisted about to kiss his cheek and give him a hug. ''Yari, Yarishka, don't worry about the future. With God's help, everything will be all right. You'll see.''

Yaroslav bit back a hopeless groan. Dear Elenishka, so innocent, so trusting . . .

So . . . naive.

His arm about his wife, Yaroslav stared out into a future that looked unbearably bleak.

XXV

ENEMIES

FINIST STOOD atop the walls of Kirtesk, his Power rippling like an arcane wind about him, and watched with psychic vision the approach of his enemy.

The long, anguished night of waiting and preparation was over at last.

Now that the moment of battle was actually here, the prince found that any fears and doubts had left him.

He had already used magical discipline to close his mind to the perilous distraction of worry about his wife and his people. The Deathless would hardly waste time destroying the fields; planting could continue after this battle was done. The peasantry had fled, at their prince's warning, into the security of the forest, where Koshchei dared not tread. The Pact should keep them safe. Maria and the people of Kirtesk were sheltered within the city, as protected as they could be so long as he lived.

And he thoroughly intended to survive.

Koshchei was radiating a cold cruelty all the more chilling because it was totally devoid of human evil: that simple indifference to pain or anguish told Finist plainly what would befall his wife, his people, all those the prince loved, if the Deathless prevailed.

Finist grimly shut his mind to those chill insinuations.

Closer, he urged the Deathless silently, *come just a little closer . . . Yes.*

Quietly Finist murmured to the wind, calling, cajoling, *Come to me, come* . . .

Somewhere, far beyond the physical, elemental presences stirred, curious.

Come to me, come . . .

A breeze rippled the still air, died, then began anew. Not enough. Finist began his summons again, knowing he could never force those basic entities of air to act against their will; no mortal could. He could only hope to tempt their rousing curiosity. And this time his cajoling words were edged with Power, fierce with will: *Come to me, come!*

Koshchei was speeding ever closer. In another moment, Finist would have to abandon this spell and try another—

The elemental presences decided, all at once: yes. And the wind came. Roaring, it nearly tore the prince from his perch before he could guide it and shape it and send it on as a savage, whistling spear, straight at the foe.

KOSHCHEI'S LIPS TIGHTENED in a thin smile. There was Kirtesk, there was the enemy, Finist, too far still for mortal vision but clear enough to the Deathless.

Feeble Power, Koshchei thought with scorn.

It was limited, after all, by what a mortal frame could bear. A fragile mortal frame. But the Deathless had no such limitations. Swiftly he pulled his own magics to him, honing them, preparing to hurl them in contempt.

But suddenly the wind-steed quivered under him, shaking his concentration. As the being danced nervously in the sky, for all the world like a restive earthly horse, Koshchei snapped at it:

"What is it, fool?"

Oh, master, the air changes! Do you not feel—Aie, no, I cannot stand before it!

"What are you saying?"

But then the full fury of the wind struck them.

FINIST, hands clenched on the balustrade, watched his enemy go tumbling helplessly away out of the range of even psychic vision, the one wind-spirit powerless against the much greater force of the wind. Disheveled, hair whipping wildly about, the prince caught his breath. Would a fall from those heights be enough to smash Koshchei's man-shaped shell? Surely the battle couldn't be over so easily.

It wasn't.

Koshchei had managed to wrestle his terrified wind-steed safely to the ground. Now he was riding once more towards Kirtesk, the wind-spirit maintaining a speed far beyond anything known to flesh-and-blood horse.

Finist sighed. The wind-summons hadn't cost him much energy, but he dared not waste any strength, not with a foe with unknown reserves of Power.

Now let me try Kirtesk's defenses.

Quietly, the prince began a new incantation, murmuring certain ancient, intricate Words, then flinging out both arms in a commanding gesture. Walls sprang into being in response, encircling Kirtesk in a wide, fields-encompassing circle, walls invisible to nonmagical eyes but very real indeed, as many would-be invaders in Kirtesk's past had learned to their regret. These were barriers of pure Power, formed from a spell first cast by the founders of Kirtesk, strengthened and renewed by each successive prince. Finist *felt* their roused magic quivering all along his nerves. And he laughed, a falcon's fierce cry, to *feel* that their sudden eruption into being had trapped Koshchei amid them.

"Fight them if you can!" he shouted silently, hoping the Deathless could hear him. *"Learn this, old Deathless: I am not your prey! I shall never be your prey!"*

AS THE WALLS of force blurred into being, Koshchei tried frantically to turn the wind-steed aside. Too late! The walls closed about him with implacable power, abruptly holding him helpless as a fly in amber. And for the first time in countless ages, the Deathless knew a stab of genuine fear. No man, no woman, could destroy the shell he wore—but these genderless, nonliving walls might crush it beyond all hope of restoration.

Seething, the Deathless caught the whisper of the words the human prince threw at him, he heard the gloating. Akh, look at the man, standing so boldly on his city walls.

"Do you think me some stupid human *foe?"* Koshchei raged. *"Wait, little man, I will show you what you've truly tried to catch!"*

THOUGH THE PSYCHIC DISTURBANCE of the walls of force kept Finist from sensing the exact words of his enemy's threat, the sheer force of Koshchei's rage could not be checked. Before he could shield himself, Finist was engulfed by the inhuman will behind the savagery. He staggered on the narrow wall, clutching at the balustrade and thinking in despair:

And this *is what I thought to fight?*

All Finist could see was horror: hideous visions of his city laid waste, of his people casually tormented and enslaved, of his wife, his Maria—

But that last obscene image was so far beyond human bearing that Finist's mind rejected it. As the inhuman despair lost its hold on him, he cried out in silent defiance:

"Oh, no, old Deathless, you don't snare me so easily!"

With a surge of will, the prince slammed down a psychic wall of will over his mind, shutting out the last cold traces of the Deathless, angry at himself for letting the other nearly get under his guard. Particularly when the Deathless was his prisoner—

His prisoner?

Not any longer.

Koshchei had given up trying to fight his way forward. In those few moments when he had confused Finist's mind with despair, the Deathless had begun prodding his wind-spirit steed backwards, step by delicate way. The walls of force, meant to keep invaders out of Kirtesk, had no power to keep them in. And now Koshchei stood free of them once more.

"Did you think to hold me captive?"

Now that the Deathless was away from the psychic

interference of the walls of force, his words came as clearly to Finist as though Koshchei had spoken them in his ear.

Ghastly thought.

"And did you think Kirtesk defenseless?" the prince retorted dryly. *"Stalemate, old Deathless."*

"Your walls will not stand. This, I promise."

"You shall not enter. This, old Deathless, I promise."

Then Koshchei attacked in earnest. The prince gasped, nearly falling, at the sudden impact of the Powerstorm—cold as the Outer Dark—the Deathless hurled at him. Somehow Finist managed to straighten beneath that onslaught; somehow his inner shields held firm.

But hope died in that moment.

There wasn't going to be any gallant duel. There wasn't even going to be any traditional, understandable casting of spells back and forth. Feeling the coldness, the terrible cruel emptiness beating at the boundaries of his will, knowing that this alienness was the very stuff of Koshchei's inhuman soul, Finist knew he hadn't the faintest hope of puzzling out the shape of that Power, of putting a name to it, of understanding it.

Without that understanding, he could shape no effective spells of defense. All he could do was what he was already doing: hold the wall of his will firm as a barrier. Stand and defend, and hope the Deathless would overextend himself, burn himself out, or grow so frustrated by resistance that he turned aside before the prince's mortal strength crumbled and failed.

Emelian . . . The name slipped through his mind like a ray of light.

There could be no true victory against Koshchei without Emelian. Finist was certain of that, though he had no idea how or why.

And then Finist stopped thinking altogether. Under the never-ending assault of inhuman Power, he simply stood and endured, holding back that terrible tide by sheer, stubborn force of will.

XXVI

ENCOUNTERS

EMELIAN AWOKE in the midst of green, sweet-scented forest springtime, stiff from sleeping on the ground and chilly from the dew, but with a feeling of *rightness* radiating all through him such as he hadn't known since that ill-fated day Koshchei had been freed.

He also awoke positive that someone was watching him. Someone warm and loving.

I . . . could almost swear it was Marya— Oh, that's impossible!

Nevertheless, for all that he felt like a fool, Emelian couldn't resist calling out softly, "Marya . . . ?"

"Yes, love, I'm here," Marya cried. *"Emelian, I'm here. Oh, please, can't you hear me? Can't you feel me?"*

EMELIAN SIGHED. Of course there hadn't been an answer. But even though he hadn't really been expecting one, the young man felt an absurd twinge of disappointment.

Yet the sense of being watched remained. With a shrug of impatience at himself, Emelian set about looking in the tangle of forest all around him, and found nothing but more berries and a crystalline spring.

See? Emelian told himself wryly. *No one's here. Of course not.*

Yet the warm sense of well-being persisted while Emelian shook himself dry of dew, working the kinks out of his muscles, then broke his fast with a long drink from the spring—its water cold enough to make his teeth ache—and a few more of the enticing berries. It persisted even as he oriented himself by the amulet and set out on his way northward.

Hey now, this was better! The bushes grew more widely separated now, far enough back from the path that he could walk without tearing skin or clothes. Relieved, Emelian tried to settle into the easy jog he had watched the peasant hunters use when they needed to cover ground quickly without wearing themselves out. But it didn't turn out to be so easy a gait for someone softened by life at court, and at last Emelian gave it up and settled for a steady walking pace.

But something just wasn't right here! How could he be feeling so good, so ridiculously cheerful and full of life while Marya was still trapped?

Warily, Emelian tested his worry about her, as a warrior prods at a wound, unable to resist even though he knows it will hurt. But now the pain seemed so remote the young man knew, with a single-minded certainty that at any other time would have amazed him, that for now at least, Marya was safe.

Safe as he, at any rate.

However "safe" that might be.

But the world around him was too beautiful for any thoughts of peril. Emelian inhaled a great lungful of clean, fragrant air, then exhaled, grinning. Surely the sky had never before been so intoxicatingly blue, or the leaves all around him so dazzlingly green? Mm, or the flowers so sweet?

Emelian shook his head. Either he was getting belatedly springtime-drunk, or there was something strange in the air. Something magical.

He stopped short, eyes widening.

Of course, magical! Magical, the way the bushes no longer blocked his path. The forest had evidently decided to allow him safe passage. Not that the forest couldn't suddenly reverse its opinion of him . . .

Eh, well, one thing he had learned from the peasants: *if they give, take; if they beat, run.* If the forest chose to give him kindness, no matter how short-lived, he wasn't about to argue.

With a courtly bow to the four directions and the unseen Whatevers that were almost certainly watching him, Emelian continued on his way.

MARYA HOVERED protectively and invisibly over her husband, pleased at his politic politeness to the Old Magic, aching to tell him so.

Ah, love, if only I could be with you in body as well as spirit!

This weightless nontouching, nonfeeling was beginning to make her nerves prickle. She had almost reached Emelian this morning . . . but of course she hadn't succeeded; he was no magician. Still, the sight of him, so near, so unreachable . . .

Marya sighed, and in a sudden burst of frustration, rushed on to scout out the land before them. Up ahead, the heavy mass of trees thinned out a bit: saplings rather than ancient, thick-bodied trunks; the brightness of sunlight here was startling after the dim green shadows. Saplings in turn gave way to a small clearing lush with knee-high grass.

Something snorted. Marya jumped, forgetting for a moment her safe, immaterial state. It was a horse, ears pricked, staring at her in astonishment. Marya raised a brow. No elegant steed, this, only a shaggy, chestnut-red farmhorse, the marks of harness still scarring sturdy legs and body.

"Now, how did you get here?" she asked him wryly. "I doubt there are any farms nearby."

It wasn't a difficult puzzle to solve. Cat-curious as all his race, the horse must have worked away at a latch till he'd freed himself, then wandered aimlessly till he'd reached this meadow. And, thought Marya with a grin, horses being supreme pragmatists, he hadn't questioned his good fortune, but had settled down to graze the lush, untouched grass.

Till now. He sensed her. He *saw* her in some mystic animal way. And while he wasn't exactly afraid, those flicking ears told Marya he wasn't quite easy about this human-nothuman, either.

"Don't worry, horse," Marya told him gently. *"I'm not going to hurt you."*

She made a shooing motion, clicking her tongue. The horse's ears pricked straight up. Then, with a nervous toss of his head, he began to walk; then, as Marya continued to wave her arms, to trot.

"Nicely done, horse," Marya called after him. *"Just keep heading south. I know someone who'll be very glad to see you."*

EMELIAN'S SENSE of well-being had slowly faded under the weight of renewed weariness. How far had he come? Oh, God help him, how much farther did he have to go? Every time he stopped for a rest, his mind kept conjuring images of Marya in terrible torment, while he could only go on walking and walking . . .

He stopped at the sound of approaching hoofbeats. A rider? Here?

No rider. A plain old farmhorse, red as a shaggy flame, was trotting purposefully down the path towards him.

"Well, hello, there!" Hardly crediting his eyes, Emelian reached out a hand. The horse obediently stopped, snuffling at him in friendly curiosity. "Someone must be missing you, for certain. But I don't know where that someone might be. Not a clue on you, or a scrap of harness, either. Still . . ." The young man grinned at this stroke of good fortune. "You're going to prove very useful to me, my friend. Ah, always supposing, of course, that you've been broken to riding as well as plow-pulling. Have you?''

The horse snorted as though in reply, and Emelian chuckled. "Now, how am I to control you? Ah, I know.'' Unknotting the sash from about his waist, the young man carefully tied the length of sturdy wool into a makeshift halter around the big, amiable head. "Let's see if this works.''

The horse very plainly wasn't used to the weight of a rider on his back, ears waggling back and forth in confusion. Emelian held his breath, only too well aware how inexperienced a rider he was. If this beast should fight him . . .

But after a moment, the horse accepted the unfamiliar situation and the familiar human scent without more than a token buck. Emelian, his legs stretched around the sides of the enormous barrel, had to laugh.

"A glamorous steed, you're not. And I must look more like a farmboy than a hero. But this will be a hundred times faster than walking!''

MARYA, SOARING SOFTLY OVERHEAD, shivered to feel the forest stirring. Aware of Emelian, uneasy, the lives within it were watching and whispering:

Human. He is human.

But he breaks no forest laws.

Not yet . . .

Human . . .

But Koshchei-foe, Deathless-foe.

Let him pass. Let him pass.

For now . . .

Marya shivered anew. The Old Magic could be so fickle, so quicksilver-fancied. If Emelian somehow gave offense, if the forest chose to rend him, there would be nothing she could do against it.

"*Emelian, be wary,*" she whispered. The farmhorse swivelled an ear around to catch her words. But Emelian gave not the slightest sign that he had heard.

BY THE END OF THE DAY Emelian had stopped smiling.
God, was there no end to this path? His legs ached from
straddling the wide equine barrel, and he shifted about
on the broad back, trying to find a less painful position.
At least they had covered three or four times the distance he could have managed on foot. The horse's stam-
ina was downright amazing; Emelian couldn't judge
time too accurately, what with the wide-branched trees
hiding the passage of the sun, but as far as he could tell
from his inner time-sense, and his aching muscles, and
for that matter, the stubble covering his cheeks and chin,
they *must* have been travelling all day.

Had they, though? The patches of sky he glimpsed
through the occasional breaks in the leafy roof were
still a dazzling blue. The light down here, the dim,
cool, greenish haze of normal forest day, showed no
signs of fading. He wasn't even hungry, though all he
had eaten so far was that handful of berries.

Enchanted berries? Emelian thought with a quick
grin.

But the grin faded just as quickly. What if his time-
sense wasn't distorted? What if the day didn't simply
seem longer? Glancing around at the unchanging forest
that held its secrets to itself, Emelian found himself
remembering peasant tales he would have laughed off
in more . . . civilized surroundings.

Could time really flow at a different pace in this forest? Emelian rubbed a hand thoughtfully over his stub-
bly chin. The *leshy* had told him:

"That is a strange realm; distance is different there."

The words hadn't made much sense at the time; he'd
been sure the *leshy* was only waxing poetic. But what
if the creature had been speaking the plain truth?

"Distance is different here," Emelian murmured experimentally. *"Time* is different."

Ridiculous! Time was time, not something that
stretched or shortened itself at will!

Just then, as though to taunt him, a butterfly blue as
twilight, large as his head, flitted across his vision, so

swiftly that Emelian, starting so badly he nearly slid off the horse's back, caught only a flash of—had those been its eyes, so bright, so full of . . . mischief? Could that possibly have been a laugh?

Oh, this was getting out of hand. He'd heard a snatch of birdsong, only that. Why, the horse hadn't even twitched an ear.

But a flicker of motion made Emelian turn his head sharply to the left. There was a quick glimpse of eyes peering at him from behind a bush; slanted, tapering green eyes like those of no animal he could name, eyes filled with definite intelligence and . . . malice? He blinked—

The eyes were gone.

Emelian hunched down on the horse's broad back, feeling sheepish. Maybe the *boyars* . . . weren't completely wrong about him. A man never quite outgrew his childhood, after all, and his had been spent around folk with a never-ending repertorie of old, pagan tales. Of course, the ones about the *leshy* had proven themselves true. But the rest—bah!

Just the same, he found his hand stealing up to nervously clutch his silver amulet. *North,* the amulet's warmth told him; and *north,* the path pointed. The too-smooth path, the too-clean path, the too-straight path— Emelian let out his breath in a long, shaky sigh.

XXVII

DARK DAYS

FINIST HAD long ago lost track of time, of place. There upon the walls of Kirtesk, Power ringing him round, he no longer had any conscious thought. All that was left to him was the will to survive, to protect, to defend . . . Dimly, the prince *felt* the forest calling to him, pleading, *Survive, destroy,* but the cry was so much nonsense: of course he meant to survive, if he could. Of course he meant to destroy the Deathless, if any mortal could.

The prince was unaware of his body's complaints. There was nothing as tangible as pain: there were no physical or psychic injuries involved in holding back the Darkness, only the weariness growing in bone and muscle held motionless while the mind within did battle. But Finist vaguely sensed that, left to himself, his mortal strength would by now be beginning to crumble beneath the endless assault. And without knowing he did so, the prince called upon the Power of the city's own protective spells, pulling it to him, joining it instinctively to his own, the force of it warm as hearthfire along every nerve and sinew, its essence his to command since his ancestors had created those spells.

But would even this enhanced Power be enough?

It would.

It must.

For Kirtesk's sake, there was no other choice.

KOSHCHEI THREW POWER AGAIN AND AGAIN against the merely human foe, and again and again felt that Power turned aside, a floodtide breaking harmlessly against an impregnable wall.

Impregnable? Impossible. The man was mortal; there must be a weakness. There *would* be a weakness, sooner or later, a crumbling from within as the human's mind or body gave way beneath relentless pressure. Koshchei, after all, could draw upon the endless reserve of the Darkness within and without, the primal Outer Dark in which he'd spent so much timeless time. What mortal being could resist? The magician's psychic wall, impressive though it seemed right now, would fall. And then . . .

Koshchei's smile was chill and sharp as ice. Finist's defiance was maddening, yes. But beneath the fury, the Deathless felt the faintest shiver of pleasure. How long had it been since anyone had tested his strength in full? How long since he had faced any genuine challenge? He would almost be disappointed when it was all over.

SILENCE HUNG over the princely city of Kirtesk, crushing silence broken only by the occasional wail of a baby— quickly stifled—or the flap of pigeon wings, loud as thunderclaps. The wood-paved streets and vast, cobbled marketplace were cold and empty as places of the dead.

Most folk in that city were staying safely home, doors and shutters bolted fast. Those folk who must do business outside did so with one eye cocked nervously at the city walls. There Prince Finist stood locked in magical battle. His hair blazed silver-bright, whipping out behind him in an arcane gale, but his tall figure was statue-still, arms outstretched. Power encircled him, shimmering like blue-white fire.

"If only we could do something!" It was a frantic whisper from Ivan the butcher, clenching and unclench-

ing his muscular hands around the haft of his meat axe.
"If only we could help him!"

Sasha the tailor, who was only out here with Ivan
because, crisis or no crisis, his family had to eat, shuddered. "And shake our prince's concentration? Get him
killed? And us and our families as well, if that damned
demon gets in?"

Ivan sketched a quick, pagan warding-off sign in the
air with one hand. "God, no!"

They were not alone in their fear. Within the city's
snug stone houses, nervous glances swept cozy inte-
riors. Nervous thoughts flickered:

Will the walls hold?
Why didn't I patch the mortar when I had the chance?
I should have reinforced the bolts.

But all the while, the city-folk knew only too well
that there was nothing they could do to fend off the
Darkness, should their prince fall.

WITHIN THE ROYAL PALACE OF KIRTESK, blazing white
and gold against the sharp blue sky, the Inner Council
of *boyars,* led by elderly Semyon, milled nervously
about the elegant Ruby Chamber.

"What do we do if he dies?" murmured a soft voice.
"The prince hasn't yet sired a child. Princess Maria
has no magic; by law she can't inherit the throne. What
happens to the succession?"

Semyon, who had been standing by the chamber's
window, staring intently at the psychic battle, whirled
in sudden anger. "Succession! If our prince dies, there
isn't going to *be* any succession."

"Uh, but Semyon," began *boyar* Andrei, "how can
we forget that—"

"Good God, man, *think!* That's Koshchei the Deathless, a creature as close to being a genuine demon as
ever might be! If Prince Finist fails, how long do you
think any of us are going to survive?"

"Surely you exaggerate the danger—"

"Do I?" Semyon drew a long, shaky breath. "I . . .

truly hope I do." The elderly *boyar* turned hastily to stare out the window before the others could see the glint of tears blurring his vision. *Akh, Finist, Finist . . .* "Merciful God, I truly hope I do."

STANDING AT THE WINDOW, Maria was unaware of her surroundings, even of her own fatigue and aching eyes. There was only Finist, so alone on the castle wall.

Ah, God, if only I could be there with you. If only I could do something, anything!

At least Finist wouldn't want for food or drink; he had once told Maria that the Power of the city-spells, if ever he should need to rouse it—as rouse it he had— would strengthen him as well as anything physical.

But what good is that? Maria cried in silent pain.

Finist was only mortal. How long could he last without rest? How long before his mind or will failed, and he . . . he died?

Maria's hand fell protectively to her stomach. Of course there wasn't any telltale curve yet; she couldn't even be sure she hadn't miscounted, or skipped a few cycles of the moon by chance or stress.

And yet, deep within her being, Maria knew . . .

Akh, Finist, I was looking forward to seeing your face as I told you . . . Now—oh, my love, will you ever see our child?

Would any of them?

Maria clenched her teeth, refusing fear. She was perfectly well aware that if Finist fell, she wouldn't survive him by very long; the prince's wife, bearing the prince's heir, would almost certainly be Koshchei's next target.

Only if she allowed it.

Maria drew in a sharp breath. Belief was a vital part of magic, Finist had told her that often enough. And yet, here she was, already half believing in failure—

"Damn you, *no!*" Maria shouted at the Deathless, eyes blazing. "I won't let you have my husband! I won't let you have my child! Hear me, demon! *Believe me!* You shall not have them!"

The silence that followed seemed deafening. Maria slowly became aware that she was clutching the windowframe, and deliberately released her grip. Had the creature heard?

Those hadn't been empty words she'd shouted. She had fought too long and hard for Finist's sake already, even in the days before they were wed, to ever surrender. She had left her home, her family, for Finist. She had travelled through wilderness and fought strange beings, had even battled a sorceress for him.

She would not abandon him now.

Alone, Maria stared out at her husband, her love, where he stood on the city wall; stared, willing strength and greater strength into him.

XXVIII

THE RIVER

EMELIAN RUBBED a weary hand over his eyes. How could he doubt any longer that he had entered a land out of fable? Time really *was* different here—or perhaps this was a realm not quite *in* time. Darkness came when it would and vanished without warning, while the moon—

Ha. There shouldn't even be *a moon in the sky right now.*

But a moon there was, full and round, and most certainly not a mortal world's moon, because there wasn't a mark upon its smooth, silver surface.

Emelian lowered his hand to scratch at the stubble on his cheeks. If he'd needed further proof of strangeness, it was right here on his face: though days and nights had passed, at whatever weird speed, his emerging beard hadn't grown at all. It was, the young man thought uneasily, almost as though he were living outside of time, as though the forest was telling him, *We let you pass. We do not let you* in.

"That would explain why I haven't been getting very hungry," he told the horse. "I haven't been living *in* all the time that's been happening around me, merely . . . passing through." He stopped with a wry laugh. "And here I am, trying to explain what *I* don't understand to a horse!"

The animal lowered its head to snuffle at him in curiosity. Emelian laughed, and reached out to scratch under the shaggy red jaw. Poor beast! The horse wasn't too happy about this strange place, either, equine senses confused by alien time to the point where Emelian had to be careful to hobble the animal with his increasingly shabby sash whenever he stopped to sleep.

Not that he was sleeping well. By now, Emelian found his body so bewildered by too-long or too-short days that it couldn't tell just when it *should* be sleepy. Besides, there was an ever-increasing sense of . . . other presences. Not quite hostile, not quite friendly, the presences seemed to chitter or murmur in words he could *almost* understand.

Emelian sighed. Once he'd awakened to find a dead rabbit carefully laid out at his side. Stifling a yelp, he had sat up just in time to catch a fleeting glimpse of what looked like a foxy tail, and heard what might have been a fox's bark—or a mocking, ''With the forest's good wishes.''

Eh, well, at least the rabbit—once he'd gotten over his uneasy scruples, and found a portion of the path wide enough to safely build a fire, and deadwood the forest actually allowed him to *use* for a fire—had turned out to be quite tasty.

Emelian yawned, stretched, and yawned again, watching the darkness around him begin to brighten to greenish-grey.

Hey now, morning already, he thought wryly, working the kinks out of his muscles and shaking out his sadly travel-worn clothing as best he could. Dew hung from every leaf, cool and delicious when he licked up a few drops, and the air was heavy with the thick, spicy smell of wet vegetation. A few tentative chirps rang out through the stillness, and somewhere nearby a squirrel chittered briefly at him, then scurried off in a pattering of twigs.

Morning, all right. Wonder how the birds here puzzle out the proper times to sing.

If they were as magical as everything else around here seemed to be, they probably didn't sing at all. They probably discoursed like learned sages.

At least his muscles had toughened. Riding no longer left him stiff and aching. Neither did sleeping on bare ground.

About to vault onto the horse's back, Emelian stopped, remembering. Just before waking, he had had the most wonderful dream, all about Marya . . . Marya standing over him and whispering words of love, so sweet . . .

"Akh, enough. Come, horse. We must be on our way."

MARYA, following invisibly after, let out her breath in a long, soundless sigh. God, how she longed to touch Emelian, to touch anything! If it wasn't for the horse, who knew she was there, or the little magical creatures, who sometimes spoke to her, she would have wondered if she'd begun slowly fading away . . .

Marya forced down a shiver. There had been times lately, usually during the night, when she was so alone from anyone human, when depression would all but overwhelm her, times when she was sure there was no escape for her, for Emelian. But, *dammit*, she was not going to give up so easily! Particularly not now that she seemed to have found a way to speak to Emelian—and have him hear her.

It had been an accident. She had only intended to talk to Emelian, as she had every night, to assure him of her love, to assure herself she still did live. But . . . somehow last night, she had almost reached Emelian. He had heard her in his sleep, no doubt about it, even though she hadn't managed to give him a true message.

If only he hadn't awakened so soon! She had nearly puzzled out the proper method of dreamspeaking.

Tonight, Marya promised herself. When his waking mind abandoned its defenses into slumber . . . *Tonight I will speak to him again, and he* shall *hear me.*

* * *

"BEWARE . . ."

The whisper came from all around them, making Emelian and the horse both start. As the animal snorted, Emelian looked helplessly around, seeing only the never-changing forest. "Beware?" he echoed. "Beware *what?*"

"You shall see . . . Soon enough you shall see."

The words broke off in a harsh little giggle and the sound of a small body scurrying away through the underbrush. The forest fell innocently silent once more.

Emelian sighed. Were they never going to grow weary of this prank? This was the fifth such warning he had received today, with never the slightest hint of what it was he was supposed to be wary.

"A jest," he told the horse. "The forest beings have decided to play 'tease the human.' I suppose I should just be glad they're only playing games, not— Hey, now, horse, it's all right. He, she, or it is gone."

The horse continued to snort, prancing nervously in place. Emelian reached down to stroke its neck, murmuring soothing phrases. But the wind changed about from the left to blow directly towards them—and borne upon it was the faintest taint of smoke.

Emelian's first, panicky thought was, *Forest fire?*

But common sense prevailed. Of course there wasn't any forest fire. The forest around him would hardly be so tranquil if it was in danger from its greatest foe.

"A campfire . . . ?" the young man wondered aloud. "Or the smoke from a chimney?"

God, maybe he was coming to the end of this alien realm. Maybe there was a farm up ahead, and good, normal, *human* farm-folk.

With a shout of glee, Emelian urged his reluctant horse onward.

MARYA, unable to smell smoke in her immaterial state, had no idea what had so excited her husband. But she'd heard the forest creatures, giggling at their own cleverness, call out warnings to him. It would never have occurred to the alien, whimsical minds that the human wasn't at all magical, that something harmless to them might mean genuine danger for him. Hastily, she rose into the air, struggling against the wind, then rushing forward to see for herself what lay ahead.

And what Marya saw made her stop in midair. *Oh, Emelian, how are you ever to get past* that?

She went soaring back to him almost as swiftly as thought, calling out to him with all her might:

"Emelian, beware! Beware the river!"

"Beware!"

Emelian shook his head at the faint, tickling intrusion. Yet another vague "beware," eh? Another prankster?

"Beware . . . river . . ."

"River? Ah. Beware the river, is it? Getting more specific with our jest, are we? Well, I'm not going to—"

Just then, the forest broke off in a steep embankment. The horse skidded to a stop barely in time, going back on his haunches in a desperate rear. Caught off balance, Emelian yelled out a frantic:

"Hey—whoa!"

Emelian snatched at the horse's mane, but the strands, slick with sweat, slid out of his grip. As the animal lurched back to safety with a sudden mighty heave, Emelian went flying off the sweat-slippery back and down the embankment. He caught one quick glimpse of what lay below, and twisted, clawing at the crumbling soil, trying frantically to slow his fall. Sure he was about to die, Emelian flung out a desperate hand— and felt it close about a tree root projecting out of the embankment. He clamped down with all his strength. His body slewed wildly around, its descent stopped so sharply his arm was nearly jerked from its socket. For a moment, he hung helplessly by one hand, gasping.

There was a creaking, ripping sound, and earth came

pelting down on him. Emelian craned his head back and saw that the root was giving way. It couldn't hold his weight, it was going to tear out of the earth and let him fall—

With a burst of panicky strength, Emelian hurled himself upward, scrambling and clawing his way up the embankment, back to the forest and safety.

For a time, all he could do was lie still on the nice, flat forest floor, hardly believing he was still alive. But at last he struggled to his feet again, scraped and shaking.

The horse, naturally, was gone. Emelian didn't blame the poor animal. What beast would willingly face . . . that?

Emelian turned to carefully look down over the embankment's edge. Below him lay the river into which he'd nearly plunged.

The river not of water, but of swift-flowing, molten, dazzlingly bright fire.

XXIX

CONFRONTATIONS

ELENA, wife to young *boyar* Yaroslav of Astyan, sat in
the garden, her needlework unheeded on her lap, and
watched the other noblewomen at their gossip. After a
time, she sighed. Look at them all, so happy, so care-
free. Why couldn't she join them? Why did she have to
go on remembering Yari's bitter words last night? He
had been so worried about Astyan being doomed because the *boyars* couldn't get along. Akh, poor Yari!
Surely he had been exaggerating; Elena was constantly
concerned that the other members of the Inner Council
worked him too hard, because of his youth.

He had been exaggerating, hadn't he?

Elena sighed again. Maybe she wasn't as quick-witted
as some of the other *boyarinas;* she knew that. But she
wasn't stupid, either, no matter what everyone seemed
to think. Whenever you were small, and blonde, and
blue-eyed, nobody took you seriously. People were always smiling at you the way they would a child, or
telling you not to worry your pretty head about anything. And not a one of them ever asked you what you
thought about something, or how you would solve such
and such a problem.

And now there *was* a problem. Whether or not Yaroslav was right about the disasters he swore would happen to Astyan what with Princess Marya missing and

the Inner Council quarrelling all the time, she wasn't going to let the other *boyars* go on treating Yari the way they were.

Elena pursed her lips thoughtfully. Yaroslav wouldn't want her to do anything. She was pretty sure of that. Yari was a sweet, dear man, and she loved him deeply. But sometimes he could be just as infuriating and patronizing as the rest of the royal court.

So she wouldn't tell Yari anything. She would just take action. What could she do, though?

Then the answer struck her: she would go to see *boyar* Nikolai. He was the Regent; surely he would know what to do. She would go to him, and tell him everything Yari had told her about what was happening, and surely Nikolai would set everything to rights.

Elena folded her needlework carefully and set it aside, then got to her feet and went looking for *boyar* Nikolai.

NIKOLAI LEANED on the windowsill of his private chambers, staring out over Astyan without seeing a thing, and feeling older and more worn than he could ever remember feeling.

Akh, Dimitri, and here you think I'm power-mad, do you? God, I'd give this all up and go off to my country estate in a moment!

Except what good would running away do? No matter what the other *boyars* might think, someone had to take command, and even without official royal sanction, who else was there? Dimitri, all bombast and gall? That cold fish, Yuri? Naive young Yaroslav, for the love of Heaven?

Nikolai drew himself erect with slow, painful care. He had been named the Regent. And, by God, he would rule.

Whether Dimitri liked it or not.

A tactful rap on the door made him turn. "Enter."

Sasha, Nikolai's personal manservant, bowed respectfully before his master. "The *boyarina* Elena Mikhailovna craves an audience, my lord."

"Elena? Not her husband?"

"No, my lord. The young lady only."

Nikolai frowned. It wouldn't do for a young woman to be here alone with him in his private chambers. And she a married woman, too! One would think the chit would have more sense than to— No, this was innocent little Elena. The word *scandal* probably wasn't in her vocabulary.

"Ah . . . my lord?" Sasha prompted.

"Yes. Tell Elena Mikhailovna I shall grant her an audience in the Council chambers. And see that some trustworthy woman—akh, your wife will do—is there, as well."

". . . AND THEN *BOYAR* DIMITRI SAID something about—about your having 'overstepped the boundaries' of authority, and that . . ." Elena's voice faded to an embarrassed whisper. "And that you were t-trying to take over the throne—but I know that's not true, my husband told me so—and when poor Yaroslav tried to defend you, the *boyar* Dimitri called him a—a boy, and almost challenged him to a duel!"

With that, the young woman fell silent, blue eyes wide. Nikolai waited a bit, but when she said nothing more, he sighed and asked severely, "You are certain this is the truth?"

"Oh, yes, Regent Nikolai. Yari told me everything."

"And everything he says to you is the truth. No, no, *boyarina*, don't stare at me like that. I'm not questioning your husband's honesty." *Of course not,* Nikolai added silently. *Yaroslav is too young and inexperienced in the game of politics to be anything* but *honest.* "Thank you, my dear. You may leave now."

"But . . ."

"Don't worry, *boyarina*. Be sure I will take action on what you've told me."

He received a grateful flash of those big blue eyes. "I—I knew you would," Elena said, blushing. "Thank you," she added, then scuttled nervously away.

Nikolai stood watching her retreating back, then shook his head. He must take action, yes. Dimitri must be set in his place, and quickly.

And so he shall be, the Regent thought grimly.

DIMITRI, comfortably asleep in his wife's plump embrace, woke with a start as a tentative rap sounded on the door of the bed-chamber.

Fool servant . . . he thought groggily, and muttered, "Go 'way."

This time, instead of a genteel rap, there came a rude, emphatic banging. With a grunt of anger, the *boyar* sat bolt upright. Beside him, Ludmilla whimpered in sleepy protest. "Dimi, love? Who is it?"

"I don't—" Dimitri began.

But before he could finish, the door was flung wide. One of his body servants, Misha, came hurtling in, eyes wide with terror, to land in a heap on the floor. Soldiers stormed in behind him, fanning out around the bed. Ludmilla clutched the bedclothes protectively about herself, and Dimitri glanced about futilely for a weapon, any way to defend himself against—

Against members of the royal guard. As he recognized their livery, Dimitri sank back against the pillows in dismay. "What do you—"

"Boyar Dimitri Nestorovich?" asked a lean, stern-faced man who was, to judge by the rich embroidery on his heavy tunic, breeches, and high leather boots, the soldiers' captain.

"You know who I am! What is the meaning of this—this—"

"Forgive us for this untimely intrusion, *boyar.* " The captain bowed. "But we have our orders."

"Orders? Who sent you? Ha, it was Nikolai, wasn't it?"

The captain's well-schooled face showed not a trace of emotion. "Kindly dress, *boyar* Dimitri, and come with us."

"Now? Good God, it's the middle of the night!"

"We have our orders," the captain repeated apologetically. "If you will not come of your own will, I'm afraid we must take you with us as you are."

"Oh, Dimi!" Ludmilla reached toward her husband, and Dimitri patted her in absentminded consolation.

The captain bowed politely. 'Forgive me, my lady. But . . .'

"I know," Dimitri snarled. "You have your orders." Trying not to show his fear, the *boyar* drew himself up as proudly as one could while trapped like this in bed. "I shall come with you. Now leave this room and let me dress."

When the soldiers wavered uncertainly, the last threads of the *boyar*'s self-control snapped. "I will be with you shortly!" he roared. "Now, get out of here! Just—*get out!*"

As soon as they were gone, Dimitri got to his feet, his mind racing. Nikolai, damn the man, was probably going to have him imprisoned as an example to the others, or maybe even slain, slain for treason . . . Treason not to the throne, but to that—that— *Damn* Nikolai!

"My—my lord?" quavered Misha.

"Yes. Bring me my clothing." As the servant rummaged nervously about in the clothes chest, Dimitri frowned. "No, fool, not those things! I will wear my holiday garb."

"But—but—"

"Don't argue, man. Just do as I say."

He forced himself to stand rigidly still as Misha, trembling so badly the clothing nearly dropped from his hands, dressed him in his finest caftan of rich blue silk stiff with gold thread, glittering with gems, and his most elegant boots of red-dyed, golden-filigreed leather. Dimitri nodded. *If I go to face my death,* he thought with a certain desperate pride, *at least I go clad as a true* boyar.

Behind him, crumpled forlornly in their bed, Ludmilla wailed. "Be still, woman!" Dimitri began sharply, then sagged under the weight of her pain.

"Akh, 'Milla, dear love, don't weep. I shall be back, my wife. Farewell."

NIKOLAI SAT ALONE in the small council chamber in the royal palace of Astyan, a faint smile on his lips. Right now, Dimitri must be arriving at the palace, unheralded, unwitnessed, save, of course, for his escorting guards—guards who knew how to keep their mouths shut about this business. He must be expecting to be faced with the grand Audience Hall, with all its multitude of candles blazing and all the court gathered, yawning and wondering, to watch a *boyar's* downfall . . .

No public humiliation for you, Dimitri, Nikolai thought dryly. *Not this time.*

A knock sounded on the chamber's door. "Enter," Nikolai said, watching, impassively, as a guard opened the door, then stepped aside. Surrounded by his escort, Dimitri entered the chamber, back proudly erect but eyes flicking nervously. Nikolai noted the *boyar's* elegant garb, and nodded slightly, satisfied.

You're frightened, aren't you, Dimitri? You must be, to dress so well.

Nikolai held silent for a long, long moment, watching Dimitri. But soon the *boyar* would shatter, and that, Nikolai didn't want.

"Dimitri. Trite as this may sound, you are probably wondering why I've had you brought here."

"Wondering! My God, man, you invaded my home, you had these—louts drag me from my bed— All right, get on with it! What's it to be? How are you going to get rid of me?"

"I'm not."

"But—you—"

"Isn't this just the way you expected me to behave? Isn't this the action of a true tyrant?"

Bewildered, Dimitri opened his mouth and shut it without saying anything.

"No, Dimitri. Were I the despot you've called me,

you would already be dead, secretly, or have been publicly paraded through Astyan, a figure of ridicule, before being thrown into lifelong imprisonment.''

The *boyar* found his voice. ''Get on with it, Nikolai.''

''Ah, but I've already finished. I'm *not* a tyrant, or a usurper. I follow the laws of the land. And so, Dimitri, please forgive the drama of this . . . little lesson. I think you've gotten the point of it. Go home, man. Since I am not a tyrant, you are free to leave.''

''But—''

''And you aren't going to stir up more dissention among the Council, are you? In these times of trouble, that could be interpreted as an act of treason. Do I make my message clear? Good night, Dimitri.''

''Wait—you can't just—''

''I can. I did. Good night.''

With a wave of his hand, Nikolai dismissed the man. Fuming, Dimitri left amid his escort. Alone once more, Nikolai sat for a long while, legs outstretched, chin resting on steepled hands. Oh, Dimitri had gotten the point, no doubt about it. But could there ever be peace between them again?

More important . . . could there ever again be peace for Astyan?

XXX

UNSAFE PASSAGE

EMELIAN SANK WEARILY to the ground. The little silver amulet was still insisting in no uncertain terms that, yes, his path still led due north, and no, it was making no allowances for any minor obstacles that might block him.

Minor obstacles like a river of fire.

All this seemingly endless day, he had been travelling up and down along the edge of the embankment, searching without much hope for a convenient narrowing of the river, or some manner of bridge. But whether he walked east, struggling through the underbrush, or west, climbing sudden outcroppings of what looked like lumps of cooled lava, the river stubbornly refused to narrow. Nor was there any sign of a bridge, natural or magical.

Akh, well, if there was a way across, he wasn't going to find it today, because in the unpredictable way time had been moving around him lately, today was almost over. Without any warning, the day was starting to grow dark.

How convenient, Emelian thought dryly. *For once, the night is going to cooperate just when I'm tired enough to need sleep.*

Disheartened, the young man dragged his weary body under the shelter of a wide-branched bush and closed his eyes. For a time, he was too tired to relax, lying wide awake, lonely enough amid his alien surroundings to find himself even missing the warm, living company of the farmhorse.

Poor horse . . . he thought vaguely. *Probably still running . . . Probably gallop all the way back to the lands of men . . . God, wish I were there, too, and Marya . . . Marya . . .*

Bit by bit, consciousness slipped away.

MARYA HOVERED over her sleeping husband, close to screaming with frustration. If only there was something she could do to aid him.

He had to cross that river of fire, no doubt about it. Cousin Finist, for whatever reasons, had remagicked the amulet to point Emelian this way. And Cousin Finist wasn't the sort to send a man on a quest that couldn't be completed. There had to be a way for a mortal man to cross that river.

And . . . there was a way, Marya *felt* it. The answer was hiding at the edge of her mind, taunting as a sound not quite within hearing . . .

The princess took to the air, soaring over the fiery torrent without feeling its heat, grudgingly admitting the fierce beauty of that flood of blazing red-orange-gold. She flew low, sparks passing harmlessly through her intangible self, and searched with every psychic sense for a clue . . .

Ah! Wait, now . . . Marya swerved in midair, circling to pass back and forth over one particular spot. There was nothing to be seen if one stared at it full-on. But if she looked without trying to look, there was the faintest hint of a crystalline glitter spanning the river in a high arc . . .

A magical bridge, needing only a certain key to bring it into sharp, safe focus.

A key that Emelian held. Hastily she swooped back down to his side, bending over him.

If ever I needed to reach you in your sleep, love, it's now.

Was she reaching him? All at once he murmured, stirring in his sleep.

"*Oh, no, don't wake up,*" Marya cried.

Emelian murmured again, incoherently. But then he settled back into deep sleep. Marya, who was holding her breath, let it out again in a slow sigh of relief.

"Hear me, Emelian," she began again. *"You can. You must. Hear me, Emelian. Open your mind to my words, my love, and remember what I tell you . . . remember . . ."*

Over and over, Marya repeated her message, all through that long, empty night. At last, with the forest about her brightening faintly with the first grey light of dawn, she gave up, drained and weary as she hadn't been since first separating her essence from her physical self.

Had Emelian heard her? Would he heed her? She would learn the answer soon enough.

EMELIAN WOKE with a start, his anguished cry of "Marya!" echoing in his ears and confusion in his mind. Where was he?

Ah. Leaves. Forest. Emelian sank back again with a faint laugh. Nothing had changed. He still had the river of fire facing him.

And Marya had been with him only in a dream.

Emelian rubbed a hand across his gritty eyes. A dream, yes, but one that had been particularly realistic. Marya had seemed to be kneeling at his side, cupping his face in her hands . . . Emelian shook his head. He could almost recall the feel of her fingers, cool as mist against the skin of his face. Marya had been trying to tell him something, repeating herself over and over. Emelian blinked, trying to remember . . . something about the river . . . a bridge . . . She had given him specific instructions about crossing the river of fire by using the amulet to—

Emelian got to his feet, stretching. "What do I have to lose?" he asked the forest around him, and started for the edge of the embankment, to stand staring at the flaming flood below him. The air stank of sulfur, and he drew back, gasping. If that . . . thing below him was natural, then he was a fool. It positively radiated magic, ancient, primitive magic at its most basic.

And, because it was magic, he no longer felt silly holding up the little silver amulet, the amulet containing a lock of Marya's hair, three drops of her blood, and the power of her love, and waving it out over the river, holding his breath. Once, he waved it, twice, thrice . . .

With the faintest sound of glassy chimes, a bridge formed itself out of the air, a bright, crystalline bridge that glittered in the sunlight and threw off dazzling clouds of rainbows.

For a long moment, Emelian was too stunned to move. For all its bizarre composition, the bridge seemed solid enough, rising in a tall, perfect arch over the river. Whoever had originally spelled it into being had created it with an eye for beauty—and with reassuringly high railings.

Emelian swallowed dryly. The dream had been true, then. Marya had magically sent him a message. The charm of blood and love and Power gathered in the amulet had been strong enough to charm the bridge into appearing.

''Thank you, my love,'' he whispered.

But how long would a bridge built of magic remain real? Emelian had a sudden, all too graphic picture of it fading away again into air while he was only halfway across, leaving him to tumble helplessly down and down into the waiting flames—

Stop that! he told himself sharply, and reached out to tap a railing with a fingernail. The railing rang out with the clear, bright sound of true crystal. He set a tentative foot on the shining surface, then gingerly put weight on that foot.

So far, so fine. The bridge seemed solid enough. Emelian took a great breath and stepped forward, climbing the bridge's arch. It wasn't easy; his feet kept slipping, and only by keeping a deathgrip on the equally smooth railings was he able to pull himself along. The heat rising from the fiery river was enough to make him gasp, but every breath brought smoke and fumes as well. His legs were beginning to ache from the struggle to maintain his footing, and his hands were getting slick with perspiration.

Grimly holding onto an image of Marya, Emelian kept going. It became more and more difficult to keep his feet under him as the angle of his climb grew sharper near the top of the arch. But at least he was now high enough above the river to be free of the worst of the fumes and heat, able to gulp in lungfuls of clean air.

A little farther, Emelian urged himself, *just a little farther . . .*

He was at the top. He could actually stop and rest for a moment, enjoying the cool breeze, and easing the cramps in hands and legs.

The view up here was dizzying. Back the way he'd come there was nothing but the endless green of the forest, but before him loomed some of the grimmest, most primitive-looking mountains he had ever imagined. Rough, jagged and grey, they surged up like the fangs of the Earth.

And that's where the amulet's leading me?

But the journey wasn't getting shorter for the waiting. Before him, far below, was the far side of the river. He thought about the struggle that descending would mean, fighting the pull of the Earth with every step. Unless he . . . No, that was ridiculous.

Emelian stared more closely, and slowly he began to grin. The bridge didn't end in rock on the far side of the river, but in what looked like a mound of sand. An idea was tickling his mind, and the harder he fought to resist it, the more it itched.

Ah well, why not? Let him be impulsive one more time.

Letting go of the railings with delicate care—the last thing he wanted to do was slide all the way back down the way he'd so laboriously climbed—the young man carefully seated himself on the bridge's slick surface. With a whoop of defiant delight, he pushed off.

And like a child sliding down an icy hill, Emelian went hurtling forward, down the far side of the crystalline bridge.

XXXI

SPIRIT SONGS

SLOWLY A GROGGY EMELIAN RAISED his head, stretched out arms and legs. Everything seemed to be attached and functional, bruised but unbroken.

Wincing, he sat up, then froze as his senses reeled and his stomach lurched. Hastily, Emelian shut his eyes, waiting till he was sure he wasn't going to be sick.

God, that had been stupid, sliding down the bridge like that. Sand or no, he had hit with enough force to nearly kill himself.

A damnably stupid thing to do. If anyone from the Astyan royal court had seen him acting like a little boy, whatever might be left of his regal reputation would have vanished then and there.

Still . . . it *had* been a glorious ride—until the end— soaring down the sleek crystal like an eagle diving from the heavens. Emelian gave a sudden grin of defiance and got delicately to his feet, trying to ignore the new bruises. He brushed himself off and craned his head back, studying the mountains before him.

And I'll bet Vyed'ma lives at the top of the steepest, most dangerous one of all.

Emelian took a deep breath and began to climb.

HIGH AMID THE MOTIONLESS CRAGS: movement. A shape, jagged as the crags, stirred slightly, then froze once more.

261

Free us . . . ahhh, free us . . .

Pleas meant nothing to the mountain, to the mountain dweller. Eyes flat and grey as the naked rock drank in the light and returned none of it, staring . . .

He was there, the small mortal thing, there on her mountain, slowly climbing.

Seeking her? Few men dared. Those who did reeked of Smallness, of cramped little human places, cramped little human thoughts: weak mortal magic, weak mortal pride. They came to her in challenge, with their little thoughts of conquest, of Power-theft or treasure-theft, or of destroying in the name of Newness and narrow ways. And when they came, when they came . . . Ahh, sweet, their flesh, so sweet . . .

A thin tongue licked at stone-sharp teeth.

Yes, Vyed'ma said silently to the mortal, *come to me.*

A flicker of motion: Vyed'ma was gone to her home. Gone to prepare.

THE WINDS MOANED and wailed and whispered all around Marya. She shuddered, overwhelmed by the loneliness all around her, one small human self amid inhuman wildness—

No, it was more than mere human reaction. Marya's eyes widened as the shock of comprehension struck her. Carefully, she opened her new magical senses to the winds, all at once *feeling* with every bit of her roused Power the very real misery in their song. Dear Lord, these were no random swirlings of air! She *knew,* knew without the faintest shadow of doubt, that these winds were alive in their own elemental way.

Marya stood still and listened. The winds were singing to her, responding to her human Power. The winds were sending her a plea, a warning, a name, and she could almost understand it . . .

Akh, useless!

"I can't help you!" Marya cried in frustration, wondering if the spirits could even hear her. *"I'm sorry, I don't know what you're trying to tell me."*

Mountain . . . whispered the winds.

"Yes, I know this is a mountain, but—"

Mountain . . . Rocks . . .

It was so faint and drawn-out a sound she almost missed it.

"Rocks?" Marya echoed dubiously. "Well, yes, there are rocks all around us, but—"

Rocks, the wind-whisper insisted, and then, almost fearfully, *Hag . . .*

"A hag . . . ?" Marya was puzzled. Surely the winds couldn't be so terrified of some poor old woman living alone! But . . . a hag amid all these rocks . . . part of them . . . The princess frowned. Something was teasing her memory, something about a hag . . . a Hag of the Rocks—

"Vyed'ma?" Marya asked. "Surely she doesn't exist . . . ?"

But the air around her had gone utterly still when she'd spoken that name, Vyed'ma.

Now that her senses had been alerted by the winds, Marya recognized the Power surging all around her.

Old Magic. Earth Magic. Akh, nothing strange about it; this whole land fairly reeked of it.

But here the force of Old Magic was stronger than any she had ever known. She started to warily open her senses to it as she had to the winds, and that force tore through her mind, raw and primitive and no more to be measured in human terms of Good or Evil than the Earth was for thrusting up these mountains from its heart. Oh, God, it was overwhelming her, crushing the essence that was *Marya*—

In her panic, the princess slammed shut instinctive psychic barriers she hadn't known she possessed. All at once there was no one in her mind but herself.

For a time she could do nothing but shudder at the smallness of being mortal.

Vyed'ma was of that crushing Power, elemental as the rocks around her.

And Emelian was going to her.

"Oh, Emelian, no!" Marya swooped down at him, struggling to stop him. But his waking mind was shut to her pleas, and her attempts to block his path were as useless as the flutterings of a shadow.

"A shadow," she cried out, *"that's all I am, a shadow!"*

A shadow who didn't even dare stay by her husband's side. Should Vyed'ma sense Marya's human aura, her human Power, about Emelian, should she mistake it for his own, the Hag would surely slay him.

There wasn't anything Marya could do now, save watch and pray.

EMELIAN PAUSED on a steep slope to wipe his sweaty face and catch his breath.

At first the climb had seemed deceptively easy, a steady scramble up a tree-covered slope. Protruding roots and a jumble of broken rocks had made for treacherous footing, but at least there had been nice, sturdy branches to help him pull his way along. But as he had continued to climb, those branches had grown closer and closer to the ground. Now Emelian found himself walking amid a dwarf forest of shrunken trees, the lot of them bent over like a frozen wave, a clear warning that storm winds swept frequently down this side of the mountain.

Not that there was much he could do about it now. Emelian took deep lungfuls of air that didn't seem very satisfying and forced himself upward once more.

Gradually the miniature forest thinned out around him, leaving him alone in a world of jagged grey rock, broken here and there by splashes of red and orange lichen.

Emelian stopped again, looking around in bewilderment. He couldn't have climbed above the timberline so quickly!

Not in the mortal world, anyhow. Here, distance could be as deceptive as time.

Emelian glanced quickly up again, half hoping to see

that the mountain had miraculously flattened itself, or that somehow he'd made a magical jump almost to the top.

No, dammit. The looming mass stubbornly continued to loom.

All right, then, he told the mountain silently. *You won't give in. Neither will I.*

Grimly, Emelian forced himself upward. Icy winds came whipping down from the summit, at times gusting powerfully enough to nearly throw him to the ground. They carried with them the scent of snow, of death by freezing.

God, how had the sun managed to sink so alarmingly far in the sky? Night was nearly here, and if he was caught here, in the open— There wasn't any shelter to be had up this high, not even the overhang of a rock. There wasn't the smallest scrap of fuel for a fire. If he didn't manage to reach the top and get safely down the other side, he would surely die.

Gasping in air that seemed increasingly lacking in strength, Emelian struggled on. But at last, drugged by exhaustion and the lack of nourishment in the thin air, he passed beyond the point of pain and weariness into a trancelike state where there was no thought, no worry, only the need to keep putting one foot in front of the other, following the pull of the amulet.

Lost in that mindlessness, Emelian wasn't aware of reaching the mountain's crest. Seeing nothing, hearing nothing, he walked blindly forward.

And he nearly walked right into a tall, terrible Something.

Roughly shaken from his trance, Emelian staggered. A rock twisted under his feet and he fell awkwardly, fumbling for his belt knife because his sword was under him and he'd never get it free in time, twisting frantically about to stare up at the demon that spread its ragged black wings and plunged forward to engulf him.

XXXII

THE HAG OF THE ROCKS

FOR A LONG MOMENT, Emelian lay frozen where he'd fallen, knife clutched in his hand, waiting for the attack.

But there wasn't any attack. The demon didn't move, save for the random flutter of a wing.

A wing? Emelian blinked. Surely that tattered thing was only a cloak, while the demon itself was . . .

Sanity came flooding back into Emelian's mind, and he struggled to his feet with a shaken laugh, sheathing his knife. The "demon" was nothing more than a propitiatory offering left who knew how many ages ago: a horse's skull mounted on a stake, swathed in weather-beaten horsehide. As a boy, he'd once heard a peddler tell of long-ago pagan folk who had made such offerings to the gods of mountain and steppe.

Emelian looked at the offering again and shrugged. Eh, well, he didn't *quite* feel foolish about his fright. God knew the thing did look eerie, particularly in the fading light; there was something about the long skull, the empty eye sockets, that raised an atavistic prickling up Emelian's spine.

Akh, he was still so weary his thoughts weren't making sense. Where was he now, anyhow? He had reached the mountain's peak, and this rocky bowl, shaped like a long, narrow oval, was it.

But even though he was out of the worst of the wind, it wasn't much warmer here than the outer slope had been. Shivering in renewed cold, Emelian started forward wearily, hoping to find some crevice or cave in which he could huddle for the night.

God, he really was tired. The rocks all seemed to be watching him.

Then the young man realized with a small shock that they *were* watching, in a manner of speaking. Those long-ago nomads had carved crude forms and faces all over every available surface. This must have been a holy place for them.

Or . . . had it been a place so dangerous the nomads had tried to summon every god they knew for protection?

As Emelian moved down the rocky crater, the walls narrowed till the nomads' carvings surrounded him at close range, figures so weatherworn they could have been men or gods or demons. They were all the more eerie for being so worn: here a face seemed to writhe in frozen torment; there empty eyes seemed to stare at him in mocking hatred.

Stop that! Emelian snapped at himself. *Just keep going.*

If only it wasn't so silent up here, so oppressively still that even his footsteps seemed muted. The air was so cold it burned his lungs, and so clear it had no scent at all.

When Emelian saw another "demon" ahead of him, he almost sighed in relief. Just another nomad monument. Maybe it was an ugly thing, but at least it wasn't more unfriendly rock. Just another horse's skull, nothing to fear—

But this time a man's skull was impaled on a post, gaping at him in an endless silent scream. And judging from the shreds of skin and hair clinging to it, it hadn't been there very long.

Emelian's sword had flashed into his hand before he'd even been aware of drawing it. But the stubborn amulet

still insisted, *Onward. Northward.* To give up now
would be to fail Marya.

Looking warily from side to side, he went slowly on
down the rocky corridor, and passed another of the
grisly posts, then another, and yet another. Each bore
a human skull, some fresh, some yellowed with age; he
counted eleven in all.

Then the corridor widened into yet another valley of
rock. At its mouth stood a twelfth post. And this one
bore no skull at all.

At the far end of the valley stood a house of sorts, a
ramshackle thing of stone and bits of wood piled up
against the side of one rocky wall. But it *was* a house,
it had a roof, and he could see the wispy smoke of a
cooking fire spiralling up from that roof.

Vyed'ma's home? The house of some pagan priest or
grisly murderer? Emelian no longer cared. To be out of
the cold, to be out of the night . . . Sheathing his sword,
the young man stumbled forward as fast as his ebbing
strength would allow. Seen up close, the hovel was even
less prepossessing than before, windowless, its one narrow doorway covered by sheets of what looked like
badly cured leather. Emelian hesitated a moment, but
a blast of cold wind decided him, and he called out:

"Hello? Is anyone at home?"

Silence. Emelian drew breath to call again. But then
the leather curtain was drawn aside, and the young man
found himself facing the most extraordinary woman he'd
ever seen.

At least, he assumed it was a woman; there was nothing particularly feminine about her, not in face or squat,
shapeless form. Her rough features looked as though
they had been carved from the stone around her by a
particularly primitive sculptor: predatory beak of nose,
jut of chin and knife-edged cheekbones. And the eyes
. . . flat as rock, hard as rock . . . There was a world
of alien knowledge in those eyes, of strength and Power
without any tempering of pity, and after a startled instant, Emelian refused to meet their steady gaze.

The woman was shrouded in flapping grey rags. Her long, coarse hair was dull grey. The young man realized uneasily that even her weatherbeaten skin had an eerie grey cast to it: she really did look more like one of the nomads' statues come to life than anything even remotely human.

Vyed'ma.

He knew without a moment of doubt that she had been the one who'd set the human skulls on their posts. He also knew, seeing the thin tongue lick across knife-sharp teeth, what had become of the original owners of those skulls. But by this time, Emelian was weary beyond caution or fear. He needed rest and shelter, and this was the only shelter to be had on the whole mountaintop.

"Good evening to you, Old Mother," he said in his most courteous voice, with his politest bow, as if she were no more than one of the peasant women of his youth. "I regret bothering you. But the night is going to be cold out here. And I would truly appreciate any corner in which I might take shelter."

Vyed'ma stared, unblinking, but Emelian thought he'd seen the faintest flicker of amazement in the flat eyes, as though she wasn't used to courteous words.

No wonder, living up here. Eating anyone foolish enough to bother her.

He wasn't going to be foolish enough to say that aloud! "I'd be willing to work for my keep, Old Mother. Are there any chores that need to be done?" He straightened. "Is that a storeroom I see, there to the side of your house? Or a stable?" It looked more like a night-dark cave, but there were hints of what might have been stalls within. "I would be happy to tend your animals, or—"

"No! There are no animals."

"I didn't mean any offense, Old Mother."

"Why are you here?"

"I . . . beg your pardon?"

"To harm me? To slay?"

That startled Emelian. Granted, Vyed'ma was—whatever she was. Manslayer, at the very least. But she'd done him no harm. "Old Mother, believe me, I am no murderer!" A new blast of wind made his teeth chatter. "And—and believe me again, if—if I d-don't get into shelter soon, I will not be anything else, either."

A grey eyebrow raised. Vyed'ma stirred again, rocking slightly on her heels, plainly bewildered by this human who treated her with courtesy and did not fear her.

Who's too cold and tired to fear her, Emelian thought.

"Come," said Vyed'ma.

It was cramped within, and smoky; Vyed'ma plainly didn't believe in such effete luxuries as a chimney for her central hearth. The weak, flickering light did its best to show how the single room was full of bits and pieces of things, worked or unworked, piles of wood presumably scavenged from the lower slopes of the mountain, even the occasional shiny piece of metal—copper or bronze, never magic-hating iron—that could only have come from human travellers or raiders. There were always men foolish enough to go after what they thought was glory, and callow enough not to care what they had to do to find it. Remembering the forest dwellers, to whom human ideas of "good" and "evil" didn't apply, Emelian began to wonder if Vyed'ma had only been defending herself.

And then again, maybe she just liked the taste of human flesh.

Never mind. Time enough to worry when he got his strength back. At least it was warm in here, even if it did reek of hot stone.

Emelian sank down beside the fire.

Must be careful . . . stay on guard . . .

It was his last conscious thought for a time. Worn beyond bearing, Emelian lost his hold on caution, and slept.

VYED'MA STARED DOWN at the sleeping human in vague unease.

He did not act the way the others of his kind had

done, the ones who had rashly challenged her. The ones whose flesh had been so sweet. They had blustered to hide—or try to hide—their fear, or had stupidly attacked. But this human who smelled of youth and weariness had made no threat at all.

Vyed'ma's stony face creased in a slight frown. She knew well enough by now the acrid stench of human terror; he never could have disguised *that*. He genuinely had not been afraid.

The puzzled frown deepened. Vyed'ma had set this snare for him, turning this keeping-place-of-useful-things into a seeming of a dwelling place—as though she, Hag of the Rocks, had need of a fire's warmth!—yet the human had not questioned. No, the youngling had treated her with courtesy, open courtesy such as no human before him had ever thought to show, had entered freely, and had fallen asleep without a single qualm, as though he *knew* she would not attack him.

Vyed'ma stirred uneasily. Such courtesy, such certainty, such unpredictability gave her discomfort. Best to end discomfort in one swift blow, then feast—

And yet . . .

No human had ever treated her with courtesy.

Then, too, the smell of him was more than young. It was male, reminding her of certain . . . pleasures. For a moment, the solid, stocky form shifted, altered, a seeming of sleekness, of cool beauty-as-humans-saw-beauty upon it. There had been no flesh-delights for her since that thief, that Deathless, had stolen a wind slave and fled her, and for an instant Vyed'ma hovered on the brink of chill desire.

No. She knew enough about human-folk to realize there would be no delights, not while the scent of weariness still lingered about the youngling.

The seeming of cold elegance faded. Herself, Vyed'ma settled back with mineral patience to wait.

She would not kill him, this disturbing young man.

Not this day, at any rate.

* * *

EMELIAN WOKE with an aching head and a complete
sense of disorientation. This cramped and crowded
place didn't look like a peasant's hut. It didn't smell
like one, either: that unmistakable mixture of herbs,
vegetables, human and farmyard so familiar from his
childhood. Instead of that strong, warm, *living* scent,
this . . . room reeked only of dank earth and stone.

As did his hostess.

Emelian froze, trying not to stare, memory returning
in a frightened rush.

Vyed'ma. God, how could he have forgotten about
her, even for a moment? She was watching him with
her flat, unreadable eyes, face inhumanly composed, her
sturdy, solid form fairly radiating the quiet, cold, implacable strength of the mountain around them, reminding him of a predator waiting quietly for its prey to
make the first, fatal mistake . . .

And I entered her lair by choice!

But now that he thought about it, there hadn't really
been a choice: enter or freeze. And Vyed'ma had accepted his attempts at courtesy, so maybe he was still
safe. At least until she learned why he was here.

Akh, well, the inevitable could only be postponed
for so long.

Emelian sat up slowly, careful to make no sudden
moves. He bowed at the waist.

"Good morning, Old Mother. May I thank you for
your hospitality? I've slept wondrously well." Which
was true enough; he had been so weary last night, he
could have slept standing. "And now I must—"

"Why are you here?"

Emelian winced. Vyed'ma's voice was as hard and
rough as the rest of her. "Ah . . . Well, that's a long
story, Old Mother."

"Tell it." A thin tongue licked over sharp teeth.
"Briefly."

He doubted very much that the Hag was going to be
moved by Marya's plight, or by any appeals to the softer

emotions. He doubted Vyed'ma even knew what a softer emotion might be. Yet if he out and out asked her for one of her wind-spirits . . . Emelian remembered that one bare, skull-less post, and fought down a shudder. But, judging from the chill force of the Hag's staring eyes, this wasn't a good time to delay. So Emelian, commending his soul to Heaven, straightened as best he could in the cramped quarters, bowed again, and said in his most formal, courtly voice:

"Old Mother, your fame has spread even to the land of we poor mortal men."

Was that the faintest spark of pleasure in those stony eyes? Did Vyed'ma enjoy flattery as much as she did courtesy? She could hear little of either up here in her chill isolation.

"Has it?" the Hag asked.

Her voice was as harsh as before, but Emelian thought he heard the slightest quiver of curiosity in it, and pressed on:

"Ah, yes, Old Mother, yes, indeed."

He had her full attention, no doubt of it. Now, to net her . . . if she didn't eat him first. Emelian took a deep breath and continued. "The tales of your might were wonderful. But . . . I . . . Well now, I doubted. Travellers tell such fabulous tales. Never did I think they spoke the truth."

"The truth? About what?"

"They claim you are all-Powerful. They claim you can hold the very winds within your grasp and bind them to your service."

Vyed'ma straightened ever so slightly, all at once a predator about to spring, and Emelian hurried on, "But of course they must have lied."

"They did not lie."

"No, no, such things cannot be the truth."

A hint of insulted anger glittered in the Hag's flat eyes. "They can. They are."

Aie, delicately, now, Emelian warned himself. *Rouse*

her anger too much, and be crushed. If I rouse it just enough, though . . .

"Oh, no, Old Mother," he said in sweet condescension, "forgive me, but no one has such Power."

"I do!"

Emelian shook his head. "Again, forgive me. To enslave the wind—I can't believe that."

"It is the truth!"

"But—"

"Come. I will show you."

A rough grey hand closed about his wrist. Vyed'ma dragged him helplessly after her out of the hut as though he weighed no more than a babe, then dumped him unceremoniously at her feet. Emelian scrambled up, trying to surreptitiously rub his newly bruised wrist, but the Hag ignored him. Arm outthrust commandingly, she called out sharp, harsh syllables that could have been Words of Power, or merely names. Emelian shivered as a cold wind swept down out of still air, briefly wrapping itself around him, then went wailing away. More winds had started up, their cries amid the mountain crags an eerie sound, almost like distant pleading . . .

Vyed'ma called out again, a flat certainty in her voice that permitted no disagreement. Emelian blinked, then gasped, staring in honest wonder as the air before him shimmered, then congealed itself into glinting, translucent, alien shapes, shifting and uncertain as sunlight through a spinning crystal.

"Form yourselves," Vyed'ma said shortly.

The quicksilver glittering deepened. Where nothing had been a moment ago, steeds of wonder stood now, pearly white, too fine of head and limbs, too graceful and slender to ever have been born of mortal stock, their proud necks arched, their luxuriant manes and tails flowing like flame in a wind only they could feel. Their eyes were wide and frightening: all the wild, empty space of the sky was in them. But the sorrow and helpless rage of slavery was there, too, painful to see, *wrong* as the imposing of shape on such creatures was wrong.

"Wind-spirits . . ." Emelian heard himself breathe.

Vyed'ma made a gesture of dismissal. The shining steeds swirled up into empty air and were gone in a whirling of wind, an illusion of freedom.

The Hag turned to Emelian, letting her arm drop. "Well?" she asked flatly. "Have I not Power?"

For a moment, Emelian couldn't find his voice. He could only continue to stare in wonder at the space that, an instant before, had been full of swift, glistening life.

Prince Finist had been right. With one of those steeds, Emelian could save Marya, he knew it. How could anyone, even Koshchei, stop them when they rode upon the back of the wind itself?

But first he had to win one of those steeds.

With that sobering thought, Emelian came back to himself. "Yes, oh, y-yes," he stammered. "Yes. You have Power, indeed." He took a steadying breath, then said bluntly, "Old Mother, I have need of one of your steeds— Akh, wait. I am no thief."

That struck a spark; she could only have been thinking about the Deathless, and betrayal. Hastily, Emelian added:

"I plan to earn one. You need only name the price— provided, of course, that it's something a mortal, Powerless man can pay."

Vyed'ma was silent for a long, long while, gone suddenly so still she could easily have been mistaken for just another rocky crag, staring at him with her flat, lustreless eyes as though bemused by his nerve, as though weighing him and the value of the entertainment he might provide against . . . hunger.

Emelian waited, trying to keep just as still, trying not to think about a mountain's strength turned against him, or of bare, skull-less posts.

"Yes," Vyed'ma said all at once, eyes unblinking. "You shall try to earn your steed."

"Ah, thank you, Old—"

"There shall be tests," the Hag continued as though he hadn't spoken. "So it was in the oldest days, so it is now. There shall be three tests you must pass, and three days in which to fulfill them, one day to each."

When in doubt, bow, Emelian told himself, and acted out the proverb. He said nothing, and after a moment, Vyed'ma continued thoughtfully:

"Mortal men pride themselves on their skill at the hunt. So be it. For the first test: you must go to Somewhere-Nowhere, and bring me Something-Nothing."

"But . . ."

"Do you yield so swiftly?"

There was a hungry edge to that, and Emelian hastened to say, "No, of course not. If you desire Something-Nothing, then Something-Nothing you shall have. Speak on, Old Mother. What of the next test?"

"Why, the second test shall be a simple one. Mortal men pride themselves on their mastery over the beasts of the field. For the second test: you must herd my shining mares in their mountain pasture for a full day, and lose not a one of them."

That sounded suspiciously simple to Emelian. Far too simple. Oh, he knew that beings of the Old Magic never lied; falsehood was a strictly human failing. If the Hag said there were mares, there would be mares, and he would have to herd them. But there was a trap here, somewhere.

But Vyed'ma was continuing in a voice hard and cold as the mountain's winter. "And the third test, ahh, the third test. Mortal men pride themselves on their mastery in the Deep Mystery of Creation. For the third test: on the third hour of the third night, young mortal man—you must lie with me."

XXXIII

CONTINUING STRUGGLES

His wife, Ludmilla, a soft, sleeping mass at his side, *boyar* Dimitri reluctantly sat up, looking blearily around at light that seemed garishly bright.

Morning.

With a groan, the *boyar* rubbed at eyes that seemed full of hot, gritty sand and fought the seductive pull of his warm bed.

No wonder he was tired. After last night's trauma . . . Dimitri had slept not at all, not from the moment he had returned from that midnight summons—

Nikolai. Dimitri sent a silent, reflexive curse the Regent's way, but was just too drained, emotionally and physically, to do anything more vigorous.

Nikolai had won. With the palace military behind him, he had made his point only too clearly last night: no matter what Dimitri thought of him—*that thrice-damned, self-righteous, arrogant son of a . . .* — No matter what he thought, Dimitri dared say nothing aloud, nothing that might reach the Regent's ear.

Dimitri felt his face redden. At least the summons had come in the dead of night. With any luck at all, no one would learn about it. No one knew about it, save Dimitri. And Nikolai, of course. And the guards.

The guards who were probably blathering their fool heads off about the *boyar* and the midnight arrest,

spreading the news all over Astyan, turning him into a
laughingstock— Oh, damn them all!

But how had Nikolai known to arrest him? How had
the man even found out about the *boyars'* secret meetings? As far as Dimitri knew, there were no spy holes
or private listening posts anywhere in that chamber.

Dimitri spat out a curse, so hotly that Ludmilla stirred
in sleepy protest. He ignored her.

Which one of the *boyars* had betrayed him? Which
one was the spy?

"Yaroslav," he muttered suddenly.

Who else could it be? Dimitri thought back to their
quarrel, and clenched his teeth in frustration. Why, that
frightened little boy must have gone running off to
Nikolai like a child hurrying to tell tales to its mother!

"It was Yaroslav," the *boyar* repeated grimly.

But what could Dimitri do about it? Threaten the boy?
Nonsense. Young and raw though the youngster might
be, he was still a *boyar,* not some peasant.

What, then? Challenge him to a duel? Dimitri gave a
snort of wry humor. Yaroslav, all prickly, childish honor
as he was, would almost surely accept. God, and
wouldn't that be ridiculous? Dimitri looked down at his
own middle-aged, wellpadded self, thought about Yaroslav's lithe youth, and shuddered. If one must die in
combat, one should, at least, be beautiful. If he died
on the end of that boy's sword, it wouldn't be tragedy,
it would be high farce.

Odd: Princess Marya—Heaven protect her—was no
older than Yaroslav. And yet Dimitri had not the
slightest qualm about obeying any order she gave. She
was . . . royal.

Unlike Yaroslav.

Unlike Nikolai.

Unlike . . .

"Oh, God."

The wave of despair swept over him without warning.
He had never been this vindictive a man, never. Hating
Nikolai, hating Yaroslav—what was wrong with him?

With all of them? Once the Inner Council had been a place of harmony. Of course they'd had their disagreements, their dislikes; they weren't saints. But somehow they had all managed to work together for the good of their city. Now . . . When had it happened? When had the Inner Council dissolved into a group of back-biting, hating fools?

That included himself . . .

No, dammit, it was all Nikolai's fault! Nikolai, and Yaroslav, and—

Dimitri gave Ludmilla a rough shove. "Wake up, wife." He shoved her again. "Wake up!"

"Dimi!" She glared up at him. "Stop it!"

"Get up, 'Milla. It's a fine, warm, sunny morning." Dimitri smiled grimly. "I want you to do something for me."

Blinking groggily, Ludmilla sat up. "Dimi?"

"I want you to do what you always do on such a morning. Sit among the other *boyarinas*. Talk to them. Listen. Listen in particular to *boyarina* Elena."

"Yaroslav's wife? But Dimi, what—"

"Listen to her. And if you hear the slightest bit of anything suspicious, anything . . . treasonous, against the Inner Council, against me, you are to report straight to me. Do you understand me?"

"But, Dimi—Nikolai's warning—I mean—"

"Never mind that! Do as I say, wife. *Do* you understand me?"

Ludmilla sighed and dipped her head in reluctant submission. "Yes, Dimi."

Dimitri's smile widened. No more surprises. No more alarms. And, should it become necessary—no more Yaroslav, either.

YOUNG *BOYAR* YAROSLAV, striding down a palace corridor, his mind full of angry thoughts about his fellow *boyars* and their stubborn insistence on quarrelling, came to a startled halt, his eye caught by a flash of yellow, a familiar yellow caftan, there in a little corner room.

"Elena!"

The young woman sprang up from her window seat, staring as though he had caught her in the middle of some subversive act. "Y-Yari?"

"Elena, love, what are you doing in here? I thought you were out with the other women."

"I was. I—couldn't stay."

"Whyever not?" Amused, he moved forward to gather her in his arms, feeling her slight figure go first rigid, then limp in submission. "Has one of those cats been teasing you again? Love, I've told you over and over not to let them bother you. You're better than any—"

"No. It's not them." Elena's voice sank to a flustered whisper. "It's . . . Ludmilla."

Dimitri's wife. Suddenly wary, Yaroslav held Elena at arm's length, studying her. "What about her?"

She wouldn't meet his gaze. "Oh . . . I d-don't know."

"Elena."

The young woman sighed in resignation. "She's been after me all morning, Yari," she said softly. "Not actually asking me anything, j-just watching me." Elena pulled away from her husband, turning away. "Watching as though she was waiting for me to—to blurt out something I wasn't supposed to know. Something d-dangerous."

"But, Elena, love, that's ridiculous."

"I know."

"Then why—"

"I—I haven't done anything wrong. Not even when I told Regent Nikolai . . . I didn't—"

"Told the Regent?" Yaroslav asked. "Told him what?"

"I—nothing."

"Don't play games, love. What did you tell him?"

"Nothing!"

"Elena!"

"I didn't mean any harm! I . . . was only trying to help you."

Yaroslav took a deep, steadying breath. "Elenishka, please. What did you tell Regent Nikolai?"

She sagged. "Just that you were unhappy. That you were worried about the well-being of Astyan."

"Ah. That doesn't sound so terrible."

"And . . . that *boyar* Dimitri had quarrelled with you," Elena added miserably.

"Oh, God . . . Elena, you didn't tell him *everything*, did you? You didn't tell him what Dimitri said about him?"

"I . . . Please, Yari, I—"

"You did tell him, didn't you?" Yaroslav shouted.

"I had to. He—he kept asking. And he's the Regent, after all."

"So you condemned a man to death for treason!"

Elena stared at him in sheer horror. *"B-boyar* Dimitri? Oh, no, that's not right, that can't be—"

"Dammit, Elena!"

Her eyes filled with tears, but she faced him in desperate defiance. "Don't you dare shout at me. He's not going to d-die."

"Now, how would you know that?"

"The servants told me."

"The servants," Yaroslav echoed in contempt.

"Yes, the servants! You should listen to them sometimes, Yari. They have all sorts of information we noble folk never learn. And this is what *our* servants heard from some of the palace guards. Those guards were *there*, Yari! Last night, they *heard* Regent Nikolai spare the *boyar.*" Elena drew herself up to her full slight height. "I thought you loved me."

"I do!"

"No, you don't. You're no better than any of the others."

"What—"

"Don't interrupt me! You think I'm silly and stupid

and—and good only for keeping your bed warm! Well, maybe I shouldn't have gone to Regent Nikolai, maybe that was above and beyond what a—a good little bed-warmer should do. But I was worried about you, Yari! I wasn't going to let anyone hurt you, not the *boyar*, not anybody!''

"Elena, I—"

"D-don't touch me.'' She turned sharply and stalked away, the folds of her silky caftan rippling about her. Her angry words trailed after her:

"You'll have your little bed-warmer, Yari. But it isn't going to be me!''

"Elena!"

Yaroslav started to run after her, then stopped short, red-faced and wavering, torn between love and his dignity as a *boyar*.

Servants were watching him, eyeing him speculatively. And, oh God, they must have heard every word.

Ignore them, he told himself sternly. *Just ignore them.*

Dignity won out. Elena might be angry now, but she would get over it quickly enough. Besides, she was at fault, not he. Yaroslav drew himself up proudly and set off for—

For where? He had already quarrelled with his fellow *boyars,* and now Elena— The young man paused by a narrow window, staring blankly out at Astyan. Things were surely falling apart. And he didn't know what he could do to stop them.

SEEN FROM AFAR, the city of Kirtesk would surely have looked all but normal, lacking only the ever-present small stream of merchants, farmers and the like, the usual comings-and-goings-forth of every city not at war. There were no besieging armies to be seen, no trampled earth or weapons of war—

There was only the one tall warrior in a dark cloak, astride a steed of shining, alien grace, there at the base of the city walls, staring up at the silvery-haired figure standing atop those walls with arms ever spread in refusal. The air between the Deathless and Prince Finist shimmered with a blue-white blaze of magic, grown strong and bright enough by now to hurt even magicless eyes. It reeked of tension, hot and sharp with the constant flood of Power.

Below, shut out from Kirtesk all this long day and night and new day, Koshchei found himself more and more frequently fighting down surges of rage that threatened to overwhelm his concentration. Who would ever have expected the human to have such reserves of strength within him?

Of course, it wasn't Finist alone who blocked him. It was the accumulated Power of the prince's ancestors as well, all poured into those damnable spells of defense, even as Koshchei was drawing endlessly upon the raw Power that was the Outer Dark.

But this had gone on far too long, this ridiculous example of human defiance.

Damn the man! No matter how much Power was feeding Finist, he still *was* only mortal. In time his body must fail him, his mind must collapse from the endless strain. And then would come the reckoning . . .

Yes, Koshchei snapped silently, *but when? When?*

Akh, no, he must stop this! Such impatience was deadly to spells, destroying the focus needed to hold them. Savagely, Koshchei won control over his mind, banishing all conscious thought, till there was nothing left once more but the cold, implacable attack.

Sooner or later, Finist would fall.

WITHIN THE ROYAL PALACE of Kirtesk, old *boyar* Semyon, head of Prince Finist's Inner Council, stood alone by the open window in his private chambers as the light brightened, and rubbed a weary hand across his burning eyes.

Morning at last.

Semyon slowly tried to straighten, and bit back a weary groan. Deny it though he might, his bones and muscles were not as resilient as they had been, once upon a time when he'd been a young man.

His head hurt, too. According to everything he had ever heard on the subject, the elderly were supposed to need far less sleep than the young, but the few hours he had snatched this night while standing this self-imposed vigil, watching his prince locked in arcane battle, seemed hardly enough to qualify as rest.

Still, they had been more than Finist had been allowed.

My poor Finist . . .

The old *boyar* stretched again, eyes never leaving the rigid figure there on the city walls, arms still outstretched, red cloak and shining hair bright in the sunlight and stirring faintly in a magical breeze. Semyon winced. If he stared hard enough, he could actually see the Power being expended, blue-white and shimmering like a heat haze all around the prince. After all the long years in service to magical princes, the old *boyar* knew only too well the danger involved in that expenditure, the risk to the magician who, for all that extravagance of Power, was but a mortal.

God, how long could Finist endure?

If only I could help him! It was a silent shout of frustration. *If only I could protect—*

Foolish, foolish. There was nothing he could do to help. There was nothing anyone could do to help, not even Princess Maria, standing her own lonely, defiant vigil.

Nothing save prayer.

And the sheer, desperate power that was love.

XXXIV

SOMEWHERE-NOWHERE

"YOU MUST LIE WITH ME."

Vyed'ma's words seemed to hang in the air between them for a long, long while. Emelian stared into her unblinking eyes in shock and tried not to flinch away.

Lie with her. With . . . that. God, even if he could manage to . . . perform in proper manly fashion with the Hag, her primal strength would almost certainly crush him.

Hey, now, what am I worried about? Emelian thought with desperate gaiety. *That's the* third *test, and I'm probably not even going to get past the first one!*

Go to Somewhere-Nowhere. Bring back Something-Nothing—what rubbish! She was mocking him, dammit, giving him these impossible tasks just to see him fail. He shouldn't let her make a fool of him. What if he refused to even try the stupid tests?

A thin tongue swept suddenly, hungrily, over the rock-sharp teeth, giving Emelian his answer without a single word. Damned if he was going to let himself end up as dinner for a hag!

"All right," he snapped. "I accept." Struggling to hold on to courtesy, Emelian added carefully, "I shall try your three tests, Old Mother, and pass them, and claim my prize."

"There need not be those accusing looks, young-

ling.'' Vyed'ma's rough voice was serene, her face totally without expression. "I keep my bargains. Pass my
tests, and the windspirit is yours. Fail, and . . . pay the
penalty.'' Again her tongue whipped over those deadly
teeth. "Now, the first test. Go.''

WARILY STAYING OUT of Vyed'ma's way, hoping the Hag
couldn't sense her presence, Marya hovered over the
mountaintop. With her heightened magical vision, she
saw the ancient offerings left by the long-dead nomads
as faint blue whirls and swirlings of human Power,
gradually being erased bit by bit by the stronger, heav-
ier mineral life-force of the mountain itself.

This was an eerie place, dangerous, pulling at her
with quiet force as it had the nomad's Power, threat-
ening to drag her down into it, to destroy her individual
essence and make her only one small once-human part
of the whole.

Shivering in the winds she sensed but couldn't feel,
Marya forced herself to soar higher and yet higher, till
the deadly, seductive pull of Old Magic was reduced to
a mild tug she could easily resist.

Akh, but Emelian was still down there, among all
that perilous force, and faced directly with the Old
Magic in the form of Vyed'ma and her three tests.

That the Hag intended Emelian to fail, Marya had no
doubt. But those of the Old Magic never lied; Emelian
knew that as well as she. There had to be a way to pass
those tests. But . . . "Go to Somewhere-Nowhere . . .
Bring back Something-Nothing . . .'' That was a challenge straight out of the old tales. It was surely nothing
that had any remote connection to the real world—

But this wasn't the "real" world, was it? There was
a trick to this first test, a riddle to be solved . . .

Oh, she couldn't think! This lonely place with all its
ancient Power was making her too weary to do anything
but wish with all her heart she was spirit-and-body
again, so that she could sleep . . .

Marya shook her immaterial head, trying to clear it. How could she rest, when Emelian was in danger?

And how could she help him, when she didn't even dare approach him?

Helpless, Marya soared above the mountaintop, circling it again and again, surrounded by the mournful winds.

"Oh, my love, be careful," she cried out to Emelian, even though she knew he couldn't hear her, *"be careful and clever and safe!"*

EMELIAN HAD BEEN WANDERING AIMLESSLY about amid all this mountaintop barrenness for what seemed like all day, though, judging from the unreliable sun of this realm, only a short time had actually passed.

"Go to Somewhere-Nowhere. Bring me Something-Nothing."

"How can a place be both somewhere and nowhere?" he muttered.

And how in the name of Heaven could anything be both something and nothing?

At least Emelian was sure it couldn't be some sort of magic formula; the Hag, being of the Old Magic, with its own antique sense of honor, wouldn't cheat by setting him a task that could only be performed successfully by a magician. This test was a riddle, no doubt about it.

Maybe, urged a small, childish part of his mind, maybe he should give up on the whole ridiculous, impossible thing, and simply run as far and as fast as he could—

No, Emelian realized suddenly, a little surprised at his own quiet certainty, he did not want to run, even though his life was in danger. He had done enough running in his life: running from confronting his father and convincing the man to see reality, running from the world of his childhood, even running (though this hadn't totally been his fault) from the regency of Astyan. Now the time had come to take a stand.

Besides, dammit, I'm not going to die.

Emelian paced back and forth over the rocky ground, barely noticing his surroundings. There was something about the first riddle that nagged at him, something there at the back of his mind, triggered by memories of childhood, of the peasants and their tales . . . ancient tales, much older than anything heard at Astyan's sophisticated court, tales that, for all he knew, dated back to the first stumbling steps of humanity.

Tales that just might be known to the primal creature that was Vyed'ma.

"Go to Somewhere-Nowhere. Bring me Something-Nothing."

That "Somewhere-Nowhere" couldn't be very far away, not if he was expected to get there and back in one short day. And as for "Something-Nothing," what if it wasn't a *thing* she wanted . . . ? What if, like the characters in those old, old tales, she was merely testing his cleverness, his worthiness to survive?

Somewhere-Nowhere.

Something-Nothing.

"Ha!" Emelian exclaimed, so sharply that the echoes flew. "Yes! Of course!"

Hastily, he went in search of Vyed'ma. But the Hag was nowhere to be found. For a panicky moment, Emelian wondered if that was her plan: to simply hide herself, leaving him with no way to tell her he'd solved the riddle till it was too late, till the day had passed and he'd forfeited any chance to pass her test.

"Old Mother!" he yelled. "Vyed'ma! Where are you? Come, Old Mother, be honest! Show yourself!"

"I have."

Emelian started. What he had thought to be no more than one more jagged tooth of rock had suddenly stirred and resolved itself into the Hag of the Rocks.

"What would you?" she asked calmly.

"Ah—the riddle—the first test." Emelian caught his breath, and started over, more coherently this time. "Old Mother, I do believe I have passed your first test."

"Yes?"

Emelian gave a laugh of sheer tension. "I have, indeed. You see, I *am* in Somewhere-Nowhere."

Vyed'ma stared at him, unblinking, and Emelian continued, hastily, before those flat eyes could unnerve him:

"Yes, I know, this place is home, it's Somewhere, to you. But this mountaintop, this whole realm, is far outside the realm of humankind—so to me, it is most surely Nowhere."

Not by the slightest quiver did Vyed'ma reveal whether or not he was on the right path. "And Something-Nothing?" she asked without emotion.

Grinning desperately, Emelian held out his cupped hands. "See? It lies right within these hands: air!"

"Air." The Hag said the word flatly, as though it meant nothing to her.

"Exactly!" Feeling like a merchant trying to convince a stubborn customer, Emelian rushed on. "For while air cannot be tasted, or seen, or smelled, while it seems to be truly Nothing, all who live and breathe know without a doubt that it most surely *is* Something." The young man paused breathlessly, watching Vyed'ma. "Well, Old Mother?" he prodded after a moment. "Is it not so? Have I not passed the first test?"

There was a long pause. Then Vyed'ma gave one dip of her grim head. "You have." She stopped, studying him, her thin tongue suddenly darting over her teeth. "Rest well, youngling," the Hag continued. "You shall not find the second test so simple."

Without another word, she turned and moved silently away.

HIGH OVERHEAD, Marya danced among the winds, rejoicing in her husband's cleverness. To solve Vyed'ma's riddle—and to solve it so easily! Marya confessed to herself that she never would have succeeded. Trained as she was in the intricacies of court politics, where even the most simple of statements must be weighed for hidden meaning, analyzed for yes or no, good or

bad, wise or dangerous, Marya would surely have
wasted the day trying to puzzle out the "real" truth
behind Vyed'ma's apparently simple words.

Oh, my clever husband! Marya crowed anew.

But she had to stop this wild whirling about. She was
growing dizzy. And weary yet again, so very weary . . .
It would be so much simpler not to fight, just to surrender and float away forever . . .

No! God, no!

All at once, Marya was seized by a frantic longing
to be *solid* once more, to *touch* something, anything.

Yet what could she do about it? Abandon Emelian?
Return to her body, back there somewhere, assuming
that she could find that somewhere again from this Other
realm? Return to her body—and Koshchei?

Impossible. Here she was, and here she must stay, at
least for now, one slight, lonely ghost of a woman wandering amid the sobbing winds.

XXXV

HERDING THE MARES

EMELIAN AWOKE aching with sorrow, wondering, bewildered, what he could possibly have dreamed to have upset him so deeply. Marya . . . Something about Marya . . .

It was gone, now. Nothing more than a dream-worry, surely, a longing to see her again, touch her, *touch something, anything* . . .

Emelian shook his head to clear it. He dare not let himself get lost in dreams. It was the second day, a bright, brave, sunny one, and it was time for him to go and herd Vyed'ma's mares.

The Hag was nowhere to be seen, but she had left him a share of last night's dinner. The goat tasted no better for having weathered the night in its half-charred, half-raw, saltless and spiceless state, but Emelian choked it down, trusting to the mountain cold to have kept it from spoiling, then went out into the crisp chill of morning, gasping at air almost too sharp to breathe. He tried a few running steps in place to warm himself and ease the kinks out of his muscles, then, reluctantly, began to look for Vyed'ma.

"Human."

Emelian bit back a yelp. Once again, she'd startled him by suddenly coming to life from amid the crags.

You do it on purpose, don't you, you old— "Good morning, Old Mother."

"Come. It is time."

She moved fluidly over the rugged ground towards the cave that apparently served as her storeroom and stable. Emelian stumbled after, nearly turning his ankle on slippery rocks that lurched beneath his feet, and peered as best he could over her shoulder into the darkness.

"Old Mother?" he began warily. "You said I'm to herd your mares, but . . . I don't see any horses in there." *I don't smell any, either,* he added silently, *or see any dungheaps, or—* "Good God."

They had appeared out of the dark mouth of the cave without a sound, a file of pale grey or glistening white horses—mares. But their bodies were too sleek, their heads and the arch of their necks too elegant. Their manes and tails streamed and streamed in a never-ending wind, and their eyes—

Emelian took an indignant step forward to face the Hag. "Now, technically, those may be mares. They're in the shape of mares, anyhow. But none of those—beings ever started out as a foal!"

"Ah?"

"Don't pretend you don't understand! I— Look you, Old Mother, I'm not a complete fool. Those aren't true horses, but more of your captive wind-spirits. And how in the name of all that's holy am I supposed to herd them?"

"That," said Vyed'ma without expression, "is for you to learn."

"But—I—they—"

"You agreed to three tests. Do you concede the second test now?"

There was a hungry edge to that, and the faintest hint of mockery. *Oh, you sly bitch,* thought Emelian, almost in admiration. Well, he'd expected a trick somewhere along the way, and here it was. Hastily, the young man considered his undesirable options: refusing, and being eaten; running, and being eaten; or actually trying to herd wind-spirits. He sighed.

"No," Emelian said flatly. "I do not concede."

"So be it. Herd them well, human. Bring them back here at sundown." Vyed'ma paused for the barest instant. "I know their number, human. Do not seek to trick me. If but one mare is missing, I shall know it at once. You will have failed. And," she added coolly, "you will pay the price. Now, be off."

MAYBE HE SHOULD HAVE FOUGHT HER. In his old, impulsive days of not-so-long-ago, Emelian supposed he probably would have done just that. But maybe he wouldn't have been so wrong. Maybe he *should* just draw his sword—

Right. And have it grate harmlessly—or worse, break—against elemental flesh that could suddenly become stony. And have the head torn from his body by powerful fingers.

Damn.

But, to Emelian's surprise, the mares, all one-and-twenty of them, were tripping lightly along after him, for all the world like mortal, well-behaved mares on their way to a morning's grazing. There didn't seem to be a shred of rebellion or mischief in them, and Emelian could, if he didn't stare into those alien eyes too closely, almost believe they were nothing more than they seemed. And he began to hope. They couldn't be very fond of the Hag who'd bound them. They couldn't want her to win. Maybe, maybe . . .

One finely shaped head, soft-skinned as velvet but cooler than mortal horseflesh, nudged him in the small of the back, making him jump. When he continued forward, a second wind-spirit pushed at him as well, blatantly steering him.

He turned to look at them. Ears up, they looked right back, and Emelian felt an atavistic shiver, primitive reaction to the unknown, run through him at the sight of the wild, alien intelligence he saw there. Trying to hide his discomfort, the young man forced a laugh.

"Don't tell me you really *do* have a pasture? And that you really do need to graze?"

Akh, well, perhaps they did. Perhaps, since they were bound into physical shape, they had some of the needs of physical beings. At any rate, the rocky landscape up ahead sloped gently downhill, opening up into a small valley that, if one were charitable and counted the few rough green tufts of vegetation as grass, might be called a pasture.

"Hey, watch it!"

A smooth body had bumped into him, nearly knocking him over.

"Watch it," Emelian repeated helplessly. "Don't—Hey!"

He slapped at one horse-form, but it darted easily out of his reach. More bodies were crowding him now, the smell of them the fierce, sharp tang of ozone, the sound of their breath the roar of the wild mountain air. Alarmed, Emelian struck out in earnest this time, trying to keep a circle of clear space around himself, only too well aware that the sleek hides about him only barely disguised the raw power within, the sheer, alien force of winds turned tangible. He frantically ducked flashing teeth and dancing hoofs, dodging this way and that as the mares flooded past him, pouring into the valley with all the eagerness of hungry horses.

Emelian caught his breath, rather amazed to find himself unbitten and unstepped-on. With luck, the beings would settle down, now that they'd arrived where they plainly wanted to be. With even more luck, maybe they would stay here all day, just like the mares they almost seemed to be. Unless he was being unduly optimistic . . . ?

He was.

For a moment, all the mares raised their heads, looking at him with their eerie eyes, empty and wild as the open sky. And then they all exploded into motion, bucking and rearing, whirling about till his eyes were dazzled trying to follow their action. Faster they whirled, faster than any mortal horse could move, a silvery blur, a whirlwind, spiralling round and round, the wind of their passing nearly tearing the air from his lungs. Gasping, Emelian lost his balance and fell to his knees, staring in sheer, impotent astonishment.

There was a wail that might have been a drawn-out peal of laughter or merely the shriek of the wind. The mares whirled up into the sky and were gone.

Emelian scrambled to his feet, still staring. For what seemed a long, long time, that was all he could do: stand frozen and stare at the empty space where one-and-twenty wind-spirit mares had been. And then, with a groan, he sank back down to the ground.

How could he ever have been foolish enough to believe the spirits might have any sympathy for him? More to the point, how could he have believed that slaves such as the spirits had any options? The Hag had probably told them, "Lull him. Lower his suspicions. Then—flee," and of course they had fled.

And now what could he do? Accuse Vyed'ma of cheating? Much good that would do! He had already accepted that fighting or running weren't going to help against an elemental being. That left only meekly admitting his failure, and throwing himself on the Hag's nonexistent mercy— Dammit, no! There must be something else he could do. After all, he had survived pretty well up to this point, hadn't he?

But this time there didn't seem to be any way out.

MARYA, FAR OVERHEAD, saw the wind-spirits abandon mare-shape and go whirling up into the open air.

Why, that treacherous bitch! Setting Emelian a task she knew *no mortal could win!*

Marya glanced quickly about, her Powerful vision picking out the shimmers of the various wind-spirit slaves easily enough. And she said the first words that came to mind:

"Now, aren't you ashamed?"

In the next moment, she realized how ridiculous that sounded, as though she was trying to scold some erring children.

But the wind-spirits evidently didn't see it that way. Their startled curiosity was a quivering in the air. *Shame?* *Human shame?* *What is shame?*

"Don't pretend you don't know. Look at you! You were created to be free things, serving no will but Air. Yet you practically tumble all over each other to obey Vyed'ma's slightest whim."

A whisper of sorrow shivered past her. *Not our fault . . . Hag . . .*

"Yes, I know that," Marya said, pitying. *"I know you don't want to be her slaves. But . . ."* She looked at the shimmerings surrounding her. *"But why are you destroying your only chance to get free?"*

The air fairly boiled with turmoil. *What? What?* *No!* *Not— Can't—*

"Oh, but it's true. The Hag told you to trick Emelian—that human man—didn't she? So he would fail her tests and she could . . . could kill him."

The winds stirred about her. *Yes . . . * *We did.* *A game, a fine game.*

Marya sighed. How could she expect morality from beings so far removed from human concepts. *"You don't understand. By helping Emelian, you weaken the Hag. Every victory of his is a victory against your enemy."*

*No . . . * *Maybe . . . * *Yes, but . . .*

"Listen to me. Think." Marya put on her most regal arguing-with-*boyars* tone. *"Who would you rather be helping? The being who pulled you down from the skies and enslaved you? Or the man who is her enemy—and, thereby, your friend?"*

She waited uneasily, not at all sure they would understand the idea of "your enemy is my friend." There was silence for a long, long while, with not the slightest stirring of the air. And then, a whisper of wind asked warily:

What would you have us do?

Ah! *"Go down to Emelian. Let him herd you back to the stables of the Hag."* Marya felt the wind-spirits resist at the mention of that name, and added hastily, *"It will be a fine trick, one played upon your foe, the finest of tricks."*

Yes . . . ? asked a wind-voice doubtfully.

There was a pause. Then: *Yes!* the others agreed.

EMELIAN HAD BEEN SITTING with his head in his hands, trying without success to puzzle out a way, any way, out of this mess, when something cool and soft rustled his hair. He glanced sharply up, and found himself staring up a long, elegant equine head.

"Well . . . hello," the young man breathed, hardly daring to move lest this mare, too, dart away up into the sky.

But she made no move to fly, only stepped aside delicately as Emelian got to his feet.

She wasn't alone. Behind her, as though they had been there all along, were the other wind-spirit mares. Warily, Emelian counted them . . . nineteen, twenty, one-and-twenty . . . He let out a shaky laugh, so overwhelmed with the sudden rush of relief that he staggered. God, he wasn't dead yet, he hadn't failed Marya, he—

"You're back. You're all back." It was an inane thing to babble, but at the moment he didn't feel up to anything more intelligent. But where had the wind-spirits gone? Why had they suddenly decided to return? Akh, no, he wasn't about to ask. *Don't question good fortune*, went the saying, and right now it sounded like a very wise saying indeed. "Now, please, *please*, just stay here!"

To his unutterable relief, they did.

And when the seemingly endless day at last faded towards night, the mares followed him meekly back, all one-and-twenty of them, to the stables of the Hag. One by one, they tripped daintily back into the darkness, leaving him alone with Vyed'ma.

She stared, only stared, but around her hung the wordless menace of the building mountain storm. Before that storm could break, Emelian gave her his most ingratiating smile and said:

"I have herded your mares for you this day, as you commanded. The second test is completed."

"You had help," Vyed'ma muttered. "You surely had help."

"What help?" Emelian asked indignantly, his sweep of arm taking in the empty mountainside. "Come, admit it: the second test is completed."

Vyed'ma continued to stare. "So it is," she conceded at last, then seemed to rouse herself. "Prepare yourself. Tomorrow you shall face the third test. Tomorrow . . . night."

XXXVI

THE CAPTIVE

HOW COULD I EVER HAVE AGREED TO THIS?

Emelian stood staring moodily out over the darkening mountaintop on this, the evening of the third day.

Aside from the fact that if I go through with this, I'll be betraying my wedding vows to Marya—

The young man broke off with a sigh. That train of thought was bordering on the ridiculous. It wasn't as though he wanted to commit adultery, most certainly not with Vyed'ma! No, what he was about to do—to attempt, at any rate—was for Marya; no need to feel guilt about it.

Besides . . . there wasn't going to be any time for guilt. He almost certainly wasn't going to survive this night. One way or another. Particularly since he didn't think even the lustiest of men could find anything even remotely alluring about Vyed'ma.

Like bedding a boulder.

Indeed. A boulder that just might crush him if he refused her, or failed to satisfy her.

Emelian winced.

Oh, Marya, my love, my heart, will I ever live to see you again?

"Human."

The grating voice made him start, and he turned reluctantly back into the hut. Time for the sacrifice.

Emelian stopped, staring. "Vyed'ma . . . ?"

299

"Vyed'ma," she replied.

Gone was the squat, solid shape. In its place . . . Akh, well, even now she could hardly be called beautiful, not with those sharp-planed features, but there were definite, voluptuous curves beneath the rough robes, and a cascade of silver-grey hair. There was also expression in the flat eyes for the first time, a mixture of hunger and hope and . . . loneliness? Could it actually be loneliness?

She's afraid! Emelian realized in shock. *She's afraid that I won't find her attractive, that I'll turn away in disgust . . .*

And, to his amazement, Emelian felt genuine pity warm him. Alien, amoral being that she was, how could she ever know anything of love? And yet she knew and mourned for its lack. Emelian found himself remembering Marya, and their first timid, wondrous night together, the night they were wed, the scent of flowers in the air and her body, so sweet, so softly revealed beneath the thin robe that was her only covering, save for the veiling of long black hair, silken and sweet-scented as the flowers . . .

All at once such a surge of longing and desire raced through him that his senses swam and he couldn't separate past from present. His body moved forward to take the transformed Vyed'ma in his arms, but his mind soared above (a dream, surely it was only a dream) to embrace Marya. As Vyed'ma pulled him down to the fur-strewn floor, Emelian lost all touch with the real, the tangible. He saw only Marya, his love, his wife, as they joined in joy.

MARYA SHIVERED in the morning light, cold with a chill beyond the physical, clinging desperately to the memory of the night just past as the only thing that reminded her that love, and warmth, and a solid, tangible embrace still existed.

Akh, Emelian . . .

Marya sighed. How wonderful the night had been, almost as wonderful as if they'd been alone together in body as well as spirit, safe and secure in their own bed in their own palace chambers . . .

But Emelian probably thought it had all been a dream. Or would think it, Marya corrected herself with a faint, fond smile, as soon as he awakened.

Just then Vyed'ma stirred, and fled the hut, to freeze amid the boulders in desperate, hating stillness, and Marya dove down out of the sky in sudden terror, sensing with every psychic nerve what the Hag intended. Emelian! Vyed'ma had never meant to let him live. Oh, she would keep to the vow she'd made, the Old Magic never lied. She would let Emelian claim a wind-spirit steed— but then, before he could escape, she would kill him!

"Wake!" Marya shouted to Emelian's mind with all her will. *"For your life—Emelian, wake up!"*

EMELIAN HAD DIMLY BEEN AWARE of Vyed'ma's rush outside. But it was only after a groggy moment that he came sharply awake, aware, though he wasn't sure how, that the Hag meant to kill him.

For a moment Emelian wavered, wondering after his survival of last night's surprising events if perhaps he really did stand a chance of successfully fighting Vyed'ma.

Ha, no. Last night's softening had almost certainly been an aberration on her part. In her normal, boulderlike, elemental persona, the Hag would crush him and hardly know there'd been a battle.

"Not if she can't find me," Emelian muttered, too sensible for bravado, and stole warily out to find himself his wind-spirit prize.

Assuming that he could persuade one of the mercurial beings to go with him.

Vyed'ma, as usual, was nowhere to be seen. The mountaintop had an *empty* feel to it, like a house with no one at home. That didn't mean she wasn't watching him, ready to spring into life in her charming fashion. Sure he felt eyes upon him, Emelian approached the cave-stables as quietly as he could, trying to pretend that nothing was wrong, just in case she really *was* watching him, trying to pretend that no, he didn't suspect a thing . . .

Nothing happened. The space between his shoulder

blades was prickling as Emelian stepped carefully into the dark mouth of the cave. After what seemed an eternity, his eyes adjusted to the darkness, and he looked cautiously about.

Nothing—at first. Fighting down disappointment so sharp it was almost pain, Emelian stared into the darkest corner of the cave.

There, now! He had seen it again, a faint glimmer of motion.

Warily drawing his sword, Emelian moved towards the glimmering, stepping carefully over the uneven surface. There was something blocking his path—bars, Emelian realized, tapping one of them gingerly with the blade of his sword.

Iron bars, he thought uneasily, *to keep anything magical trapped behind them.*

And behind them, the pale whatever-it-was shuddered at his approach. Emelian caught a flash of eyes wide with terror and defiance, then the creature was cringing away, pulling itself into so small and tight a ball that he couldn't make out anything more about it than its sleek, sickly-white hide.

Its terror hurt his heart.

"It's all right," Emelian whispered gently. "I'm not going to hurt you."

The creature only shuddered.

"Really, it's true." With sudden inspiration, Emelian added, "Look, I'm human, mortal; I'm not . . . ah . . . on *her* side."

The creature uncurled ever so slightly. Wide eyes studied him for a silent moment. Then, with a sudden flurry of motion, the captive was completely uncurled, staring. Emelian stared back, fighting not to wince. Akh, what an ugly little thing! Limbless, pretty nearly shapeless, its hairless hide slick and moist, it looked like nothing so much as a giant slug.

But . . . its eyes were lovely, wild and wide, the echoing freedom of the skies within those depths. And all at once Emelian knew the truth.

"You're a wind-spirit, aren't you?" Remembering the flash of challenge in the being's eyes, he added, "Maybe you defied her, refused to do her bidding. And she shut you away to repent."

Yes . . . The sudden faint shiver of non-voice tickled through his mind. *I . . . I would not serve her, be her slave . . .* The spirit shuddered violently. *Punishment,* it whispered, *darkness . . . closed-in . . . rock . . .* and in the words was terror so sharp it echoed in Emelian's mind. *No-sky rock, no-life rock,* it continued in an anguished rush. *Closed-in, closed-in, dying—*

"Easy, now, easy," Emelian soothed, shaking from the emotional backwash of the spirit's pain. He could only guess at its torment, an infinite creature forced into a finite shape that could be bound by iron, crushed into a finite space.

And all because it had tried to defy Vyed'ma, the one who had torn it from its proper place.

Rage blazed in Emelian at the thought, rage at the Hag, at Koshchei, at all that Marya and he had been forced to undergo, rage at all those, human or Other, who would harm the innocent out of power-greed or cruelty. And he knew in that sudden, intense moment that even if he didn't escape Vyed'ma, at least he would see she didn't have this innocent wind-spirit.

White-hot with the force of his will, Emelian told the wind-spirit, "Don't be afraid. I'm going to get you out of this."

As the wide, wild eyes followed his every move, Emelian crouched down to study the iron bars holding the spirit in its narrow prison.

"They're not really set into anything," he murmured to the wind-spirit, "just jammed into a wooden frame. I guess the Hag can't handle iron too well, either."

He gripped one of the bars firmly and gave it a tentative push. The wood made faint, weary creaking sounds. Mm, but if the bar fell in on the spirit, the poor creature would surely be hurt by the touch of iron. Emelian took a new grip on two of the bars, and began pulling backwards instead, using his whole body weight. "Or else," he continued, "she just doesn't have a proper ironworker's tools . . . Ah!"

There was the faint, dusty splintering of wood, and all at once Emelian went staggering back, nearly landing on his rump, the two iron bars clenched in his hands.

"Ha, knew it would work!" He glanced at the narrow opening he'd created.

"Think you can edge through that?"

I . . . can try, came the wind-shiver answer. Delicately, the white worm-figure squirmed its way along, quivering with tension as it worked its way past the dangerous iron.

Then, all at once, it was free, and rejoicing, its wild, non-vocal song twining and dancing about Emelian's dazzled senses. He finally managed to gasp out:

"Hush, oh, hush! There's no time to celebrate, not yet. First we've got to get you out of here."

Ah. Yes. The strange psychic wind-whirling ceased. *Sorry. Freedom—I never dreamed— Now, free of that cursed cold metal, I should be able to rid myself of this foul shape . . . Yes.*

The ugly worm-form blurred, grew. Dizzy, Emelian blinked.

It was gone. In its place stood . . . it could hardly be called a steed. A pony, perhaps, or a badly grown colt, all bony angles and ragged fur.

I . . . am still weak from captivity, the wind-spirit apologized as Emelian stared at it in mingled pity and dismay. *But I am still strong enough for what must be done.*

"Akh, yes, hurry. I don't know where the Hag's hiding, but surely you don't have much time. Get out of here before she finds you!"

The being never moved.

"Go on! Get out of here!" But then Emelian paused uncertainly. "You *can* escape, can't you?"

A shudder raced through the shaggy form. *No,* it admitted, so softly the non-sound almost couldn't be sensed. *Not truly. Not while she still holds my not-name, Sv'istat, the . . . shaping name she forced on wind-shapelessness.*

Sv'istat? "Ah," Emelian said doubtfully.

But that does not mean I cannot try for escape, Sv'istat added. *Now, while her attention is gone. She does this now and again, sinks her essence into the mountainside and forgets the world without.*

"Goes into trance, you mean?"

The wind-spirit stirred impatiently. *Words,* it said. *Maybe, maybe not. She is your foe, too? Yes? As you would say, we have not much time. Come.*

"Come where?" asked Emelian in sudden despair. "I can't fly or—"

Come, Sv'istat insisted. *Mount.*

"But—"

You wish to escape? Then, hurry. Before she stirs and knows—I owe you my freedom, my existence. Come!

Emelian vaulted onto the thin back, feeling the wind-horse's ribs prominent between his knees, wondering if the being would collapse under his weight. "Are you sure—"

Then the wind-spirit leaped forward, and his words were lost. He buried his face in the rippling white mane, feeling the wind tear at any exposed skin and whip tears to his eyes. He had a quick, blurred glimpse of the nomads' offerings, then Sv'istat was plunging headlong down the mountainside in great, terrifying bounds, and Emelian could only cling to his slippery-skinned mount.

I cannot soar, the wind-spirit said sadly, *not yet.*

"This—this is good enough!" Emelian swallowed convulsively, his stomach protesting as earth and sky whirled together in a mad rush of color with every near-to-flying leap and landing. "Just don't forget I'm only human, and—ah—breakable."

For reply, he received only a wind-whisper tickling in his mind. It took Emelian a moment to realize that Sv'istat was laughing.

XXXVII

PURSUIT AND CHALLENGE

THE MOUNTAIN SLEPT in the chill morning light, its rugged peak still and empty as though life had never touched it. But of a sudden, one boulder amid the many moved, resolved itself into Vyed'ma.

A thief! A thief had been here! While she had been one with the mineral quiet, absorbing its unchanging peace, the disturbing human had stolen a spirit away from her.

He would not keep it. Vyed'ma surged to her feet, calling out a Name. A wind-spirit came to her, reluctantly forming itself into steed-shape, shuddering as she mounted it.

"Fly," she ordered it. "Catch me the thief."

Bound to obedience, the wind-steed sprang forward. But in the next moment, it slowed its pace with a piteous wail.

I cannot fly! Mistress, you are Earth, Mountain, you weigh me down.

"Run, then," Vyed'ma told it flatly. "Overtake him."

As the wind-steed sped down the mountain, the Hag ran her tongue over her rock-sharp teeth, forgetting the pleasure-pain the human had given her; savoring only the taste to come, the taste of hot, fresh man-flesh.

EMELIAN SENSED PURSUIT even before he saw it. Crouched low over Sv'istat's scrawny mane, half-blinded by wind, he risked a glance over his shoulder.

306

"Sv'istat! The Hag's after us!"

I know. The non-voice quivered with strain and fear. *I feel the aura of the kin she rides—I know that one. Ae-e, so swift it is! I—I am still weak, I may not be able to outpace it.*

You'd better *outpace it!* Emelian thought frantically, and told the spirit, "Don't start doubting now. Just run."

And run Sv'istat did, its thin body struggling gallantly on.

But the other wind-steed was sleek and shining, unweakened by the torment of close captivity. Beneath the incongruous hump that was Vyed'ma, it fairly radiated glistening strength. With every mighty leap it made, the margin separating hunter from prey grew smaller. Ahead of him, Emelian saw the wavering heat haze that meant the river of fire, and arcing over it the thin, faint glitter of crystal that was the magic bridge. But it was still so far away, and the Hag was now so very close.

Emelian drew his sword, determined not to die meekly.

Marya, he thought in a surge of longing. *Akh, Marya, farewell.*

TIRED . . . She was so tired . . .

Marya roused herself from her torpor with an effort. Something was wrong . . . someone was missing . . .

Emelian! The realization hit her with a shock. Emelian was gone from this grim mountaintop—and so was the Hag.

God, how could she have faded out of consciousness like this? How much more had she missed? Was Emelian already— No, no, of course he was still alive, she would surely know it if he—if the Hag had—

Marya soared down the mountainside, hunting. Thank Heaven, there was Emelian, astride a poor little starvling of a wind-spirit, his sword glinting in his hand.

And the Hag pursued him.

My love, my love, what good a mere mortal blade, even an iron blade, against the power of the Mountain itself?

Vyed'ma was close behind him now, hunger sharp on her face, reaching out with her rough arms to pull him from his mount.

"Oh, no," Marya shouted to her, *"you shall not have him!"*

She thrust herself, keen as an avenging blade, straight at the Hag. Vyed'ma's wind-spirit reared up with a cry, startled (or perhaps pretending to be startled), and its rider tumbled to the ground. As the spirit whirled away up into the sky, the Hag surged to her feet.

"Human-thing."

Marya held her ground. If Vyed'ma could see her, the Hag could probably hear her, too, so she said as calmly as she could, *"Quite human."*

"Not as you are now. Spirit-thing, stand aside."

Marya refused to be alarmed, even though Vyed'ma's sharp teeth flashed most alarmingly. *I'm not tangible,* she told herself. *She can't harm me.*

No? This was the being who had captured the wind-spirits.

Hastily blocking that line of thought, the princess said firmly, *"You shall not pass."*

Vyed'ma made no reply. Instead, she raised her arms from her sides, slowly, as though they weighed as much as the mountain, and pointed at Marya. And the mountain's weight seemed to descend on the princess, forcing her essence just as slowly down into the rock on which she stood, crushing that which was *Marya, human,* forcing her into a soulless yet living part of the mountain, forever lost, forever aware—

No! God help me, no!

How had she ever thought to challenge Vyed'ma? The Hag *was* the Old Magic, or a part of it, while *she,* oh, *she* was no trained magician, she barely knew how to wield any Power at all!

Marya frantically searched through her memories for the spells her father had so laboriously taught her in her Powerless childhood. God, God, why hadn't he taught her any *useful* spells, any that would work against the other-than-human? The merciless pressure was driving her further and further from what she was. In another moment, she wasn't going to be able to think. Her sense of self was going to dissolve, and it would be all over. She flailed about mentally, hunting outside herself in a last drive for survival without knowing what it was she sought—

Power! All at once she felt a source of Power, wild, wonderful, there to be drawn. And Marya pulled it into her in one uncontrolled rush, crying out in painful ecstasy as it flooded through her like molten fire, bringing fierce new strength. She nearly sobbed with relief as she felt the terrible pressure on her being cease instantly. Vyed'ma staggered back, plainly drained for the moment, staring.

Marya didn't wait. Emelian and his wind-spirit mount had already crossed the crystalline bridge, and the princess prudently fled after them.

"You have not yet escaped."

Marya felt Vyed'ma's words rather than heard them, prickling along her nerves. She glanced back to see the Hag surging her grim way up the steep slope of the bridge, the angle slowing her not at all. She reached its apex—

Marya, hanging frozen in midair, cried out in disbelief as the bridge silently broke apart into a bright shower of crystal shards. Time seemed to cease for an instant, holding Vyed'ma transfixed in empty air.

And then, without so much as a cry, the Hag of the Rocks plummeted into the river of fire. Great waves of flame blazed up in a terrifying parody of water, flashing, blinding. Then they settled, and the river flowed smoothly once more. Vyed'ma was gone.

I did that, the horrorstruck Marya realized.

That soul-saving Power had come from the bridge. She had drawn the strength right out of it, leaving behind only a glittering shell—

A shell that collapsed the moment stress was placed on it. Oh, dear Lord . . .

Even the river's heat couldn't seem to warm her. Shuddering, wishing she could weep, Marya hurried away after Emelian.

XXXVIII

DOMESTIC WARFARE

"Boyar Semyon. Boyar!"

Boyar Semyon of the Inner Council of Kirtesk started awake, gasping. What— Who— He blinked at the small, wild-eyed figure invading his chambers. Then his sleep-fogged mind cleared, and the *boyar* struggled to his feet from the chair into which he had sagged and managed a courtly bow.

"Princess Maria."

Semyon was bemused to find himself vaguely ashamed at her having caught him asleep, as though she'd surprised him in the middle of something not quite nice. He certainly hadn't intended to sleep; he had meant to keep vigil, even as poor Maria, with her red-rimmed eyes and wan face, had been doing.

For how long? Semyon risked a quick, nervous glance out the window. Nothing out there seemed to have changed. The Prince of Kirtesk still held his city's foe at bay. It was still an incongruously bright, innocent day (though, the *boyar* admitted, a good bit later than it had been before weariness had conquered him).

"My Princess?" Semyon began politely. "What—"

"I—I can't stand here and watch any longer. We have to do something to help him. We must!"

Semyon recognized the desperate glitter in her eyes as the result of too little rest and too much strain, and

310

winced in sudden guilt. Akh, the poor child! When was the last time she had let herself eat or sleep? No matter what she'd commanded, he never should have let her stand watch for so long, not all alone and uncomforted. But there was a limit to the body's endurance, and right now, lost in walking sleep, Maria wasn't at all responsible for anything she said or did.

Trying to steer her towards the door of his chambers so he could summon one of her ladies to help her, Semyon said, very gently, "I'm afraid there isn't much we can do. You know that."

"No, I don't!" Maria's voice shook. "He's up there on the city walls all alone, risking his life, maybe even his soul, to keep all of us safe—and we're not doing anything to help him! He's s-so alone up there. Maybe you and all the others can abandon him, but I can't." She stared at Semyon with wild, wide eyes. "I'm going up there, too."

"Oh, no, my dear!" Semyon was too alarmed to worry about proper titles. "You mustn't. You know how magic operates: if you suddenly join him, you'll shake Finist's concentration. If he loses control, the shield about the city will fall."

But Maria wasn't hearing him. "Oh, Finist, I won't lose you, not now, not ever!" With a strangled sob, she turned and ran.

"Wait! Come back!" Semyon shouted uselessly, then gave an impatient shake of his head and went looking for the palace guards instead. Princess Maria must be stopped before she reached the prince—before she destroyed them all.

BOYARINA LUDMILLA, wife of Dimitri of the Inner Council of Astyan, sat with the other ladies and their needlework in their pretty garden, there in the royal palace. It was only now growing near to midday, but the air was already sleepy, heavy with the rich scent of freshly turned earth and the mingled sweetnesses of apple and cherry blossoms, and many of the women were

drowsy-eyed, their heads nodding. The only sounds were
the echoing chirps of nesting birds in the palace walls and
the distant whistling of one of the palace gardeners.

And Ludmilla wasn't aware of any of it. Frowning,
she pondered the matter of her husband, her Dimi, who
lately had been such a different man from the one she'd
married so long ago.

Granted, dear Dimi had always been a bit . . . officious whenever anyone pressed him about his duties as
a *boyar*. When left alone, though, he was an easygoing
man. Comfortable, Ludmilla decided. So relaxed at
home as to be downright sloppy. He loved her, she had
never had occasion to doubt it. He loved her, and their
children, even taking little Misha from his nurse's arms
to play with the boy himself. But in these past days . . .

The *boyarina*'s frown deepened. Yes, Dimi had been
quarrelling with Nikolai, but that was nothing new.
Rigid, so very proper Nikolai and her Dimi were always
finding *something* over which to quarrel; the good Lord
knew they never had seen eye to eye on anything. There
had even been that terrifying midnight summons,
though after the first shock had worn off, Ludmilla had
been positive things would end peacefully. After all,
Nikolai and Dimitri were both members of the same
Inner Council; Nikolai could hardly go and eliminate
another *boyar* without due proof of a crime. And, sure
enough, the matter had been peacefully resolved. Even
if Nikolai had actually threatened Dimitri . . .

Ludmilla snorted. At least she assumed it had been
a threat. Dimi might be a love, but he could be infuriatingly condescending at times; he had balked at giving
her many details, refusing to, as he put it, "Worry you
about matters that don't concern you."

Wasn't that typical of a man? As if what happened to
him at court wasn't going to affect their private lives as
well.

"A matter of politics," he'd added loftily. "Not
something for women."

She had tried to argue with him that Princess Marya,

after all, was undeniably female. But Dimitri had ended all debate by shutting his ears to anything she said.

Politics. Politics was a game, no more. A foolish game played by men who had never quite grown up.

"As most men have not," she muttered, feeling quite daring. "Children, the lot of them."

Including, alas, her Dimi. Of course, he was upset about poor Princess Marya, God be with her wherever she was. Everyone at court was upset, from the Regent on down; that was the reason the *boyars* were all so short-tempered with each other, though none of them seemed willing to admit it. But worry about the princess didn't give a man an excuse to—to abuse his wife!

Ludmilla straightened indignantly. Why, in these past days, he had had the nerve to order her around as though she were one of the servants, commanding her to do this, do that—setting her to watch poor little Elena as though the girl was a danger to the realm and she, herself, was nothing more than a lowly spy!

Politics.

"What nonsense."

Oh, but here came Elena now, rushing blindly along like a runaway child. And, judging by her reddened eyes, she had been weeping, too. The *boyarina* sighed, glancing about at the other women, who hadn't noticed the girl yet. Elena probably wouldn't want all these cats nattering over her business. Ludmilla set aside her needlework and rose to meet her.

Elena stopped short. For a moment she stood frozen, staring at the older woman as though Ludmilla was the very last person she would ever want to meet.

Small wonder, the *boyarina* thought, *considering the way I've been watching her at Dimi's request—no, his order.*

Then Elena let out a wail and turned to flee. Ludmilla moved hastily to block her path. And in the next moment, she found the young thing in her arms, Elena sobbing against her bosom.

Oh, dear. Now what?

The *boyarina* murmured stock soothing phrases for a time, the gentle, mindless sort of things she remembered murmuring to little Misha or her other children when the nurse had brought them to her with a toothache or a skinned knee or some other small disaster. And at last Elena seemed calm enough for Ludmilla to ask:

"What is it, child?"

"I c-can't . . ."

"Here. Take this." Ludmilla handed her a square of linen on which to dry her eyes. "Ah, I know," the *boyarina* said gently. "You've had a fight with your Yaroslav, haven't you?"

"No. Y-yes. I—I mean . . ."

For a moment, Ludmilla feared that was going to start a fresh torrent. But to her surprise, Elena straightened with red-faced dignity, sniffing, and said, "Your pardon, *boyarina* Ludmilla. I did not mean to trouble you."

"Oh, nonsense. Come, child." Ludmilla took her by the arm, pulling her into an antechamber. "No one will hear us in here. Now, what is the problem?"

Elena took a deep breath. "I only wanted to help my Yari . . ." she began.

". . . AND MAYBE I SHOULDN'T HAVE GONE to Regent Nikolai," Elena concluded breathlessly. "Maybe I shouldn't have told him about the fighting among the *boyars*. But—but *somebody* had to tell him, and it looked like none of the *boyars* were going to do it. Besides," she added defiantly, "whatever I did, it doesn't give Yari the right to treat me like a—a stupid little girl!"

"No," Ludmilla agreed grimly, thinking of Dimitri and his officious commands. "Indeed it does not." She drew herself slowly erect. "Now, isn't this ridiculous? Here we women sit like a group of fools, docilely sewing, while those . . . grown-up boys of ours play their games, toying with our lives and the futures of our children, refusing to see that while they play, Astyan is sinking into the mire." The *boyarina* stopped for breath, lips tight. "Well now," she continued sharply, "matters aren't going to go on like this any longer. Not if *we* have any say about it."

Elena was staring at her in open amazement. "But what can we do?"

"Talk to the other women, for a start. I suspect we'll find that they're just as tired as we of the way things have been around here."

"Yes, but—"

"Come, child." She took Elena firmly by the hand. "We have some convincing to do."

"BUT DO WE DARE?"

"Dare!" Ludmilla glared at the offender, and the woman shrank back behind the others. "Haven't you been listening to a word I've said? You have children, Sophia. Do you want to see your Andrei starved and hopeless as a peasant? What about Xenia?"

"She—she's just a baby!"

"Not such a baby some bastard wouldn't drag her to his bed."

"Boyarina!"

"That's right, look shocked." Ludmilla glanced sharply around at the cluster of women. "Look as shocked as you like, but be prepared, because if things go on the way they are, Astyan is going to fall. Come, you know it as well as I."

"She's right." Elena's voice was shy but steady. "My husband talks to me about what's going on at court, and— Oh, please, listen to the *boyarina*."

"Thank you, love. Now, ladies, we all know that what Elena's saying is the truth. We may not be trained counselors, but we're not blind and deaf, either. There are always envious princes out there, just waiting to expand their holdings. If our men can't unite and Astyan falls, just what do you think is going to happen to us? To our children?"

"Yuri isn't the most patient of men," murmured Feodora. "If I anger him, he might . . ."

"Might what? Beat you? Come now, Feodora, you've been married ten years now. Has Yuri ever once raised a hand to you?"

"Well, no. But—"

"Ladies, please. If we're going to huddle here like—like chickens frightened of the hawk, we might as well come right out and say we don't care what happens to our children. Do any of us want to admit that? Well? Do we?"

There was embarrassed silence. Triumphant, Ludmilla smiled. "So now, ladies. Are we agreed? Then—let us go into battle!"

REGENT NIKOLAI SAT before the assembled Inner Council, solemnly discussing trade routes, trying to ignore the glares *boyar* Dimitri was giving him or the patent unease of the others.

"And so," he continued, "we must—"

Just then, the door to the Audience Hall flew open, crashing against the inner wall. A guard came stumbling in, as though propelled against his will.

Nikolai sprang to his feet. "What is the meaning of this?"

"Uh . . . forgive me, my lords, I didn't want ta disturb ya, but the ladies insisted—"

"We did indeed," said a regal voice. "Stand aside, guard."

As Nikolai and the other *boyars* stared in disbelief, Ludmilla sailed majestically into the hall, closely followed by a small sea of women.

"Elena!" cried Yaroslav. "What are you—"

"I'm sorry, husband," she cut in demurely. "But we have something to say to all of you."

"Ludmilla." Dimitri's voice quivered with rage. "How dare you intrude into men's affairs?"

"Good Heavens, husband, *somebody* had to do it." She moved serenely forward to dip her head courteously to Nikolai. "Now, my lords, if we may be seated . . . ?"

* * *

LUDMILLA SMILED to herself in satisfaction. She had
warned the other women to be prepared for noise, even
for threats, but the insulted male shouting hadn't gone
on for nearly as long as she had expected. The threats,
of course, had been totally illogical. After all, though
a man did have the legal right to beat his wife, as Feodora had so timidly reminded them, he certainly didn't
want to sleep alone, or with a cool and unresponsive
bed-mate. And a woman did have *some* rights; she
couldn't be arbitrarily cast aside or—Heaven forbid—
imprisoned or maimed. She waited for a suitable pause,
gave the men her most dazzling smile (Dimitri, to her
delight, reddened), and asked quietly:

"Now that your opening remarks are concluded, my
lords, may we discuss the matter of Astyan?"

"There's nothing to discuss," muttered Dimitri.

"Your pardon, husband, but there is. My lords, normally we women wouldn't dream to intrude on your
affairs. But I have three children, my lords. And I would
like to see them grow up in peace."

"So would we all, *boyarina*," Nikolai said courteously. "Surely you can't doubt that."

"Oh, but I can." Ludmilla glanced around at the
other women, who were nodding. "We all can."

"I'm sure you didn't mean for this to happen," Elena
broke in softly, all big blue eyes and innocence, and all
male attention went straight to her.

Why, the little flirt! Ludmilla thought, delighted.
Never thought the child had it in her.

But Elena was continuing earnestly. "It's just that
you're all so strong, so wise . . . It must be very difficult for you not to fight."

Oh, now that's a bit overdone, my girl, Ludmilla cri-
tiqued silently.

Still, the *boyars* did seem to be hanging on Elena's
next words:

"But—but you've got to try, don't you see? If you
don't try, if you can't get along . . ." She trailed off,
the lovely blue eyes all at once welling up with tears

that Ludmilla was surprised to see were genuine. By God, the girl really *was* innocent enough not to realize her power over the male animal! "If you can't g-get along, run Astyan till Princess Marya returns—and she will return, I . . . I know it!—then . . ." Elena stopped again, blinking frantically, then lost the battle for control, bursting into tears with a wail of, "Then what happens to us all?"

"Now, my dear young woman," Nikolai began uncomfortably, "surely it won't—"

"I d-don't want to lose my Yari! I don't want our b-baby to grow up somebody's slave!"

"Our baby!" Yaroslav exclaimed. Forgetting propriety, he dashed from his place to catch his wife in his arms. "I didn't know— Eleniskha, is it true?"

Burying her face against his chest, she nodded. "I . . . wanted to tell you later . . ."

"Oh, Elena!" With an apologetic glance back over his shoulder at Nikolai and the others, Yaroslav led his sniffling wife from the room, leaving in his wake a group of stunned, uncertain *boyars*.

Ludmilla settled back in her chair, nearly choking on stifled laughter. God, men were such sentimental fools! If they'd heard a minstrel sing a tale like this, they would have scorned it as fit only for females. But face them with the truth, with something as normal, as prosaic, as a pregnant woman—and, God's mercy, a young, pretty one at that—and they fell apart!

Aware of Dimi's glance on her, Ludmilla determinedly repressed another laugh. From now on, every time the men tried to quarrel, all their wives would have to do to stop them was piously refer to that innocent little babe-to-be and watch them flounder to a stop!

Ludmilla gave her husband a charming smile. Akh, yes, Elena and her pregnancy had just given Astyan a better push towards peace than any logical arguments she ever could have devised.

XXXIX

FLIGHTS AND ALARMS

EMELIAN TWISTED about on Sv'istat's back, staring through the forest's leaves in disbelief as the crystalline bridge dissolved into glittering shards, and Vyed'ma fell.

"Look!" he gasped, too stunned to be coherent. "I don't—It didn't—"

But Sv'istat had gone wild beneath him, bucking and plunging and all the while making its mind-tickling laughter, and Emelian went sailing unceremoniously off its back to land with a thump on his back, the sword flying from his hand. As he struggled up to a sitting position, he heard the being shout without sound:

Free! We are free!

"But—what's going on? The Hag nearly caught us—"

No, no, I was too swift for her!

"—but then she fell back and I'd swear she was fighting with someone, but I didn't see anyone— Yes, and what about the bridge? We crossed it safely—"

Oh, I barely touched it, Sv'istat crowed. *I put no weight upon it.*

"But what made it shatter? And what about Vyed'ma? Is she . . . dead?"

Ae-e, who knows? the spirit laughed, continuing its exuberant dance. *Such as she do not die easily. Of rock, of mountain as she is, was, will be, she will prob-*

319

ably just melt and be re-formed, reborn, some other age. It whirled joyously up into the air. *But now the Named are unNamed again, free of her, free!*

With that, the wind-spirit soared up, losing all tangible shape. Pelted with leaves from the speed of its passing, Emelian craned his head back, helplessly watching the last shimmering fade into empty air. Certainly it was nice that Sv'istat was no longer a slave. But, dear God, now what? How could he ever rescue Marya and escape Koshchei without something as swift as a wind-steed?

Without warning, something glistening white came plunging down through the leaves. Heart racing, Emelian snatched up his sword as the thing took shape—

"Sv'istat! I thought you were—"

Free? No. I still am Sv'istat.

"I don't understand. I thought the spell had broken when the Hag . . . when she fell."

Not quite. The wild, empty eyes stared at Emelian, unblinking, alien. *The name upon me still exists. I told it to you. As long as you know it, it still binds me. You bind me.*

"I can't very well forget it at will! Human memory doesn't work that way."

Sv'istat said nothing. But all at once its wide, cold stare seemed to hold a touch of speculation in it, of . . . was it menace? *As long as I know its name,* Emelian thought uneasily. *If I can't forget it, there's only one other way the name can be destroyed . . .* He tightened his grip on the hilt of his sword, and saw Sv'istat glance at the blade in sudden unease; as long as the wind-spirit bore tangible form, iron could hurt it.

"Believe me," Emelian told it sincerely, "I had no idea this was going to happen. I'm sorry."

There was a long silence. Then the faintest whisper of wind tickled his mind as Sv'istat sighed. *Yes,* it said reluctantly, *I know.* It shook itself in a sudden shimmering of white, form blurring dizzyingly. *Eh, well, I still do owe you a debt for getting me out of the*

Hag's iron-trap. That was a purely physical thing; it would have outlasted her destruction. If you hadn't come, I would have passed from existence in there. So. What would you?

"I . . . need a steed," Emelian said carefully, "someone far, far more swift than a mortal horse."

Sv'istat preened. *I am that.* It stopped to stare at Emelian. *You doubt?*

"Ah . . . no. But—"

Ha! I have been regaining my strength with every instant away from the Hag. Watch.

The ungainly starved colt form blurred once more, growing, changing . . . It solidified. The colt was gone. In its place a true wonder-steed stood before Emelian, tall and sleek, fiery elegance in the curve of the proud neck, the sweep of the flowing, flaming tail.

Am I not splendid? Sv'istat crowed. *Am I not fine?*

"Fine, indeed." Emelian hesitated. "But can you run in mortal lands?"

What difference does it make? Wherever there is sky and wind, there I can be. Now, come, mount. And we shall fly!

FOR ALL SV'ISTAT'S CASUAL BOASTING, the wind-spirit still wasn't as strong as it claimed, unable to gain any altitude at all while bearing a human passenger. But Emelian had no quarrel with its land-bound abilities. Hunched low over the straining neck, he felt his arms and body slashed by branches, whipped by leaves and bits of twig hurled at him by the speed of their passing. It wasn't so easy to stay on the slick, smooth back, but after a quick, wary glance at the earth flying by in a dizzying blur beneath Sv'istat's hoofs, Emelian winced and clung to the wind-spirit like a leech. They virtually flew through forest and meadow till his muscles ached from the strain of holding on and his mind swam. God, Sv'istat might be tireless, but he was not!

But just when Emelian was about to call to Sv'istat

to stop—to beg it to stop!—there was a sudden dizzying sense of hitting something unreal, of dashing through a barrier that wasn't really there—

And returning to the warm, living, mortal world again.

Emelian let out a whoop of joy as he felt *real* time wrapping itself around him, accepting him, as the warm afternoon sun poured down on him and he caught glimpses of normal, springtime forest all around him.

Springtime?

I would have sworn I'd spent at least half a year in . . . wherever I was. How can it still be spring?

Unless . . .

Emelian nearly lost his grip on Sv'istat's mane as the idea struck him. Could it be that between his entrance and his exit from that Other realm no mortal time had passed at all?

It sounded like a peasant tale. But then, here he was sitting astride a wind-spirit in the shape of a horse of wonder, after having escaped from an elemental being who wanted to eat him—and he was calling something *else* fantastic?

Oh, but let no time have passed! he prayed.

For if that were true, then he still had hope.

IT WAS BECOMING a nightmare journey. Confused, unable to focus on reality, intangible body aching with cold, Marya was able to fasten on one thought only: she must stay with Emelian. It cost her almost every bit of her remaining strength, but desperation drove her on, forcing herself to keep pace with the wind-spirit, letting the wave of speed surrounding it help pull her along.

There wasn't much choice. She must keep pace. If once she relaxed, if once she let Emelian and that dazzlingly swift wind-steed get beyond her psychic range, Marya knew that would be the end of things. She would be lost amid the realms forever . . . or at least till the essence that was *Marya* dissolved away into the air.

It was starting to seem only too likely.

Marya cried out as without warning she struck the non-barrier between the realms and was dragged back and pulled forward at the same time. For a horrifying moment, she was sure her being was about to be torn apart. Then she was through, sobbing with relief, back into the normal, mortal world.

Oh, but how weak she felt, ill . . . dizzy . . . remote . . . Unable to cling to fear, or hope, or any human emotion, Marya drifted helplessly in empty air and wondered vaguely:

Is this death? It isn't so dreadful after all . . .

XL

SACRIFICES

THERE WAS NO GRANDEUR to this attack, here below the walls of Kirtesk, no drama, no sense of vast and terrible magics being loosed. Indeed, Koshchei mused darkly, there was nothing at all of note, except for the undeniable fact that, for all his Power, for all his deathless strength, he still stood out here, blocked beyond the city walls, just as he had from the start.

And his foe, the mortal human prince, still stood up there upon the city walls, just as he had from the start, outlined against the afternoon sun, motionless as though turned to stone but continuing to repel whatever Power Koshchei hurled at him.

Damn him! Damn—

The Deathless broke off, feeling the floodtide of his concentration ebbing beneath the sudden blaze of hatred.

No, not hatred. Frustration. Sheer, useless, *human* frustration.

"No." It was a soft, chill whisper. "I am no longer human. I will not be human."

Why should he need to keep asserting it? Why were his emotions slipping into melodrama so easily? He had thought his essence fixed, immutable. But . . . what if it wasn't? He was old, endlessly old. What if his essence was starting to crumble from sheer age? What if the basic *he* was starting to fall apart and—

"No!"

Koshchei took a new grip upon his will, prepared to hurl a storm of Power from the Outer Dark at the motionless, tormenting figure of the prince. Unlike his human opponent, he could carry on a separate train of thought and still hold his concentration firm, but there were limits. Right now, if he didn't rechannel all those thoughts on destroying that opponent—

Then Koshchei felt his wind-spirit slave quiver at his side, throwing its head up. *Master . . . ?*

Koshchei too felt the change: a sudden whisper of psychic wind. And he let out a hiss of disbelief.

The man who'd freed him from the royal prison was alive. Koshchei must have left a crumb of life within the broken body. Somehow Emelian had healed (who knew, maybe that accursed *leshy* creature had aided him). And now he was moving swiftly to steal away the woman-captive—

"No!"

It was a primal roar, deep and harsh enough to shake the city walls and send birds spiralling wildly into the sky, shrieking. Koshchei broke off his attack, casting aside the force of suddenly unbalanced, unbound Power with a savage sweep of his arms, sending it past him on either side in two blue-white bolts that seared into the ground with a stench of burning. Then he leaped astride his wind-steed, forcing it to its full speed, and soared like a dark comet across the sky.

BY THE TIME MARIA HAD REACHED the city walls, waking sanity had returned to her in full. She stopped short, terrified that she might already have shaken Finist's magical concentration by her presence. Sounds of pursuit echoed through the deserted streets behind her, and she pressed one hand protectively to her stomach. Dear Lord, if she really was with child, this mad racing about would do no good to the babe.

She looked up the dizzying height of the walls to where Finist stood motionless, locked in combat. Now that she stood so close, she could feel the force of Power burning and straining all about her, so strong the air seemed too thick to breathe. Power dazzled her eyes and prickled painfully along every nerve, stirring the hair at the nape of her neck and along her arms as a cat's fur is stirred before a storm. She could feel the evil just outside the walls, cruel without pleasure, cold beyond all human comprehension, and with it, the sense of a presence so . . . empty that she sobbed, wondering how Finist could endure its touch.

Without any warning, a raging roar seemed to tear at the very foundations of the city. Maria staggered, hands over her ears, shaking with the force of Koshchei's hatred.

But . . . it was gone. Koshchei the Deathless was gone. And with him had vanished the crushing force of Power as well. Frightened anew by the too-sudden change, Maria glanced hurriedly up to where Finist stood.

She couldn't see him.

"Oh, dear Lord, no . . ." Gathering up the skirt of her full caftan, Maria scrambled up the nearest stairway to the top of the wall as fast as she could move.

"Finist . . ."

There he lay, crumpled like a child's toy. She moved slowly forward, terrified of what she would find.

And then, as she reached his side, her legs gave out from under her and she sank to her knees in sheer, wordless relief.

The Prince of Kirtesk was asleep.

THE WIND-SPIRIT TRAPPED into the name Sv'istat cocked an equine ear back in curiosity. For some time now, it had been aware of the bodiless essence following them through the forest. It had been mildly amused to identify the essence as human, and—most puzzling to a sexless wind-spirit— gendered.

And it was in trouble, too, showing signs of imminent dissolution. These odd flesh-and-blood beings apparently couldn't live without their fleshy shells for very long.

"Help me . . . Please, help . . ."

Was that the essence's mind-voice? Was she trying to call the male human? Such odd creatures. Sv'istat twitched an ear, slackening its speed just a bit, and said casually to its rider:

She had best find a solid body quickly, or dissolve.

AS THE WIND-SPIRIT'S INDIFFERENT WORDS WHISPERED through his mind, Emelian jerked upright. Beneath him, Sv'istat, feeling its rider go suddenly off balance, came to a hasty stop. Instead of falling over backward, Emelian was thrown roughly forward, almost smashing his nose against the being's neck, and tumbled helplessly to the ground. He scrambled up, sputtering:

"She? She who? Sv'istat, what are you talking about?"

The one who follows.

"That's no answer! Who is it? The—Hag?"

Oh, no, that one will not be back for long and long. This female seems to know you.

"Of course I know him!" came a faint, desperate mind-voice.

"I heard that!" Emelian gasped.

Naturally. Sv'istat was smug. *I . . . have my abilities. Here, now. Listen.*

"Emelian? Oh, my love, can you hear me?"

"Marya . . . ? Dear God, Marya, is that you? Are you all right? Where are you?"

"Ah . . . here, love. At—at least part of me is here."

Her essence, Sv'istat interjected. *The female has some Power, it would seem . . .*

But neither Emelian nor Marya were listening to it. Lost in a whirlwind of excitement, they exchanged broken, half-hysterical phrases of joy and longing.

At last the first wild storm faded. "You mean, you've been with me all the time?" Emelian asked.

"Almost from the start. When I— When I thought you were dead, and—"

"I . . . nearly was dead. Cousin Finist saved me and—"

*These gendered-creature words are very interest-

ing, Sv'istat cut in. **But Marya wastes strength. Without a body, dissolution is certain.**

Emelian's heart gave a leap of shock. "No!" he protested.

"That's impossible," Marya argued. *"I—I feel quite strong again."*

The last strength before the spirit dissolves.

"Dear God, Marya! Leave me, get back to your body—"

"I . . . can't . . ."

"Marya . . . ?"

"Strange . . . All at once, I . . . can't . . . seem to . . . think . . ."

"Marya!"

Too late, Sv'istat interjected. **She must have a body** now. **Dissolution is here.**

"No! Dammit, Sv'istat, there must be something I can do—"

No.

But . . . there was. Emelian straightened slowly, steeling himself. He had never wanted to live so much as in this moment when Marya was near, and he felt his youth and strength coursing through every vein of his body. But a love that thought only of itself was no love at all. "Yes," he decided.

Sv'istat shivered. **Is this emotion what you mortal folk call love? Odd . . . It isn't at all like the passion-force of Vyed'ma—may she melt forever. It's . . . almost as wonderful as soaring through the gold of sunrise.**

Emelian ignored the being. "Marya, hurry. I welcome you. I—oh, come, you must have a body. Take mine."

He felt her horror pour through him. *"Emelian, no!"*

But he could also sense her losing struggle; the drive for survival was stronger than any will. As her essence rushed towards him, flooding him, Emelian added in silent resignation, *If this means my death, my love, so be it. At least I'll die knowing you will live.*

KOSHCHEI, speeding down the windways of the sky, suddenly sent his wind-spirit down to a stop on the ground, listening intently with more than mortal senses. After a moment he frowned, bewildered. Up to this point, rather than waste time returning to his mansion, the Deathless had been following a thin but easily read psychic trail, the two auras of his prey, man and woman, the *feel* of them distinct and unmistakable to anyone with Power. But all at once those two auras had become dizzily entangled, like two tapers suddenly run together.

"No matter," he mused aloud, urging his mount back up into the sky. "Death will untangle them."

EMELIAN AND MARYA CRIED OUT TOGETHER. There had been a wild pain, a dizzying shifting of senses, a confusion of sight and sound and smell, as *he* looked through *her* eyes, *she* looked through *his* eyes— No, they were one and the same, two human souls trapped within one body—

No! It was a frantic declaration of identity. *I am* myself!

I am me, *no other!*

The two terrified mental voices shouted as one. Two frantic essences fought to keep themselves separate and apart within the confines of one body, clinging desperately to their own senses of self as the memories and emotions of each washed over them both. Emelian shared Marya's pride as ruler of her city, suffered with her the childish pain of having failed her father, of wielding no Power till now, too late to tell him . . . Marya shared Emelian's grief for his father, the old man who had shut himself off from the real world, living only in the past, endured with Emelian the childhood fear that he would never fit in anywhere, never find a place that was truly his—

Till now. You are my life, Marya, my world, and I—

—never could have another in your place. Now and forever, you are mine, I am yours, and I—

—love you, Marya.

—love you, Emelian.

How could something as petty as fear stand between them? For a moment they were silent in shared joy. Then Emelian warily tried his vocal cords.

"Well," he said in deliberate understatement. "Things didn't work out quite the way we expected, now, did they?"

Though right now they had no need for vocal speech between them, the sounds were comforting, reminding him that he was still tangible, human.

Marya must have felt the same way. Emelian felt his lips move without his will—an eerie sensation, as though he had suddenly become a puppet in a master puppeteer's hands—as she took temporary control. "It . . . is strange, isn't it?" Marya stopped short, and Emelian felt his body shudder as she fought not to be alarmed at the sound of her words spoken by his voice. After a moment, she continued bravely, "Do you think we'll be able to . . . ah . . . go our separate ways?"

For all his love for her, Emelian couldn't hold back a twinge of fear that he wasn't going to regain control over his own body. Marya, feeling what he felt, quickly backed away into his mind. Fighting down a surge of relief, Emelian said, "Oh, surely. Eventually. I . . . hope. After all," he added with a desperate laugh, "this is carrying the concept of togetherness a bit too far!"

Sv'istat, who had been watching with ears pricked, the very image of equine curiosity, shook its waterfall of mane with a whisper of laughter, untouched by human emotions. *Still, this is one way to keep the female alive!* it said.

All at once, it tensed, eyes wide and sightless.

"Sv'istat?" Emelian asked. "What's wrong?"

Slave . . . Kin-slave . . .

"Another wind-spirit? But I thought you were the only one still—"

No, no, another Named one, held by . . . Aeee . . . It was the wind's own wail. *The Dead-Alive one, the Deathless—is here!*

XLI

CONFRONTATION

KOSHCHEI CAME PLUMMETING DOWN out of the sky on his wind-steed, grim as Old Death himself, black cloak snapping and whipping about his powerful form. As he forced his mount to a swift landing in the clearing, Sv'istat gave a wail of terror and whirled up and away into empty air, hovering about Emelian's body as a barely visible shimmering.

He knows my name! it shrilled to the humans.

That's impossible, Emelian told it. *Vyed'ma wouldn't have told him. Don't—*

He knows! Sv'istat insisted. *His Power is not of the living Elements—He knows things! If you die, he will bind me forever—*

"Hush," Marya cut in sharply. "Don't distract us. Emelian, Koshchei means to end things here and now. We can't let him gather his Power."

I know. We have to strike now.

There was a moment of tense confusion as two minds tried to control one body. Koshchei watched without expression, then gave a soft, humorless chuckle, plainly sure his prey was paralyzed with fear.

Like hell we are! Emelian thought.

Not that there were many alternatives. Marya could hardly fight the Deathless with magic; her newfound Power didn't have a chance of being as focused or refined as that of someone with ages of arcane skill behind him. But

331

trying to battle Koshchei by normal human means hadn't
worked so well in the past. (*"Not for me, either,"* Marya
mind-whispered.) Still, it was a far better choice than meek
surrender, so Emelian, overcoming his body's two-master
confusion by sheer determination, whipped out his sword.

In the next moment, Marya almost made him drop it
as she impulsively tried to lunge. *Stop it, love!* Emelian
snapped. *You'll get us both killed.*

"Dammit, Emelian, I'm trained as a warrior—"

And I'm trained as a— Oh, good God, look out.

Koshchei had drawn his own sword in one swift, skillful
motion, a thin smile on his cold face. (*Almost,* thought
Emelian, *as though he finds weaponry a diverting change
from magic.*) With one lithe leap, the Deathless sprang to
the ground and began stalking slowly forward.

"Ah, now I see how it is," he said, his deep voice
almost gentle. "At first I thought I faced only one of
you: the foolish young man who has lived to regret the
mercy he showed me."

"There *is* only one of me!" Emelian shouted.

"Don't think me a fool, little ones." Koshchei's tone
was still mild. "You two have been playing with Power,
haven't you? Both of you are caught in one body." His
smile was a terrible thing. "Convenient."

The Deathless lunged forward, ferociously graceful.
Emelian and Marya simultaneously tried to bring their
sword up to parry, but the force of two wills in one
mind overbalanced them. Emelian's body went tumbling—and the inhumanly swift stroke that would have
cut him in two passed instead harmlessly over his head.

God, he's fast!

Emelian, knowing, after all, what his body could and
couldn't do, hastily seized control and scrambled to his
feet, steadying his sword in both hands. Koshchei stared
at him, eyes black and empty as the Outer Darkness
. . . the endless, lifeless, hopeless Darkness . . . pulling at him . . . drawing him in . . .

"Don't look!" Marya hissed in his mind. "He's trying to snare you—Emelian!"

In the next moment, she wrested control away from him, this time much to Emelian's relief. Dazed, consciousness slowly returning, he rode as a passenger in his own body as Marya brought their sword up to parry. At the last possible moment, she sprang to the right, letting the Deathless's forward motion carry him helplessly past her, then darted in again, sword outthrust.

It's not a thrusting weapon! Emelian protested.

"It has a point; good enough!" she snapped back. *"Get out of my way!"*

The mental exchange had taken less than a heartbeat, time enough for Marya to complete her lunge. But before the sword could touch him, Koshchei recovered, twisting about so sharply that the flat of his blade delivered a stinging blow to Emelian's sword arm.

Dammit, Marya, I told you that wasn't going to work!

"Got any better ideas?"

No, he hadn't. If only they could somehow pool their skills, act as one, not two—

Impossible. Even though they were trapped in the same body, they couldn't act as halves of a whole. They were two complete entities.

Koshchei, smiling faintly, drove Emelian's body back across the uncertain ground with powerful slash after slash, his cold eyes glinting with pleasure. Desperately, Marya and Emelian each tried to stop their helpless retreat, but separate, simultaneous efforts at defense did nothing but jerk Emelian's body dangerously about, sending it crashing into bushes and stumbling over roots and rocks. Koshchei continued his drive, forcing them back and back—

Right into the unyielding trunk of a tree. The Deathless raised his sword for one final blow, and Emelian and Marya knew there wasn't going to be time to escape. Cornered against the tree, they stared into Koshchei's face, and saw it as the face of Death . . .

And in that final, intense instant, barriers crumbled. In that instant, Emelian and Marya saw their inner selves more clearly than ever in their waking lives.

Emelian: running from his father, from his child-

hood, from all that would force him into someone else's mold, into being no-longer-me.

Marya: fiercely holding her own, independent will, the once-child forever proving to her father that if she couldn't wield Power, she could, at least, still be of worth.

But at the end, there was no time for pride or fear. Only one basic fact remained: *stay separate, and die.*

The will to live was stronger than all else; time enough to rebuild inner barriers after, if there was an after. As one, Emelian and Marya abandoned the limitations of *self.* United in body and skill, they leaped sideways, away from the tree, raising sword against Koshchei with a confident new grace, dodging lithely aside as his blade swept down, lunging in again before he could recover, slashing open a cut on his forearm—

No. Though the sword had undeniably struck something, there was no wound, no blood.

Koshchei smiled. "Hopeless, little ones. United though you are—and a pity such skill must be wasted— you are still, alas, quite human. Fatally human. This shell I wear can be destroyed by no one of your kind."

"Why should we believe your lies?"

"No lie."

Without so much as the visible tensing of muscles in warning, Koshchei brought his sword whistling down again, with all the force of his powerful form. Caught off-guard, Emelian and Marya took the brunt of the blow directly on their sword. The incredible shock of impact shot up their arms to the shoulders, nearly tearing the weapon from suddenly numbed hands.

As Sv'istat whirled wildly around them, shrieking desperate encouragements, they staggered back, frantically trying to recover their balance, as the Deathless continued to coolly rain blows upon them.

Dammit, enough!

They threw their body forward into a roll, past Koshchei, springing up behind him, and slashed out at him with all their united strength even as he whirled to face them. It was a blow to cut a mortal man nearly in half.

Unfortunately, it was a blow that recoiled harmlessly off rock-hard skin, sending them stumbling helplessly back. Sv'istat whirred about them, so close that it nearly passed right through them, crying hysterically, *No, no, no,* confusing their senses.

Sv'istat! Get out of the—

Koshchei's sword came flashing down again, turned this time with deliberate malice—prolonging the fight— so that it would be the flat of the blade, not the edge, that struck the side of Emelian's head. But the Deathless misjudged his own inhuman power. The sword slammed against the side of Emelian's head with blinding force.

White-hot confusion blazed up within two linked minds. Two mortal essences cried out in terrified loss within that flash of time at the sight of the solid human body crumbling tenantless to the ground, even as they spun away into a dizzying tangle of *tangible-intangible*, even as they *felt* a brief, frantic cry of:

* No! You can't— We aren't—*

Suddenly Emelian and Marya were aware of the world again, but through vastly altered senses: nothing of *scent* existed now, nothing of *touch*. There was only color, pure and dazzling, and free, empty, endless space in which objects registered merely as *dense* or *not-dense*.

Only the Power inherent in Marya's essence kept two mortal minds sane. Desperately, they grappled with the truth:

Sv'istat had hovered too near. When the stunned, helpless essences of the humans had literally been hurled out of solid flesh, it had accidentally drawn them into the only other refuge open to them:

Itself.

There was an instant of stunned silence. Then the calm erupted into a frenzy of panic, a wild psychic swirling of *Emelian, Marya, Sv'istat,* as the terrified wind-spirit tried to free itself from the touch of mortality, as the two human minds fought just as fiercely to cling to their sanctuary, aware of Koshchei's slow, sure approach.

Sv'istat! Emelian managed to snap out the name, relieved to find he could still communicate, that for all these bizarre intertwinings of spirits, his basic essence was still his own. *Sv'istat, stop it! He'll kill us—and you with us!*

That horrified the wind-spirit into momentary quiet. Emelian took advantage of the lull to gather his dizzy senses to him— Akh, no, not all his senses, not with the blunting of some of them and the complete distortion of his vision— He could endure it, though, if he didn't fight it, if he just accepted it for what it was, a look through alien eyes.

God, he was wasting precious time. Better to concentrate as Marya was doing on remembering Koshchei's exact words:

"This shell . . . can be destroyed by no one of your kind."

"*My* human *kind*," Marya amended softly.

Indeed. But right now, they were hardly . . .

Hope sparked through two mortal minds.

Sv'istat, Emelian began again. *Would you remain a slave? Or—would you be free?*

Free . . . It was a whisper of anguished longing. **Ahh, free . . .**

Then, aid us.

Against . . . the Death-Life-One? the spirit asked. **I . . . can't . . .**

"Think of the wild winds, Sv'istat," Marya tempted. "Think of the open, boundless sky—"

That you will never know again if Koshchei wins, Emelian cut in. *Decide, Sv'istat: eternal slavery or the freedom of the sky?*

For one dreadful moment, he was sure Sv'istat was too terrified to act. Then a tremendous shudder shook the wind-spirit's being. **Freedom!** it gasped in anguish. **Oh, by the sky, freedom!**

Then aid us, now!

KOSHCHEI STARTED as a shining white wonder-steed condensed itself out of the air before him. Of course the surprise was momentary; he had sensed the wind-spirit's presence from the first. But he had thought nothing of it; the slave breed snared by Vyed'ma's Namings had little courage against their masters. The Deathless waved an imperious hand and spat out a Word of Confinement. It would have no actual power over an intangible creature, but the aura of closeness, of dank, narrow prison walls, that clung to the Word would be enough, surely, to send the rash wind-spirit fleeing for its terrified life.

But though the wind-steed shuddered, it made no move to flee. And its scream was pure rage. Open-mouthed in shock, Koshchei barely leaped back in time to avoid its gleaming hoofs.

This was impossible! The spirit folk could *not* act against their natures. And yet this raging creature showed little sign of its race's inborn terror of confinement. More amazingly, it was showing no signs of being bound by his hastily shouted spells, either, spells that should have bound any of the spirit kind.

Koshchei stumbled back again, dodging the being's wild-eyed fury, the first twinge of alarm prickling through him.

What if this was no longer a true wind-spirit? What if it had become something more?

The alarm deepened into something that was almost true fear. Koshchei could always sense a living human essence, but it was virtually impossible to actually read one if the human in question was unconscious, unaware. When he had struck down his foes' shared body just now, there'd been no reason to think they weren't still within. But now that he had reason to be truly aware of this unnatural wind-spirit's aura, the Deathless realized there was something strange about the *feel* of it—

No, impossible! They never could have survived the shock!

They could. They had. Koshchei staggered back and back, shouting out spells that should have wrenched apart a wind-spirit, crushed a human soul, but had no effect upon a threefold creature not human, not spirit—

Not human.

At the realization, Koshchei cried out in wordless rage and slashed out with his sword. Let cold iron do his work!

But the triple being was quicker even than he. In a whir of wind, it sprang up into nothingness, and the deadly blade swept harmlessly through empty air. Whirled about by the force of his blow, the Deathless recovered balance by sheer will. Dropping the useless sword, he rummaged frantically through his vast mental storehouse of Power for any spell, any Words, that would be of use against this impossible hybrid. But the same lack of control that had troubled him in his battle against Prince Finist, that had kept him from decisive action in his capture of the princess, returned in full force. In this moment of terrible need, Koshchei's mind insisted on focusing only on his own interminable age, his endless gathering of Power, the emptiness of past and present and future . . .

Not now, not here!

Ignoring his inner struggle, the Deathless continued to search—and found nothing that worked amid all his magics, nothing of any good at all. His shell was invulnerable against any human attack, but this foe was not human—

The being plummeted with the speed of a stormwind, a flashing white steed with deadly hoofs aimed right at his head. Koshchei tried to leap aside, but his mind and body, still caught in the confusing sense of too-great age, too much Power, felt sluggish, fatally slow. All at once, his ears rang with the whispery, triumphant laugh of a *leshy*.

Hallucination.

Then a gust of wind brought a branch stinging across his face. As Koshchei staggered helplessly aside, an upward-thrusting tree root snagged his foot. He fell heavily—directly under the wind-spirit's plunging hoofs. There was time for one last flash of hatred, one flash of terrible, hopeless fear, as the endless Darkness loomed before him—

And then the shell that had held Koshchei the Deathless within it was crushed and broken.

XLII

UNTANGLING

PRINCE FINIST WOKE with a start and a cry. Someone was catching him in warm, gentle arms: Maria. She was up here on the city walls with him, her eyes dark with concern. Finist stared past her up to the clear blue sky, and let out a weary laugh.

"Finist . . . ?"

"It's all right, love. It's over. He's dead."

"But—"

"Oh, maybe not dead in our mortal sense." Finist broke off, feeling the forest outside Kirtesk's boundaries celebrating with him. "But he's gone, Maria. Koshchei the Deathless is gone back to the Outer Dark forever."

*AND SO, when we couldn't get me—Emelian—back into my own body, we managed to get it onto my back— *Sv'istat, that is*—and went to recover Marya's body.*

The triple being gestured with its head back to where the two bodies were stretched out on pallets there in the Audience Chamber in Kirtesk.

Prince Finist leaned forward in his chair, chin on hand, his wife standing protectively at his side. Emelian, who had recovered enough of his own senses— even though still part of Sv'istat—to see relatively clearly, winced inwardly at the changes in the prince.

The elegant face was gaunt now, the skin drawn tightly over the high cheekbones, emphasizing their sharpness, making the prince look more than ever like the falcon he also was, and dark shadows were painfully evident under his amber eyes; Finist had plainly been through his own ordeal. But those eyes were bright with magical curiosity.

"You couldn't get back into your own body, either, Cousin Marya?"

The triple being shuddered. *"No,"* Marya said softly. *"So we did the only thing we could think to do, and came to you."*

"And *that* must have been a struggle worth watching," the prince murmured. "Two mortal bodies to be carried, and not a useable pair of hands among you."

I reshaped myself somewhat, Sv'istat interjected. *We managed.*

"But you . . . c-can help us, can't you?" Marya asked.

"Oh, my dear, nothing simpler! Under the normal course of things, you three never would have been able to join into one at all. Marya, cousin, it's your own roused Power that's keeping you trapped."

"What should I do?"

"Nothing."

"But—"

"I mean it quite literally. Untrained in Power as you are, as long as you're awake, you won't be able to relax it. Once you're asleep, however—"

"But—but I can't sleep, not in this bodiless form!"

"You can. You will."

"Finist . . ." Maria murmured in a cautionary tone.

He grinned up at her. "Don't worry, love. I won't exhaust myself. I'll be careful for you." His glance dropped to her waist. "And . . . for our little newcomer-to-be."

Such warmth flashed between husband and wife that Emelian, embarassed, wished he could look away. But then Finist turned his attention back to the triple being.

His suddenly Powerful words, aimed strictly at Marya's ears, meant nothing to Emelian but so much gentle gibberish. But all at once, he felt Marya's essence slide softly away from him.

Marya!

Then, speechless with delight, he saw her body stir, her chest begin to softly rise and fall. In the next moment, Emelian's own senses blurred dizzily. There was a wild, terrifying moment of *intangible-tangible*—

And suddenly Emelian realized he was blinking up at the high, vaulted ceiling, staring with wonder at the details of the plaster-covered stonework. Why had he never noticed how splendid such things could be? Look at the neat joints, without a rough edge to them, and the bright paintings covering them, the red and gold flowers entwining on their stems clear even through the bluish shadows . . .

"Hey!" It was a cry of pure joy. "Look at this! I'm back in my own body!"

"Emelian, please . . ." murmured a sleepy voice. "Don't shout . . ."

"Marya? Marya!"

Her eyes flashed open. "Emelian? I—"

More she couldn't say, because her husband had reached out to her, the two of them clumsy in their newly restored bodies, and kissed her with all the pent-up passion in him. Laughing breathlessly, Marya pulled away, trying to smooth down her tangled hair. "Akh, I must look a horror."

"Oh, love, you look splendid."

Marya laughed again. "Dear heart. I—oh, Emelian, it's so wonderful to be *solid* again!"

Well and good, whispered a plaintive wind-voice. *But what about me? I am free of the human-invaders now. But . . . I am still a slave.*

"What's this?" asked an intrigued Finist.

"Ah, well." Emelian explained as best he could the problem of knowing the name of a being never intended to be named. "And Marya and I can't very well just forget it. I don't suppose you could . . ."

"Make you forget? Cousin," Finist said reproachfully, "I'm not a god. I can't set things to right with one casual wave of a hand."

"Sorry. I didn't mean—"

"I . . . could excise part of your memory, yes . . ." The prince broke off with a negating wave of a hand. "But it would certainly be a larger chunk of your past than one name. Do you want to risk forgetting meeting each other? Or falling in love?"

"God, no! But . . . poor Sv'istat. You can't do anything to help?"

"I didn't say that." Finist got to his feet, swaying slightly with weariness, steadied by Maria. "Let me rest a bit, and ponder a bit. And then we shall, as the saying goes, see what we shall see. Meanwhile, my dear Cousin Marya, don't you think you'd better let your people know what's become of you?"

"Oh! Oh, yes, of course."

"I've taught you the spell. A perfectly good mirror can be found in the next chamber. Till later, friends."

BOYARINA LUDMILLA, strolling down a corridor in the royal palace of Astyan, her servants trailing docilely behind her, was nearly bowled over by her head-down, forward-striding husband.

"Dimi!" The woman glared at him in indignation, smoothing the folds of her brocaded caftan. "Dimitri, please be careful."

He stared at her as though seeing her for the first time. "Sorry." It was a grudging apology. "I didn't mean—dammit, wife," he added, "it isn't you, it's just—I don't know how much longer I can stand it. Being polite to that sanctimonious— Thinks he's a god, not a mere Regent, and—"

"Dimi. You know there's nothing you can do, except—"

But she stopped short, listening. "Now, I could swear that was cheering."

"Yes . . ." Dimitri frowned slightly, puzzled. "Sounds like young Yaroslav's voice. Yes, and that high squealing can only belong to his Elena."

"They're getting louder. And closer. And—"

In the next moment, the crowd overtook them in a dizzying blur of color, *boyars'* bright silks flashing with red and blue and gold, servants' duller browns and greys, all of them, nobles and commons, tangled together, alike in their laughter.

Nikolai was in their lead. And for once his lean, proper face was creased by what could only be described as a foolish grin. Before the astonished Dimitri could pull away, the Regent caught him by the shoulders and gave him a ritual kiss of peace, right cheek, left cheek, right.

"Nikolai! What in the name of Heaven—"

"She's alive! I've just spoken with her!"

"What *are* you— With whom? Princess Marya?"

"Yes! Our princess is alive, and well! She's with her cousin, Prince Finist, in Kirtesk right now, but we'll have her back with us soon enough."

Ludmilla heard herself give a positively girlish squeal of delight. Beaming, she watched Nikolai and Dimitri, their differences forgotten in the impact of sudden joy, embrace each other like long-lost friends.

"So, NOW." Finist looked about at Emelian, Marya, and the dimly visible Sv'istat. "I promised you I would look for a way to free you, Sv'istat. Akh, yes, I know your name now, too, but it's all for the good." The amber eyes sparkled with excitement. "Believe it or not, I've found a way in an ancient peasant ritual of banishment. Don't give me that stare, Cousin Marya. There's a good deal of wisdom to be garnered from the old folkways."

Marya glanced at her husband. "So Emelian has always told me. I . . . think I believe him now."

"Good," Finist said absently. "Come, stand here before me, all three of you, and listen. Believe. Now, then:

"You are Sv'istat. Be Sv'istat."

Finist's voice rang with sincerity.

"You are V'isat," he continued. "V'isat. Be V'isat."

What is *he doing?* Emelian wondered.

The wind-spirit, at least, seemed to have no doubts, staring at Finist as though the prince held the secret of existence. Which, as far as the spirit was concerned, Emelian realized, he probably did.

"You are V'iat," the magician-prince said, his eyes aglow with Power. "V'iat. Be V'iat."

Ahh, I get it! He's peeling letters off the name, bit by bit. But we'll still remember the original. Will that matter?

Apparently not. "You are V'ia," Finist told the spirit. "V'ia. You are V'i. You are V'i. Be V'i . . . V'i is nothing . . . no meaning, no binding . . . the empty wind . . . V'i is the empty wind. You are the wind. You are unNamed, the name is gone in the empty wind . . . You are unNamed . . ."

With a start, Emelian realized that the peeling away of the wind-spirit's name had worked on his mind as well. He made one instinctive attempt to remember, then quickly set his thoughts to a safer subject—Marya— rather than risk accidentally recapturing the spirit.

"You are unNamed . . ." Finist continued to croon.

And all at once, with a great shout of joy, the wind-spirit danced up into the air. Formless, it shrieked, *Free! I am free! I am!*

With that, it soared up into the sky, thinning, melting, dissolving into the wind with a thoroughness terrifying to a finite human being. But the final wind-whisper of thought Emelian caught was a joyous *I am home at last.*

Left behind on the solid palace floor, the humans all let out their breath in simultaneous sighs of relief, then burst into laughter.

"That's that," Marya said at last.

"Not quite." Finist sat back in his chair, studying her, his head tilted at a birdlike slant. "Cousin, now that you've awakened your Power, it can't be allowed to grow wild. You've already had some small proof of that."

Marya smiled a wry little smile. "Yes. I can't exactly put it back into its cage, can I?"

"Hardly." The prince chuckled. "Eh, don't look so grim, cousin! Once you learn to deal with it, you'll find Power more a gift than a curse. Besides, I'll be happy to train you in its . . . ah . . . proper care and feeding."

"I . . . wasn't really worried about that."

Emelian raised an eyebrow at the hangdog look she gave him. "You're afraid for me?" he asked incredulously. "After all we've been through, dear heart, the thought of Power doesn't alarm me in the least." He paused. "Or were you thinking of our court, perhaps? Marya, love, after dueling with Vyed'ma and battling the old Deathless himself, do you really think I'm going to let any mere courtiers bother me?"

Marya grinned at that. "No. Certainly not. Heaven help any *boyar* who dares condescend to you now. But— my poor husband. Life won't be easy for you now, not with a—a princess-magician-warrior wife!"

"I'll risk it," Emelian said, laughing, and pulled her into his arms.

JOSEPHA SHERMAN is that rarity: a resident of New York City who was actually born there. Her short stories have appeared in the *Sword and Sorceress* anthologies, *Dragon* magazine, *Fantasy Book,* and elsewhere. In addition to several books for children, she is the author of *The Shining Falcon,* which won the 1990 Compton Crook Award.

Ms. Sherman earned her M.A. in Ancient Near Eastern Archaeology at Hunter College. She writes, ''I have participated in such salvage excavations as the ones taking place in York, England—where we discovered that ancient Roman cesspools retain an amazing amount of aroma. Ah, the romance of archaeology!''